On Mars
Pathfinder

The Mike Lane Stories
Volume 1

By Jim Melanson

On Mars: Pathfinder

The Mike Lane Stories, Volume 1

Printed by CreateSpace

Available from Amazon.Com
Available on Kindle, Kobo and other devices

ISBN: 978-0-9937565-6-6

Melanson Publishing

See more books from this series at
www.on-mars.ca

More titles available at:
www.melansonpublishing.ca

Editorial service provided by Dorathy Gass
www.metwritingservices.com

Cover Illustration © 2015 Jonathan Hunt
www.huntillustration.com

Acknowledgement

I thank God for giving me the ability to afford the luxury of writing, and the skill to write with.

There are several people who helped make this book a reality, and I'd like to thank them for their efforts, friendship, and contributions.

First, I'd like to thank my son Gaelan, a student at the University of Guelph. Working on his PhD in the field of Cancer research, he helped me understand cloning, recombining genes, and other various gooey things. Any mistakes are entirely mine. A big thank you to Rick Fearnley and Kenneth Lord, two men I've worked with for years. As I watched them go through the process of publishing their own books, they inspired me to pursue my own dreams of writing. Therefore, anything I produce from now on is *totally their fault*! Thank you to David Leung, pastor of the Lighthouse Church of Newcastle, who helped me deal with some of the weightier theological issues hidden in the story. Thank you to Dorathy Gass, my editor of choice. A special thanks to Jessica Smith, for making sure I had the girly mindset correct. A really big thank-you to Guillaume Ruch, my test reader extraordinaire. He caught many things that the editor and I both missed. His honest criticism (and complements) are gratefully appreciated! Last but by no means least, a very old friend, Roxanne Paquette. She helped me out in a pinch with the French translations when my long ago language skills failed me, and Google Translate didn't look quite right.

There are a few places in the story where I mention Tim Horton®, my favourite Canadian coffee chain. I have done so with their permission. My place is littered with the cups they used to get me up early and kept me up late, so that I could write this book. Feel free to send me a large steeped tea with one cream, double cup.

The inspiration for this book and the volumes that follow comes from my love of sci-fi, but my disappointment at it always being "out of time". Currently, there is a vision of colonizing Mars that has been made a possibility by the Mars-One Corporation. I guess that was the kick in the butt I needed to finally start writing this book. I have no affiliation with that organization; other than being an applicant (Pick me! Pick me!). I do not intend this work of pure fiction to represent that company, comment on the company, or profile that company in anyway. They have my respect and gratitude for what they are going to achieve. I have been in touch with the Mars-One corporation and am pleased to announce that 10% of the authors profits from this book will be donated to their mission. I must, however, restate that I am not affiliated with Mars-One and they are not affiliated with this work of fiction.

Further inspiration comes from the sci-fi big boys in my life like Kim Stanley Robinson, Isaac Asimov, Gene Roddenberry, Terry Pratchett, and George Lucas to name a few. The biggest salute to authors must go to the memory of Edgar Rice Burroughs for introducing me to John Carter, Tars Tarkis and Deja Thoris: they captured my imagination years ago, and hold it firmly to this day.

Ultimately, this story would never have been written without Yuri Gagarin, Alan Shepard, and Neil Armstrong (just to name a few), for making the fiction of yesterday, the history of today. They not only took great leaps in the advancement of mankind and science, they provided dreams and fantasies for millions of unnamed boys and girls around the world.

Jim Melanson
Cobourg, Ontario
April, 2015

Dedication

The book is dedicated to the one person that has kept me sane and connected these last few crazy years. She is also the woman who saved my life.

Monique Altmann, my dearest friend … even though she doesn't understand a *lick* of what I'm writing about.

Disclaimer

All Tim Hortons trademarks referenced herein are owned by Tim Hortons. Used with permission.

All Coffee-Mate trademarks referenced herein are owned by Nestle Corporation. Used with permission.

This is a work of fiction. Names, characters, businesses, places, events, and incidents are either the products of the author's imagination or used in a fictitious manner. Any resemblance to actual persons, living or dead, or actual events is purely coincidental.

Preface

Why would a man go to Mars alone? I mean, really, why?

I think the answer to that question is the same as asking why someone would go on vacation alone. Why do some people accept remote outpost jobs alone? What about Forest Rangers? They're a solitary lot. Lighthouse keepers too; lighthouse keeping has to be some *mad* alone time. Taking a ten year posting to one of the deep void listening posts between here and Epsilon Eridani, now *that's* some kind of commitment to being alone. I had a friend many, many years ago who had been a geologist in the earlier stages of his life. He loved nothing more than packing his pack, and hitting the tundra in search of elusive peculiarities. He would then take those peculiarities home and squirrel himself away; studying them, surrounded by his books. He would do this for weeks; sometimes for months at a time.

Anyone I've known who has gone into an intensely isolated field, or work location, including those who first went to the Jovian moons; were running from something. I think we all run from something at some point in our lives. Those of us who seek solitary lives are running just a bit harder, a little bit farther. That begs the next question, especially for a guy who goes to Mars all by himself; with no possible way to return to Earth: what do you do when you stop running?

I wasn't running from someone. I wasn't running from the law. That would have been difficult, considering I spent years as one of the most recognized faces on the planet. I certainly wasn't running from taxes, bank debt, insolvency, the courts, or allegations of unwanted paternity. It was much simpler, and much more ... pedestrian.

I was running from a ghost.

Loreena: my love, my life, my wife. She was so much. She was all of it. She was everything. Then she was gone; but she wasn't. She is always in here (picture me pointing to my heart). She is always in here (now, pointing to my brain bucket). The memories of her are mostly pleasant. I would see her often, after she passed, in ways that were sometimes startling, and sometimes supportive; sometimes, just funny. She appears to spend as much time smiling and laughing in the postcorporeal state of existence, as she did in the pre-postcorporeal state of existence. At least, in my mind.

I knew, however, that no matter how much I regretted, missed, loved, treasured, her memory; I should have been moving forward with my life. I wasn't though. She haunted me. Every day and everywhere, she was there. I had tried dating in the years after her passing. It was like I was cheating on her. I just couldn't do it. Everything they said and did, I had an anecdote about

Loreena saying or doing something similar. Apparently that gets old, and fast, for another woman.

Finally, I just admitted to myself that there was one and only one great love of my life; that I had already had that great love, and it was never to be repeated. Well, there was Carrie. Carrie was nice. It was easy with her. I grew very fond of her and her two boys. I don't know if I could say it was the "L" word. By the time I met her though, I was already preparing to go to Mars. It wouldn't have worked out. So again, I was checking out, I was on the lam, I was on the run.

Running is never the right thing to do; yet sometimes, it's the *only* thing you can do.

"Wherever you go, there you are." *Buckaroo Bonzai* got it right. As soon as I arrived on Mars, all alone, with no return ship, I discovered the Buckmeister had it going on. In the early days after arrival on the Red Planet, I realized, *yep, there I am.* I didn't escape her. I didn't escape me.

Don't get me wrong, I wasn't sad about coming to Mars. I wasn't upset about coming alone. I said, "yes". I said it for all the right reasons too. Just, perhaps, maybe out of the laundry list of right reasons, there was that one or two that might not have been quite so right. Like thinking I would escape those painful memories; the visions of Loreena at the oddest times; the aching emptiness in my heart that used to be so full of, well, her.

Sigh. Enough maudlin verbiage.

I came to Mars all alone to prove one thing. I came to prove that humans can survive on Mars. I had to do this so that the corporation that sent me would be allowed to send more people. If I hadn't survived, well, the whole interplanetary species thing would have been temporized. Humanity's first steps as an interplanetary species almost did come to a crashing halt when I made planet-fall, landing in the mouth of Chasma Boreale, near the Planum Boreum. Six minutes after I arrived, my ship blew up! With me in it! I mean, *damn*, not exactly welcome wagon … know what I mean? It's only by the grace of God, and the competence of some very, very good German engineers, that I managed to survive.

I quickly realized that I wasn't alone on Mars after all …

… and I wasn't welcome.

The Story Begins...

The battered, but mostly intact airlock wreckage bounced once and skittered to a halt. The lone Pathfinder was alive but unconscious within its twisted, protecting walls; while the wreckage of the exploded Lander burned around him.

Chapter 1

Descent Day

Every Terran January 15th, humans around the solar system and beyond celebrate "Descent Day". It celebrates the first time a human arrived on a planet other than Earth. On Mars, it also celebrates the survival of what happened almost immediately after landing … and those first few months afterwards.

That human was me. My name is Mike Lane, and I am the original Pathfinder. I gained that title by being the first spacefaring explorer to set foot on a new world, a new planet. The planet Mars to be specific. Humanity had sent dozens of exploratory robotics to the planet, but I was the first flesh and blood to arrive. While I followed in the footsteps of Yuri Gagarin, the first man in space, and Neil Armstrong, the first man on the Moon: I was the first human to go to another *planet*. That seemed to capture the imagination of all generations, everywhere. Humans were finally on their way as an interplanetary species. While I have great respect for those other two firsts, I identified more closely with Cortés. For me, there would be no going home. The fact that Cortés had destroyed his ships upon arrival in the modern southern California (formerly Mexico), would later, strike a very eerie chill down my spine.

I arrived in orbit without any fanfare. My transit vehicle took up geosynchronous orbit about 15 degrees south of the Corporation's Mar-Sat (Mars Satellite), which had arrived twenty months earlier. The 246 days in transit had been both a very long, and yet a very quick journey. I bemoaned how long it was taking while I was on the way to Mars, but when I arrived, I found it hard to believe that I had gotten there so soon. The massive amount of studying, daily science experiments, and the regimen of strength and aerobic exercise that I did twice a day while in transit was probably why time flew by for me.

The plan that had been released to the world was that the Mars Transit Vehicle (MTV), which I somewhat affectionately referred to as the "Jalopy", was going to be abandoned as space debris since it was too big to land. We told everyone it would eventually enter a decaying orbit, and burn up in the atmosphere of Mars. We lied.

We had a secret plan to leave the transit vehicle in orbit as a secondary communications satellite and observation deck. It had to be a secret, because of a few other capabilities that I'm not ready to talk about yet. In case something ever happened to Mar-Sat, it could also function as a secondary communication satellite. Redundancy in space exploration is always good. There is an old saying amongst survivalists, "Where you have two, you have one; where you have one, you have none." It applies to space travel as well!

While the full capabilities of Jalopy-Sat left a distinctive bad taste in my mouth, I liked the whole cloak and dagger aspect of it too. It appealed to my inner-action movie junkie. Less than forty people knew about this plan for Jalopy, and the off-site contractors that supplied the extra "stuff" were not in the habit of being loose lipped. They were all hired and controlled by an external government agency of a foreign power that I'll talk more about later.

The most difficult aspect within the secret part of the mission was getting the nuclear mini-reactor installed without the media catching wind of it. However, the mini-reactor was needed to power Jalopy-Sat reliably for many years to come. Relying on solar power for this was not within the mission parameters for Jalopy-Sat, officially known to *those in-the-know* as "The Mars Platform" or more simply as "The Platform".

After ascent and reaching orbit, I went into the trajectory burn. The final burn of the remaining big engines positioned, and placed me on a ballistic trajectory to meet up with Mars just over eight months later. After the transit vehicle (I hesitate to call it a ship - it was metaphorically just a big hollow bullet with a man inside) was on its way, we deployed the solar panel wings. We did this for show. We didn't want the world to know we had a nuclear power source. As well, we were also testing out some new energy technology for future missions. The new solar technology worked so well in fact, that I ran everything off the solar cells, and didn't have to fire up the mini-reactor until I reached Mars.

The last three days before descent were filled with a lot of stuff to do. Now that I was in orbit, I had to retract the solar cells. This was to give the impression that the Jalopy was now debris, *and* make it harder to find. The hull of the Mars Transit Vehicle (and eventual satellite/platform) was made of a product developed in Canada. It returned no radar image, no matter how close the radar was. It also had zero magnetic presence from the hull. The transit vehicle was also painted non-reflective black, which assisted in making it harder to find optically. In reality, the only way you could find the transit vehicle, even if you were in orbit around Mars, was if you knew where it was, or you bumped into it. We told everyone it was black, like my Activity Suit,

2

so that it would absorb energy; part of the new technology being tested. I think most people actually believed us.

Now that I was getting ready to leave the Jalopy behind, I ran through the power-up sequence on the mini-reactor. When its systems were nominal, I moved the ship's electrical system from solar to nuclear. The cabin lights winked out, and then back on. They were on direct feed circuits to give me a visual cue of a power problem. Everything else was on a dual power source controller, so nothing reset or was interrupted.

Most of the trip to Mars had gone smoothly. I still managed to have a few exciting moments. I did have to spend a few boring days in the water cell to avoid the effects of a radiation storm … twice. I had an interesting few moments in the space toilet when I had finished my business, and couldn't get the closet door open. I left it open after that, live cameras be-damned. Aside from that, and a slight course correction after the midpoint, the trip had been flawless until now. This was going to be my glitch of the trip, and it was a big glitch.

I ran the sequence to retract the solar wings, one at a time, and store them back in their original resting bays. The starboard wing retracted as planned; it took 52 minutes. I felt, more than heard, a light *thunk* as it snapped into its cradle. The hatch swung shut, the green lights on the seal came on, and the indicators locked. Awesome. The port side solar wing was a different story. I ran the retraction procedure on the computer, and it showed the retraction was in progress, but when I looked out the port window, nada. Nothing was happening. It was not folding up into its original accordion shape. It was extended, and just sitting there. I re-started the computer sequence and again, all showed working fine. I looked back out the portal and the solar wing sat there, doing nothing, mocking me. I let out a string of expletives under my breath, and sent a quick message to Terra. I went on with some of the other work until the reply came back from Earth. They told me to look out the starboard window; the solar wing that I had successfully packed up was fully extended. The string of expletives got a little bluer.

They responded that it was a software glitch. The port wing retractor was actually firing the starboard wing extender procedures. They said to retract the starboard wing, and then retract the port wing manually. My mood brightened a bit at that. While I had trained for it quite extensively, I never had a reason to go EVA during the trip as of yet. *I was finally going on a spacewalk*!! *Yayyy*!!

I ran the retraction procedure again for the starboard wing, and looked through the portal to make sure it was indeed moving. While that was in progress, I got into my pressure suit, ran the prewalk checks on the environment controls of the space suit, and made sure the oxygen bottles were full. Why don't they call them nitrogen bottles anyways? The air we breathe

3

on Earth is 78% nitrogen, 20% oxygen, and a handful of other gases including carbon dioxide, neon, methane and helium: so really, why don't we call them nitrogen bottles? I digress. I pulled on the lower body torso and legs of the space suit, and then wiggled into the upper torso and arms of the suit. The waist seal got a solid lock the first try. I put on the helmet, powered up the suit, and checked the diagnostic readings and oxygen flow. All was good. I shut down the system and then waited for the starboard wing to finish retracting, again. Finally there was the soft *thunk* sound of the cradling. I confirmed visually that the hatch was closed, and then shut down the program that controlled the solar wings. I didn't want it's "glitch" to decide to re-launch the starboard wing while I was out working on the port wing.

I made sure the water bag was full in my space suit. This was a device that allowed me to drink water through the sippy-hose; not to be confused with the other water bag, which would be almost full by the time I was done. I filled the pressure suit with air, and I put on the helmet. I had to re-set it twice before I could lock it in place. I put on the gloves, sealed them, and then closed my visor. Reaching around behind my helmet, I tightened the locking screw on the visor armature. I didn't want to wind up like Nick Piantanida.

I may have made the whole space suit thing sound easy, but it's not. On Earth I had three people helping me to put it on. In zero-g it was easier to get into; but it still had its challenges. The pressure suit underneath the space suit took almost 20 minutes to put on. The rest of the suit took about an hour to get on and hooked up properly. I always wondered why astronauts in space looked like rag dolls with their arms and legs splayed when resting. It's because of the pressure suit. The pressure suit is pumped up with gas to keep your innerds, from becoming your outerds. Combined with the space suit it makes movement very unorganic. You have to be physically strong and have a good deal of stamina to work in a pressure suit/space suit. If the space suit itself had been pumped up to pressure, it would be useless for movement; hence the two suits. A few hours of EVA, and you can lose a few pounds from exertion against the pressure suit itself. Thankfully I'd be using a mechanical Activity Suit on Mars. Developed by MIT, the Activity Suit was going to be much easier to use. However, for now, I was in the real space suit that was provided to us almost last-minute by NASA, and had to get moving. I say almost last-minute because to this day, each and every NASA space suit is custom-made and hand stitched by a small company in the Mojave desert. They did, however, deliver mine in record time.

Powering up the suit environmental system, and getting all nominal readings, I floated into the smallish airlock on the Jalopy, then shut and sealed the inner hatch. The depressurization was about ninety seconds. I took a deep breath of anticipation, and then I opened the outer hatch.

I stood there in the open hatch, just taking a moment. I was a Pathfinder. I was an Explorer. I was travelling through space and going to a new planet. I was alone. After years of training and months of travel, now, at this moment, about to take my first step into the void: I felt like I was finally a real, honest to goodness astronaut. I laughed quietly; I was giddy like a school boy with a new toy rocket ship.

I looked all around the hatch opening. I could see beautiful Mars in full rise just above the horizon line. I looked down to see distant stars with a lot of nothingness in between them. My tether was securely attached to the airlock's inner anchor point, my tool bag was clipped to my utility belt, and I was ready to go. Holding on to the frame of the hatch, I lifted a foot to step out into the void, and had to stop. I had to suppress the urge to vomit. I knew I was safe, I knew I wasn't going to "fall"; but somewhere in my brain, the animal instinct that preserves most of us from acquiring a Darwin Award kicked in. I took another moment, breathing deeply a few times while still taking in the splendour before me, and then decided to fool my brain. I turned around, facing the interior of the smallish airlockairlock, holding the door frame. Then I just let go and hung there, floating in the open hatch.

I gave a little toot on the manoeuvring jets on my space suit, and flipped upside down slowly. Now Mars appeared below the horizon and suddenly, I didn't feel ill any more. I manoeuvred out about four feet, turned to the right (which was aft now that I was turned around and relatively upside down), and then another little burst on the manoeuvring jets sent me back to the solar wing which was about fifteen feet from the hatch.

I looked down into the cradle-well for the manual release on the solar wing armature, grabbed it and pushed it. Sticking up perpendicular to the cradle, it had to be moved all the way down flush with the cradle to disengage the locking mechanism that would allow me to fold up the wing manually. Of course, it wouldn't budge. I tried again. No movement at all.

I had tools for nuts, bolts and prying things open; but nothing to lever another lever. *"Well, wasn't this a pickle,"* I thought to myself. I can't leave the wing extended. I was already four hours into my orbit time, and only had about sixty-eight hours remaining until descent. While I wasn't in a rush, I wasn't going to dilly-dally either. I put one hand on the frame of the wing-well opening, and swung my body around. I grabbed the frame with my other hand and then swung my body, foot first, down towards the locking mechanism. If you can't turn it or force it ... then kick it! The darn thing didn't even pretend to move.

I repeated this about a dozen times. At some point I started giggling. I knew the exterior wing camera would be trained on me, and in eighteen minutes the live feed would start reaching Flight Control. I knew I would be a sight to see: the astronaut on his multimillion dollar space ship, on a spacewalk, trying to kick a lever closed. To make it even funnier, would be the audio of me grunting and groaning with every kick and calling the mechanism a few choice names; questioning its parentage, like I did with my snow blower during a particularly rough winter, years before on Terra.

After giving up that plan, I re-oriented myself. I floated down to the lower side of the 2 metre long hatch, hunkered down and pressed the back of my pressure suit and PLISS pack (air tanks, etc.) against the frame. I then placed my foot on the lever, and started pushing. I was straining hard, grunting, and then started kicking again, "Close! … Close! … Close!" Finally it gave. The lever moved forward like there had never been a problem. The tight wing went slack, and a sudden *"Oh, shit"* sent me scrambling out of the wing-well. I had visions of the solar wing fully retracting on me, and sealing me in the wing-well like a tomb. Of course, it didn't retract. It had just gone a bit slack without the tension of the locking mechanism.

The rest of the process was easy. Crank in the tension cable a bit, fold the first solar panel flat, crank in the tension cable a bit more, then fold the next solar panel flat; but in the opposite direction. I started out thinking it was easy work, even though it was slow. The solar wings were 49 metres long, and had 156 solar panels. The crank, fold and placement for each panel took about five minutes. However, my nitrogen bottles (hey, I'm a rebel), only lasted a little over four hours. The stowage process took thirteen hours. Then you had to add in the time it took to get the wing unlocked, get the hatch finally sealed shut, stop to fill my nitrogen bottles *four* times, and take a break for lunch during one of the refills. In total, my port wing debacle was a nineteen hour exercise. At the end of it, I was exhausted. At first I thought manual labour in zero-g would be easy, but it's not quite the walk in the park you would think. If anything, you spend more exertion keeping yourself anchored and oriented, as you do the actual work.

There was a whole list of things to do on a clock that was getting smaller, but I had to sleep at this point. I set the alarm for four hours, but wound up sleeping through it and waking up after six. A dozen messages were waiting for me from Flight Control. Hans Gohs, the on duty Mission Director, was beside himself. He didn't outwardly show it, but I had spent a lot of time with the man back on Terra and I could tell he was ready to chew bubble gum, and kick ass. Mainly the ass of the person who programmed the software for the port wing retraction, but I knew I better be a bit "Yes, Sir. No, Sir. Three bags full Sir", or else he might turn his attention to *my* ass.

Roughly forty-six hours until descent, and the next glitch struck.

After waking up and listening to Hans' messages, I had to hit the head. In my haste (both to get to business, and to get this particular business done), I failed to notice the absence of a negative pressure lock when I sat on the space potty. You see, when you make nice-nice in space, the toilet actually has a slight negative pressure inside. It basically suctions itself to your butt or your penis (separate hose for peeing), so that what you eliminate from your body goes down into the small tank that holds it until you vent it to space. However, like I said, I failed to notice the absence of negative pressure.

The Mission Control propeller-head weenies informed me later that when I had been sitting in the wing well with my suit pressed back against the frame for leverage to move the lever of the locking mechanism; my suit had damaged the controller that held the negative pressure in the holding tank. The wing well was right beside where the transit vehicles' head was, and some knob of a designer had put the controller in the port solar wing well.

I finished my business and moved away from the toilet seat (which was supposed to snap a cover closed when you moved away from it); but the cover never snapped shut because there was no negative pressure. As I was working my way through the ESA approved nine step "Sanitary Maintenance Post Evacuation Procedure" (wiping my ass), I noticed an odd smell. I started to turn around and came face to face with something roughly shaped, brown, and very moist. Ewwwww. Space turds …

With the cover not snapping shut, and the lack of negative pressure, everything in the holding tank over the last three days (since the last outboard dump, no pun intended) was slowly floating out of the toilet, and into the small compartment. Yes, I tried to scream in frustration. Tried, being the operative word. IT WAS A BAD CHOICE OF THINGS TO DO IN ZERO-G. When you scream, the first thing you do is make a large inhalation of air. Not wise with "stuff" floating so close to your face in this kind of environment.

The cleanup took two hours. Thankfully there was two small bottles of mouthwash available in the toiletry supplies. At the end of the two hours I had a floating plastic bag full of … well … *you know what it was full of*. I also had a non-functioning toilet that I had to manually close and permanently secure the lid on. It was a small mercy that this happened at the end of the journey, and not at the start. It was no small mercy, however, that in my disgust and haste to clean things up, I had completely forgotten about the live feed cameras sending images back to Flight Control; and from there, out to the internet. Apparently several million viewers saw me exiting the space toilet with my bare ass hanging out, floating space turds around me, and of course, me, spitting and hacking. Yep. The stuff legends are made of. Even now, eighty-three years later, it's still considered one of the most hysterically funny videos of the entire Terran space program; especially after some tech head re-cut the feed and added Strauss' Blue Danube Waltz as the audio track. I still don't think it's so funny. There are certain events in a man's life that he just has to accept he will *never* live down. It just leaves a bad taste in your mouth. Hell, even the Hybrids had seen it; but that's another story completely.

While the video I received from Flight Control was a room full of people laughing so hard I thought they were going to suffer renal failure, the image of Hans was different. He had gone from upset, stopped for lunch somewhere around supremely pissed, and was now driving forward at breakneck speed to the town of, "Apoplectic With Rage – Population 001". His message that I watched after the cleanup indicated that if I was done turning the mission into a Keystone Cops' routine, and that I might want to get on with the shutdown procedures as I was due to descend in approximately 45 hours. "IF, you don't MIND," was his acerbic and cutting closing statement as the vid ended.

Seeing him like that gave me a case of the giggles. The whole absurdity of the situation compounded it, but I knew he was right. Tempus was indeed Fugit-ing, and I was on the clock. I ate some rations quickly, and sipped a lukewarm plastic bag of coffee as I got on with the business of transitioning the MTV to satellite mode.

I had to transfer some supplies and equipment to the Lander. The transit vehicle had brought enough toiletries, food, water, consumables, and medical supplies for a round trip. This was for show. Had I arrived at Mars, and there been a problem with the Hab (Habitat) and other systems on the ground (AtmoGen, Solar Farm, Water Plant, etc), OR there had been a problem with the Lander; then I would need the supplies to do a free-return trajectory shot back to Earth. This step was solely for the happiness of the politicians, government bureaucrats, and the media pundits. Those in the program knew that if we were to do a free-return trajectory on this mission, the position of Mars and Terra at this point meant that the transit vehicle would in fact never reach Terra in time for me to survive. Terra would always be out of reach for the time the supplies would last (all that we had room for), and the transit vehicle would take almost two years for the orbital alignments to allow Terra and the transit vehicle to cross paths again. They only loaded an extra eight and a half months' worth of supplies. Even if I went to half rations on a diet that was low cal and very basic to begin with, I'd still wind up four months short of the time needed to return home safely. This meant there were extras for me to take to the planet. It took me a full day to get everything bagged up and moved to the Lander, then securely stowed. It was a complete waste of time as things would turn out, but I didn't know that then. Work like this *is* easy in zero-g, much easier than the heavy work outside: but it's *slow* work nonetheless. This completed, a stop for lunch and two uses of the ESA approved Emergency Biological Evacuation System (basically eliminating into double thick plastic bags, cameras off), and I was ready for sleep. Thirty six hours until descent and I spent four hours in slumber to rest up for the next phase of preparation.

Awake, refreshed and fed, I had T-Minus 31 hours 20 minutes on the descent clock. It was time to get back into my pressure suit and space suit for my second (though the first planned) EVA. This was a secret part of the Jalopy-Sat's future, so the live feed cameras were turned off. Mission Control would be getting delayed telemetry as usual, but they would not be getting any video, nor would the world. Only a small handful at Mission Control knew what I was up to. As far as the rest of the flight control crew were concerned, there was a problem with the relay satellite, Relay-1, in Terran orbit.

Opening the floor compartments, I pulled out the five square boxes and the one very long box which had been stored there by a "special" night shift crew of "experts", shortly before assembly of the transit vehicle to the booster rockets. I put the long box and one of the square boxes in the airlock, finished getting my suit sealed and running properly, then went into the airlock and depressurized. I was installing a 1.5 metre long telescope on a mounting unit on the exterior dorsal portion of the Jalopy. This was a small telescope, but very powerful. Completely outside the Terran high atmosphere and just that much further from the sun, there was high hopes for what it would provide, in secret, to those planning future space missions. It's true that the Martian thin atmosphere extends farther from Mars than the Terran atmosphere extends from Terra; however, the differences in atmospheric composition made it an insignificant consideration. The mounting platform for the telescope was hooked into the ships power and COM ssytem to allow the telescope to be remotely controlled from Terra or Mars. They had made it idiot proof (a good thing, with me doing the installation). Other than a few mounting bolts, it was plug and play. Well, the secure point screws on the power and communication lines were a bit fiddly, but they had designed it well so I got it done the first try. All I had to do as a last step was run the power-up sequence. It worked like a charm, thankfully.

Finishing this installation, I went back inside, re-pressurized, and exchanged the empty containers for the four full ones which I had tethered together. Back in the airlock I depressurized and went EVA again.

The four boxes contained four cameras. One camera was a bit beyond Ultra-Hi-Def. It would be able to read the output of my suits control panel on my left forearm, when I got to the surface of Mars. Its capability was beyond what NASA or the NSA had, and had been developed in secret by the ESA as a contribution to this mission. They had plans to go commercial with it, but not just yet. The second box contained a targeting camera. It was part camera, part radar, part optical motion-tracker; and all American made. It was hooked up to some very powerful targeting software on board the Jalopy's main computer. It could track any moving object on the surface of Mars larger than 2 centimetres in diameter or within a relatively close (750,000 kilometres, twice as far as Luna is from Terra) approach to Mars from space. It was going to be used for directing and focussing the Ultra-High-Definition camera. It had another use too, but I'll get to that later.

The first two cameras were mounted on the port side, which would always be oriented towards Mars. The final two boxes contained duplicates of the ones I had just installed. These were installed on the starboard side, pointing away from Mars. When that configuration came up in the security briefing, half a dozen questions came to mind; but I decided not ask any of them. I really didn't want to know. When the ESA agent finished his briefing he walked over to me, looked me right in the eye and said, "Is there anything, anything at all, that you need to ask me?" I looked him squarely back in the eyes and said, "No sir. Not a thing. I have my instructions." He reached out and gently slapped me on the shoulder and said, "Good man." Then he walked out of the room, and I never saw him again.

The exterior "package" installation, in total, was fourteen hours. Of course, some of the fourteen hours was me, a-hem, doing a bit of cavorting about. Hey, it was the last time I'd ever walk in space; I was entitled to a bit of frolic. Had there been any audio or video feed of this going back to Flight Control, the "yee-haws" and "woo-hoos" would have done nothing to improve Hans' state of mind. Thankfully, he was spared that challenge by the inherent secrecy of what I was doing. When I came back inside, I got out of the space suit/pressure suit combo and had a bite to eat; there was only 17 hours and 5 minutes left on the descent clock. There was only about four hours of real work left to do, so Flight Control told me to grab as much sleep as I could. It was getting harder to sleep, this close, after so much preparing and travelling. I was almost on Mars! This time, even though I was dog-tired, sleep came with a bit more difficulty. I finally managed to get a surprising seven hours of solid rack time (you have no idea how good you actually *do* sleep in deep space, until you've been there), and woke up with 7 hours and 45 minutes on the descent clock. I ate, used the emergency evacuation system for the last time, and moved the final three small bags of supplies into the Lander, securing them in place. Again, unbeknownst to me, this was a complete waste of time.

At T-Minus 6 hours I began the final system conversions. This officially converted the Jalopy from transit vehicle to satellite. While I had been asleep, Flight Control was busy conducting tests on the camera packages, and everything checked out. They also got the Lander powered up and full diagnostics performed. They were able to do a portion of the systems conversion, but there were parts of it that had to be done locally.

Finished with the software, I made the final hardware configuration changes. I ensured all the hatches, compartments, and storage bins were secured, even though empty. I was ready to leave the Jalopy behind. It had been my home for the last 246 days, and I was glad to be rid of it. It had been a comfortable ride, but in the last couple months the walls had been closing in.

It was time put my Activity Suit on. It was quite different from my space suit. The Activity Suit was designed by MIT astronautics professionals for use on Mars' surface. The Activity Suit did not need a pressure suit, as it maintained pressure mechanically (through fabric pressure) as Mars was not a total vacuum. It was much lighter and flexible than the pressure suit/space suit, and allowed freedom of movement. It was skin tight. There was still an inter-suit heating system, though it was only rated to -30 degrees Celsius. This was all that was technically required by the developers. Because of the harshness of the surface of Mars, especially the blowing sand and the winter temperatures at our colony site that would reach -120 degrees Celsius; I had an exterior jump suit that went over the Activity Suit. The two were attached at certain points so it was like having one of those jackets with the lining you could detach. The exterior jump suit was also air tight when worn properly, but it wasn't pressurized. The exterior jump suit also had a heating system to provide the comfort and protection the Activity Suit couldn't. Okay, maybe the jacket analogy isn't great, but the two functioned as one as far as I was concerned. You could not wear the exterior jumpsuit without the Activity Suit because it wasn't pressurized. If you did, you would die a relatively quick (though not instant), and painful death.

The exterior jump suit was five layers of carbon nano-tube reinforced Kevlar fabric. It even had an optional cowl with faceplate to protect my Activity Suit helmet during high winds and other hostile conditions. The exterior jump suit formed hard seals with the Activity Suit at the collar, wrists, and ankles. The Activity Suit had to stand up to the abrasive environment on the Martian surface, the bumps and falls of a klutz (yours truly), and it had to last a long time. The exterior jump suit was a vital part of the design. The actual Activity Suit and exterior jumpsuit I was putting on now had extra features for use in the space craft, but there was a day-to-day suit combo waiting for me in the habitat. Like the exterior of the MTV, the jump suit I wore on top of the Activity Suit was also black, not white like traditional space suits. The argument was this would absorb more heat on the daytime surface, making things easier on the suit's heating systems. More than once, in the coming years, I would enjoy the benefit of the stealth properties of a black suit. The next time I took this suit off, I would be in the Habitat on Mars. The helmet and gloves were waiting for me in the Lander. The gloves and booties had to have some pressurization though, as there are simply too many bone joints in those areas for the mechanical aspects of the suit to be as effective as needed. Of course, I had Kevlar work gloves to go over the Activity Suit gloves. The boots themselves would have been the pride of any steel worker. After the suit was on, and the initial system check performed, I headed to the Lander tunnel and hatch.

After reaching orbit around Terra on ascent day, part of the long flights configuration was to detach the nose of the space ship from the transit vehicle and turn it around to re-dock it. I rode that candle up into the sky in the Lander craft. The Lander was the nose portion. In orbit we detached, moved the Lander forward about forty feet, manoeuvred it into the proper position, and then docked it with the Command Module. This procedure was almost identical to what the original Apollo astronauts did with the Lunar Lander when going to the moon. Of course, my ship was more spacious (designed for four people to be comfortable on an extended mission), and it was prettier.

During my journey, I rarely went into the Lander. There was no life support running in there, and the heat was kept to the bare minimum (15.6 degrees Celsius) to conserve energy and prevent condensation. When I arrived in Mars orbit, Flight Control had remotely turned everything on, powered it up, and ran all the system checks for me. All I had to do was stow the luggage, as it were. There was a short, one metre tunnel between the Lander and the Command Module vehicle with air tight hatches at both ends. The last two things I had to do were: turn out the lights, and transport the portable waste elimination system to the Lander.

I moved forward to the crawl hatch and hit the master light button near the opening. The transit vehicle went dark. The only light that was available was coming in through the port side, ventral, and dorsal portals; as well as the light coming in through the hatch. The starboard portal was dark as it was pointing away from Mars, and that side was not facing Sol, the sun, at the present time.

The final item was to export the portable waste system. I looked down at the thick plastic bags in my hand. Double bagged and tied off with plastic ties. I had a vision of those bags bouncing around in the Lander during descent, and knew there was no way I was going to take that risk. Travel 120 million miles on my own in a glorified tin can, no problem; take thick plastic bags of human waste into the Lander, no way. I lifted my hand, and let them float aft in the Jalopy. I backed into the hatch to the Lander.

I sealed the Jalopy-Sat hatch, floated backwards into the Lander and then sealed the Lander hatch. I hit the hard-seal button. This turned the pressurized seal into a hard seal by turning four small screw engines that inserted four tapered plugs through the door jamb, and into the hatch rim. By the time they were fully inserted, that hatch wasn't going anywhere. The same process repeated out of sight on the Jalopy-Sat hatch. In the Lander, each insertion point had a small mechanical confirmation device. When the small glass window showed a red panel that was clear, it meant no hard-seal and no soft-seal. When I engaged the soft seal, the red turned to light green. When the hard-seal screw stopped turning and everything was tight, the plain green turned to a darker green barber-pole pattern. Four barber poles. It made the heart feel good.

Twelve minutes left until the descent sequence. I grabbed my helmet, put it on, and plugged my Activity Suit's umbilical into the Lander's life support system. Nothing happened. The suit heater was supposed to be on, and I was supposed to feel the life support systems oxygen flow in my helmet. Crap. I unplugged and plugged the hose back in. *Still nothing*. I started to run a quick diagnostic, but when I lifted my left arm to look at the suits control panel attached to it, I realized I hadn't turned the suits system back to the "On" position after completing the initial diagnostic during suit-prep.

"Oh for Pete's sake", I said out loud. I imagined Loreena laughing at my chagrin, and smiled.

I set the control to "On"; immediately I felt things start to warm up, and instantly felt the oxygen flow in my helmet. I put on the gloves, pressurized them and the boots, and then re-checked the closures and seals on the boots, helmet and gloves. Everything was good. I snapped down the visor, tightened the screw on the locking bar, and then turned up the air pressure in the Lander cabin. The additional air pressure was required to strengthen the stability of the Lander while it tore through the buffeting forces of descent through an atmosphere that, by its very nature, wanted me to die.

I strapped myself into the seat, which was more of a purple cushioned chaise-lounge with pretentions. Flight Control had transmitted the final descent guidance package from Terra, they sent it directly to the Lander's Computer: all systems had been setup, and were ready to go. All I had to do was press the "Go-No-Go" button. It was the only part that I played in the descent process. The Lander would not actually detach and descend unless I pressed one small, but oh-so-important green button on the small panel in front of me. However, pressing the button didn't make it actually "go" per se, it was more of a button to tell the computer that it was okay to go; when it decided in its inestimable silicon wisdom that the actual millisecond of departure had arrived.

My friends on Terra had made a big deal about me getting to "fly" a space ship. However, ever since the end of the original Space Shuttle program, astronauts didn't technically "fly" anything. During launch, the spaceship was on top of a ballistic projectile. In transit, the guidance system directed and auto-corrected the ships course faster and more accurately than a human could. During descent, you were basically riding inside a large metal can that is being "lobbed" by the computer in the right direction. I wasn't "flying" anything. I was just along for the ride. I was luggage.

Chapter 2

399 Days Ago

I tried to grasp what I was hearing.

"Just one person?"

"Yes."

"In twenty weeks?"

"Yes."

That flew in the face of everything we had been working on. It also meant I'd be going to Mars six years before anyone else ... *alone*.

Jayden, the CEO of the Corporation continued, "You are the only real choice for this, Mike. I can't make you do it of course, but the whole program depends on someone going."

I stared at him, slack jawed I'm sure. I stared at him so long, it started to get uncomfortable.

"Mike, I need you to do this. I need you to say yes. No pressure of course, but if you don't do this, I have to send someone I don't have 100% confidence in. You are the only one that I think ... that *we* think, can handle going to Mars alone."

The meeting was being held in Jayden's spacious office. He was the CEO of the Corporation behind the Mars colony project. Along with Jayden were Hamish, the VP of Technology, and Clarissa, the CFO. It was a small and cozy group. There was good coffee from from the Tim Hortons coffee chain back home in Canada. It was my one weakness, well, the only one I was willing to admit.

I didn't know why I had been called to the CEO's office. Whenever I got called to see the boss, I was always nervous I was going to catch hell for something. It was inherent because of my upbringing, and would probably never go away.

We sat at one end of the not-so-small conference table. Jayden at the head, I was on his right side, while Hamish and Clarissa sat on his left side. Jayden toyed with his pen as they made small talk before he started addressing the issue at hand.

With the small talk out of the way, Jayden cleared his throat and began a speech that would forever change my life, which would forever change humanity's future in space; which would ultimately change a lot of things.

15

Chapter 3

Four Years Ago

The Corporation was planning a one-way mission to Mars, according to their webpage. The most difficult part about a manned Mars mission had always been the delivery of the equipment, but more importantly, the fuel, to return a crew back to Earth. The Corporation simplified the process and the technological aspects (relatively speaking) by making it a one-way mission.

The plan was that they were going to begin colonizing Mars with volunteers on one-way missions to the red planet. Every two years, they were going to send a crew of four or six colonists on the eight-month journey. Each manned mission would be preceded by supply and equipment missions delivering consumables, medical supplies, habitats, exploration and building equipment. They planned to start manned these missions in ten years.

Another unique element to this endeavour is that it was totally private. That is, commercial. This was a private corporation with no political or governmental ties. Therefore they didn't need to do things the government way; they weren't limited by government bureaucracy or the voting public. Based in Sweden, they enjoyed a freedom that most corporations located in a super power would not enjoy.

To the excitement of a great many sci-fi fans, scientists, and thrill-seekers everywhere, they opened up the colonist application process to everyone in the whole world. They only needed to have good health, and be able to speak, read and write in English. Any age was welcome to apply. Training would be provided.

As soon as I finished reading this on their website, I found the appropriate online form and submitted my application. It cost me thirty Euros to apply, but it was well worth it. I was forty-seven years old when I submitted my application. "Fat chance I have," I thought at the time. However, the thought of applying was in itself, a high of its own. It might help me forget, too.

As I was filling out my application, I thought of Loreena's face, how she would have burst out laughing if I told her I wanted to go to Mars. She would have then kissed me slowly and given me a few very good reasons not to go. It was a dumb thought, that it might help me forget; I would simply take that empty aching space in my heart with me, no matter where I ran to. For a long time now, the only important thing left in my life had been my son. He was the result of some heavy petting that got out of hand with my teenage sweetheart; a very welcome product, mind you. She and I had never married.

We were just kids ourselves. Close to twenty years later, I met Loreena on the day she furloughed out of the Navy. A year later we were married.

My son was an adult now, following his career, dating someone I hoped would become his wife. I couldn't stop moving forward just for him, not that I was moving forward then anyways. I didn't have the strength or desire to be with anyone else. I didn't want to face the potential for that pain again. Sometimes running away is the only option left.

When I told my son about Mars, he was supportive, though I think he was inwardly rolling his eyeballs. I told my best friend about it, Mary. She just closed her eyes and shook her head. She was used to my hair brain ideas and plans.

When she asked what I was thinking, my diatribe started.

Yes, it's a one-way trip but wow, what a trip! Once on Mars, I would never, *ever* be able to return to Earth. I would never sit on green grass, under a tree, or by a river. I was okay with that. I would never be able to step outside and take a deep breath of air; because outside on Mars, the air is deadly. I was okay with that too. I would never be able to nip off to the convenience store, stop at Tim Hortons for a coffee, go to a Cineplex for some popcorn and the latest thriller, have a pet or any one of the thousands of things we take for granted daily. I could give those things up. All my life I had shared my living space with cats; so not having a cat with me would be troubling to my sense of calm ...but I'd get over it. I hesitated as I rhymed off these things to Mary, as she smiled supportively. I wouldn't be able to put flowers by Loreena's headstone anymore. I was okay with that ... I *was* okay with that ... barely. Mary's eyes filled with compassion for my silent thoughts. She just sat there quietly, sipping her coffee; she didn't say anything. Twelve years had dulled the pain, but Mary remembered how I had cried myself to sleep every night, for almost three years.

The most daunting aspect was going to be leaving my adult son on Terra. Yes, he was an adult and studying to be a scientist, but I would never see him again in person. That was going to be hard. Even more daunting, he would marry someday and have children, my grandchildren. While I would see images, video, sound recordings; I would never be able to hold them, hug them, kiss them, or bounce them on my knee. Hmmm ... okay, that was going to be harder. I didn't know then, that one of my future unborn granddaughters, *his daughter*, was going to join me on Mars; but that's another story.

For the success of the mission, I believed that at forty-seven years of age I had something important to offer that a lot of the younger folks applying didn't have. I had a vast amount of life experiences behind me, I had emotional strength won through some very tough emotional battles, and most importantly: I had perspective. While my life was by no means even relatively close to being over, I had done a lot of living and knew that the worldly diversions we all enjoy would be very easy to give up. I had already given up a lot of them after that hot August night in 2003. Well, they better send *coffee* with me, or else heads would roll …

The reason I wanted to go to Mars, aside from the fresh start, was both very simple and very complex.

When Hernán Cortés landed on the coast of Mexico (now part of Southern California), he destroyed his ships so his people would work harder to survive. On Mars, there would be no rescue mission. The ship that took the human colonists there would *not* take off again, effectively putting the colonization team in a similar situation to Cortés and his men.

Survival meant work, commitment and determination. My life had been full of those. The history of the world was full of people with these traits and characteristics. The history of the world was filled with people who went on what they thought, or knew would be one-way journeys. People like Gaspar and Miguel Corte-Real, Percy Fawcett, Peng Jiamu, Benjamin Smith and others had already set the example. Of course, they all probably met their fates in bad circumstances; but the important part was the courage, the commitment, and the dedication.

Man had gone from Terra to the Moon, but never ventured farther. Conspiracy theorists surmised humans were warned off by aliens, but in fact it was merely economics and the lack of political will; or so I thought. As this was a private corporation and not a political entity, political will was not a factor. All that remained would be funding.

I guess the thing that really drove me the most was that I was a sci-fi fan since childhood. In saying that, most sci-fi involves Earthlings becoming an interplanetary species. I remembered old movie classics like *Mission To Mars*, *Journey to the 7th Planet*, *Kronos*, *Buck Rogers* (the original, and the remake with Gil Gerard). These, and many others made childhood exciting, with dreams and imaginings of incredible adventures beyond the bounds of Earth's orbit. As an adult, shows like *Firefly*, *Andromeda*, and *Farscape* fueled my imagination. Perhaps the most powerful one for me was *Star Trek*. The crew of the good ship Enterprise, on its five-year mandate to explore strange new worlds. As much as these fictional stories and characters drove my imagination, and were probably the fuel cell for my desire to go, there were also the very grown-up and practical considerations of my adult mind.

The only way we were going to be an interplanetary species was if we went to another planet, period.

Someone had to get off their lazy ass and go. Someone had to make the first step. Someone had to step up. That was going to be me: I was going to step up. Besides, I knew in my heart that if I was selected to go to Mars, it would be because God intended me to go: and that would be enough confirmation for me that it was the right thing to do. No matter what challenges, dangers, and difficulties I faced, I had full confidence walking with the Lord at my side. American astronaut Col. Mike Good seems to have expanded upon wartime columnist Ernie Pyle when he said, "They say there are no atheists in foxholes, but there are probably no atheists in rockets".

It was time for humanity as a species to move forward. It was time to take another giant leap off of Neil Armstrong's "small step for man". We were going to move forward by standing on the shoulders of giants like Alan Shepard, Neil Armstrong, and Yuri Gagarin. It was time for humans to begin their interplanetary existence. Sign me up.

Chapter 4

Jayden's Pitch

"We had a visit from the Swedish Minister of Foreign Affairs a few days ago. The Minister himself came to see us. He wanted to express some concerns about the Corporation's plan. Why this is coming five years into the program, we can't say for sure, but it's something we have to deal with."

Jayden adjusted his seating, looked at Hamish and Clarissa, and then continued on.

"Bottom line Mike, is that they want to shut us down. The Minister said we were recklessly endangering human life, and that there was no proof any of our technology, or any of our systems would get a person safely to Mars; and if it did, he had very little doubt they would perish from system failure in a very short time. He says that unless we abandon this project ourselves, or at least scale it back to a research project, his Ministry was going to shut us down."

I was shocked. I had given up my entire former life for this, and here Jayden was telling me it was for naught. "Isn't this exactly why you spent so much money lobbying for the changes to the Outer Space Treaty?"

"The Minister isn't claiming primacy of the space endeavour; they are going to shut us down for more mundane violations. He didn't specify which, but it doesn't really matter. They are the government of the country in which we reside. They can do whatever they want. Legal department has assured me that yes, they can shut us down for just about any reason they want to; but we would have a very good chance of having that overturned by the courts."

I smiled.

"Unless the government issues a parliamentary decree that is notwithstanding the court's ruling."

The smile faded.

"Fighting this would be successful in the long run, but our chief advocate says it could be tied up for as long as the government wants to tie it up. It could be tied up for years. He also said that we should find out what is really behind this move by the Minister."

Until now, the Swedish government had been fully behind us. They were proud we were based there, and happy to ride the publicity coat tails. What Jayden was telling me was coming as a shock, and a surprise.

"We know the Americans, the Chinese, the French, and the Russians are all actively pursuing a Mars colony program, but they are pursuing it with a 'return the crew' mentality; they are not committed to one-way voyages. The board has been talking about this, and we believe that one of these governments is behind the move by our Minister. Only the Chinese or the Americans have the clout to do this, but even still, Sweden has always been a neutral power, so we still can't figure out why they are playing along.

"We did corner his Excellency on one important point though; we got him to agree that if we could offer irrefutable proof that a human colony could survive on Mars, they would then remove the barriers. He expressly agreed that given irrefutable proof, the government would not stand in the way. For now though, they said we both scale down operations and give up the plans to go to Mars, or they would come in and shut us down."

I was stunned. I sipped my coffee and looked at Jayden. Everything I was working for and wanted, was being taken away. The "man" was going to step in and screw things for the little guy. Part of me wanted to cry; part of me wanted to hit something. Clarissa started to talk, but I got up and walked over to the coffee maker. I poured another coffee, turned and waved the pot at them. Hamish lifted his cup. I topped it up, and then returned the coffee pot, setting it down a little too hard - but not hard enough to break it. I added some powdered Coffee-Mate (I preferred it over cream or milk in preparation for a 100 million mile trip to the corner store), and went back to the table. I sat down, looked at Jayden and said, "Go on."

"We've come up with an idea to work around this. To be honest Mike, it's illegal given the Minister's direction, it could get us thrown in prison, and it all hinges" he paused, "On you".

"Me?" Suddenly confused I said, "Why me?"

Jayden set his pen down, leaned forward in his chair, tented his fingers in front of him and said, "Mike. I need you, *we* need you," He paused, took a deep breath and continued, "We need you to go to Mars alone. We need you to go as a proof of concept mission. We need to do this in secret; you need to leave in twenty weeks, and we need to start today."

Chapter 5

May 1st, 2018 09:06 GMT

Mission Time 29 Hours, 12 Minutes

I looked over all the readings in front of me for the umpteenth time. I had been sitting here patiently for hours. I didn't really have to "do" anything now that the Lander had docked nose first with the Command Module. Still though, I couldn't enter the Command Module again until after the Trajectory Engines finished their trajectory burn. I had been in it once after the turn around, I had to power it up and make sure all the life support systems were working; and I had to run a local hardwired diagnostics program. Everything was good to go. After shutting down the non-critical systems, I floated back to the Lander and resealed both hatches. I turned my flight couch in the opposite direction, so I would be facing relative forward when the Trajectory Engines fired for the transit orbit insertion, and the eventual trajectory burn.

Getting me to Mars was a little more complicated than the old Apollo missions. In the last twenty weeks the Corporation had prepped, loaded, and lifted six supply missions; all successfully launched, and then sent on their way to Mars in the last two weeks. The two Habitats had gone two months ago, along with the AtmoGen plant, all in separate launches and transit profiles. Those systems were still six months from landing, and if there was a problem with them, it would be pucker time.

I had to travel to LEO (Low Earth Orbit) with another supply mission. My Lander piggybacked the supply mission on top of a Boeing Delta IV Heavy. The last-minute nature (yes, 20 weeks is very last minute in the space program), and rush of this mission had caused the need for some creative and outside the box thinking. It also required our mostly silent benefactors in pulling some strings, and I'm sure, doing some leaning on people and businesses.

I was riding right now, in the Lander which was also the nose cone of the supply mission, which had been carried up by the last of the Delta IV Heavy launches. We were using the Dragon Lab 5, from the Falcon Corporation, as the Lander. It was roomier, a full metre wider than Dragon Lab 2. It had been modified heavily, of course, to land on Mars. We couldn't use a simple parachute retrieval in the ocean because: a.) there are presently no oceans on Mars, and b.) there was no one on Mars to retrieve me from the ocean, had an ocean presently existed on the red planet.

This version of the Dragon Lab 5 had been modified with a proper airlock and a three stage RAD (Rocket Assisted Descent) assembly to keep the capsule from crashing into the surface while under parachute. The airlock had been installed because once on Mars, the Lander was going to be my lifeboat in case anything happened to the Habitats. Because this was going to be an option for an extended mission, they also did a last-minute installation of an enclosed Head in the Lander, opposite the airlock. I guess the Head also served to balance out the weight profile of the craft.

The Lander was on top of the PDV (Payload Delivery Vehicle). The PDV was basically a big tin can that you could put stuff in. It also had a parachute, and RAD system - but it was a *big* tin can; so it had bigger parachutes, and a bigger set of landing rockets. The PDV also had a set of Trajectory Engines to get it into Geosynchronous Transit Orbit (GTO), and then on its way to Mars from High Earth Orbit (HEO). The PDV was the standard supply delivery system the Corporation was using for supplies and equipment to Mars, this one was just a bit bigger. Each of those flights to Mars cost approximately US$185 million. Its useable internal size was just over 3 metres in diameter, and almost 6.8 metres in length. It was the largest payload system ever launched that was capable of landing on a planet. The composite MTV (Mars Transit Vehicle) was larger; however, the MTV could not land, so I guess it was semantics.

I'm afraid I may be making something complicated, seem overly simplified; but it really was quite complicated. Personally, I think it was more amazing that we went at all, rather than just that we went. How everything was pulled together was a salute to human ingenuity, dedication, perseverance, and American intimidation. The rush to get this Mission on its way was what had made it more complicated than it needed to be; but when someone else takes you to a dance, you don't usually get to choose the music. It was far more complicated than a routine supply and colony mission would be in the future, as future missions would not have the US Air Force having any sway over them … we hoped. For today, however, they did have a stake in this particular launch, yet oddly no stake in our colony mission itself. Future supply and colony missions would only need the Falcon Heavy; they wouldn't need the Delta IV Heavy.

Getting the mission on the road had five parts to it. First we had to get all the necessary parts (Payload Delivery Vehicle, Lander, Command Module, Support Module, and two sets of Trajectory Engines) into Low Earth Orbit (LEO). Second step was to re-assemble the parts in the right order. Third step was to enter a Geosynchronous Transit Orbit (GTO), to get the two flights to a High Earth Orbit (HEO). Fourth step was re-alignment and orientation for the final trajectory burn. Finally, the fifth step would be the trajectory burn itself, which would accelerate the PDV and then the MTV into coplanar heliocentric (around the sun) orbital trajectories: delivering us to the red planet. Not surprisingly, it was the fourth step - the re-alignment and orientation - that was the most critical and sensitive part of this process.

As I said, the first part of this was getting all the necessary parts into LEO. This required three separate launches from Vandenberg. The third launch was the Lander on top of the Payload Delivery Vehicle (with one set of Trajectory Engines). This launch was brought to LEO by a Delta IV Heavy. The second launch was for the oddly large Support Module, also lifted by a Delta IV Heavy (I should point out here, that both of the Delta IV Heavy rockets and launches were secretly paid for by the U.S. government). The first launch had been the other set of Trajectory Engines and the Command Module or more precisely, the living module. This first launch was lifted to LEO by the Falcon Heavy. This Command Module is where I would spend all of my time while in transit to the red planet.

The order of the launches facilitated the second step, the re-assembly of the Mars Transit Vehicle (MTV) components. The Lander, the Command Module, and the Support Module were, collectively, the MTV.

The Trajectory Engines were like a mini-version of the Falcon Heavy. It was just the nine Merlin engines and fuel tanks in an open framework (no cowling). The fuel tanks only burned for five minutes and the Trajectory Engines didn't have to lift anything off the ground. This allowed the fuel tanks to be significantly smaller than the original, but the engines were no less powerful. This Trajectory Engine only had to get us out of HEO, and up to speed. Mass, momentum, Newtonian physics, and a properly calculated heliocentric transfer orbit would get us to Mars. While the whole Mars Transit Vehicle had significant mass, it had very little gravity to overcome from High Earth Orbit. Naturally, there was also no atmospheric drag to compensate for either.

The Support Module had to be a separate launch because of its size. Its surprising size was due to the U.S. Air Force, and hence why the U.S. Government paid for it, but more on that later. After all three sections were in LEO, they had to be "reconfigured". This was when I might have the opportunity to do the only real bit of "flying" I was going to do in the mission. The computer made it way easy, but I still had to punch some buttons (*just call me Yorick*). I had a joystick for manoeuvring so that the human luggage could take over in case the computer failed, but it didn't.

After I attained LEO in the third launch, I spent half a day waiting for the orbits of the three lifts to get into close proximity. It was a relief when the orbits synchronized, and the Delta IV Heavy's cowling was jettisoned. We could now separate the Lander from the top of the PDV. The Mission plan had programmed a few hours during this time for me to get some sleep, but really, would you have slept?

After separating from the PDV, the Lander used manoeuvring rockets to move forward about forty feet, turning one hundred and eighty degrees, so the nose of the Lander was oriented to the rear. Small thruster rockets moved the Lander fifty feet to the port side of the PDV. This all happened as the other half of the reconfiguration was taking place.

The Command Module (the first launch), had the Support Module (the second launch), approaching it from behind. As retrorockets on the top end of the Command Module fired short bursts to slow it down; the Support Module fired manoeuvring rockets and attitude rockets to align the two immense bodies. Over the space of about an hour, the two modules drew closer and closer together until finally, in a minutely controlled ballet of retrorockets, attitude rockets, and manoeuvring rockets; they hard docked together. The mechanical male/female connection points fit together perfectly. The internal mechanics of the hard dock points immediately drew the two Modules tightly together, becoming inseparable. There was an airlock collar that also aligned between the two, so that I could enter the Support Module if necessary. With much breath holding, and a really big collective sigh afterwards, this docking and connection of the two modules went flawlessly.

As this ballet in space was playing out, the PDV, with the Lander as a sidekick, travelled abreast of the partially assembled MTV. Then it was my turn to join up. The Lander used thrusters and attitude rockets to move another four hundred and fifty feet to port from the PDV, putting it directly in front of the Command Module. With some more minutely controlled firing of retrorockets, attitude rockets, manoeuvring rockets, and a bit of breath holding; the Lander flawlessly hard docked with the Command Module, nose first. The nose of the Lander contained the pressurized tunnel that would allow me to move back and forth between the Command Module and the Lander.

The Command Module and the Support Module made up the MTV proper (Mars Transit Vehicle). The Lander was considered part of the MTV; operationally it was just really big luggage on the roof-rack. The MTV is where I would live for the next eight and a half months, rarely entering the Lander prior to descent day. Once all three sections were securely joined, and remote system checks performed, I entered the MTV Command Module to do the full system power-up, local status checks, and then return to the Lander for the GTO burn.

An hour after the in-orbit assembly finished, the PDV and the MTV had a small burn on the Trajectory Engines to put both rockets into an elliptical GTO (Transfer Orbit). A few short hours later, and we were coming up on the GTO apogee. The point of apogee was in High Earth Orbit, and it was from there that we would have the final burn of the Trajectory Engines to get us on our way to Mars.

The transfer orbit burn had been eleven hours ago. After the gentle GTO burn, I was nothing but a tourist again for those eleven hours. I went back into the Command Vehicle to give everything the once over, a second and a third time. I also spent an embarrassing amount of time in the zero gravity doing somersaults, spins, playing with my floating flashlight, and then a small box of Smarties. I had put the Smarties in my flight suit's pant leg pocket, expressly for this reason. Yes, I ate the red ones last. My mind had ample time to wander, as I floated there; counting down the remaining Smarties, counting down the remaining minutes until I left Terra forever. Such a moment of mental freedom was something of a novelty after the last twenty weeks of non-stop effort.

As I floated there amidst the few remaining Smarties, said red ones, a big smile erupted on my face. I had a flash of Loreena, clapping her hands and smiling, showing nothing but joy and happiness for me. I guess I was lucky that most of my memories of her were good ones. Floating serenely in the silence, I unzipped the breast pocket on my fight suit and pulled out the small plastic folder. I flipped it open and gazed with fondness, and longing at her picture: My red-headed Amazon. She was 193 cm tall, almost 11 cm taller than me. She looked back at me, her soft green eyes peeking out from under her flowing red curly hair; the wild hair that she refused to tie up, falling down over her shoulders; over her one shoulder white dress; she was as radiant in the picture as she had been in person. That picture, taken on our wedding day, in the back of the limo, showed us very happy and very much in love. It was how we lived almost every day, almost. With the military assistance in getting us on the way to Mars, it was natural I would think of her at that moment. She had served most of her career as an Interdiction Specialist on the Restigouche class destroyer HMCS Terra Nova. Loreena spent her last year instructing future officers in Interdiction tactics at the Royal Military College of Canada. That she had been such a fearless and effective warrior, a truth supported by her nightmare screams; the way she died was beyond tragic - it was just stupid. That son-of-a-bitch just *had* to stop off for a cold one after work. I put that thought of my head, I needed to focus. I gave the picture a soft kiss, and then put it back in my pocket, over my heart.

The Smarties were still floating there. I ate the last of the red ones. It was now time to get back to the Lander and get strapped in for the final trajectory burn. Before the return to the Lander, however, upon being alerted by Flight Control, I went over to the Port portal (window) and watched the Trajectory Engines burn on the PDV. The distance between the PDV and the MTV had been widening over the eleven hours, but I could still see where it was. We weren't close by ground standards, but we were close by space standards, though still a safe distance apart. Because of its stealth properties, I couldn't actually see the PDV until the engines lit up. Being relatively close, it was a bit of 'Shock & Awe' to watch those nine Merlin engines ignite, and witness the space ship move off slowly at first; but very, very rapidly gain speed. In a few seconds it was gone from sight, and all I could see was the fading light from the engines. The Trajectory Engines burn for only five minutes, exactly. That gets the rocket up to supersonic speed. After that, the Trajectory Engines are jettisoned and it is Newtonian physics that gets the space ship where it's going. All three Laws of Motion at play.

Presently, I was now in the final leg of the GTO and coming up on the rapidly approaching apogee. Because of the MTV's higher overall mass, the MTV trajectory burn was from a bit higher orbit. I had been awake now over thirty hours, but the thought of sleep still wasn't anywhere on my radar. With the PDV finally en route to Mars, I was strapped in my seat again and was impatiently waiting for the Mars Transit Vehicle to be on its way.

The size of the MTV had caused some comment. The Command Module itself had just over 30 feet by 12 feet of interior space (minus cupboards, equipment, and storage areas) for the occupants. It was designed for four people to spend over eight months inside that small area. For just one occupant on this journey, it was positively palatial by comparison to the Apollo 11 Command Module. However, as a proof of concept mission, there were a lot of concepts I had to prove. That was why they sent me in the full size Command Module.

The Support Module had caused a small stir. Most space designers (Roscosmos, ESA, Falcon, etc.) agreed it only needed to be about eighteen feet long; however, the Support Module on the MTV was forty feet long. That had caused some pause and more than a bit of commentary when images of the MTV were revealed during the launch day video feeds. The fact that the Lander, Command Module, and Support Module were almost ninety feet long in total, and that they were all matte black, raised quite a few technical and military eyebrows. We simply told everyone the Support Module was full of new technology for space travel that we needed to proof and validate for the safety of future flights of humans to Mars. I was the first human going to Mars, after all. That seemed to keep most people happy in the long run. *Most people*.

The day after the trajectory burn, the Science and Space reporter for Fox News appeared on the early morning Fox & Friends program, and raised some questions. He made some suggestions about secret military missions, and government cover-ups in how the mission was planned and announced so suddenly. He then went on to suggest that the mission was solely to establish a weaponized military presence on Mars. He even referred to me as the "expendable package". It was a pretty farfetched accusation considering this was a one man colony mission. I like to think that most people would have just snickered at him from behind their coffee cups, and got on with their day.

However, John Portland had a reputation. He was the reporter known for some outlandish views and opinions that invariably turned out to be true.

Mr. Portland went straight to his suburban home after that early morning appearance. He arrived in time to see his young daughters off to school, and his wife off to work; kissing each one in turn. It seemed like his wife had only just pulled her car out of the driveway when his doorbell rang. There were two very tall and solidly built men standing at the door when he opened it. They hovered in his doorway in black suits and black fedoras, perfectly trimmed crew cut hair, very square jaws, wearing Ray-Ban sunglasses. After a brief discussion, they suggested to Mr. Portland that he should refrain from reporting any further wild speculation on the nature of the colonization mission, particularly the components of the space ship; the Support Module specifically. He informed them his opinion was protected by the First Amendment and that he would report on that which he chose to report on; including his own opinion and speculation. He further informed them that now he was even keener to investigate this topic, *and* that he would indeed continue his reports of said investigations, *and* that they did not intimidate him from finding out the truth about what was being sent to Mars.

The next morning, Fox News reported the unfortunate passing of John Portland. They reported that he had apparently committed suicide, by jumping from the balcony of his home, thus tragically ending his life. They judiciously chose not to report that it was a second floor balcony, and he fell only ten feet to the lawn at the back of his house. They may have been incensed and outraged, but there wasn't a single executive at the news agency that wanted to fall from their second floor balcony as well.

The medical examiner, while unaware of the circumstances of the man's recent on-air commentaries prior to his untimely demise, had a lot of unanswered questions on his hands. These questions were soon taken care of by a couple of visitors. As the two large men in black suits and black fedoras, perfectly trimmed crew cut hair, very square jaws, wearing Ray-Ban sunglasses hovered in the doorway of the medical examiner's office; he somewhat nervously edited some observations out of his final report. Specifically, he removed reference to the observations that the 3 metre fall had apparently caused Mr. Portland to break an eye socket, a cheek bone, his neck, his left arm, six fingers and both legs. After Mr. Portland's death, there were no more serious media stories *anywhere* concerning the Support Module.

Shortly after Mr. Portland, *ahem*, committed suicide, another incident of little note took place involving Brenda Finney, an acquaintance of Mr. Portland and a high level civilian clerk at Vandenberg Air Force Base. She was a sweet middle aged woman, single with no children, winsome in appearance as my grand-mother would have said. She had a passion for retro 50's clothing, and bought far more than she could afford, even though she had the ample pay grade of a high level clerk in the requisitioning office. Her passion caused her to have a significant debt load and financial problems that she kept hidden from everyone. The shame of her compulsive behaviour was too much to share. Shortly after Mr. Portland's as yet undiscovered demise, she answered the phone ringing on her desk, and was summoned to the main gate. She was told there were a couple of men there to see her. Not expecting anyone, curiosity eating at her, she arrived at the gate minutes later to find two large men in black suits and black fedoras, perfectly trimmed crew cut hair, very square jaws, wearing Ray-Ban sunglasses. They had offered the Duty Officer the ID of another government agency, but the D.O. didn't say which agency, when he led her to them. When questioned later he said he hadn't slept well the night before, was kind of bleary-eyed that morning, and didn't really remember what agency they were from. That was his story, and he was sticking to it. All he remembered was that Brenda had spoken briefly with the two men, and then appearing to be fighting back tears, she accompanied them to the nondescript black sedan that they had arrived in. Brenda Finney was never seen again. By anyone. Ever.

Of course, I didn't know any of that had transpired while I was waiting, a bit impatiently, in my rocket ship. I didn't find out until years later.

As the time for trajectory burn was closing in on me, I fastened myself in the flight couch, pulled the restraints really tight, and did a final COM and video check with Flight Control. The Flight Control centre with the imported German Flight Director and my friend, Hans Gohs, was in the Falcon-X facility in Texas, although we had launched the rockets from facilities at Vandenberg Air Force Base in California and Cape Canaveral in Florida. After the final trajectory burn, control would be handed off to the Mission Control centre set up at the Corporation's offices in Sweden. Hans would then board a private jet to return there. Florida, California, and Texas were far beyond the reach of the Swedish or Chinese governments so they could not stop the launch. The Americans were not too keen on someone stealing their space-race thunder, particularly the Mars-race thunder; but they got more joy out of screwing over the Chinese, whom everyone thought (wrongly) was behind the Swedish government's announcement to us twenty weeks ago. They also had certain requirements, that I have alluded to, for permitting the launch to be hosted on U.S. soil, but again, I don't want to get ahead of myself.

While I was gritting my teeth through the boredom of the last hour, the Corporation was holding a news conference. They were announcing to the world that less than a day ago I had been launched into space, and in the next few minutes I was going to be propelled towards Mars. We waited until this moment for the announcement, because once that last candle lit up, there really would be no stopping it.

Not soon enough, Flight Control took me through the final local checklist, and then I was ready to rock and roll. Hans came over my headphones, "Flight Control to Pathfinder, we're ready to begin transmitting live to the world." I gave the camera two thumbs up. My own video feed from Flight Control flipped over to a stage at the Corporation's auditorium in Sweden. It was 9:00 A.M. (GMT) in Sweden. Jayden and the brain trust of the company were on the stage. My son and his wife were there, and my BFF Mary as well. I could see in my own video monitor that the large screen behind them had gone from the mission logo, to showing the live feed from the Lander, with a close up of yours truly. I smiled and waved at the camera, watching my smiling waving image, behind the image of Jayden looking off stage, and of those around him. Even in HEO there was no signal delay.

What I couldn't see was who Jayden was looking at. He was looking at the Swedish Ministry official who had just arrived and was standing in the wings of the stage, surrounded by six very large Swedish Federal law enforcement officers. They stared at each other, the Minister scowling and chewing on his lip, and Jayden looking resolute. Finally Jayden just nodded at the Minister who after a pause let out a deep sigh, nodded back and then turned around leading his entourage out of the building. He appeared to have decided it would be easier to beg forgiveness from the cabinet, than do what it was that he had probably been ordered to do; but didn't want to go through with. Many years later, the official confessed to Jayden, over cognac and cigars, that he had been incensed that his government had given in to the threats and sabre rattling from Pyongyang. *Screw the North Koreans,* was his thought du jour as he stomped out of the building ahead of the six, very relieved, Säkerhetspolisen.

The world had not expected anyone to be going to Mars for another six years and there had been plenty of speculation and talk about who would actually be first: the Corporation, or one of the superpowers vying to be first on Mars. The fact that the Americans were helping us out (not the least by not interfering) was surprising to everyone, and as events would later play out, a bit ominous in its prescience. Everyone in the auditorium had been stunned when this press conference was called, with short notice, and no warning. The crowd, mostly media, was certainly in a pandemonium of enthusiasm.

Jayden had explained to them that this was a "proof of concept" mission, and that the courageous lone astronaut was setting the path for the future colonists; that I was setting the path for all future interplanetary and exoplanetary exploration. He explained that I was taking on the incredible risk of this one-way mission to show the entire human race that it was possible to get safely to Mars and to live there. If one man could do it, then a colony would thrive. He then called me the "original Pathfinder of the human interplanetary space effort". That was how the term Pathfinder became synonymous with me, Mike Lane. It was also the name of the Lander, the name that I alone had picked, but the name was forever associated with me, as a person.

From that moment, I became the most famous person on the planet, or more precisely, off the planet. Jayden delivered a brief biography about me that he had committed to memory. He introduced my son, Gary, and daughter-in-law, Amy. They had married four weeks ago, after I told them what I was doing. They insisted on advancing their own plans because they wanted me to be at the wedding. Jayden didn't introduce Mary, my closest friend, but that was at her request. She was there to show her support for me and have one last chance to say good-bye.

One of the not totally unexpected offshoots of my departure was the media attention that would soon focus on my son and his family. With the talk shows, a book and movie deal that would come from this event, the press conference began the process of his financial independence for life. As that news eventually worked its way to me over the coming weeks, I was glad. I was relieved and it felt good that I had been able to give him a parting gift that would last forever. I had unknowingly been, as the Canadian rock group Bachman Turner Overdrive put it, "takin' care of business".

Jayden was wearing an ear piece that was providing him with an audio feed from Flight Control. He and I both heard the anonymous voice:

"GTO Apogee in 15 seconds, Three minutes to trajectory burn for Heliocentric Orbital Insertion."

The smiling Jayden put his hand up to stop the media's questions. He then asked me a couple of sound-bite questions for the media's benefit.

"At GTO apogee, two minutes, forty-five seconds to trajectory burn. Heliocentric Orbital Alignment procedure running."

"OMS engaged."

My son and my friend Mary, stepped up to the microphone. They wished me a safe journey and Godspeed. They told me they loved me and were proud of me.

"Alignment procedure completed, trajectory alignment lock activated. NavCom final update in progress."

The audience politely laughed when my adult son pulled off his sweater and revealed a red t-shirt with yellow lettering that said, "My Dad went to Mars and all I got was this damn T-Shirt".

"Forty-five seconds to final trajectory burn, OMS to ready state."

"Final alignment confirmed. NavCom confirmed."

Flight control then asked the all-important question, *"Pathfinder, Flight. Confirm Go-No-Go."* It was my last chance to bail on the whole thing.

"Flight, Pathfinder. We are go for transit burn."

Jayden asked if I had any final words before leaving. I adopted a comical southern twang and replied, "Well that's a big 10-4 good buddy. I think it's time we kick the tires and light the fires! Let's get this puppy off the porch and see if it can bark with the big dogs!"

The audience and the stage all laughed and applauded at my élan. The image cut to an external view of the MTV and Lander, courtesy of a USAF Mil-Sat. There was a PIP in the corner still showing me, and the anonymous voice of Flight Control was now loud over the auditorium speakers. My son, his wife, my friend Mary, and Jayden all had tears in their eyes: all for different reasons. The auditorium went dead silent except for the Flight Control voice.

"OMS cut-off, final alignment re-confirmed."

"Trajectory Engines prelight warm-up commencing."

"Five."

"Four."

"Three."

A sudden flair of light from the nine Merlin engines as the ignition sequence began.

"Two."

"One."

The brilliance on the screen flashed blinding white. The long lens aperture screwed almost shut so that a viewable image was still on the screen.

"Ignition confirmed. Final trajectory burn in progress."

The screen flared orange and yellow as all nine Merlins fired full throttle at the same time. Much of what I saw out the portal when the PDV went on its way was what the auditorium audience and millions of television viewers saw, except that the USAF Mil-Sat was a bit further away and taking a long shot with the camera.

"Main engine ignition, re-alignment engines enabled."

Having much better optics than my eyes, the camera was able to effectively follow my rocket for almost two full minutes before the engines' flaring became a small burning spec in the distance.

"Approaching mid-burn."

"Mid-burn. Engine number one planned cut-off, trajectory alignment re-confirmed."

The on-board camera was now showing a static laced feed of me in the cockpit. It showed me pressed into the couch. You could see the skin on my face slightly distorted by the massive g-forces from the powerful thrust of the engines.

The ship had gone from being relatively still (though it wasn't really, not in orbit) at apogee to a speed of 33,800 kilometres per hour, or 9.6 kilometres per second. That would be like travelling from Toronto, Canada to London, England in under ten minutes. My flight Activity Suit had a built-in pressurization system for the flight. It had pumped up and did its best to keep the blood high up in my body so that I would not black out from a brain starving for oxygen.

We had done extensive testing and training on this one aspect of the flight, and while I was prepared for it, I wasn't ready for it. With no real gravity to speak off, trying to fight the engines thrust, this burn was like a whole passel of wild horses going hell-bent-for-leather towards the stars. A few seconds into the burn I felt like several of those horses had decided to sit down on my chest. The pressure kept up for almost five full minutes. I was absolutely convinced at one point that my brains had liquefied and were leaking out of my ears. I had planned to keep up a narrative during this part of the acceleration, but all I could do was make guttural grunting noises. When I first tried to talk there was so much grunting, groaning, and squealing that Flight Control had muted the audio transmission from the capsule to the auditorium, and kept up a running narrative of their own so the audience wouldn't notice.

"Final engine cut-off in three."

"Two."

"One."

"Final engine cut-off."

"Stand by to jettison Trajectory Engines."

"Trajectory Engine separation successful."

"Final trajectory alignment confirmed. The Mars Transit Vehicle has been successfully inserted into a Heliocentric Transit Orbit."

"Pathfinder is now en route to Mars." There was loud cheering in the background, *"Flight Control to Pathfinder, bon voyage Mike, and Godspeed."*

I managed to croak out, "Thank you, Flight."

"Flight Control to Mission Control for hand-off."

"Mission Control to Flight Control, we have assumed active control status. Thank you for your assistance."

The horses lounging on my chest had stood up since I was no longer accelerating. I was able to breathe without a struggle; the pressure suit relaxed its death grip on my legs and lower torso; the ringing in my ears finally subsided. WOW! What a ride. The Space Shuttle alumni I had spoken with had never really let me know how intense that acceleration was going to be. Of course, none of the Space Shuttle alumni had ever ridden a Falcon Trajectory rocket out of Earth's orbit either: no one had until that day. So just a word of caution to any future Pathfinders, when they "prepare" you for that trajectory burn, smile to yourself. You will *never* be fully prepared for that ride! It's just an order of magnitude worse than the ascent g-forces.

"Pathfinder, Mission Control. We have assumed control of the mission. We are ready for you to move to the MTV."

Chapter 6

An Aside: The Outer Space Treaty

The document called the Outer Space Treaty was agreed to by the United Nations in 1966 (resolution 2222 [XXI]). It was largely based on the 1963 United Nations Declaration of Legal Principles Governing the Activities of States in the *Exploration and Use of Outer Space Including the Moon and Other Celestial Bodies* (resolution 1962 [XXVIII]).

This treaty was created during the height of the cold war. Given the climate of détente between the superpowers, I can't blame some of the decision makers believing it would be for the benefit of all. However, their thinking on the matter was flawed. In The Space Review, in 2007, John Hickman argued that this treaty evolved from, "the fear that either superpower would achieve a decisive military technological advantage over the other in outer space, the fear that competition for the best 'real estate' on celestial bodies might itself result in war between the superpowers, and the fear that the superpowers might cooperate in a duopoly over all of outer space." So as you can see, we still have the biggest cause for war and sabre rattling, real estate, being a concern for outer space as well.

The Outer Space Treaty had the purpose of making both corporations and States (Nation States) responsible for what they do outside the atmosphere. The treaty stated that any corporation privately operating in outer space would be operating under the flag and auspices of that corporation's host country; that is, the country where the corporation's head office paid their taxes. Actually, it says that States (Nation States) are responsible for space activities carried out by governmental or non-governmental agencies (corporations); so ipso facto, my first statement was correct.

There is quite a bit about the treaty that makes sense; common sense, actually. It's unfortunate that the world at the time was a place where they felt it was necessary to codify common sense in legalese but hey, we're humans. If we didn't have government and lawyers, we'd all sit around with too much money in our bank accounts, and not enough things to complain about.

The Outer Space Treaty says that outer space is for the use and benefit of all. That makes sense. It says that States (Nation States) are responsible for any damage caused by their space junk. That also makes sense. It says that astronauts, of any state (Nation States), shall be considered envoys of mankind. Yes, still making perfect sense. It also says that States (Nation States) shall not place nuclear weapons or other weapons of mass destruction in orbit, in space or on other celestial bodies. Ah-ha! Now we find the crux of the impetus to wrest control of that which is beyond our borders, which God

37

created, and which we actually have no hold over. I think that the whole sentiment is wonderful, given the cold war stalemate of the day, but they should have left it at "in orbit". Why would mankind not want the ability to defend itself against all enemies: foreign, domestic, interplanetary *and* exo-planetary? So while, as I said, it was a good sentiment, this wording doesn't really make as much sense.

Moving right along, we find that the treaty also says that outer space (which includes the moon and other celestial bodies), cannot be appropriated by means of claim, use, or occupation. That means that no nation can assert sovereignty over anything in outer space. So this is where the treaty stops making sense completely.

If mankind cannot claim sovereignty, why would mankind want to expand to new uninhabited planets? If mankind were to set up bases on the moon or bases on Mars, would mankind not inherently have claim to at least a goodly portion of the surface around them? Would they not be able to say, "No, our base is already here, go build your new base over there." Does that not make sense?

If corporations were going to go into space, the most likely economic benefit would be production of low-g chemicals, medicines and building materials (asteroid ore mining, etc.). Granted, no one could tell them to "shove off", as no one would have the sovereignty to. However, the corporation would not have any claim to not be *shoved off* by someone that wasn't adhering to quite all of the sections of the treaty. Therefore, the treaty was, if I may be so bold, stupid.

Within the aforementioned article in *The Space Review*, Mr. Hickman presents us with an understanding of the anticommons. The anticommons arises as a direct result of the treaty establishing that everything beyond Earth was *res communis*. By virtue of this assertion, the treaty had ensured that since it had, "eliminated the possibility that States could claim territory on the final frontier it also extinguished an important motivation for States and private firms to engage in exploration and development."

With this understanding of the Outer Space Treaty in mind, we can see that the Corporation, with Jayden at the head, had to do some work to actually get the mission off the ground (no pun intended). In 2016, with a 50 person lobby group, the Corporation, with the assistance of their host country, Sweden, had successfully introduced amendments to the Outer Space Treaty through the United Nations Office for Outer Space Affairs. Specifically, the amendments were to Article 1 and Article 2.

Article 1 of the treaty was amended from, "and there shall be free access to all areas of celestial bodies."; to read, "and there shall be free access to all *unclaimed* areas of celestial bodies."

Article 2 was a bigger change, but took less arguing. Article 2 stated, "Outer space, including the moon and other celestial bodies, is not subject to national appropriation by claim of sovereignty, by means of use or occupation, or by any other means." The lobby team argued from the position that this would allow an enemy from beyond Earth's orbit to establish a colony or base of operations anywhere in our galaxy, including our solar system, or even our own Moon. The military lobbyists worked around the globe. It was an easy sell for military ears; they pushed for larger countries' military establishments to talk sense into the politicos of the day. Finally, after several months of discussions and private talks, with the assurance there would be no media coverage of the changes or which Country had voted for them, a closed session of the United Nations General Assembly passed the edits to Article 1, and the complete withdrawal of Article 2.

With that *fait accompli*, our own Corporation was now free to pursue its goal, without encumbrances by any Nation State or treaty of law.

Chapter 7

Descent Day: T-Minus 90 Seconds

Eight and a half months later I was orbiting Mars and ready to descend to the surface. All the indicators are green, all the readings are nominal. I cast my eyes around the Lander cabin to make sure everything looked secure. I felt like I was in my uncle's old Woody packed with suitcases, bags, and odds and sods on moving day. Every available surface had either canvas bags, or heavy duty plastic equipment boxes strapped, lashed, and tied in place. I had three large duffels, and two plastic foot lockers that were filled with personal clothing and other items. Getting those on board had been a bit of a battle, but eventually I played the, *I'm going there forever and giving up my life on Earth* card. I won. I got to take some stuff from home. In that "negotiation" I also won a commitment for just over a half cubic metre of space in every supply mission that they would fill with whatever I asked. They said they would do it for me, but they could not do that for the following colony ships. I said that was okay, I'm going to be the first man on Mars. I'm a special case. Besides, I planned to use that for tastes of home that would help keep me sane. There was no Dépanneur on Mars, how the hell else was I going to get any Twinkies there? I chuckled to myself thinking thankfully that there were no garbage bags full of bedding or clothing, and that I didn't have to stick my arm out the portal and hold a mattress on the roof.

I had brought a lot of stuff in the Lander with me because I had to make up the weight of the three people I didn't have on board. There was even about 20 kilograms worth of scientific experiments for some university students I had befriended in the Swedish town I had been living in. There was even a rumour circulating in the rocket assembly building, that there were two cement bricks in the Lander to make up the weight difference. The configuration of the Lander was for four people to descend to the surface of Mars, so it had to have the same mass as four people.

Audio and video transmissions with Terra were delayed about 18 minutes and a few seconds each way with the current position of Mars in its orbit. In another four months, Mars would be at apogee, and transmission time would be 22 minutes. I wasn't able to hear Mission Control counting down or providing a running narrative. When I left Terra there had been a lot of chatter for me to listen to. Now it was silent, except for the ever-so-slight hiss of air in my helmet. Everything concerning the actual descent had been programmed into the Lander's navigation computer. It would have been nice if the computer could carry a conversation with me but hey, this is real life, not science-fiction. All it could do was respond to direct requests and alert me to preplanned events. I found that silence was kind of creepy, yet the moment was still very exciting!

The "Go-No-Go" button winked at me. It was time to put on my big boy panties. If I didn't press the button in time, I would be given the chance again next orbit; and then again the following orbit after that. If I missed pressing it for three orbits, then the MTV would execute a preplanned burn with its final bit of remaining fuel, and enter a free return trajectory to Earth. Of course, I would never be able to survive that trip. I pressed the button.

The display on the computer in front of me gave me the countdown: I was at seventeen seconds. One last look around, I re-tighten the straps holding me to the couch, squint my eyes shut, and quickly recite a portion of the 23rd Psalm.

When I opened my eyes, the countdown was at three seconds. When it reached "one", I heard the tunnel between the Lander and the MTV depressurize; I also heard the Lander/MTV mechanical couplings *thunk* open (the mechanical couplings that had held the Lander to the Command Module for the whole journey). There was an ever-so-slight jolt and barely a sense of forward momentum as manoeuvering rockets moved me away from the Command Module. I was now completely detached from the MTV. Looking forward through the dorsal portal I could see the MTV moving away from me, or more accurately, me moving away from the MTV. With a sudden twinge of nostalgia, I raised my hand to my visor and gave it a salute, "Goodbye old friend, old *smelly* friend."

I reached out to the COM panel and transmitted the confirmation signal for successful detach. Telemetry would provide the technical information on the procedure. I was just sending the human confirmation. I think they just wanted me to feel useful in this fully automated descent stage of the trip, like every other fully automated stage of the trip. I said a quick prayer for a safe landing, then after a pause, I yearningly whispered, "Look out Barsoom, here I come."

Everything I said and whispered was being relayed back to Terra, and broadcasted on the internet. I learned from Hans later on, that this statement had caused all those in Mission Control to go sombre for a few moments. Shortly after being informed of this proof of concept mission, I had bought a dozen copies of *Princess of Mars*, and put them into circulation at the Corporation's head office. A lot of the Mission Control staff had already read it. Those that hadn't already read it fell in love with it. It was about a time and place when men were honourable, women were strong, and adventure waited at every turn of the page. The words I whispered had struck a chord with everybody for the monumental nature of what we were doing, the dreams that we were turning into reality, and that we were doing all of it *right now*. That I was doing all of it, all alone.

My couch was oriented to a normal upward position. I was on my back facing the top of the Lander, which meant I could only see where I had been, and not where I was going. When the Orbital Manoeuvering Package (OMP) fired, the downward force thrust me upward, in the direction I was facing. It was like a big hand reached down and was trying to pluck me out of my seat, but the restraints held me in place. The OMP burn only lasted a few seconds, and then I felt normal again. I could feel a distinct sense of motion, but once more, my ship was ballistic and no longer under power. It was up to physics, Martian gravity, and prayer to get me where I needed to be; to get me there safely. I took care of the prayer part, and left the rest to Newton. I was roughly twenty-five minutes from touchdown in Chasma Boreale in the North Polar region of Mars, only a kilometre above the northern edge of the Hyperboreae Undae region of sand dunes. Specifically, I landed at 81° 40' 27.28"N and 44° 32' 24.92"W, West of the Martian prime meridian.

This site was selected for its proximity to the North Polar ice fields that covered thousands of square kilometres, and were estimated to be two to 3 kilometres thick. The site presented excellent drilling opportunities for water, and the test drilling carried out by robotics indicated a reliable source of water was possible. My ability to extract water would be the difference between life and death; the difference between mission success and failure; the difference between a colony and no colony. I was arriving in the latter half of the summer, so spring sublimation would have evaporated most, if not all, of the frozen carbon dioxide that settled over the North Polar region in this hemisphere's winter season.

The landing and habitat site was less than 2 kilometres from a 500 metre ice wall. With good recycling technology in place, these frozen fields would supply a fair sized colony indefinitely. We planned the water mining and collection so that I could use up to 50 litres of water a day, not that I would ever use that much. With the advanced recycling technology I had in the Habitat (*everything* got recycled, if you know what I mean), and proper maintenance of the water storage tank, I would only lose about two litres a day. The two five hundred litre water storage tanks in the Habitat meant I would only have to water-mine two or three times a Martian year; only one or two times per Terran year. The water mining transport tank would also act as a backup. Provided it was kept properly insulated and heated, that water mining process could be done only once or twice every *two* Terran years after its first fill-up. Of course, once the first colony arrived and set up the hydroponics, that might change. By then, I planned to have a piping system with automated recovery in place so that it would be something no one had to actively go out and attend to as often.

The flat, open nature of the landing site also presented excellent opportunities for the wind farm that was going to be an important and extensive project. I needed to set up ten wind collectors soon after arrival for my own needs for the next few years. While the wind collection system would keep the Habitat batteries fully charged, the mission planners wanted the Habitats to use the DC conversion as much as possible, given the almost continuous wind patterns at the colony site. I needed to set up thirty wind collectors in total to supply all the colony needs prior to the next crew arriving in six years. No problem. The wind turbines had already been delivered, and were waiting to be unpacked and set up. I only needed to set up four for my immediate needs, then six more before my first Martian winter. Mission Control relayed daily updates to the Command Module after our equipment started landing on Mars. Since the Habitats' arrival, Big Dawg and Little Dawg (the large and small rovers) had moved the Habitats into close proximity, and then deployed and connected the solar collectors. These required frequent attention as they seemed to be dust magnets, and even a little dust drastically affected their efficiency. Little Dawg was almost exclusively dedicated to keeping the solar collectors dust free. After the wind farm was up and running, the solar collectors would be rolled back up and held in reserve as a backup to the wind farms.

The Lander started buffeting slightly in the thin atmosphere of Mars, only about ten percent as dense as on Terra. I could feel the buffeting turn into a thrumming feeling coming through the couch. Eventually that thrumming became a teeth chattering sensation. Thin atmo or not, this was going to be a ride!

There would be no ionization blackout for telemetry during re-entry. Mission Control would continue to receive the stream uninterrupted. Both the Mar-Sat and the Jalopy-Sat had a TDRS installed. The Tracking and Data Relay System was able to transmit and receive telemetry signals from the forward (topside) antenna array on the Lander, through a small space in the ionization envelope created by the shape of the Lander itself (topside was pointed backwards during re-entry). Otherwise there would have been almost a full minute of blackout as the Lander was on a very shallow trajectory to the landing site. I would be completing almost a full half orbit before touchdown. The Landers descent needed this extra distance due to the very thin Martian atmosphere being such an important part of the aerobraking/deceleration process. As I was heading towards the planet surface, the Jalopy-Sat was already moving itself to a more northerly geosynchronous position, to have better oversight on the colony.

I had been orbiting Mars at roughly 6 kilometres per second. That meant the descent time was going to be about 25 minutes to cover the low angle distance, and slow down the Lander. The robotics packages that had arrived in the past few years landed much faster. They also had significantly less mass than I did. The supply drops and systems delivery (Habitat, Atmo-Gen, Hydrazine Plant, etc.) had all taken almost a full 50 minutes for descent. Maximum use of the thin Martian atmosphere was required because of the exceptional mass of those objects. The Habitats alone were about seven tonnes each. However, all had landed safely and intact according to telemetry and visuals from the rover, Big Dawg. Big Dawg and Little Dawg had been dropped in the first investigation package to land at Chasma Boreale, four years ago.

The pressure system in my Activity Suit was activated around my upper body (as opposed to lower body during ascent), but it wasn't squeezing me like a tube of cheese, as the pressure suit had during ascent, and trajectory burn. The pressure suit was primarily needed for acceleration and the descent of the craft was all deceleration.

I began to see a faint red glow outside the windows. The aeroshell on the bottom of the Lander was getting extremely hot from the friction of the Martian atmosphere. Even though at this altitude it was about 1% as dense as the Terran atmosphere, there was still a thin atmosphere that was dense enough to be using it for the initial braking effect.

Fourteen minutes into the descent, the next critical phase came up on the timeline. While the atmospheric friction had slowed down the Lander considerably, it was still going too fast to deploy the three parachutes. If they were deployed at this point, they would rip right off the top of the Lander, and probably taking the top of the Lander with them. What came first was the firing of RAD assemblies (Rocket Assisted Descent engines). There were two disposable RAD assembly frames on the bottom of the Lander, plus the final third assembly attached to the Lander itself. These RAD assemblies had the brunt of responsibility for getting me safely to the surface.

Before any of that could happen though, the aeroshell had to be discarded. I was now moving slow enough, and in a thin enough atmosphere that the aeroshell was no longer needed as a heat shield. I felt a slight jolt from the jettison rockets after the control system had blown the couplings to the aeroshell, propelling it out of the path of the ballistic Lander.

When the first RAD assembly ignited, I was slammed into the flight couch again. This lasted for seventeen seconds. After the seventeen second burn elapsed, the first stage RAD engines cut out. Almost immediately, tiny launching rockets fired three, one pound metal Monkey's Fists from three points on the top of the Lander. These small weights pulled and arched the drogues for the parachutes out far enough to not get tangled in each other. The larger than normal drogues, catching the thin atmo filled out; and pulled out the much larger than normal three main parachutes right behind them. All three parachutes deployed simultaneously. After the first RAD assembly cut out, I went back into free fall for about seven seconds (an eternity it seemed), before I felt the parachutes give drag to the Lander's descent. Ten seconds after the RAD cut-off, the first RAD assembly ejector units released that first frame. It fell from the bottom of the Lander, engines, and fuel tanks attached to them.

The release of the parachutes was a pivotal moment. They had been pressure packed and frozen in the cold of deep space for over eight months. There was the ever-so-slight risk they simply wouldn't deploy. I didn't hear anything, but I did feel them and see them deploy through the dorsal portal. Aside from them deploying at all, the concern was that all three of them should deploy, and that they should all deploy at the same time. If one had failed, I would still survive the landing but I would have gone wildly off course, winding up too far from the Habitat to make it there on my own. Thankfully I could see all three had snapped into full shape. The effect was like being suddenly slammed in the back as my own body's momentum dug into the flight couch; the flight couch which was again no longer travelling as fast as I was. This only lasted about two or three seconds. I started breathing easier as the speed of the couch and the momentum of my body came into balance.

These parachutes were not for a straight descent purpose. The Lander was tilted backwards, moving forward through the thickening atmosphere, the aeroshell absorbing the increasing friction heat. It was still going quite fast. The parachutes were providing the necessary drag to slowly bleed off more speed from the forward momentum. The mass of the Lander and its initial speed compounded by the thin atmosphere meant that the parachute assisted aero-braking was still going to take some time. I was going to be under canopy, relatively speaking, for another ten minutes. In the final 50 seconds of the canopy braking, the Lander had slowed enough that it was now under a direct parachute descent over the colony site, over my new home. However, the parachutes, while fine for braking, were woefully inadequate for straight descent. I started picking up speed again, slowly.

Roughly twenty-four minutes after separating from the MTV, the second of three RAD rocket assemblies would fire. The Rocked Assisted Descent motors took over, and did what the atmosphere and parachutes couldn't do. They would get me safely to the surface, and on target.

A full second before this next RAD assembly fired, the flight computer fired three tiny rocket propelled guillotines, which cut the parachute harness for each of the canopies. That one second of time allowed the Lander and parachute canopies to move far enough apart, that the falling parachutes would not interfere with the rest of the Landing sequence.

With the second RAD assembly engines instantly coming to full power, I was thrust deeper into the flight couch as the ship slowed dramatically in the space of a few seconds. These engines burned for twenty seconds as they positioned the Lander over the final landing site, and slowed my descent considerably. On cue, three small explosions jettisoned the second RAD assembly. At that instant, because I was so close to the colony site, two rockets on the second discarded RAD assembly came to life. Those small rockets carried the assembly several kilometres down-field where it crashed into the sand dunes of Hyperboreae Undae. Had I been able to look out the starboard portal, I would have seen it crash in the distance. I thought briefly about the amount of litter I was creating. I was going to have to go around and pick this stuff up some day. Yeah, I could still hug trees even if there are no actual trees to hug.

The second RAD assembly had slowed me drastically, almost to a complete stop of downward motion. With the second RAD assembly jettisoned and flying off to the south, the Lander began a vertical free fall descent.

Very quickly, at 60 metres above the surface of Mars, the third and final RAD cluster fired. As this final assembly was attached directly to the hull of the Lander, I could hear the three engines, and they were *loud*. I soon heard another mechanical sound or perhaps I just felt it. This was the six landing struts being deployed. My excitement was becoming unbearable. The firing of the third and final RAD assembly brought me to a complete stop at 3 metres above the surface. As the RAD quickly burned out, the Lander settled with a hard jolt onto the surface of the planet, the design of the landing legs causing them to act as shock absorbers, cushioning the final drop.

I scanned all the instrumentation and took a deep breath. It hit me hard as the sound of the RAD engines faded. I was finally on Mars. I WAS FINALLY ON FREAKING MARS!!! I let out a war whoop of joy, and pumped my fists in the air. The good Lord had delivered me safely. I was finally here and I couldn't wait to get out of the tin can, to put my space-suited foot on the surface. I pulled the three restraint release levers, and bounded out of my seat. I came out of it so fast I almost went ass over tea-kettle, catching myself just in time. Oh yes, one-third gravity. It had been a long time since I had been in gravity (almost eight and a half months), so I took a moment to let my body, brain, and organs get used to the concept again; and let the brief wave of accompanying nausea pass. I pulled up the Mar-Sat image of the landing site on my tablet. I was only off by 17 metres. That's a lot, but again, Chasma Boreale is a windy place. I was only about half a kilometre from the Hab (Habitat) as planned. In retrospect, being only 17 metres off target after travelling over one hundred million miles wasn't that bad at all.

I touched the COM button on my suit controller and transmitted a message to Terra. I said, "Mission Control, Pathfinder. I'm happy to report I touched down about a minute ago. It was completely successful and went according to plan. I'm preparing to exit the Lander now." The message system was on live feed so as I talked, the Lander uplinked the signal to Mar-Sat. The audio was on its way to Terra as fast as I was saying the words. The worlds wouldn't arrive though, for another 18 minutes and 20 seconds (approximately).

A shadow passed over the port side portal. I glanced that way but couldn't see anything. It had to be one of the parachutes following the Lander down.

I moved over to where the handheld camera was stored, unboxed it, turned it on and made sure it was recording. It had been hooked into the ships system and began to top off the battery charge when the Lander powered up in orbit. The battery was full, and would record for twelve hours non-stop before needing to be recharged. The handheld camera itself could record over three hundred hours of video imagery before I had to download it. I had two cameras on my Activity Suit as well. One was outboard on the helmet recording wherever I turned my body. The second was inside the helmet recording my face with a tiny fish-eye lens. I grabbed the tablet that was providing my Lander system readings, undocked it from the panel in front of the flight couch, and did a quick system query with the Habitat's COM over a guest connection. That limited guest connection would be replaced with a full connection once I had time to pair my tablet and my suit's COM system to the Habitats. That wouldn't happen, though, until I was inside the Habitat, out of my Activity Suit and chillaxin' on Mars! For now my suit was uplinked to Mar-Sat through the Lander. All systems showed operational, 3000 Kg of oxygen, 500 liters of water, full electrical charge in the batteries, and the solar collectors were operating nominally.

I moved over to the airlock. I had put a bunch of personal stuff in there while transferring supplies when I was still in orbit. They were still securely attached to the anchor points provided. As I was about to shut the inner airlock door, I stopped and thought a moment about the U.S. Air Force briefing I had received prior to departure. I turned back into the cabin of the Lander, found the two elongated cases with no markings, and detached them from their straps. I put them in the airlock, and then shut the inner airlock door behind me.

I checked to make sure both my suit cameras were recording and began a brief statement that was also being uplinked to Mar-Sat in live-time through the Landers COM array. In eighteen minutes and a titch, they would see it on Terra.

"Hello Earth! This is Mike Lane reporting to you from the surface of Mars! My Lander safely touched down just over five minutes ago. I'm in the Lander airlock now, I'm ready to depressurize, and open the outer hatch." I reached over and pressed my gloved hand against the button to cycle the airlock to a pressure equivalent to that outside the Lander. As the pumps whirred and sucked the atmosphere from the now cramped airlock, I continued. "I have to tell you that I'm humbled today. I stand on the shoulders of giants and I'm able to reach even further because of what they did. Yuri Gagarin, the first man into space, paved the way for all who followed him. Neil Armstrong, Buzz Aldrin and Michael Collins, well, they fired our imagination with Neil's one small step for man and one giant leap for mankind. Today is going to be the follow-up, the sequel to what those brave men did. Today we are one step further into the Verse."

Pressure balancing was complete, and the hatch was ready to open. "In just a few moments I'm going to open the outer airlock hatch and take humanity's first step on a planet other than Earth. I'll be making that first step on the planet that has so often been the subject of science-fiction, speculation, poetry and prose. It's no longer a dream though folks. With this first step, mankind will truly be an inter-planetary ..."

The airlock was filled with a flash of light so bright that my breath caught in my throat, and I closed my eyes reflexively. This was compounded at the exact same moment by the loudest sound I had ever heard, and the feeling of my body, my whole world, being catapulted and turned upside down. I screamed as I slammed into the rear of the airlock; or more precisely, the rear of the airlock rushing towards me slammed into my body. I blacked out as my head dangerously bounced around inside my helmet.

Chapter 8

Mission Control

It was just after two in the morning in Sweden. There was a chill in the air, and large snowflakes gently fell through the night sky; the sticky kind of snowflakes that clung to everything. They clung to Carrie Oolsen's tightly braided blond hair, as she ran into the Corporation's night entrance, just down the hall from Mission Control proper. She had to wait for her babysitter to arrive at her home, a fifteen-minute drive from the Corporation's complex, before the thirty-seven year old widowed mom of two could leave for work. She had been due in at midnight, and had wanted to get there even earlier. It was Descent Day after all; everyone was wound up and excited. That plan didn't quite work when the babysitter got there late. A traffic mess had been created by a transport truck on a slippery curve in the road.

The self-trained computer genius and video expert ran to her shared office to throw her coat and briefcase into the corner, she picked up her travel mug, stopped to fill it with rich black coffee, and then bolted for Mission Control. As she burst through the door, one of the media lackeys jumped in surprise, and sent an explosion of paperwork falling around him. Hans Gohs, the Flight Director and now one of the Mission Directors looked over at her, smiled and touched his nose. She smiled back in embarrassment, and headed to her workstation. Her skill, commitment, and dedication bought her leeway with Hans; but she still did not like taking advantage of that.

The afternoon shift tech was still sitting there and wasn't in a rush to leave. He gave up his seat for her, but grabbed another nearby chair and hunkered in beside her. Arno Lidstrom was as excited as Carrie was. He also thought she was kind of cute, in a frumpy way, so he didn't mind the cramped seating. While he didn't mind sharing the workstation with her, he had to keep reminding himself, she was on duty; it was time to let her do her job, and keep his hands to himself … in more ways than one. They had four Ultra Hi-Def monitors at their workstation, which had much clearer and crisper images than those that were being displayed on the large screens at the front of the room. They were probably the only two people in the room that were not watching the big screens, because their pictures were better. Tonight Carrie's focus (and it would seem Arno's as well) was to ensure continuity of video feed, and address any problems that came up with it. Because this computer handled the image processing to the bigger screen, there was just over half a second lag time from what they saw, to when everyone else saw it.

She could see the image of Mike Lane in the Lander. Slightly distorted by the curve of his helmets face plate, she could see his teeth were gritted, and he was focused on the instrumentation in front of him. The second screen was the downward camera on the outside of the Lander. The last two screens were images from Mar-Sat, one long range and one upclose on the descending Lander. The targeting systems kept the Lander in the centre of the screens all the way to touchdown.

"Down angle camera please," Hans Gohs' voice came from across the room. Arno started to reach towards the console, but Carrie slapped his hand away with a smile. She made the adjustment and the down angle camera on the outside of the Lander now replaced Mike's image with that of the Martian surface rushing up to meet the Lander. Unfortunately there was a fair amount of rocket engine flaring obscuring the view. Carrie looked over her shoulder and Hans shook his head. *Too much flame and not enough pizzazz,* she interpreted. She switched back to the feed arriving from Mike's helmet camera, giving a point of view shot from the interior of the Lander. Wow, she thought to herself. Could he have crammed any more crap into that little thing? She then switched the long camera view from the satellite to appear on the big screen, replacing the boring view of the interior of the Lander.

She saw the parachute canopies jettisoned on the big screen and turned her head slightly to focus on her smaller screens in front of her. Shortly after that, the second RAD assembly fired. After that assembly was depleted and jettisoned, she put the image from the outboard camera up on the big screen. There was a chorus of "ooos" from around the room. There was a clear shot of the Martian surface rushing towards the camera that lasted for moments before the flare of the final RAD assembly. She looked over her shoulder and Hans gave a slight nod.

Arno leaned in and was using the station to modify the long shots from the Mar-Sat. She leaned a bit sideways to let him do this and then nudged him. They both watched the engine flaring out as the downward movement stopped. The long shots confirmed it, Mike was on Mars! With the final engine cut-off a roar of cheering, backslapping, and general carrying-on occurred, lasting almost a full minute. They all settled down to their stations after that, there was much to do, and more celebrating would begin shortly. The bubbly was on ice, caterers were making final preparations in the large conference room, and the media gallery was jammed. The inevitable celebration party was in a programmed hold and ready to blast off when given the word.

Arno had reached over Carrie and changed the outboard view back to the Landers' internal view. They saw Mike standing up with his hand against the wall. He was bouncing up and down a bit, obviously getting his sea legs back after so long in zero-g. Had he been on Earth, he would not have been able to stand so quickly, but the low-g of Mars made it basically, a non-issue; or at least, not much of an issue. Of course, the three hours of daily strength training while he had been in transit had benefited him greatly.

Carrie didn't have much to do at this point. Her sole area of concern for the evening was on the video feed, which due to the DSP innovations by NEC Laboratories made her job easier. The video arrived with only a fifteen second lag behind the digital telemetry feeds.

While the Mar-Sat upclose image filled one screen, most people were watching Mike on the other. Carrie and Arno both leaned forward at the same time with furrowed brows. They looked at each other and looked back at the feed. They had both seen the shadow pass over the Lander and the ground near it, transiting basically Martian west to east. They couldn't figure out anything that would have caused it at first glance. They had seen the parachutes jettisoned farther down field. Carrie noticed a small point of shimmering distortion on the screen and started to work at clearing it up, but then it disappeared. At the same time, they both came up with the thought that it was probably a weather anomaly. Arno stood up to look at the meteorology station directly in front of them. It showed clear skies, and no clouds in the landing area; winds were at norm, and the Mars local temperature was holding steady at -23 degrees Celsius. The Mar-Sat long shots didn't show any clouds either. Carrie was about to pull up the record of the second longer shot from Mar-Sat to review it when they heard Mike's voice over the loudspeaker in the room.

"Hello Earth! This is Mike Lane reporting to you from Mars ..." Carrie made a quick feed adjustment, and then they both looked up and watched the helmet cam feed of Mike in the airlock giving what would be a much replayed speech. This was a historic moment; the playback could wait a few minutes. Shortly after Mike's speech began, a bunch of techs on the other side of the room started talking rapidly, Carrie and Arno looked over as one of them put both of his hands up in the air and turned towards Hans, "Herr Gohs, we've lost all telemetry from the Lander."

"What do you mean lost telemetry?"

"I mean we are not getting ..." The room turned orange, then yellow, then white, with the brilliance of the silent explosion on the large screen at the front of the room. Everyone looked at where the Lander had been, now it was just a fireball and mushroom cloud of smoke forming as the ejecta of debris spewed upwards from around what would come to be known as "Cortés Crater".

The smoke cleared quickly and the flames were rapidly dying out. Martian atmo was not conducive to fire. There simply wasn't enough oxygen in the Martian atmosphere to sustain it. Fire requires three things, fuel, oxygen, and heat to be sustained. While it had fuel (there was still some rocket fuel and

53

vapours in the third RAD assembly attached to the ship), and the burning was indeed with enough heat, the lack of oxygen in the atmosphere meant the fires did not last long. While man had figured out how to extract oxygen from CO2, fire could not do it on its own. It would seem that as an act of contrition by nature, the black smoke from the smoldering debris did last a very long time. The mushroom cloud of smoke quickly dissipated, and they saw that what had once been the Lander, was now a gritty red field of alien regolith strewn with chunks of twisted, burning, and smoking debris around a blackened depression. Arno made the satellite camera zoom in closer on the site of the explosion. They watched silently as a green-and-white baseball cap (one of the Swedish bandy team caps, Hammarby from Stockholm), untouched by flame or soot, was blown across the debris field. It was blowing end over end, drunkenly. Carrie felt her heart ache. It was the baseball cap that her oldest son, Hindrik, had given Mike the last time he had spent the weekend; the weekend he took her boys to see the ball club play. That was a year ago. She fought back the tears that burned like it had been yesterday. There were a few large chunks of twisted metal that hadn't been thrown far, and they watched as everything that had gone up, was now coming back down close to the explosion site. Spinning Wheel; cue Blood, Sweat & Tears.

The room stayed silent for a long time. You could have heard a snowflake drop, it was that quiet. Someone eventually gasped and started sobbing. There was a lot of breath holding that got let out at the same time. Almost on cue, the place broke out in pandemonium and everyone started shouting at once. Hans was shouting orders, most of them at Arno and Carrie to start with, before he started moving on to the techs that had raised the concern about no-telemetry. Uplinks from the Habitats and the AtmoGen were all transmitting properly and completely. The rover signals and video feeds were all working fine, uplinked through the W-Hab. Medical had zero telemetry from Mike himself, however that data stream would have been uplinked through the now non-existent Lander antenna array. There was no signal degradation from the Mar-Sat. A mousey little man in the far front corner of the room did a discrete check on the Jalopy-Sat signal which was also strong and without interference. He looked up, caught Hans' eye, then raised his hands palm up and shrugged his shoulders at what had happened.

Arno responded to Hans' request on the video feeds, while Carrie took over one monitor for herself. She had pulled out the secondary keyboard and was now working in a separate system from Arno. As Arno was playing back the imagery of the explosion for the room, he nudged Carrie with his elbow, "Did you see that dull flash just before the explosion?" he almost whispered.

"That's what I'm looking for", she replied under her breath.

An infinitesimally short moment before the big explosion, both Carrie and Arno had seen a twinkling of light on one of the RAD fuel tanks (the outboard auxiliary tank), via the close-up from the Mar-Sat. Hans had seen it too, but it barely registered when the big explosion had hit. He just thought it was part of it the big explosion. It was part of it, in fact, it was the trigger. Both Arno and Carrie new something wasn't right, but they had to be careful about what they said and had to be absolutely sure. If they ran off half-cocked saying that they had seen the reflection of an energy beam, they would be jobless. The meaning of saying such a thing would be both shattering and catastrophic, with world-wide implications, if it were true. They both had completely forgotten about the shadow and the distortion they saw a few minutes earlier.

Chapter 9

In The Wreckage Of The Airlock

I groaned as I slowly woke up. I felt like I had been hit by a car. My back hurt, my arms hurt, my legs hurt, my head hurt. The only sound was the hiss of airflow in my helmet, a sound that would be part of my day for the rest of my life, however long or short that was going to be. It was a sound that would come to mean life itself. I was still alive. That was a good thing. I knew coming to Mars that there was the chance I would die on the way or after I got here. I had never said to anyone that all it would mean to me was that I got be with Loreena again, sooner. Ah, well. I was alive. That was a good thing. Obviously the good Lord had a reason to keep me that way.

There was some light around me but not much, the internal lighting in the airlock wasn't working. I lay there for a moment and took stock of my body. I was sore, but I didn't think anything was broken. I was breathing okay, which was always a good sign. Slowly lifting my arms, I felt no pain in my ribs or my chest. I ran a diagnostic on my suit systems, everything was fine, and my oxygen tanks were still at 98.4%. I turned on the HUD to keep an eye on system readings, and then turned on the LED area light in my chest plate. It was too bright for the small space so I shut it off again.

"So what the hell was that?" I asked myself. It had to have been an explosion, *duhhh*. I was still oriented relatively upright in the airlock but I was lying horizontally on my back. I looked up at the internal airlock hatch which was almost directly above me. There was light coming in through the portal in the hatch, but it looked like it had been mostly blackened out by soot, by something burning. I groaned as I realized this meant I was probably lying on top of the outer airlock hatch. That meant that I could not fire the emergency explosive bolts on the outer hatch to open it, not if it was face down on the Martian ground with the bulk of the airlock on top of it. The blow back would probably finish what the original explosion failed to accomplish, killing me. I was very grateful at that moment that I had depressurized the airlock *before* whatever happened had happened.

I surmised that because the airlock was a late addition and reinforced in its construction, this must have kept the airlock mass intact when the explosion happened. I couldn't tell if the whole Lander was on its side, or if the airlock had come apart from the Lander. However, the sunlight coming through the soot smudged interior airlock portal, almost directly above me, didn't give me much hope that the Lander was intact. Either way, it was probably not going to be serviceable, in any fashion..

I looked upwards, but only saw the inside of my helmet. I had to slowly and gingerly re-orient my body and push back on the top of my helmet so that I could look up at what was the actual ceiling of the airlock. There was some light coming through holes in several parts of the ceiling. "Okay, definitely not going to be serviceable," I muttered to myself.

I didn't have any welding equipment big enough to handle ship repairs. The Habitat had a small TIG welder for small repairs to mechanicals and equipment, but it wouldn't handle this much of a job. Of course, at this point I was still hoping the ship was mostly intact with some holes in it.

I rocked back and forth a bit, then a bit harder. It seemed prudent to test the stability of the airlock, to see if it would roll; but it wasn't budging an iota. That's promising. I gingerly moved so I wasn't between the wall and transport bags, and tried to stand up. The airlock wasn't wide enough to allow me to fully stand up though, so I crouched down, resting my butt on one of the transport bags. Reaching above my head, I rotated and pushed hard against the handle on the inner airlock hatch, which was now top-side. It only moved part of the way and then stuck. I pushed hard on the handle, and tried pounding on the hatch with my fist, but it wouldn't budge. I changed my body's seated angle a bit, and looked closer at the airlock door. It was deformed slightly. *Great*. It would never open again, not with what I had at hand to try and force it. The pulse-energy rifles I had put in the airlock just before closing the door would be useless, they didn't work that way. Using them in such a confined space would probably backfire on me anyways.

I turned my attention to the "ceiling" of the airlock and the light coming through it in several places. There seemed, oddly enough, to be a bit more light coming through than I had originally noticed. I guess I was adjusting to the gloomy interior of the airlock wreckage. I shuffled around a bit, detached and moved a couple bags, and then braced myself in a semicrouching position with my back against the reorganized cargo. I pulled both feet up as much as I could and kicked hard. The ceiling panel buckled in the middle and moved outward about 10 centimetres. This pulled it away from the sides in a few places and let more light in. I hunkered forward a bit closer and then I kicked again, and then again. I was getting somewhere. I moved myself closer again, drew up my legs, and gave a massive thrust with them. The entire ceiling panel came apart from the airlock and fell forward, very slowly. I looked down through my feet and could see both of the Habitats in the distance. Between the Habs and my position, there was an extensive debris field of smouldering, twisted metal, and other smouldering things. I could see equipment bags half burned, and utility boxes smashed apart; contents bare to the atmosphere.

"Frak me"

I collapsed backwards and wanted to cry, part with relief and part with disappointment. Everything had gone so well. So why this? Why did the ship explode? The HUD showed all my suit systems were nominal, so I lay there for a few minutes going over in my mind the events of the last hour before the explosion. I went right back to when I closed up the tunnel from the MTV to the Lander. I recalled everything I saw, checked, did, and re-checked. I recalled all the readings as best I could, nothing was off. Using my helmets HUD display, I even replayed the video file of what I had been recording with my helmet cam at the time of the explosion. There was absolutely nothing from separation, descent, and landing that indicated any problem that would have caused an explosion. Well, that left two possibilities. Either there was a problem with the propellant system that didn't surface until after engine shut down or it was sabotage ... or perhaps a third possibility ... no ... I didn't have time to think about that. There would be time later for speculation absent any evidence.

I was well aware of the security precautions taken by both the Corporation and the Americans. I doubted the Chinese or anyone else could have planted a device in the Lander. However, it's said that everyone has a price. Perhaps they got someone who already had a security clearance, and a need to do it. There was undoubtedly going to be a big investigation back on Terra. However, my money really was on a mechanical fault. In fact, my money was on the primary and secondary couplings to the auxiliary RAD reserve tank. A lot of us thought it was useless, but the astronautic engineers had insisted on it.

"Oh shit, they probably think I'm dead."

I detected the COM presence of the Work Habitat COM system, but I could not access it or pair with it until I was physically standing at the control panel inside the Habitat. The guest connection I had used previously would not process communications, only data exchange. The Lander system had automatically connected upon touchdown, but I didn't have the Lander interface anymore. Same with the Mar-Sat and Jalopy-Sat signals, I could detect their presence but could not do anything with them until my suit system was authenticated via the Habitat system. The Landers COM relay was obviously not functioning. This suit was going to be effectively mothballed once I reached the surface. I guess no one thought it was worth putting an automatic pairing procedure in with the descent preparation procedure either. That would definitely have to be changed for future manned missions.

I started to shuffle my body downwards, to exit the airlock debris through the ceiling when one of my internal mantras came up in my mind, *economy of effort*. I started moving the other way, then worked slowly at detaching the large duffel/transport bags, the two foot lockers and the two weapons boxes. I then moved them a little awkwardly, but fairly easily towards my feet. *Got to love the low-g.* I kicked the bags out ahead of me and shuffle-slid the boxes towards the opening. Last thing I grabbed was my tablet and the handheld camera, hooking them both to my utility belt. I finally went through the impromptu exit and was able to look up.

There was a large hunk of the Lander's shell that looked like a dull can opener had pried it up. It had flipped over the airlock wreckage forming a canopy over my egress solution. I took a moment to check my HUD and other Activity Suit systems.

I crawled on my hands and knees from under the wreckage canopy and lifted my upper torso, still on my knees. My back twinged a bit, but I felt a lot better now that I wasn't in the tin can that had almost become my coffin. As my eyes adjusted to the relatively bright Martian light, I rested in the kneeling position with my hands on my hips looking around. I could see the blackened crater that indicated where the Lander *had* been sitting. The airlock, as I suspected, had remained mostly intact and had been ejected about 30 feet from the Lander by the force of the explosion. I could see on the other side of the small crater that there was another large chunk of ship still intact. Dollars to donuts, it was the Head. I later found out I was correct in that assessment. Odd, the two safest places in a Lander are the airlock and the shitter. Damn.

For about three hundred metres in every direction there were smoking hunks of metal and other ship components. There were no fires, although the scorching indicated there had been, at least briefly. I guessed they had burned out pretty quickly in the thin atmo. The debris was still hot enough that what would have burned was still smouldering, thus, smoke. I could see a lot of the supply bags and equipment boxes. It was also raining debris over the whole area, and probably would for several more minutes. The debris was small enough, falling slow enough, and far enough away that I could get out from under this canopy and stand up. I started crawling forward on my hands and knees but just as I was about to stand up, I took dizzy and nauseous all of a sudden. I stayed motionless on my hands and knees until the dizziness and nausea passed. It didn't take too long. I didn't think it was a concussion, but with head trauma that was a possibility.

I slowly stood up and then turned in a slow circle looking at the smouldering wreckage. Not so oddly, the sight of the wreckage was conflicting with the sheer beauty of the setting I was in. To the west was the ice wall. I could see it clearly, the reds and dark greys of embedded sand on the face of it. North was the flat, slightly rolling and rocky terrain of Chasma Boreale proper. To the west and east were the sand dunes of Hyperboreae Undae that stretched for hundreds of kilometres. The sky was the yellowish gray I had been expecting. The atmosphere had no thick ozone layer to make it blue when the sun was high in the sky. Blue sky didn't happen until evening time on Mars. Since I was in the latitude of the summer long midnight sun, I wouldn't see an evening sky for another two or three months. The rocky ground, of course, was red and brown.

It hit me again at that point, I was really here. I was really on Mars. I had done it. We had done it. God had done it; He had brought me safely across the dangerous expanse of space between the two planets and He landed me safely on *martis firma*. He had even kept me safe when the small world of the Lander blew up around me.

The time reading on the HUD brought me back to reality, with the realization that I had been on the surface for over forty minutes before emerging from under the canopy. I can't communicate directly with Mission Control, but the Mar-Sat will undoubtedly be trained on the wreckage and looking for signs of life or signs of death. I leaned back as far as I could and looked up at where I roughly guessed the Mar-Sat to be. I clenched my hands into fists and raised them, then crossed my arms above my helmet. I held the pose for ten seconds then lowered my arms and surveyed the debris again. I raised the hand camera and slowly panned 360 degrees, so that I could record a POV (Point of View) shot of what I was seeing. There is nothing like boots on the ground to investigate an accident scene. I slowly shuffle stepped through the debris closer to the crater, and took some more footage of the blackened ground; hopefully the blast pattern would give some assistance in their investigation. There was a large, mostly intact hunk of the final RAD assembly, but with no sign of the engine nacelles; I guessed they had been pretty well vapourized by the blast. I took a minute to do an upclose recording of the remaining RAD components in the wreckage. Finished with this, I lowered the camera and strapped it to my utility belt on my jet-black Activity Suit outer shell. I left the camera recording.

I shuffle walked back to the impromptu egress point on the airlock. I picked up a weapons case, two of my duffel bags, and a metal foot locker; then set-off towards the Habitat, walking strongly and without hesitation. Of course, forgetting to shuffle step, I took only two Terran style strides before I was face down and sprawled on the ground. I laughed to myself, stood up, brushed the dirt off my knees and chest, and then checked my systems. All were nominal. I gave the Mar-Sat an impromptu hand signal to let them know I was still okay.

I had forgotten for a moment I wasn't walking on Terra. I thought back to my Martian training sessions, using slings and fast-response servo's to simulate walking in 38% of the gravity I was used to. I picked up my load of bags and boxes and then decided to do myself a favour. I went and picked up the other bag, foot locker and the second weapon box. It was really awkward, but it gave enough weight that I felt sort of like I was walking on Earth. That was a blessing because I was still feeling a little out-of-whack from the explosion, and from being back in a gravity environment. I stepped off again, more cautiously this time, and didn't fall down again. I'd be in the Hab before that embarrassing bit of video reached Terra.

Chapter 10

Mission Control

18 Minutes, 2 Seconds Later

Carrie and Arno had been working independently, but in concert. They had been sweeping the debris field with the Mar-Sat cameras looking for Mike's body, or less likely, signs of life. The Lander touched down forty-two minutes ago and it had been thirty-six minutes since the explosion had stunned the world. Carrie and Arno could overhear Jayden on his cell phone calling Gary, Mike's son. This was his third call to him. He continued to offer words of comfort about what had been seen and tried to offer him hope. The video feed going live to the world had been cut off after the explosion, but not before everyone saw the fireball and ejecta. Once they confirmed there was no body in sight, they opened the feed to the world again.

From the look on Jayden's face, Carrie and Arno were both glad they hadn't been the one to make those phone calls. After the explosion, Jayden had the phone glued to his ear almost constantly making phone call after phone call. The phone calls were probably keeping him busy enough not to let his mind settle on the full magnitude of the loss, personal and corporate. In the few years Mike had been at the Corporation, he and Jayden had become close friends.

All of the telemetry techs were huddled over two workstations playing back each telemetry feed, moment by moment, trying to find a clue. They all agreed that everything was two thumbs up until the readings suddenly all went to zero or null, all at the exact same moment. After playing the multitude of data feeds individually, they were selectively playing them side by side. This was a first look, but it was still possible something may jump out at them. They were looking for fast answers but they also knew the investigation would last for months. Most of the world would never really know what had happened; what had *really* happened.

"HE'S ALIVE!" Carrie screamed at the top of her lungs as she leaped clear out of her chair, pointing at the large left-side monitor at the front of the room. The room went dead silent as every head snapped around to look at the screen. They could hear the pounding of feet coming down the corridor, as the three dozen people in the conference room, who had also heard her scream, were running full-tilt towards Mission Control.

After a quick glance, and not seeing what she was seeing, Jayden yelled at her, "Where is he? I don't see him?"

Carrie continued yelling, but not quite as loud, "The large chunk of debris in the lower part of the screen." Arno was zooming in the camera. It wasn't actually the camera zooming, he was manipulating the viewable area of the Ultra Hi-Def video image, reframing it, and enlarging it. This made it seem like the camera was being zoomed. Carrie continued, "Watch that flap of metal." She had been looking right at it, when the first duffel bag/transport bag had come tumbling out from under it. She sat bolt upright and took half a second to savvy the meaning of what she had seen, then she leapt to her feet yelling.

Everyone saw the second duffel bag come into view, propelled into the opening from under the canopy of hanging metal. It landed by the one that had been sitting there. Then a third bag came tumbling out. Two metal foot lockers slid into view as well, one at a time, skittering further than you would think they would. Next were two longer cases, Jayden and Hans sharing a look at each other when they saw them. A few moments afterwards, they saw a gloved hand, then a helmet, then the torso of a black Activity Suit emerging on hands and knees from under the flap of metal. The room erupted in a roar of cheering. Jayden already had his cell phone to his ear, he was calling Gary. "Your dad's alive. I'll call you back when I know more." He hung up.

Since this feed was going out live on TV and the internet, Arno pulled up the subtitle screen and added text to the image. *Mike Lane has survived the explosion! Awaiting communication from Mike, no uplink at present.* Within moments this video feed, and the text, was displayed on almost every television that was turned on, all over the planet. All the major networks and their affiliates had been carrying the live feed of the landing. Most of them were still conducting posttragedy interviews and commentary when the word went out that Mike was alive.

Hans was on the phone again, and so were several other people. Everyone else was laughing, backslapping, crying, and hugging. The whole air of the room had changed instantly to joy and elation. Everyone, on the phone or not, watched intently. They saw the space suited figure stand up, with hands on hips looking at the debris around him. A widespread conversation started immediately on how he had managed to survive the explosion, and how injured he would be. It seemed like Mike must have heard that question, because just then he leaned back, looking almost directly at the Mar-Sat camera and lifted his arms and crossed them above his head, holding that pose for a long time. There were several cheers from the hobby divers in the room. Hans said out loud, "That hand signal means, 'I'M OKAY'. It means he's not seriously injured."

More cheering and backslapping erupted in the room. They watched while he held something up in his hand, it looked like a video camera. He started slowly turning in a circle. He slowly walked, with small steps, towards the

64

small blackened crater, and then over to a hunk of blackened and twisted metal debris. They watched as he finished taking his video recordings and then returned to where he started. Jayden and Hans looked at each other again, smiling. Even now, after what he had just survived, Mike was thinking details, thinking about the overbearing, he was collecting evidence.

The figure of Mike, on the big screen, reached the stuff he had tossed from the airlock. He gathered up some of the items and then stepped towards the Hab. There was a large gasp and then a wave of laughter swept through the room as he went down face first on the surface. Those who knew Mike could imagine him laughing to himself in the privacy of the suit but being fully aware the satellite captured the whole moment. When he stood up, he looked skyward and with his gloved right hand, made an "L" shape on his helmet over his forehead. It was indeed a funny moment after so much tension, but it still wasn't as funny as the toilet failure video on the MTV … but it was close, given the context of the situation. It became apparent to everyone that whatever happened on Mars wasn't necessarily going to stay on Mars.

Hans, the on-duty Mission Control Director, let the conviviality go on for a few more minutes. Then he clapped this hands together a few times to get everyone's attention.

"This has been a day of extreme emotions. First, our work of the last few years came to a realization with Mike landing on another planet. Then we had disaster strike and assumed a tragedy. We watched all our work, and as we thought, our friend, go up in a fireball. That sense of tragedy has, thankfully, turned to joy now that we know our friend is alive and well. At this point everything else is secondary to Mike's survival. Indeed we need to find out what happened, but that is secondary to the fact that we now need to move into the planned mission support mode. Mike is 115 Million miles away, he's alone and he needs our support to get life back to Mars normal for him again; whatever that might be. Carrie and Arno, excellent work on finding him for us. Hab support team, I want absolute scrutiny on the incoming telemetry. Mike will be inside by now and if not already, will be transmitting a message to us shortly. People, let's go to work."

Everyone went back to work with enthusiasm. Carrie began running playback of the landing and explosion looking for clues, while Arno ran system checks on the video and audio signal systems. They enlisted the satellite team to check on the status of Mar-Sat and Relay-1, which was in GSO (Geosynchronous Orbit) relaying the Martian Signals to the Corporation's antenna array half a kilometre away.

Chapter 11

The Habitat: Arriving Home

I finally made it to the Habitat, dropping my gear about twenty feet in front of it. The Hab was actually two individual units, soon to be connected by a tunnel. One was a work habitat and one was a living habitat. The large rover that had been here for four years had moved the living habitat into close proximity to the work habitat. One of my first orders of business would be to complete that alignment between the habitat structures and get them fully operational.

I picked up one of the duffels and walked up to the Work Hab white, soot covered, skirting. The soot was from the final RAD engine when the Habitat structure landed. The airlock hatch to this Hab unit was about seven feet off the ground. The final RAD assembly and engine nacelles were still attached. Once we removed them, after the first colony crew arrived, we would be able to lower the Hab closer to the ground. There was a landing and stairs packed in one of the supply drops, but setting that up would come later. For now I just needed to get inside. There was a small grey panel in the exterior wall just below and to the left of the Hab's airlock door. I was able to reach it easily, being six feet tall myself. I turned the inset grip to the right ninety degrees, pushed it in, and then turned it left ninety degrees. The panel popped open. I reached in and first pressed the power button (the lights came on). Then I pressed the "Release" button (which brought online the rest of the controls for the airlock). Finally I pressed the "Extend" button and got out of the way fast. A small panel just below the airlock door opened. It was about 20 centimetres high and the width of the airlock door itself. A metal ladder extended from the opening. As the first joint came into view, I stepped forward and grabbed the bottom portion of the ladder as the low gravity had its effect. The ladder continued extending a few more feet then stopped, gravity tilting it downward now that the second hinge was clear of the storage well. I dropped the end of the ladder that I was holding into place. The first three feet were at a slight angle and then it was a straight climb to the airlock door. I reached in the panel, powered it down and shut the panel hatch, repeating the opening sequence in reverse. As I was doing this I leaned back a bit so I could look up and confirm that the handhold rail had extended from the Hab wall on the left side of the airlock door.

I climbed the ladder enough to reach the airlock entry system. I removed the transit cover over the large keypad and tucked it under my arm, discarding it when I got inside. The keypad allowed me to enter a six-digit number that unlocked the security bolts on the airlock hatch. I wouldn't have to do that again unless it became locked. I pressed the dimly glowing green "Entry" button and waited.

Pressing the "Entry" button did a number of things. First, it confirmed the inner airlock door was closed and properly sealed. The outer airlock door would not open if the inner airlock door was open. If the inner airlock door was closed and sealed, then the system activated the decompression pump that extracted the human breathable atmosphere and replaced it with Martian atmosphere at the Martian atmosphere pressure level. Once this was done, the yellow light came on and the airlock door was unlocked. Then all you had to do was grab hold of the inset door handle, rotate it ninety degrees, and push. This unsealed the outer hatch and unlocked the mechanism keeping it shut. The hatch swung inward and I climbed up a bit more for a peek inside. All appeared in order so I tossed my duffel bag and the keypad hatch through the opening, then took a few moments to climb back down and toss all the other bags inside. Thankfully, low-g allowed me to do this quite easily without going up and down the ladder. Once the bags and cases were inside, I climbed up into the airlock, shut the hatch behind me, and rotated the inner door handle to the latched position. I crossed the small airlock and activated the dimly lit green button beside the inner airlock door. The outer door sealed, the Martian atmo was replaced with human breathable atmo; and I could finally get out of my black monkey suit.

Opposite the outer airlock door were four racks for hanging Activity Suits. There were also extendable rack assemblies to hang up to four more of them; my every day Activity Suit was packed in a crate on the airlock floor. I took of my helmet and gloves and put them on the shelf to the left of the suit racks. I was glad to feel that the Work Hab's heating system was running, the airlock was chilly from the door being open, but I could feel a flow of warm air from somewhere. It would heat up to about fifteen degrees Celsius, not as warm as the Command Module had been, but a lot better than outside. Once I had the wind collection farm set up, I'd be able to raise the temperature a few more degrees. After wriggling out of my suit and hanging it up, I removed the transport strapping and opened the transport box on the airlock floor to have a look at my every day Activity Suit. I would have to dig it out later and get it ready. Right now I was too tired, so I just shut the box and left it where it was.

I did have one important piece of business to attend to before going any further inside. I lifted one of the long unmarked cases onto the small workbench in the airlock. I turned around to where the first suit hanger was located, the one on the left, next to the helmet and glove shelves which were above the air bottle racks. I found the joints for the wall panel and on the leftmost panel. I pressed hard on the top right corner and then pressed hard again about 7 centimetres below the corner. The panel popped open. I went back to the workbench, undid the clasps on the case, and flipped the lid up. I took out the bulky pulse-energy rifle and went back to the hidden compartment. I placed it in the holding cradle, took that cradle's electrical feeder line, and plugged it into the connection point on the hand grip for the weapon. I repeated this with the other pulse-energy rifle in the other long unmarked case. Each case had two spare power units that I also inserted in their cradles, and plugged into the power system. I closed the hidden compartment hatch and turned to the inner airlock door.

The pulse-energy weapons were something I hoped I'd never have to use. However, there were some very real concerns about the Chinese or Russians coming to Mars and wiping out the colony to establish their dominance. This had been some sketchy intel that came to the Corporation through some very back channels in the German military. There were only six people in the Corporation who knew I had brought these, and two of them were the highly trusted and vetted techs that had done the initial loading of the MTV; the same ones who had loaded the optical equipment. The rifles themselves had been provided to us by the Deutsches Heer, the German Army. The plans for them had been stolen, ironically enough, by the Russians from the U.S. Air Force. German agents had gotten hold of them from the Russians and they were then developed and tested in secret. Someone at the Deutsches Heer contacted the Corporation and well, I was now armed with two of what were, ostensibly, ray guns. I had to chuckle. Then I stopped chuckling as I remembered the other things I had been told by someone else.

I turned the lever on the inner airlock door and it didn't budge. Stunned for a moment, I sighed with relief as I realized I had not entered the unlock code on this inner hatch. On the keypad by the inner airlock door I entered the same six-digit sequence I had done outside. I would not have to do that ever again either, unless the door got locked somehow. I grabbed the handle and this time it turned easily. The seal broke, the door opened in towards the center of the Hab. While the airlock was relatively spacious, room enough for four people to suit up at the same time, the rest of the lower level was quite cramped. The center of the structure was filled with a spiral staircase that led to the upper level. To the right of the airlock door was a suit repair workbench. There was a small set of cabinets and shelves next to the staircase. Everything was wrapped in plastic and braced by metal brackets. All that packaging and bracing would have to be removed later. With everything looking so brand new and still in its packaging, I had a passing chuckle, not my first, about the place being furnished by Ikea.

Opposite the airlock, on the back of the Hab, there was a good sized storage room. I opened the hatch and looked inside. It was fully stocked, and everything was wrapped in plastic. Beside the storage room was the electrical room. It had the power management and power distribution equipment. This room would bring in electricity collected by the solar collectors and wind collectors, and then redistribute it through this Work Hab; and up to three more Habitat units, two of which would not be arriving for another fifteen months. Right now it was drawing power from solar cell reels that had been extended and hooked up by Big Dawg and Little Dawg, the day after this Habitat unit had been moved into its current position. The same had been done to the Living Hab so that it was powered up and ready for my arrival, even though it still had to be moved a short distance to its final position. The other Hab unit managed its own power when hooked up to the solar collectors, but its power would be supplied via the work Hab once the wind farm was online.

The last room, occupying the left side of the lower level of the Work Hab was the mechanical and life support room. The AtmoGen, water and life support controllers, all fed into and were distributed from this room. This is also where the two 500 litre water tanks were located, full of Terran water. It made the Work Hab a lot heavier to get here, but it was necessary as the water mining would not start until after my first Martian winter. The recycling system, which allowed only a two litre per day expenditure, made this necessary delay viable.

I walked back around the staircase. The steps were directly opposite the airlock door, yet very close to the airlock door in fact. It was a cramped space. The steps were fairly spacious though, about 70 centimetres wide. There was a column in the center for the steps to attach to. This column went right up to the ceiling of the second level. It was also the channel for the feeds from the mechanical room to the second level for lighting and life support. Electrical and water went through the ceiling/floor between the levels. I stepped back into the airlock and grabbed one of the duffel bags, the video camera, and my tablet; both of which had been hanging off of my Activity Suit utility belt. I turned the camera off, and then I headed upstairs.

I emerged into the second level and took a good look around. It smelled funny. Funny as in odd, not funny as in "ha-ha". Sort of like a new car smell, with a bit of staleness. There was a portal (window) at the "front" of the Work Hab, above the outer airlock door. There was another portal directly opposite, looking out into what would come to be known simply as the "back yard", with a view of the distant ice cliff.

Looking at the rear of the workspace, on the left were two small rooms. One was an equipment room for the satellite uplink gear and the computer servers, etc. The other was a small storage room. It contained office supplies, spare laptops, a small water tank (full) for the mini-sink, some emergency rations, plus various other odds and sods. There were enough emergency rations to last four people for two weeks. Starting at the rear portal and moving right was the COM station and a workbench with hookup for computers. The computers were all in cushioned boxes strapped to the floor at

70

a multitude of anchor points. There was also a small moveable work table and several chairs waiting to be unpackaged and put into use.

Continuing on to the right was the active breezeway hatch with small storage closets on each side. Next, was a small workbench and workstation with a worktable/island in front of it. There was a small storage closet on the wall again, and then the conference table with unwrapped chairs. Dominating almost a quarter of the floor was a small glassed-in examination room/treatment room that could also perform the duties of an emergency operating room. To the right of the small medical bay (known to the future residents as Mini-Bay), was the passive breezeway hatch, and then back to the storage room: completing the tour of the second floor circle.

The conference table was about six feet long and would also double as a workspace, games table and the site of many late night discussions once the first colony ship arrived. It was permanently attached in place, but there were some comfy chairs lashed to the floor and wrapped in plastic, just waiting to be used.

The Work Habitat and the Living Habitat were to be attached by breezeways. These were air-tight tunnels that I would use to move back and forth, pressurized but not heated, without having to go outside. While it had an escape hatch, the Living Habitat did not have an airlock proper. The tunnel would extend from the active breezeway point and connect hermetically to the passive breezeway hatch on the other Hab unit. Each Hab unit had one active breezeway and one passive breezeway. This would allow an unlimited number of Habs to be daisy-chained together. I couldn't connect these first two Habs until I moved the Living Habitat into its final position. Yes, there was a lot to do before I'd get a chance for some sleep, but right now I had to send a message and get some food. I was starving. I was also really tired. Did I mention that my re-acquaintance with gravity, even at one-third of Terran gravity, was getting real old, real fast? The lethargy I was feeling in my limbs made me long for the much easier weightlessness of space travel.

I went over to the small sink, took off the wrapping material and primed the pump from the small tank in the store room. There were some plastic tumblers secured to the shelf above. I freed and unwrapped them, and then drew a small glass of water and drank it slowly. It had a plastic taste as it had been in the tank a long time, travelling all the way from Terra. One of the last tastes of Terran water I would ever have.

I went to my duffel that I had carried around with me, opened it up and took out a package wrapped in a couple sweaters. It was a box of meal replacement bars. I had hoarded them during transit just for this purpose. I sat at the COM station, hooked up my tablet and initiated the handshake to properly pair it with the Habitat COM system. The handshake failed though. It took me a few minutes of cussin' and typin' to get the system re-initialized and configured to recognize the tablet. The pairing was completed easily after the configuration issues were addressed. Almost immediately my laptop message system popped up with several messages from Mission Control. I started reading those postexplosion messages while I slowly chewed on a meal replacement bar and sipped precious Terran water.

Finishing the bar, feeling sated for now, and putting the hunger headache at bay, I turned the laptop tablet towards me. I activated the record function on the secure video software. The built in camera and microphone came on.

"Hey there Mission Control. Mike Lane reporting to you alive and well from Mars! Can someone please tell me *WHAT THE FRAK HAPPENED?* Holy fireworks Batman, I'm standing there minding my own business, about to go walkabout on an alien planet and *WHAMM*, I get smacked from behind by a two-ton truck. I mean really, guys, come-on, is that piece of *feh wu* still under warranty? Can you get a refund? Damn." I lowered my head then looked up with a smile. "Okay, got that out of my system. The good Lord delivered me safely, and I never had any doubt about that. I just didn't realize how exciting He was going to make it."

That was when the giggles struck, and struck hard. They quickly became rib shaking laughter. Looking at the camera again, blue indicator light waiting for me, I continued, "I mean really, I take eight and a half months to travel 115 million miles in a tin can, and when I safely land on an alien planet … *BAM*! My ship explodes." I laughed a few moments more until I got control of myself. It was time to finish and get some work done. The sun was past the high point in the sky and I needed to get the Living Hab set up. "Well, I guess it's like Q said to Picard, *if you can't take a little bloody nose maybe you ought to go back home and crawl under your bed. It's dangerous out here.*" I raised the remnants of the tumbler of water in a toast. "I've got work to do. I'll be in touch after I move the Living Habitat."

I clicked the finish recording icon and then sent the message back to Earth without any encryption. I just didn't care at this point.

Chapter 12
Walkin' the Casbah

How the Living Habitat was going to be moved was partially my idea. When I first joined the Corporation, one of the first things we did was tour the Habitat manufacturing facility in Karlsruhe, Germany. It was a small privately owned enterprise just north of the Automobilwerk Wörth on the west side of the Rhein River. Very picturesque area, very capable staff, very serious about every bolt, nut, joint and seam. They knew our lives would depend on every single thing they did.

Six of us spent two weeks living in a mock-up Habitat to get a feel for what we would be living and working with. After that, three of us spent a day with the engineers talking about how the Living Habitat (or any Habitat) systems integrated, and how it was going to be put precisely in position. We knew it couldn't land closer than 200 metres to another Hab, because wind shear might blow it into it, and the rather large RAD engines could damage another Habitat quite extensively. The engineers' solution was four titanium discs, like train wheels, which would lower down after landing, slightly lifting the Habitat from its landing struts. Big Dawg, the rover, would then attach to the Habitat structure and very, very slowly drag it into place. The big wheels were to have some power to them, so that they could rotate the Habitat structure if necessary, but they would not be able to traverse any distance on their own, even though they did assist Big Dawg's towing ability.

This discussion quickly revealed certain misgivings about how precisely they could achieve alignment, and what would happen if Big Dawg had to move it over rough terrain, or a worse scenario, too steep of a rise in the terrain; which would render the whole operation impossible. The darn thing did weigh seven tonnes on Terra after all.

As I had stood there listening to the engineers, I had a stroke of genius. Okay, I thought it was genius. I outlined a radical, although not too complex, solution for the engineers. I thought for a moment they were either going to cry or shake my hand completely off my arm. Those German engineers certainly do get excited about their work. My solution was simple, allow the Habitat to *walk* into position. The mechanics of the solution were simple in my head. It was a bit more complicated in actualizing the idea but still something that could easily be done on Terra, and easily done on Mars. Instead of the complex computer programming for positioning the Habitat, the Rover would simply drag the Habitat on its train wheels as far as it could, and then the colonist on site would hook up a remote control unit and use pneumatically controlled legs to "walk the Habitat unit".

With its present position, I needed to move the Living Habitat (L-Hab) five feet closer to the Work Habitat (W-Hab), move it 45 centimetres to relative "left" and then rotate the L-Hab about 15 degrees. This positioning was too precise for Big Dawg's rough towing ability, and I was glad I didn't have to do it by hand (which it could be done, but with a *lot* of effort … by many people, with lots of block and tackle).

I went back to the airlock and suited up again in my flight Activity Suit. Everything checked. I tore open the plastic on the first storage cupboard below the small bench in the airlock. I detached the flight restraints and removed two items. One was a heavy canvas bag that contained the small set of tools necessary for the exterior work around the Habitat structures. The second was the controller that would control the movement of the L-Hab on its mechanical, stubby legs. I depressurized the airlock, pulled the outer airlock door inboard. I leaned down to the floor to cut the restraints and pick up a large packaged coil of umbilical cables, to connect the two habitats, and tossed it out the door. It was kind of a jaw-dropping moment to watch it fall to the ground, so much slower than when things fall on Earth. "Neat-O," I said to myself, and then climbed down the ladder. The airlock had a fail-secure system on the outer hatch. If no one passed through the outer airlock door for ninety seconds, the servos would kick to life and shut the door automatically. This was so one person wouldn't leave and accidentally strand the others inside. I paused a moment, looking out over the not-so-distant sand dunes, and let the hatch close itself to make sure it worked, and it did.

I walked around the W-Hab and headed towards the L-Hab. I stopped midway to look out over the debris that not so long ago, I had almost been part of. It had only been ninety minutes since I climbed out of the airlock wreckage. The smouldering had stopped. I sighed heavily, I was dead tired but had miles to go before I could sleep.

The L-Hab was only ten feet away. Big Dawg had finished moving it there weeks ago. Little Dawg, with Big Dawg's help, had uncoiled the solar collectors. Big Dawg's manipulator arm had been used by Mission Control to plug in the solar collector power feeds. I walked the length of the five collector strips and removed the ground pegs holding it in place. Little Dawg was close by, so I walked over and deposited the pegs, 60 in total, into its utility tray. I didn't want to lose them, and the rover might as well make itself useful.

The L-Hab was almost in alignment but it needed to be five feet or less at the nacelle skirting and within three degrees of axis alignment with the W-Hab. First order of business was to remove all of the sections of the nacelle skirt. The walking process needed to extend the walking legs from underneath the L-Hab to accommodate the mechanisms of motion. I also needed to be able to see what was happening underneath to properly control the "walk".

I set down the controller in a safe place and then opened the canvas tool bag. I took out the universal wrench and went to work. All exterior coverings, ports, joints, etc. used a bolt with an inset head. For simplicity's sake, the exteriors of all the equipment sent to Mars used six sizes of bolt, using three different size heads. The universal wrench had three attachments. Selecting the correct head size; it was like a backwards ratchet set. I placed the universal wrench head attachment into the depression in the bolt head, and turned it counter-clockwise. There was a power feature for this wrench, but I had not had time to charge it up, so I did it the old fashioned way. I moved a small slider on the side of it to put the power head into Manual-Ratchet mode. There were eighteen bolts to remove in each of the nacelle skirt sections. There were twelve nacelle skirt sections to be removed.

I did this carefully and step-by-step according to the procedure I had memorized. All the bolts went into the pockets on the legs of my outer jumpsuit. Everything had a procedure for the mission, and for living on Mars. I had memorized most of them on the trip here and I knew from jobs I had in the past that a good procedure keeps you safe and protects you. I was not only a leader, I was a good follower. Life had shown me that all good leaders are at first, good followers.

I moved the large pieces of metal away from the L-Hab and placed them together, leaning one on the other, in the order I removed them. I wasn't worried about them going anywhere as the wind was only gusting around 20 km per hour according to the readout I checked before coming outside.

I returned the wrench to the tool bag then walked over to the controller, picked it up and walked back to the L-Hab. Now it was pucker time. I knew the L-Hab had enough power for this, the batteries were fully charged, and I was moving it such a short distance that I didn't need to disconnect the solar collector. It would just drag a bit with the L-Hab as it moved the few feet into position. I would re-align it afterwards. The pucker moment was going to be whether or not the "legs" responded. They were pneumatically powered and that pneumatic system was about to check out nominal, but it was still -20° Celsius. I had some concern that the low temps would affect the legs, even though the German engineering team assured me these temperatures, summer temperatures for this latitude, would not be a problem. They had guaranteed the legs and pneumatic system to work to -114° Celsius.

There was close to six feet of space under the Habitat structures. The three very large RAD engine nacelles occupied most of the space. Eventually we would remove the RAD assemblies, but that was not scheduled until there was a larger team on the ground. There was a small box that had once been white but was now covered in soot. It was under the L-Hab bottom and directly beneath the active breezeway, which for today's orientation was at the "rear" of the Hab, insofar as today's movement considered the passive breezeway to be the front.

I went back for the wrench and then used it to remove the cover plate from this previously white box. I remembered there was a pocket on the leg of my Activity Suit specifically for the universal wrench. I slipped it into the pocket and then uncoiled the cable attached to the controller. The box I had uncovered had two things in it, a USB port and a hardpoint clip. I snapped the metal protective cover off the USB port then plugged the controller into it. There was a small chain on the controller cable which I attached to the hardpoint clip, to keep the USB cable from being unplugged while we moved.

At present, the L-Hab was resting on its landing struts. After Big Dawg finished moving the L-Hab, the train wheels had retracted and left the L-Hab on its landing struts for stability. The train wheels would never be used after today, so long as we didn't have to move the L-Hab any great distance.

I powered up the controller and checked the walker system, everything was in order. I activated the first step in the walking sequence.

The first step in this process was to extend the four leg assemblies laterally. Each leg assembly had two legs that were on independent vertically mounted swivels. These were attached to the articulation controller, which was mounted under a third horizontally integrated swivel assembly. This allowed the legs to be turned in any direction and walk forwards or backwards. This entire leg assembly was on a strong piston arm that would extend them laterally beyond the base of the L-Hab. The legs had to unfold into position and the top swivel point could not rotate fully upward until the assembly had cleared the edge of the L-Hab itself. While it sounds complex, the design is fairly straightforward, and it allowed the L-Hab to be moved 360°.

The mechanics of walking was simple. Lower one of the legs on each corner to raise their respective assembly to an individual height that would keep the L-Hab relatively level. Then move each legs paired leg, so that it was 10 centimetres higher than the first leg. Next, activate all four ground-contact leg swivels, through a simple series of pneumatic pistons so that the L-Hab would appear to be falling forward on those legs. They moved slowly but faster than you would expect as stopping in mid "fall" could severely damage the walker mechanism. As the L-Hab "fell" forward, it came to rest on the legs that were a few centimetres shorter. Next, retract the legs that had just walked, extend the resting legs to the proper height, reset the tilted legs to upright orientation, and set their height to 10 centimetres above the now supporting legs. Then the process repeated. After the legs were lowered in initial position and had taken the weight of the L-Hab, I sent the command to raise the landing struts. Then I began the *not-as-slow-as-you-would-think* process of walking the big Habitat structure a short distance across the surface of Mars.

We kept going on like this for several minutes. At some point it was going so fast and flawlessly I started humming a tune and thought to myself, "Yep, we're really *'Walkin' the Casbah'* now." Gotta love those German engineers.

Each walk cycle took about three minutes to complete and moved the L-Hab about 8 centimetres. I could have taken bigger steps, but I preferred, after the day I had already had, to play it slow and safe. In between each walk cycle, the procedure was to examine the footing in "front" of the legs to make sure there was nothing that would appear to make the next step unstable. The legs had one 10 centimetre square solid titanium *shoes* to distribute the weight and not sink too far into the regolith. The "walking" procedure made each step in the walking process about five minutes long, including the actual walk cycle. It took a little over an hour to move the L-Hab the five feet that brought it within five feet of the W-Hab. The pneumatics were, by nature, sealed systems, but I had expected to hear *some* sound. Mind you, the little sound it did create, was hard enough to hear within the thin Martian atmo to begin with. Compound that with the insulating properties of the Activity Suit, and it was like watching a TV show with the sound turned all the way down. I didn't even feel any ground tremor at my feet. I turned on the external microphone on my helmet and then I could hear it. It wasn't very loud at all in the thin Martian atmo. It took almost fifteen full minutes to lower the train wheels, lift the walker legs and orient the axis to align it with the W-Hab. Then it took just over another thirty minutes to walk the L-Hab relatively "sideways" to put it in final alignment. That final movement was very fiddly and precise, so each step took longer.

Chapter 13

Achael HofPin

Her name was pronounced with soft sounds. The "h" in her name was very soft; more like a gust of breath, a breathy "uh" sound. The "ch" was soft as well, throaty, like in the word *Chanukah* or the German word, *Achtung*. Ah-ch-hail. The capital "P" in her last name had a soft "sh" sound in front of it. HofPin (Uh-off-shpin), was a hereditary Eben family name. It meant "daughter of Hof". If she had been a boy, her family name would have been HofPen (son of Hof). It has often been noted that listening to the Eben speak in their native tongue is like listening to people whispering in another room

She leaned back in her chair, short legs and long arms stretching. She rapidly blinked her very large, by human standards, oddly shaped eyes. Eyelids fluttering, she yawned and then rubbed her neck as she sat upright again. The bangs of her jet black, soft yet thick, straight collar length hair fell into her eyes. She jutted her bottom lip outwards and blew upwards a few times to move it out of the way. She had more success in tickling her human shaped nose, than moving the hair, so she used her hand to brush the bangs aside and scrunched up her face to stop a sneeze from happening.

She was watching the monitor with the co-opted Mar-Sat video playing ("pirated signal" was such a nasty phrase for this situation). She suddenly furrowed her brow and looked closer. "Oh, wow. That's cool."

Her sister, Hlef HofPin turned from her workstation and said, "what you got there sweetie pie?" (Same breathy "uh" sound, Uh-oo-Lef. The extra vowel sound, because the "H" was the first letter, and was followed by a consonant. Eben pronunciation rules are very complex ... and meaningful. Calling her Oo-Lef would get you a punch in the face.)

"Watch this. He's making that structure move with the leg supports, like it's walking", she paused then said again, "That's *so* cool."

"TransMat would be easier," Hlef commented as she squinted at the screen. It really was kind of cool, she thought as well. She just didn't understand why her sister was so interested in this human idiot who, of all the stupidity in the Verse, came to Mars *alone*. "I still think he's an idiot," she said as she turned back to her own work, never one to mince words. "You don't really think they're going to let him live do you?" Achael knew she meant the Eridani, she certainly didn't mean her own people.

The term *sister* was complicated. They weren't actually born to Hof. His sperm, which is almost identical to human sperm, was used to fertilize human ova, which produced quintuplets, in a test tube. After millennia of cloning, it was only relatively recently that the Eben had begun playing around with (and quite successfully I should note) hybridization of Eben with other species. Technically it was just cross breeding, but hybridization sounded more sexy. The human eggs they fertilized in this, the fifth iteration of the experiments, resulted in Achael, her fraternal twin Hlef, and three brothers. They were then grown in laboratory conditions. Soon after the initial conception, they were transferred to purpose-centric, Eben-designed, gestation tanks. They were officially born on Earth date August 31st, 1979. The five of them had recently turned 39 Terran years old, but were still considered adolescents by the True Blood Eben. All five that had been born that day had been raised as a family unit, and knew each other as family. Since the sperm was from the same Eben male and the ova were all donated willingly by the same Terran woman, the five were in fact all brothers and sisters by any biological definition. The only difference between normal births (human or Eben) was that they didn't share a womb.

The birthday party thrown for them last year had been nice. A few of the humans from Earth had imported the decorations, and they took care of the music and booze. The Base Commander, a human dominant hybrid like Achael and Hlef, had insisted on bringing out his karaoke machine, despite everyone's assurance he really didn't need to go through that effort. However, he was the Base Commander and he insisted it was absolutely no bother at all, no matter how much they protested.

Their three brothers, who were also turning thirty-nine that day, had gone to great length to prepare authentic spicy food, from what they all thought of as their "authentic" homeworld. While the two sisters were both human dominant hybrids, two of the brothers were Eben dominant. It had long been known by the humans that were aware of them, no one could party like a Human-Eben hybrid. They drank like fish and owned the dance floor, especially Hlef.

"He's got balls," Achael muttered. "And he survived the attack on the ship he arrived in." She thought for a few moments watching the third walk cycle start, "I wouldn't count him out just yet".

Yeah, right. Hlef kept the thought to herself for a change. Achael could be real sensitive when it came to pets and simpletons. One well-placed pulse sabot, and this lunatic's living space would be a charnel house. She shook her head and wondered why the Eridani commander hadn't finished him off yet. For that matter, why hadn't he finished off the other ship that had also just landed?

Chapter 14

Meanwhile, Back At The Hab ...

Once in the proper place, with the proper orientation and axial alignment, I lowered all eight legs and levelled the L-Hab. The final step was a few small adjustments to make the floor of the L-Hab exactly the same height as the floor in the W-Hab. Once this was done, I lowered the landing struts again and locked them in place. They would give lots of lateral stability, especially when the winter winds hit the Chasma.

I walked around to the actual rear of the L-Hab to re-adjust the solar collectors, but I saw that Little Dawg was already on the job. Two of the five collector strips had been adjusted and he was on his way to the third one. "I love you Mission Control," I muttered.

I turned around and continued what I was doing. I had seen Big Dawg sitting back from the action, near the solar collector for the W-Hab. He was pointing straight at me. Its head, made up of the mast camera and atmo-sensor, was going up and down just like it was nodding, and its manipulator arm hanging slack in front of it. I guess Mission Control was sending their approval. As I had not yet got the full W-Hab COM system up and running, I could not receive messages on my HUD. I guessed one of the Mission Control techs had put Big Dawg in a position to get some video of the walking process. I wondered for a moment if it was Carrie. I shook my head after a moment, "no sense thinking about the impossible."

Carrie and I had grown quite close for a time; and it was the first time I had grown close to someone since Loreena. I think part of my mind knew it could never turn into anything, not with me going to Mars, and that made it okay. It *was* dishonest of me; and it was unfair to Carrie. I ended things as nicely as possible. Carrie had her own misgivings anyways. She was growing close and so were her boys, totally irresponsible of the both of us. She was glad when we had "the talk", and I think, relieved that I had been the one to bring it up. I stayed friends with her boys, and I stayed friends with Carrie as well. We never stopped caring, but it could be nothing more. It wasn't Mars that would have eventually kept us apart. Love could never be fully in my grasp until I let go of the past that I didn't really want to let go of it.

All totalled, moving the L-Hab was about three hours work, probably the easiest thing I'd have to do in the coming months. I smiled to myself at the thought that I had just moved a seven tonne Habitat using just a small remote control hanging around my neck. It was about this time the thought struck me that here I was, on Mars, living in a mobile home much like I had many years before on Earth. The laughter came in waves. It lasted a couple minutes before

I could continue. I made a mental note to check the CO2 filter on my Activity suit. The big job left after moving the L-Hab into position was re-attaching the skirting; but I was tired, and I was gravity fatigued. I was hungry too. I decided to re-attach the nacelle skirting in the morning. Right now I needed food and oh, yeah, *sleep*!

I disconnected the USB connection for the walker controller, closed and re-bolted the covering panel on its housing. The last step in the process that I was going to complete before some sleep was the easiest part of the whole thing. I uncoiled the umbilical cables and hoses, all wrapped in armoured sheathing, that I had tossed out from the airlock. I opened the access panels on W-Hab and L-Hab, making sure I had the colours right (blue connected on W-Hab, and yellow connector on L-Hab - matching the interior colours of the connection boxes); I then attached the umbilical cables and hoses that would feed power, water, and breathable atmo from the W-Hab to the L-Hab. There were also a few fiber optic connections that tied the two structured computer systems together and allowed direct access to the COM equipment and array from the L-Hab.

The three COM array dishes were on the roof of the W-Hab, as well as the UHF and VHF arrays, and the two, four axial-mode, Helical Hi-Gain antenna arrays. One hi-gain was pointed towards Mar-Sat, one was a dedicated and undocumented link for the Jalopy-Sat. It was possible to communicate with Jalopy-Sat directly from a suit COM unit if you had a line of sight, after the suit COM unit had been authenticated. The day-to-day Activity Suit had miniature helical hi-gains built into the top of the helmet. So long as there was no obstruction, this miniature antenna could provide a clear communication channel with the Jalopy-Sat. I hoped I never had to utilize the full capabilities of the Jalopy-Sat, just like I hoped I never had to use the pulse-energy weapons I had stored in the airlock secret compartment. The image of a bloodied face popped into my mind.

I had found the guy in the car-park beating his already bloodied girlfriend. Normally a pacifist, I interceded, aggressively. He was in the hospital for two weeks. I eventually beat the criminal charges based on the woman's testimony and some fancy footwork by the Corporation's legal team. Thankfully the victim had stepped up when it was necessary, they usually don't. I abhorred violence. I was a very peaceful person. In all my years with the Police Service I never drew my weapon once. I didn't want to break his nose, eye socket, cheekbone, and left arm; but he kept coming at me. It turned out he was on crystal meth at the time, so he didn't feel the beating until much later. I knew I would step up and do what was needed to defend others. I knew I was capable of doing it. I just didn't like it very much. I stood looking towards the ice-wall in the distance, through the ultraclear Martian atmosphere. I couldn't foresee today that those hopes of non-aggression on Mars would not be realized. They would not be realized sooner than I would ever have contemplated.

I picked up the walk controller, put the universal wrench back in the tool bag, took one last look around, and then headed back to the airlock. Climbing the ladder, I just had to hit the dimly lit green button and confirm low-pressure interior. I reached up higher and moved the locking arm clockwise (which had been closed by servo mechanism when I exited earlier, testing the auto-close system), and then climbed in through the hatch.

While the airlock was re-pressurizing, I put the tool bag and controller away. I had the binding from the umbilical cables bundled up under my arm and looked around but there was no trash receptacle in the airlock. *Damn.* I stuffed the strapping refuse in one of the under-counter cabinets and promised myself I'd do something with it, sometime before Colony-1 arrived. "Why do today what you can put-off until tomorrow," I chuckled to myself. Procrastination was *so* not in my nature ... not since being selected by the Corporation. I was just too frakin' tired to care at the moment. I got out of my suit, plugged the environment pack into the maintenance port so it could recharge the batteries, and then I swapped out the nitrogen bottles (I had to, sorry) so fresh ones would be ready to go. Finally, I set the suit computer to perform a full diagnostic. Tomorrow I would unpack and charge up the primary Activity Suit and fill its air bottles. The one I had been wearing was the flight model, with the pressure system for g-forces. My primary Activity Suit did not have the pressure system, so it would be a bit more comfortable and easy to move around in.

I looked at the amount of dust on the exterior jumpsuit I had just removed. I could feel some sand on the deck under my feet. I walked over to the vacuum system and pulled the plastic wrapping off. I picked up the hose and turned it on. It worked like a charm. I spent a few minutes vacuuming Mars dust off my Activity Suit, something I would need to do almost every time through the airlock. I also vacuumed up all the red dust and sand that was on the floor.

Leaving the airlock, I slowly climbed the spiral staircase to the upper deck. Climbing the stairs was almost effortless in low-g unless you're as tired as I was. Today had been my first gravity of any kind in months, and my energy was draining fast: I needed rest. When I got to the upper deck, I grabbed some more water to drink, and another couple of meal replacement bars from the dwindling stash in my duffel bag. I was preparing, in my head, what my video report was going to say as I slowly chewed the first bar when I glanced over at the Habitat Environment Control (HEC). I did a double take. The W-Hab batteries were at 86%, but the rate of charge read zero. That meant the battery charging system was getting no juice. I went to the rear portal to look out at the array.

There it was, all laid out. The solar collector strips making up the array started about forty feet from the Hab units, and stretched almost one hundred feet; anchored every ten feet with metal pegs installed by Little Dawg. I had checked the power lead connection on both Habitats while taking a wee break during the L-Hab walk. I knew there were some mini-binoculars packed away somewhere in the room, but didn't have the urge to go looking for them. I'd have to go out and do a visual inspection. Big Dawg was sitting there by the power harness, still nodding its head unit up and down.

"Fraking moron."

There were messages waiting for me from Terra, but I decided to get back to them after I investigated this situation. I was getting a bit bleary-eyed at this point in the fatigue, but if I didn't take care of this right now, I could be in a real spot of trouble. I recorded a quick report for Mission Control regarding the L-Hab walk and the power situation. I reported that I was not going to activate the feeds to the L-Hab until I had investigated and hopefully corrected the power issue.

I sent the message and finished the second meal replacement bar as I thought about all the things I needed to do. Reinstall the L-Hab nacelle skirting; connect the two Habitats' Breezeway; install the steps and landing outside the W-Hab; unpack and install at least four of the wind collectors; set up and activate the AtmoGen connections; inventory the smaller items of the supply drops; unpack food supplies; unpack and install the computers in the W-Hab; boot up the Habitat servers; unpack the kitchen and living areas in the L-Hab; unpack my clothes; have a wash-up; and make my bed ... the list was almost endless. I downed the last of the water in the tumbler and headed to the airlock to suit up again. I was tired as heck. I had been going non-stop for fourteen hours on a day I should have been taking it very easy to get reacquainted with my old friend, gravity. The only rest I'd had was when I was unconscious in the airlock wreckage. I was super tired, I was so tired I wanted to cry. I felt nauseous, my arms and legs were aching, not to mention my back. I just wanted to fall down, and fall asleep.

Tired as I was though, I was still ... *tired on Mars*! WooHoo! With the outer airlock opened again, I turned around backwards and did a little bunny hop into the open. As I fell, quite a bit slower than I would have on Earth, I grabbed the ladder with my hands and did a Navy-slide down to the surface. So cool.

I walked around the Hab to the backyard, and over to the solar collectors power lead connection. It looked tight. I unhooked it and re-connected it. I turned around, and Big Dawg had moved. It had backed up about four feet, and its head unit was no longer nodding; it was motionless and at a downward angle, looking down at its outstretched manipulator arm. The head unit wasn't moving any more. "Great, after four years it picks *now* to quit?" I walked over to look at its head unit, maybe some sand gummed up the works. Not likely though, as that hadn't happened in the four years it had been here. Nothing appeared wrong with the head unit on visual inspection. I leaned behind the mast to look at the unit from behind. Looking down the axis of the head unit, I finally saw it. The head unit camera was pointed directly at the end of the manipulator arm, which was almost touching the power cable from the solar collector array to the W-Hab. The cable was completely severed. No wonder the W-Hab wasn't getting any power flow. I moved around Big Dawg and knelt down for a closer look. A shadow passed on the ground ahead of me. I looked up but didn't see anything. It was probably just some debris from earlier today, blowing around in the ever-present wind. I looked back at the severed power cable.

Power cables don't just cut themselves. I thought maybe Big Dawg had run over it, but then rejected that idea. Big Dawg had four track units with small blades for gripping the surface, so it would have chewed up the cable - not cleanly severed it. Besides, the cable was designed to be strong enough to handle the rovers traversing over it. Getting down on one knee and leaning in close I saw what had happened. Right below the end of the manipulator arm, there was a thick, sharp piece of ejecta from the Lander explosion. It had impacted right on the cable, and sliced cleanly through it. I could see part of it sticking out of the ground. I brushed away some of the regolith and very carefully took a grip on it so that it would not cut my glove. I had Kevlar gloves to go over my Activity Suit gloves, but they were packed away with my day-to-day suit so "careful" had to be the watchword of the moment.

I tugged gently several times, and pulled it out slowly. It wasn't that big, but it was solid metal framework from under the bottom of the Lander. It was ragged, slightly warped on one edge, and blackened. It must have been blown at great velocity from very close to the actual point of explosion. As the Lander site was slightly behind the medial axis of the Habitats' placement, it would have had a straight flight path right to this point. Even the slightest variance in its path, and it would have missed. It had to have been going at one heck of a velocity to travel that distance and sever the cable as well. Why this cable wasn't armoured was beyond me. I'd take that up with the development team later. Thankfully it hadn't hit either of the Habitats. It had to have passed within centimetres of where the L-Hab had been sitting, before I walked it closer to the W-Hab. Great. I was going to have to do a full inspection of the L-Hab before rest would come. Tears started to well at the frustration of wanting to sleep, but knowing I couldn't. I leaned over and put my hands on my knees, waiting for the urge to barf to pass.

I walked back to the storage bay for the solar collector. It was a 60 centimetre hatch on the bottom of the W-Hab proper, above the nacelle skirting. I could barely reach it. I turned around and walked back to Big Dawg, wishing once again that I had paired my suit with the W-Hab COM system. I reached down to the control unit on the large rover, unclipped and lifted the cover on the keypad and typed in the three-digit "follow me" command. From that point on. I would be able to simply give it the "follow me" hand signal. I closed the keypad cover and walked back to the solar collector storage port. Big Dawg followed me dutifully. I pointed two fingers to a spot close enough to the hatch, and Big Dawg rolled to the spot and dutifully obeyed the "park here" hand signal. When Big Dawg or Little Dawg were in "follow me" mode, they could respond to a series of hand signals rather than stopping to type in the interface every time you wanted them to do something simple. I then jump-stepped up to the small cargo deck of the rover's back. This allowed me to reach into the solar collector storage bay easily. There were two spare power cables stored in there, one on each side. I sighed and shook my head. Both of these replacements were wrapped in armoured sheathing. It only took me a minute to get the left side spare unstowed.

I unwrapped the carefully protected male connection on the cable, twisted and unplugged the dead cable at the W-Hab connection point, then replaced it with the new cable connector I was holding. I jumped off the rover's cargo deck, uncoiling the line as I walked, and then finished replacing the power cable to the W-Hab's solar collector array. It only took a few seconds to unsnap the old connector and replace it with the new one. I coiled up the two sections of old cable, pulling the anchor points out of the regolith along its path, leaving them on the ground. I tossed the coiled up damaged cable down on the ground by the W-Hab nacelle skirting, and turned around to see Little Dawg dutifully installing the first ground anchor on the power lead. I do so love those German engineers.

I could see the L-Hab power lead was not protected either, but I didn't think I had to worry about any more explosions in the near future (wrong), so I left it as it was for now. I spent the next twenty minutes slowly walking around the L-Hab doing a visual inspection. I found a few tiny dents and chipped paint with the offending impact debris lying below them on the ground. The Habs were tough buggers for sure. Still though, fixing the chipped paint was going to be a priority in the coming week. The paint was a very important part of the radiation protection, and even a small bit of damage to it needed attention sooner rather than later. Since I was already dressed up with nowhere else to go, I did a visual inspection of the W-Hab as well, for my own peace of mind. I didn't see any debris damage at all, and the coating over the paint was in excellent condition on both Habitats; other than the small chips from the debris impact. There was no environmental erosion from the wind and sand. The paint protected the Habitats from radiation, the coating over the paint protected *that* paint from the Mars sand storms and whirling dust devils.

Finally done, I headed to the airlock and went back inside. When I got upstairs I sat at the desk where I had unwrapped one of the chairs. Looking up at the Environmental Control panel, the charging time indicated was forty-five minutes. Good, everything was fixed. I picked up the tablet to record a message for Mission Control, and looking first at the list of messages the top one jumped out at me:

HANS SAYS OPEN THIS NOW!!

I opened a video message. It was Hans and he looked a little less than pleasant. "Mike, I know it's been a long and eventful day but checking the messages has to be a priority. We were trying to tell you about the power problem and we moved the large rover into place to show you. We also have a system fault in your atmosphere controller that needs to be reset, and it needs to be done quickly. Now please review the other messages, fix the system fault, pair your suit with the COM system and then...." he softened his expression a bit and smiled slightly, "... and then get some sleep buddy. There is a lot to do but you can't do it all at once."

Chapter 15

The Drone

The Eridani Drone sat in the cramped space of the small vessel. The vessel was holding position over the ice ridge, low to the horizon from the perspective of the human's site. The Drone was waiting for a new command from the Master, or for more outside activity by the human. The instructions had been to get close-up images whenever the human was outside. When the Drone saw the human moving, a rapid fly-by was initiated by the Drone to capture 3D moving images of what the human was doing. Most of the time was spent taking long range 2D images to keep out of sight. Stealth and secrecy were as much a part of a Drone's make-up as was absolute and unquestioning obedience to a Master's command. If a Master told the drones to jump into a tunnel of whirling blades, the Master's bevy of drones would race, each one trying to be the first one to their death, jumping into the blades, simply to prove they were most obedient. Obedience is life.

The Drone lifted the tube of nutrient compound, squeezed out some more of the tasteless paste, and stuck it in the tiny mouth set low on the Drone's face. The Drone hated the paste. This was the only food the Drone needed or was given, being that the Drone's body was closer to vegetable than animal in composition.

The Master had said that the human should not see the Drone in the small vessel; so the Drone always flew over when the human was not looking in the direction of approach. The shadows on the ground were not something the Drone gave any consideration to. They weren't real, they were just shadows. Shadows, strangely enough, didn't equate into the Drone's concept of stealth. This Drone, and thousands of others, usually operated around humans in the middle of the night; at that time, there were never shadows to deal with.

The Drone missed the feeling of fulfillment from earlier that day. The Master had commanded the Drone to fire the small vessels energy weapon on a vulnerable point of the spaceship that the human had arrived in. That felt ... fulfilling. Unfortunately for the human, the Master had meant for the Drone to fire the weapon after the human had exited it, thereby stranding the human. The Drone failed to grasp that major part of the Order of Action in its haste to be on with its mission. Luckily for the Drone, the human hadn't been killed.

The Drone could only feel hatred and the varying degrees of hatred. There were no other emotions for the Drone, except the desire to serve and look after the Master, and a feeling of fulfillment in obeying the Master's commands. Killing things was good. A purpose was truly being served when the Drone killed things. The Drone awoke from each sleep cycle hoping something would have to be killed that day. Unfortunately, the Drone had much disappointment in this perpetual hope. In the last few years there had not been a command to kill. The last time the Drone had been ordered to kill was on the humans' planet. It was in a facility under the ground in that dry, barren, lifeless, arid region of the planet; a region that reminded the Drone of the planet the Drone was assigned to now. Even the attack on the human ship earlier had not been a kill order, just an attack order. The two orders were very different, and following the Master's orders precisely was like walking and breathing to all drones. The fact the Drone had mistaken part of the order only served to deeply infuriate the Drone when it came to the human. However, if the human had died, so much the better. It was inherent to an attack order that something *might* die. The difference being that in a kill order something *would* die, or the Drone would die trying to fulfill the order. Such a failure was never a consideration for the Drone. The concept that to die in an attempt, without success, was itself failure, was not something the Drone's simple brain could extrapolate. In reality though, mistakes were sometimes made in the drones' overzealousness to carry out their Master's orders.

Previously assigned to the human planet experimentation detail, this Drone was one of the most effective at capture and retrieval. The Drone especially liked doing those things in the dead of night when the humans were asleep. Such timing inflicted maximum terror, and inflicting terror, an expression of the hatred, the Drone felt for all things not of the Master, was fulfilling. The Drone really didn't understand why they had to return the ugly giant bags of mostly water after the experiments. The Drone didn't understand why the Master wiped the ugly humans' memories, but it was not a drone's place to question the wisdom of the Master, and the Master's equals. The Masters were smart. The Masters took care of the drones. The Masters gave the drones purpose. The Masters gave fulfillment to the drones' existence. Obedience is life.

The human would probably be entering a sleep cycle soon. Perhaps Master would ask for capture and retrieval of the human. The Drone shifted in the small seat with a bit of anticipation. *PLEASE MASTER, PLEASE GIVE AN ORDER, PLEASE GIVE THE CHANCE TO SERVE MORE.* This was usually the prevalent thought in a drone's mind, but this Drone was a little more strident in the thought when envisioning how much abject terror would be experienced by the human, if the Master would only wish it to be so.

The Drone really didn't have a concept of "I" or "me". There was no such concept amongst any of the drones. The Drone merely considered the hive to be a personification and actualization of the Master's will.

A small blip appeared on the Drone's futuristic version of radar, and almost immediately disappeared, but not fast enough to escape the notice of the Drone. The Drone bared pointy teeth, and the permanent scowl deepened.

EBEN DIRTY ROTTEN EBEN; KILL THEM; KILL ALL THE HYBRIDS; KILL THEM; PAIN; TEAR THEM APART; POUND THEM; BURN THEM; DESTROY THEM; ANNIHILATE THEM; MAKE THEM NOT EXIST KILL; EBEN KILL EBEN; KILL HUMANS; KILL EBEN; KILL; PAIN; KILL; PAIN, PAIN, PAIN; KILL ... the Drone's linear thought process got stuck in a loop for a little while, the blip on the radar being something that offended and infuriated the Drone beyond human understanding, unless the human was a psychopath.

Eventually returning to a state of normal seething hatred, the Drone checked the relatively simplistic, yet futuristic instrumentation in the small vessel for any other infuriating things, and found all in order. Unlimited fuel status, full charge on weapons, camouflage skin activated.

The small vessel was almost perfectly spherical in shape, about 3 metres in diameter. The 1.3 metre tall, slender grey body of the Eridani drone did not need much room even with the surface suit and helmet. Comfort was not a consideration given to drones by the Masters.

The vessel had a camouflage system that changed the hull's colour to match the colour of the background from the perspective of the viewer. This system worked great for anyone looking straight at the vessel, yet not looking *for* the vessel; but not quite as effective for those with an oblique view. Regardless of viewer orientation, the camouflage was still *mostly* effective. If you weren't specifically looking for the vessel, it was highly unlikely you would notice it. The camouflage did nothing for Earth style radars. Since the human didn't have radar signals present at the Habitat site, the Drone was not worried about being detected. The small craft still cast a shadow though, and the camouflage system didn't work at all when the vessel was moving at high speed.

Chapter 16

Getting some sleep

I finished reviewing *all* the messages from Mission Control. Next I fixed the stuck relay in the atmosphere controller on the lower level of the W-Hab. At least that had been an inside fix and I didn't need to suit up again. Tomorrow's work manifest had been sent, but it was a planned low effort day so there wasn't much on it. I was still getting used to gravity, albeit low gravity, after the eight and a half months of zero-g in transit to Mars. I looked at the active breezeway controller for the Breezeway that would be joined to the L-Hab. However, that was an hour long process, and I was getting more nauseated with tiredness. Truthfully, I could barely stand at this point, and seriously gave consideration to just laying down on the floor and passing out. Instead, I pulled the plastic wrap off the conference table that was forward of the medial axis of the W-Hab upper level. I opened another duffel bag and took out a vacuum pack with three fleecy blankets in it. I couldn't get the zipper open, so I dug deeper into the duffel bag and pulled out my K-Bar.

Many people have asked why I brought a K-Bar with me. It was an authentic U.S. Marine Corps fighting knife. It was also a renowned survival knife. I had absolutely no realistic use for it on Mars. However, I'm a boy and sometimes a boy just has to have a knife. I planned to use it as a utility knife, and also as something that was totally mine, and that I could put under my pillow at night … just in case.

I didn't have to tell Mission Control I was going to sleep on the conference table. The internal Habitat cameras were operating and sending a continuous stream of video and audio signal back to Mission Control. This was part and parcel of the mission, providing live-ish video feed so that paying customers could watch everything happening on Mars. There were internal cameras on both levels of both habitats. There were none, however, inside the sleeping quarters. All the colonist candidates had been of one voice on that matter. There was a camera on all four quadrants of the outside of both habitats, one pointed directly down over the airlock. There were two on top of each habitat. The two on top of each Habitat structure operated differently. The panning camera (Camera #W1 and #L1) constantly swung back and forth through a 340 degree arc, the missing 20 degrees being directly over the active breezeway. The other was a controllable motion sensor camera (Camera #W2 and #L2) that could be operated manually from the COM area of the W-Hab. The second camera responded by default, when not being manually controlled, to a primitive motion detector. Both of the motion sensor cameras (#W2 and #L2) could also be set to follow an Activity Suit's IFF signal. The

Activity Suit systems had IFF built into their COM unit. This was merely to identify who was in the suit, and act as a locator beacon if they were lost. Unfortunately (or fortunately as the case may be), the IFF only operated line of sight. If no IFF signals were identified, then cameras #W2 and #L2 defaulted back to its 1.0 motion sensor tracking system. We did get a lot of dust devil footage off those two cameras. There is also a redundant COM system in the kitchen area of the L-Hab allowing full system operation from either Habitat, including all of the cameras.

Since the small release valve on the vacuum pack wouldn't open, I stuck a small hole in the package with my K-Bar. The vacuum pack, with the blankets, tripled in size as it sucked in the air around it. I was then able to open the zipper without a problem. I put two of the blankets on the table, folded in half and one on top of the other. I grabbed two sweatshirts (I had brought three) and rolled them up into a ball. I paused a moment as I smelled a bit gamey. I really tried to form a coherent thought about the way I smelled and that fact that I should wash up. However, I was now tired beyond the point where I could have reasonable lucid thoughts. I shrugged my shoulders and said, "Frak it". I sat on the edge of the conference table, rolled over onto the folded blankets and pulled the third blanket over top of me. Giving a prayer of thanks to God for the safety and strength he had given me this day, I quickly fell asleep. The K-Bar, back in its sheath, was still in my hand.

Chapter 17

Mission Control

Earlier

Ernst sat back in his chair and scratched his head. He was a quiet and mousy little man that had worked for Interpol for years as a tech investigator. Short, a bit dumpy, with graying hair and glasses, he had an incredibly sharp eye and mind for details. He also had an eidetic memory, making him both a value and a curse as an intelligence agent. When the Mars mission was in its planning stage, he accepted a job offer from the ESA for a very special assignment. Being old enough to retire from Interpol, but young enough for a new career, he took the retirement package offered by Interpol and then increased his income significantly with his new posting. No one at the Corporation really knew what Ernst did, except for a small handful of people. Everyone initially thought he was just the ESA representative. Only four people in the program knew that he really worked for the Bundesnachrichtendienst, the German foreign intelligence directorate. Even the ESA didn't know about that. The Germans had been very good to the Mars colony program, so Jayden just accepted the presence of him and his team of spooks. There were three, working in shifts.

Ostensibly though, he *was* the ESA representative, who did work for the ESA (hey, three pay cheques, take it if you can get it), independently monitoring the mission for efficacy. His presence in Mission Control was simple and easy to explain. His workstation, in the forward corner of the room was angled so that no one could look over his shoulder and see what was on his screens. The screens also had angle blocking filters hanging over them. You had to be viewing the screens almost perfectly perpendicular to see anything on them. A few commented that he seemed to have a lot of monitors and equipment for someone simply there as a token presence. Anyone who pushed the questioning though would find themselves in the Mission Director's office getting dressed down about making inquiries on things that didn't concern them.

In reality, most had figured out that Ernst was a spook. They just weren't sure exactly what his tools of spooking were with the Mars colonization, or who exactly he was a spook for. They simply surmised he was an intelligence gatherer, and since he was there in the room, it had to be okay with the brass upstairs. If it was okay with them, it was okay for everyone.

Ernst had total task control over Jalopy-Sat. That infuriated the U.S. Air Force who had basically paid for over half of the damn thing - but they didn't push too hard. They had someone who could assume total control and lock out everyone else if the particular need arose; the particular need that caused them to do everything they did to get it in orbit around Mars. As far as Hans was aware, Mike was the only other person with control over Jalopy-Sat.

Ernst could retask the satellite, as well as access its telemetry, sensors, imaging capabilities, and its other more specialized capabilities. Other capabilities that made him a very useful friend as far as those on the surface of Mars should be concerned. The only thing he could not do, the only thing that really cheesed him off, was he could not override commands to Jalopy-Sat that came from Mars' surface. Those commands had been given priority. He and the ESA had argued against it, but they lost the argument. However, Ernst didn't think that would ever be something to worry about (he was wrong), at least for several more years until there was a larger colony presence (he was wrong again).

At this moment, he was scratching his head because of the tracker camera being activated. The Jalopy-Sat Mars facing tracker camera would automatically activate when something was moving more than 500 metres from the colony site. It had the algorithms and data feeds from the other camera, so it was very good at distinguishing between windblown ground matter and something moving under power. The tracker camera was focused on a 5 kilometre square area over the ice field, just a few kilometres from the Habitat site. Ernst had been zooming in and zooming out, panning, scrolling and doing whatever he could to the available raw image feed, to find what held the tracking software's interest. Whenever he followed the tracker zoom itself (the built in process that zoomed right in on what was being tracked), all he saw was frozen ice. Like Carrie and Arno, he could only manipulate the image/video, as he was looking at it, over eighteen minutes old. Even Ernst couldn't manipulate the cameras live. Any retasking of the cameras would take over thirty-six minutes to show him the results.

He looked up and across the room. Carrie was at her station, and he thought about piping the feed over to her computer. She had much better resolution on her monitors, and her software may be able to figure out what it was that the tracker camera was targeting. Perhaps he just needed to have her come look at his monitor rather than share the feed, share the power. Having her do this though, would be letting her in on a secret that very few shared so far.

Ernst knew just about everything about everyone who worked in this room, regardless of their shift cycle. He knew that Carrie was divorced: that she spoke Romansh, German, English and French; she had two young sons; she lived comfortably but not ostentatiously; she had won prizes for her Streudel at the local fair; she had one parent living in the same town as her; she had one brother who lived in England. He also knew that she and Mike had a "fling" a year before he departed, and that they were still close as friends.

Hans and Jayden both seemed to hold her in high regard, so Ernst finally made up his mind. He picked up the phone, dialed her desk phone and waving his hand at her as she answered he asked her, "Können Sie hier bitte kommen, Frauline Oolsen?"

Chapter 18

Bolt Upright

I sat bolt upright in the makeshift bed on the conference table. It sounded like someone was knocking on the Habitat wall, *outside*. As my eyes focused to the room, which was still light in the Martian summer's midnight sun of this latitude, I started to relax. It must have been part of a dream. I smiled sheepishly and laughed a bit at myself. I was about to lay down when I realized I had to pee. Uh-oh.

Of course there was a bathroom. The bathroom was almost fully functional, having been powered up and tested as part of the preparatory post planet fall procedures. It just needed the water system primed now that I had the umbilical feeds connected. However, the bathroom was in the L-Hab. I was in the W-Hab. I had not connected the breezeway. Connecting the breezeway was an hour long process provided everything lined up, and I didn't have to go outside to manually force things into place. The sense of urgency about making No. 1 increased. It wasn't going to wait an hour. I looked around. Nothing was unpacked, even if it were, there wouldn't be any empty pop bottles. Some relief then came in the form of a stroke of brilliance. I hoped off the table, and quickly went down the spiral staircase and into the airlock. I stepped into my Activity Suit from the Lander; I hadn't unpacked the day-to-day one yet. I then hooked up the urinal catheter and found blessed release as a small smile and quiet, "ahhhhhh" escaped my lips. I was almost done, standing there half dressed in my Activity Suit, making wee-wee when the knocking sound came again. Right behind me, right at the airlock outer door. I almost jumped right out of my skin as I spun my head around, half expecting to see a space suited figure in the portal; half expecting to see something dragged out of the dark corners of my imagination, recalled from childhood nightmares. It was at this moment I decided that I would take my K-Bar everywhere with me. I remembered I had left it lying on the conference table. I was standing there in my long johns and t-shirt. I was too far from the corner to retrieve one of the weapons I had stowed. Yup, I was feeling pretty vulnerable at that moment.

Looking towards the outer airlock hatch, I could see there was nothing on the other side of the portal except the view of the Martian landscape beyond it. I heard the knock once more, loud, right below the airlock hatch, like someone was standing on the ground trying to get my attention. *Yea, though I walk through the valley of the shadow of death, I will fear no evil for thou art with me.* I hurriedly got out of the catheter and Activity Suit, pulled up my long johns and hightailed it back up the spiral staircase. I was going out of my mind trying to figure out what the sound was. It simply could not be someone knocking. I was the only person on Mars. A quick look through the outer hatch portal before fleeing the lower level had not revealed anything, so I was headed for the camera interface at the COM station. At least I didn't feel quite as exposed as I did standing in the airlock. Of course, I realized I was still half asleep, and that my thought processes weren't quite in the realm of *cogitando aperte* at the moment, but still, it was a very queer situation to say the least.

I went to the COM panel and activated the camera control icon. I then selected the exterior airlock camera, the one that is aimed straight down outside the airlock. I couldn't believe what I was looking at. It certainly explained the knocking sound. I walked over to the forward portal of the upper level, and looked out over the ground in front of both Habitats. I leaned against the wall and started laughing. I seemed to be doing a lot of laughing on Mars. As I was laughing at the source of the knocking, I remembered there was a camera in the airlock. I thought about the infamous space turd video. *Oh man, why does everybody have to see me going to the bathroom.* I smiled with chagrin, especially at how I had reacted to the knocking sound.

I looked back at the COM panel video feed of the nacelle skirting that was blowing around. I flipped screens on the COM panel and checked the weather data. The winds were gusting at 70 km/hour. One of the nacelle skirting sections that I had decided to leave until morning had been blown around in the wind. It had landed at the foot of the airlock and got hooked up in the airlock ladder. The knocking sound was the piece of metal banging against the top of the ladder, near the point it connected to the Habitat. Sleep would have to wait. That skirting had to be secured so that it would not blow too far away for me to retrieve, and so that it would not damage something critical. It would be another four hours before I got back to sleep again.

This job wasn't hard; it was just hard because I was so physically fatigued. This whole idea of gravity, I realized, was definitely for the birds. Only three of the panels had blown around in the wind, and they hadn't blown far. I had to drag them into position, and then use my body as a brace to hold them while I used the universal wrench, still no charge on the battery, to replace the bolts. I did have one close call going to pick up the fourth panel, the one on top of the pile that had not blown around. As I was approaching it, a strong gust of wind picked up the far edge and sent it tumbling straight at me. Man oh man, I've never jumped so fast in my life, not even in Terran gravity. John Carter would have been proud. Lesson learned. When picking up deadly hunks of metal in a windstorm on an alien planet, approach them from upwind, not downwind.

After the nacelle skirting panels were all back in place, I returned to the airlock and this time I dug out, unwrapped and plugged in the charger for the universal wrench. I climbed back upstairs, hopped back on the conference table, rolled over, and was almost instantly asleep again.

Chapter 19

Mission Control

18 Minutes, 22 Seconds Later

Everyone had heard the knocking/banging sound and saw Mike's sleeping figure suddenly sit bolt upright. Everything went quiet, techs huddled around telemetry feeds, Arno panned and zoomed cameras. He very quickly found out what was making the banging noise, looked over his shoulder at Hans, gave him thumbs up; then transferred the exterior airlock feed to the big screen. Everyone breathed a sigh of relief. Then they realized that Mike hadn't seen the image. Things got interesting because Mike jumped off the table and ran down the spiral staircase. They all watched intently to see the reaction when he found out it was one of the pieces of skirting. Arno switched to the airlock camera, and everyone watched with amusement, expecting him to run to the portal in the airlock hatch. Instead he put both feet in the Activity Suit as someone muttered, "Look out the window!"

There was a collective gasp as Mike whipped down his long johns and everyone had a view of his bare ass while he starting fiddling with the catheter tube. Everyone was still holding their breath when they heard, "Ahhhhhhhh…." over the speakers. The meteorological tech stood up and announced, "Full moon over Mars!" He sat down quickly to Hans' withering glare.

Honestly, no work got done at all for the next few minutes. The laughter was almost deafening. Two techs actually fell out of their chairs they were laughing so hard. Three cups of coffee got spilled on the floor. Two people had to leave the room to catch their breath. Even the ever serious Ernst, the ESA spook, had tears running down his face. Hans Gohs' face had gone from pink, to red, to what was a pretty scary hue of aubergine. Those around him stopped laughing and tip-toed away. Finally he roared in frustration, threw his headset on the desk in front of him, and clomped out of the room. No one had thought, yet again, to pause the internet feed.

Arno had seen Hans reaction and seen him leave. *Poor Hans*, he thought to himself. *It would be a miracle if Mike didn't make the man stroke out.* Twenty minutes later the whole video from waking up to the spin-around-in-terror-staring-at-the-airlock-portal was re-cut and being distributed with the sound of the "Ma-Na, Ma-Na" song dubbed in. They never did find out who did it.

Chapter 20

Foo-Fighter

The next day wasn't supposed to be filled with activity for me. The plan was for plenty of rest to be able to further acclimate back to a gravity environment. So much for the best laid plans of men, and mice. After waking up and having some water and my last meal replacement bar that I had in my duffel, I connected the Habitats.

The active and passive breezeways had both outer and inner doors but once the breezeway was extended, the outer door could not close again. In the most extreme conditions I could retract the breezeway to close the outer door, but that was an unlikely scenario. The breezeway was airtight but could not function as an exterior airlock. I powered up the active breezeway's standalone system in the W-Hab, and did a handshake with the system in the L-Hab. Everything was in order so I commenced the five step sequence to connect the two Habitats, which I was now starting to think of as buildings, instead of what they technically were, spaceships; or more precisely, fairly complicated cargo containers.

First, open the outer doors. There was a small portal in the breezeway inner airlock door and light immediately streamed through. I had unpacked and initialized a desktop computer and now held up my tablet PC, which I had finally paired with the COM Panel. I had one camera from each Hab aimed at the breezeway points and watched the process. The W-Hab outer hatch settled inward, and then lowered into the wall of the Habitat below the breezeway. I then triggered the same process in the L-Hab's outer door, receiving both telemetry and visual confirmation through the camera. After a quick double check of alignment, I went ahead and crossed my fingers, then extended the breezeway. I heard support screws retracting underneath the breezeway entrance ramp, and then heard the whine of giant servomechanisms extending the breezeway. The four sided and solidly built breezeway tunnel was my only path between the two Habitats that did not require an Activity Suit and an airlock. Watching the cameras on my laptop with occasional glances through the portal, it took ten minutes for the breezeway to extend the 86 centimetres to the other Habitats passive breezeway connection receptacle. Taking my time with the walk had paid off. The breezeway slipped right into the open hatch on the L-Hab perfectly. The servos stopped whirring, and I heard the support screws under the ramp re-engaging. I ran the processes then, to first secure and create an airtight seal on the L-Hab passive breezeway entrance. I then repeated this with the W-Hab active breezeway entrance. All totaled, thirty minutes. Before opening the hatches, I took a few minutes with my tablet PC to run integrity check on both the Breezeway and the L-Hab. I pressurized the Breezeway and then waited another fifteen minutes, per procedure. At the end of the waiting period, there was no variance in the breezeway pressure so I was good to go. I released the locking mechanism on the interior breezeway hatch at my end, and then spun the arm that would allow the hatch to open. It swung inward, as there was very little available room in the breezeway.

The breezeway was mighty darn cold, but it would warm up soon enough. It got its atmosphere and temperature from the ambient environment in both Habitats by leaving the doors at each end ajar. At night time, or if everyone (future crew) left the Habitat, or there was a severe weather condition, then the doors at each end had to be sealed (a good procedure to follow). I walked through the hatch, gingerly stepping and testing my weight on the breezeway. There was no bounce or give to the floor. I hopped up and down a few times in the middle, and everything was solid as a rock; thanks mostly to the low Martian gravity, as well as the exquisite design and construction. Gotta love those German engineers. I approached the inner hatch on the L-Hab end, peered through the portal, and then swung the arm to open the door. It swung open inward as well.

Stepping into the upper level of the L-Hab, I looked around. Toilet and shower, mech room, storage, kitchen, and table and chairs (still needing unwrapping) with auxiliary COM panel over the table. There was a couch and sitting area, a workstation, book cases and storage cabinets, recessed lighting, and carpeting on the floors; all the comforts of an austere hotel room. As both Habs were only twenty-five feet in diameter, slightly less inside, things would certainly be cozy. No worries, it would feel like home soon enough. I went down the spiral staircase to where the sleeping quarters were located.

There were three sleeping units, plus a linen cupboard and a small but very, very efficient washer and dryer in the lower level. The rooms were not large, but they were designed for efficiency and comfort. The main bedroom (and the largest),was at the back of the Hab. It was designed with a double bed. There was plenty of closet space with below bed and overhead storage. There was a dresser; one section of wall was drawers from top to bottom. There was also a small desk. To the designers' credit, they had gone to great lengths to not only make things functional and utilize all the available space; they had also gone to great lengths to make the rooms practical, comfortable, and appealing.

On the front of the L-Hab sleeping level, the second largest bedroom was similar to the larger one, but it had no wall of drawers, and no dresser. There was lots of shelving and hanging baskets in one of the storage cupboards though, so you could get by without drawers. Both the front and back sleeping quarters had portals looking out over the austere but beautiful Martian landscape.

The final bedroom, on the side of the L-Hab directly underneath the passive breezeway, was a smaller bedroom with bunk beds. There was one big closet, a small dresser, a desk, under bed storage and overhead storage. The bed was a bit wider than I had originally expected, so it looked like it would be comfortable. All the beds had thick memory foam mattresses, wrapped in plastic. I unwrapped the mattress in the small bedroom on the lower bunk then unclipped all the doors and drawers. I had decided this would be my room. It had no portal but that was okay. I didn't have to worry about waking-up in the night and seeing someone staring in at me, ha ha ha! Above the desk was a large removable decorative panel. Behind it was this Habitat's emergency egress point. The walls for the small bedroom were a bit thicker than the others; and the door was a proper airlock door. I thought about this choice for a few minutes, but realized that when Colony 1 arrived, they would need the two other bedrooms. That mission of four people was two women, two men; two couples. I might as well get used to batching it in the pseudoairlock from day two.

I spent the next 15 minutes grabbing my duffels and two foot lockers from upstairs; and unpacking my clothes and some personal items. I had brought three fleecy blankets, three crochet afghans, and three thick down pillows with me: all in vacuum bags. I had to fight hard to bring those with me. I was told the provided sleeping bag and environmental controls would be enough. My counterargument was these things made me feel comfortable and at home, and I needed them for the days when I was having a hard time handling that fact that I was *all alone on Mars*. I probably played that card more times than I should have, but in the end Jayden relented and basically said I could bring anything I wanted, so long as it fit in the available space and didn't put us over the weight limit. Now I just had to find which of the transport mission units had my guitar in it! The last item I took out of the third duffel bag was a cardboard box. I opened it and slid out the faux leather bound Holy Bible that had belonged to my mother. Well-worn and a bit frayed on the edges, I held it for a few moments, thinking about the woman that had so long ago, gone home to Glory. I smiled and wiped a tear from my eye as I imagined her face in laughter at some stupid joke I told. She always laughed at my jokes, no matter how bad they were. She always loved me, without reservation, no matter what I had done or what decisions I had made. I could only imagine how she would have reacted to Mars, but I know in the end she would have supported me. I smiled and said, "I brought you with me Mom. Welcome to Mars." I opened the bible, and in between the pages was her picture. I smiled at her smiling at me. I flipped forward a few pages and found the picture of my son and his wife on their recent wedding day. I flipped forward a few more pages and found the picture of Loreena, taken the day I proposed to her. I put the snapshots back in between the pages. I put the Bible under my pillow. Its words would bring me a lot of comfort in the coming years.

I spent the rest of the morning on that first full day unpacking and setting up the other computers and getting them hooked up to the servers; which I also had to unpack and setup, in the W-Hab. Luckily computers and software were one of my strengths so it was pretty mindless work. To make it go easier I launched the music app on my tablet and worked along to the tunes of Canned Heat, and then zoned out to some Yngwie Malmsteen. Listening to him shred arpeggios was blissfully relaxing when you listened to it loud enough. At some point I even played the very first, ever, Martian Air Guitar. Thank you. Thank-you-very-much.

Once the computers were set up, networked and working as intended, I moved on to unpacking the kitchen and living space. The L-Hab had three months' worth of food supplies so getting food out of the supply drops was not a priority at present. I finally found the small Bullet Blender, and was able to mix up a chocolate protein/meal replacement shake for lunch. I put in some water, peanut butter and a bit of cinnamon and stood at the living room portal, sipping it slowly. It was a bit of a surreal moment. I was on an alien planet, by myself, and sipping food that was familiar and comfortable to me.

While getting a hydroponic facility up and running was on the to-do list, it was going to be a slow process just here by myself, and I was going to have to wait until the beginning of the next Martian summer to do it. It was too close to winter for that work to begin. That meant I had to bring all my food with me. In fact, I had brought four years' worth of food, spread out amongst all the supply drops. I was going to get another two years' worth of food every two years until Colony 1 arrived. This was one of my deals with Jayden. This food was all, of course, protein shake powder and meal replacement bars. It packed into a smaller space than prepackaged food and the weight, per meal, was comparable. I had used this stuff for years back on Earth to maintain a good weight and health. I was perfectly happy for it to be my diet. Another one of my battles though was peanut butter. The stuff is so damned heavy. However, we got the Kraft company to foil package individual 1.5 tablespoon servings, so we cut down on the weight of the packaging. I had enough of these food supplies for four shakes and four meal replacement bars per day. That would be too much in the winter when I would be fairly sedentary, but in the summer, when I would be outside and busy; it gave me a bit extra for the days where I really worked up an appetite. As I emptied these packages from a transport container into one of the kitchen area cupboards, I found a small cardboard box in the bottom of the container. I opened it up and there were six triple-packs of Twinkies and a note. All it said was, "Love, Carrie". Bless her. I stashed them in my room downstairs.

I was feeling so peaceful, happy, and in the moment, that I made a second meal-shake and went to the kitchen portal to look at the distant ice fields. I looked out over the topography between the colony site and the ice wall in the distance. Calmness and pure, simple happiness settled over me. This was it. I was here. I was on Mars. We had done it! I looked at the play of the dust in the wind and the diamond like sunlight glinting off of the reds and grays on the ridge of the ice wall. I was doing something special. I was doing something that was going to benefit humanity. I was making a sacrifice to begin a long journey that the human race would embark on. It wasn't pride I was feeling at the moment, it was gratitude. I was grateful that I was making a difference, and that I could make a difference. I was grateful I had been chosen. When I first applied for this adventure, I had the thought in the back of my mind that I might be running away from something. Standing here today and looking out over Mars' surface, I realized that perhaps, instead of running away, I really was moving towards something: towards a new life, and towards a new chance to find simple happiness.

I focused my attention back on the beautiful sand coloured striations on the ice wall in the distance. The ice wall was both gray and red at the same time. The colours coming from dust from the Chasma plains permanently embedded on the ice wall face. I looked up at the sky that wasn't blue. During the day time, the sky was a scarlet or bright orange-ish colour (from the iron oxide in airborne dust particles); and in the evening, even though it was still the time of year for a midnight sun at this latitude, the sky became blue-ish. The Martian sky colouring ran almost opposite to when you would see those colours on Terra. Regardless of the colour, the atmosphere was always crystal clear and would remain so until the winter humidity started forming, or there was a sandstorm. While the Martian atmosphere has ozone layered into it, there is no protective ozone layer like we have on Earth. No proper ozone layer, no blue skies.

I was still amazed at how bright the sun was here on Mars. Being so much farther from the Sun than Terra was, I wasn't really sure what I had expected, but it was nice. It was like a bright but cloudy day on Terra. During the North Polar summer, there were no clouds. In the winter time, this place would be a cloud factory. Hence, the need to get a wind farm up and running was one of the more pressing items of construction. Beginning that installation was on this week's work manifest; but not on today's.

I smiled to myself again. I was on Mars. My dream and hard work of the last few years had paid off. I used to be a very large man. Life curves, a couple back injuries, and some depression had taken its toll. When the Corporation first announced its plans, I weighed over 300 pounds, had high blood pressure, and was diabetic. I lived a sedentary life and was a bit of a hermit. The whole idea of being selected to go to Mars and of having a purpose really changed my life overnight. I started hitting the gym six days a week, and with careful guidance and assistance from the doctors, I lost 120 pounds in eleven months. I got my blood pressure back to normal without medication, and the Type II diabetes went away with the weight loss. I did miss out on the first round of selections by the Corporation, but I made it through when they opened the second application process. A few short years later I was sitting and listening to Jayden's pitch for the proof of concept mission. Now here I was, on Mars, sipping my lunch, and looking out over the …

What the frak? *Something just moved on the ground.*

I squinted my eyes and looked just off axis and to the right. There was a shadow on the ground and it was moving slowly towards me. I pressed my face closer to the portal glass and peered upwards. I didn't see anything at all in the sky. I was expecting a floating piece of cloth or something from yesterday's Lander explosion. Was that only yesterday? So much had gone on, it seemed longer.

I watched the shadow as it slowed down and then stopped. Freaky man, really freaky. What was causing it? I had found the small binoculars while unpacking, so I went over to the first workstation's top drawer and took them out. Back at the kitchen portal I opened the mini-binoculars and found the shadow, refocused and then slowly panned up and down around it. After a few moments, I finally found something. It was chunk of air that was distorted. It looked like a mirage. You know when you are driving on a hot summer day, and on a rise in the road ahead, the heat makes the air shimmer? That was what it was like. Looking directly at that spot, it was like heat was shimmering the air. I looked over at the environment controls and it was -23 degrees Celsius. It wasn't heat shimmer at that temperature, but maybe something was causing a severely localized temperature inversion which would mimic a heat shimmer. Could the solar collectors focus enough heat on one spot to cause this? I set the binoculars down and looked through the portal again as I tried to make sense of this. It must be some really weird weather phenomena. I'd have to see if the cameras picked it up. I'm sure the planetologists and climatologist back on Terra would be interested in this.

On a lark, I grabbed my tablet and hit the key sequence to bring up the Jalopy-Sat controls. Much to my surprise, the Targeting Camera was active and focused down to a 50 metre resolution on the shadow, on the ground. It seems that this shadow had also piqued the interest of the onboard targeting system. While it would usually ignore anything within 500 metres of the Habitats, it would relentlessly track anything moving into the 500 metre exclusion zone if it originated outside that zone. This was just getting weirder and weirder. I could accept a momentary weather phenomena creating some ice-world version of heat shimmer; but how was something, ostensibly translucent, casting a shadow? Furthermore, how did it have enough substance to activate the advanced weapons tracking system of the Jalopy-Sat? Perhaps this shadow simply had enough definition to be targeted?

I looked up and out through the portal again. I watched the heat shimmer as it disappeared and a round grey ball about the size of a large cargo van shot straight up in the sky. I pressed my face on the portal glass and tried to follow it. I didn't even bother trying to suppress the rather loud, "FRAK ME" that came out of my mouth. Those Frakers at the U.S. Air Force weren't full of shit after all. I stood back from the window, fighting the nausea and the greying periphery of my vision, I looked around for a chair and then thought, as the greying field of vision grew smaller, "Frak it". I fainted where I was standing.

Chapter 21

Jayden's Office: 134 Days Before Launch

I had been called to Jayden's office at 4 A.M. I guess the term "called" is a bit misleading. I was sound asleep in my apartment, buck naked on the bed, and probably drooling on the pillow to the sound of my heavy breathing. I was rudely woken by a rough hand shaking my shoulders, and was blinded by the glaring ceiling light just switched on. My right arm came up swinging with a clenched fist on the end of it. The smile on Karl's face changed to one of surprise as I punched him squarely on the jaw, making him stagger backward a bit - more from surprise than power. Karl and his brother Johann stood by the bed making placating gestures and telling me in their thick German accents that *"alles in Ordnung ist"*, that everything is okay, that I had to *"beruhige dich bitte"*, to please calm down. I was standing on the other side of the bed in a fighting stance by the time I realized who was standing in my bedroom in the middle of the night; and that yes, indeed, everything was *in Ordnung*. Their security uniforms were jet black, but their faces were friendly and neither one had drawn their weapons.

I looked at Karl rubbing his jaw and instantly felt bad. I really liked the guy. I just really, really didn't like anyone touching me when I was asleep. Even my ex-wife knew to get out of the bed and step back before waking me up. I considered it an autonomic response, based on conditioning from a childhood event.

After my heart stopped trip-hammering in my chest, I had a quick wash-up, and threw on some clothes from the day before. They said I was needed in Jayden's office most *Riki-Tik* (Johann's favourite expression from American TV), and I didn't have time for a shower and *jah, ve vere,* in a hurry.

Now semiawake, and holding a coffee that Johann had picked up for me on the way to my apartment, the brothers sped me to the Corporation's headquarters. The lack of traffic at that time of the morning made the trip very quick. Karl and Johann were good guys, and I felt even worse about punching Karl. I kept apologizing - and he kept saying it was okay. They were two members of the security team that had been assigned to me two weeks ago, after the meeting in Jayden's office. They were also twin brothers. Standing almost 2 metres tall, and each one weighing in around 240 lbs of solid body builder, I always felt very safe with them. The SIG Sauer that each carried on their hip helped as well. There had been a few threats from nut-jobs ever since the project started. I was glad they were so forgiving about the sucker-punch; or else I would have been in a world of hurt. I was no stranger to the gym, but

113

these guys were the true embodiment of the term, "built like a brick shithouse". I had heard others refer to them collectively as *The Berlin Wall*.

They drove onto the apron at the front of the building, the building still mostly in darkness. It was still too early for sunrise. When I got out of the car, I did that same thing I did every morning after waking up. I would walk outside in my housecoat and take a deep, lung filling breath of crisp, clean Swedish air. For some reason, the air was just different here. I could never define it. Maybe it was the local vegetation aromas, or something to do with the temperature, or the latitude. I just know that taking that first deep breath of Swedish air in the morning was like a lightning bolt of feeling *awesome*.

Johann swiped his card in the door and they hustled me inside, and straight to the elevators. They hadn't said much on the way except that I was needed, immediately. Aside from my apologies, we drove in silence. I was sipping my coffee, Karl was rubbing his jaw from time to time, and Johann was trying not to snicker at Karl every time he rubbed his jaw.

The elevator stopped on the third floor and we walked down the long hallway to Jayden's office. Karl and Johann stopped in unison on each side of the office door, executed a crisply perfect about face, and then both stood at ease; hands folded behind their back, looking straight ahead. I looked closely at them to see if they were having me on. "Please enter ze office Herr Lane, you are anticipated," said Karl very formally.

Suddenly, my stomach started feeling a bit queasy. I got rid of the final sleepy cobwebs, downed the last of the coffee in my styrofoam cup, and started being very curious. I opened the door and walked in without knocking.

Jayden and Hans both stood up, as did their guest. "Good Morning Mike, I'm glad you could join us so early." I looked at Jayden who wasn't smiling, neither was Hans. Their guest, a woman in her 60's wearing the blue uniform and decorations of a Lieutenant General in the U.S. Air Force was standing on the other side of the table. Oddly, she had no Aide-de-Camp or other hangers-on with her that one would expect a Staff Officer to have.

I walked over to the table, set down my empty coffee cup, and shrugged off my jacket. Jayden made the introductions. "Mike Lane, this is Lieutenant General Gilda Rosewood of the United States Air Force. General Rosewood, this is the man we are sending to Mars, Mike Lane."

She leaned over the table slightly and shook my hand. Her hand was warm, but very firm. I had no doubt in my mind this athletic, attractive, and pleasantly smiling, brown eyed woman in her 60's, with beautiful platinum blond hair done up tightly, was an absolute bitch-on-wheels when she wanted to be. The fact that she was still in uniform in her 60's made her someone who was obviously very special, and very important.

We sat down and with no platitudes or small talk she said, "Mr. Lane, I'm here to give you an Article Five briefing."

"Article five?" I interrupted.

"Yes, Article 5 of the Outer Space Treaty. I understand you are going to Mars in eighteen weeks. I'm here to advise you that if you go to Mars, you will be committing suicide." She leaned forward and stared me straight in the eyes, "Now let me tell you why."

A shiver ran up my spine at that. I looked at Jayden and held up my drained styrofoam cup, "Boss, you got any hot-hot? I think I'm going to need it." Jayden nodded. I looked at the General and asked, "Would you like some ma'am?" She nodded her head. Jayden stood and reached for her coffee cup. She smiled disarmingly, put her fingers on the rim of the cup she had been drinking from, and pushed it slowly across the table towards me. When I say she smiled, I mean that her lips curved up into what is physiologically defined as a smile, but there was no real smile behind her lips curving up. "One cream, no sugar. I'm sweet enough". Hans almost choked on the last sip of his china coffee cup as she very surgically let everyone at the table know exactly who was in charge of this early morning tête-à-tête.

I smiled and walked over to the Keurig with Jayden, holding her cup in my hand. We didn't say anything as the individual Timmies K-Cups brewed for all of us. Jayden had brought out the good china for this early morning meeting. I could hear the General and Hans quietly talking about his favourite restaurants in the area, to fill the silence if nothing else. I added just the right amount of cream to my cup and the Generals cup, and walked back over to the table. Handing her coffee to her with a smile and a nod; a nod that acknowledged this meetings pecking order, I sat down across from her.

I tried to come up with something pithy to say, but I decided this really wasn't the time. I knew deep down inside that I was going to have to make an ally of this tough old bitch, and that I was going to have to do it fast. She was the type that would most likely appreciate an intelligent person who knew how to respect and follow a chain of command.

I began the meeting-proper, "Thank you for your patience ma'am. I appreciate your travelling half way around the world to meet with us this morning, and I recognize the importance and urgency that such a meeting must bring with it. Shall we proceed?" Playing the dutiful and respectful peon had its advantages some time. We would see if this had been the right call on my part.

She looked at me for a moment, sizing me up. She looked at Hans and Jayden. They had probably already had more than one mental dissection under her gaze already. By the look of the two of them, plus legal pads and folders on the table, it appeared they had already been there for hours.

"I'm the second-in-command of the 88th Air Support Wing at Wright-Patterson Air Force Base. We are part of the United States Air Force Materials Command. Our *cover* is responsibility for the procurement and disbursement of all aircraft related materials for the United States Air Force. Our true purpose is the housing, investigation, and replication of alien flight technology. We build it and then we test it at Area 52 in Nevada."

"Area 52? Not area 51?" I grinned.

She didn't grin, "Area 52."

After a brief pause to let that sink in, after scanning our faces again, she continued, "This planet has been visited by aliens for thousands of years. The bulk of this visitation activity has been since the beginning of the 20th century. Some of the visitors are our friends. Some are not. There is one race in particular that we are in a state of détente with. That particular race, the Eridani, have made it clear that they will not appreciate any human presence on Mars, just as they will not appreciate any human presence on the Moon. If you go to Mars, they will probably kill you."

The look on Jayden and Hans face was predictable. I wanted to tell them to pick their chins up off the floor, but didn't. I picked up my coffee cup, took a sip, and then looked squarely at the General again, "Please continue ma'am."

"Isn't that enough?" she replied.

For many years, I had been a YouTube conspiracy video junkie. I loved watching all that fakery. People went to so much trouble to make fantasy look real. There was the popular Rendleshem Forest incident, Skinny-Bob, underground bases, a supposed alien war at Dulce, New Mexico; and these were only the tip of a massive iceberg of internet litter. It had always been entertaining, but nothing more. Until now. What she was telling me was that some of those videos might have had some truth sprinkled into them. I was a bit shocked at that but wasn't overwhelmed, especially after my own alien abduction as a six year old child. I smiled briefly, and leaned forward putting my forearms on the table. "No ma'am, it most certainly is not enough ma'am. You've called me in here out of a dead sleep to tell me all my plans and dreams are bust because some aliens exist, of which we do not yet have any proof. You then expect me to toss my hands up in the air and say, *Oh, my. That's that then. I guess we're not going.*" I paused a moment. I knew speaking to her like this was risky. I leaned a bit more forward, "This is compounded with the fact that we know that NASA has moved beyond just the planning stages of a manned mission to Mars, and so have the Russians, the Chinese; and if rumour is correct, then the French have aspirations of

116

going to space as well, Mars in particular. Having a private corporation put a man on Mars first, with no political or military affiliation, will be a sty-in-the-eye for everyone planning on going there. It would be to the benefit of everyone, including the United States Air Force, if I did not go. So forgive me ma'am if I humbly suggest that no, that certainly is not enough. You're going to have to do better than that. I wasn't chosen for this proof of concept mission because I was a low down, yellow bellied, weak willed, knock kneed, lily-livered, scaredy-cat, panty waist," then after a brief pause I finished with a punctuating "Ma'am", and then sat up ram-rod straight in my chair.

She continued to size me up with her eyes and I could see she was making decisions in her head. I thought Jayden was going to have a coronary, and Hans looked like he wished he had chosen another line of work. Finally, she pursed her lips and nodded once. "What I'm about to tell you is above top secret. I'm going to share some things with you that even our President doesn't know. This information is so protected, that what I reveal to you cannot be revealed to anyone outside of this room. If you speak, whisper, pillow talk, or even hint of this information, you will disappear and your body will not be found; and yes, I have both the ability and the authority to make that happen." I could tell she wasn't being melodramatic. She was simply stating a fact.

The General turned to the other two and said, "Mr. Lane has to hear what I have to say. You two do not. However, given your pivotal positions in this endeavour I will permit you to be part of this briefing. The choice of whether you remain for this briefing is up to you. However, if you do choose to stay, you stay for the whole thing. Of course," that smile that wasn't a smile appeared on her face again, "you will be subject to the same caveat and addendum that Mr. Lane is subject to."

Jayden and Hans looked at each other, and then they looked at me. I shrugged and made a 'what the hell are you thinking, of course you're going to stay' face. I said, "Guys, come on, stay." They both nodded and indicated to Lieutenant General Rosewood they would stay for the briefing. She reached down beside her and lifted her black briefcase to the table. There was a keypad on it, and she entered a nine digit sequence of numbers. The briefcase unlocked, she lifted the top and I saw inside the rim what looked like not-so-small explosive charges of C4. I was glad she entered the right sequence of numbers. The Lieutenant General took out a beige folder with red bold writing 'EYES ONLY - ULTRA' and 'AQUARIUS' printed on it. She also took a small black box 2.5 centimetres thick and 7.5 by 5 centimetres. It had a green light, white light, and red light on it. The red light was on. She touched two fingers against unmarked spots on the box, and the white light came on. She sat it on the table and said, "Something from our friends to make the meeting more secure".

Folding her hands in front of her, she began the most interesting diatribe I've ever heard with a question. "Have you heard of a UFO crashing at Roswell in 1947?"

"Ma'am," I nodded my head.

"There were two ships that crashed that night, during an electrical storm. They were flying in close formation when ionization between the crafts hulls and a very large nearby lightning bolt caused their flight control systems to operate erratically, and then fail completely. One crashed north-west of Roswell, closer to Corona, in New Mexico. The other one made it further away, and crashed in the mountains near Datil, New Mexico. This was in 1947. That night, nine aliens died in those crashes. The tenth one, a mechanic of all things, survived." She opened the folder, took out a black and white 8x10, and placed it on the table in front of us.

The three of us leaned forward and looked at a bald, smooth headed creature that had a lot of human characteristics to its face. *Damn it,* I thought silently, *Skinny-Bob IS real!* Its eyes were a lot bigger, and more almond-shaped than oval. The bald head looked a bit bigger than you would expect, but the cranium looked very similar to a human cranium. The creature had a long neck that attached the head to a short body. The head was slightly disproportionate to its body, but then again, it probably thought we had really *small* heads given how big humans are in comparison. The creature's legs were short like the body, but it had very long arms, and four long fingers with, like humans, opposable thumbs. The creature was standing by two human men in American military uniform. It was shaking one of the men's hands. The alien was only a little over four feet tall. It wore human clothes; they appeared to be a two piece warm-up suit, circa 1940, a couple sizes too large.

"His official designation was EBE-1 but we just called him Bob. He lived for another five years, passing away from, as far as the doctors of the day could tell, natural causes. This alien was an Eben. The Eben are a 10,000 year old civilization that come from a planet called *Sapro* that is close to 40 Light Years from Earth in the Zeta Reticuli system, in the Cygnus arm of the Milky Way." Given the brief but interesting astronomical training all the candidates had received, that actually meant something to me. "Through that lone survivor, we developed a relationship with the Eben, and eventually an exchange program: exchanging technology and personnel. They have helped us understand our place in the Milky Way, and what other friends and foes are out there." She pulled another 8x10 black and white picture from the folder and put it in front of us. I snapped back from this one a little too fast. This one I knew.

"There is a star system," she continued, "not that far from Earth, only ten light years away, called Epsilon Eridani. There is a race of aliens from that star system; we simply call them the Eridani. This image is one of their intelligentsia cast that you would know from popular culture. This one in particular is from a race called the Vesna." She pronounced it, *vesh-nah*. She let the image sink in.

The queasy feeling in my stomach was coming back. "I don't have a picture of an Eridani Master, the Voiya they are called, but they are the masterminds responsible for human abductions and the cow mutilations you read about in the tabloids. We stop the more serious events from making it to print, but its good disinformation to let the occasional ET story appear next to Bat-Boy or the latest Elvis sighting." Again, the smile that was not a smile.

Hans touched my arm, "Are you okay?" he inquired? I had gone pale white.

I wiped my mouth with a shaking hand, and sighed deeply. I nodded my head. You have to understand, I'm a very composed and unflappable person. I take stress, misadventure, and crisis in stride. When disaster strikes and some people run around doing Chicken Little impressions, I'm the one standing there stroking my chin and saying, *Hmmmm, isn't that interesting*. It had often been noted in the program training how unflappable I was. In fact, I'm the only person to ever fall asleep during the three day sleep deprivation test. I tell you this, so you will understand the full impact of this picture lying before me. Hans told me later my complexion had gone ashen, sweat formed in beads on my forehead, and my hands were both shaking. I looked up, and the General was looking at me dead pan. "We know," she said. "January 9th, 1973." I had never known for sure if it was a real memory or a nightmare. What she just said was a confirmation; it was like a kick in the balls. How could she know? I was five years old during that terrifying night, the night that was locked away in my subconscious until it all came flooding back to me when I was in my thirties. If she had known, could she have stopped it? Could they, the U.S. Air Force, have stopped it? Did they let it happen to me? The nauseating fear started to be replaced by a quite different feeling.

She pulled that second picture back, and put it back in the folder. She resumed speaking while I got up to refill my coffee cup with my still shaking hands.

"We had formed a tepid relationship with the Eridani, but it was against the advice of the Eben. The Eben and the Eridani are bitter enemies which is odd, because the Eben genetic experiments are responsible for the existence of the Eridani to begin with."

"Genetic experiments?" Hans said out loud. He was shaking his head. "Cloning?"

119

The General looked at him for a moment without acknowledgement and then continued, "The Eridani and our human liaison team saw a great number of things quite differently, and while we tried to work together for a while, our visits to the Moon did not make them happy. They didn't want to share that base of operations."

Hans and Jayden both did a double take and in unison said interrogatively, "Share?"

Nodding, she continued, "Eventually, we started to lose patience with the Eridani and the Lectra, another race we've had dealings with. In 1978 a brief but defining war broke out in one of several underground bases at Dulce, New Mexico. Forty-four of our scientists were killed, along with a handful of the Special Forces there to police the facility. When I say killed, I mean most were shot with pulse-energy weaponry, but a few of them were physically torn to pieces." She pulled two more black and white 8x10s out of the folder, and put them on the table. Back in my chair I leaned forward to look with the others. One picture showed a hallway covered in what could only be blood and viscera. Blood stained white lab coats, and some military clothing were jumbled in with the bits and bobs that had once been living humans. From the looks on what was left of the faces of the two corpses that were merely dismembered, they died slowly.

The General continued, "Eridani weapons cause a human body to internally come to a boiling point, instantly, and then explode. The others, well, the Lectra like to use their claws." I think only John Carpenter or Quentin Tarentino could have come up with the gruesomeness depicted in that image. The second picture showed two Special Forces members holding up what was obviously a dead "grey" alien, one of these Eridani, specifically the Vesna, which are more employees of the Eridani, than Eridani proper. Part of its skull was missing from a bullet blast, and it had two large calibre bullet holes in its body."

"Only two of the roughly twenty Eridani contingent were killed. The dozen Lectra escaped unharmed. Since then, we have broken off all formal relations with the Eridani, though we do keep some back-channel lines of communication open. They are untrustworthy, violent, and don't really have any positive qualities. They see humans as chattel; and have no regard for our wants or needs. They tolerate us, and not very well at that. The Lectra, well, they're another story, and I'm not going to tell you anything about them other than they have no interest in Mars." She had no pictures of the Lectra, but the dismembered bodies in the photos on the table said enough.

"After this battle at the Dulce underground base, the Eridani have steadfastly warned us not to return to the Moon. The fact that the Corporation plans to send a colony team to Mars is known to them", Jayden was pale white by this point. "They have told us that you will be most extremely unwelcome. Oddly enough, they didn't come right out and say they would kill you, like they have in the past about us returning to the Moon; however, we all think that is what they mean. It has been our experience that the Eridani are very precise in what they mean through being very precise in what they say. Sometimes things just get lost in translation."

Thankfully, she put the pictures back in the folder. They were like a train wreck, you didn't want to see them, but you couldn't look away.

"The Eben pulled back from formal relations with us in 1985. They are a peaceful, compassionate, and caring race. They are the friendliest beings you would ever meet, even friendlier than Canadians", she looked right at me. "The Eben said that there was too much Eridani activity on Earth for their comfort level. Despite their pacifist mentality, they urged us to kill and destroy the Eridani at every opportunity; or else the Eridani would do it to us."

"So Mr. Lane, if you go to Mars, it is likely you will be killed before you land, or when you land. Hell, they might even preemptively just blow your ship to bits on the way there. If you go to Mars, we are confident that there is a high probability that it's going to be a suicide mission."

She looked like she wanted to say more, but she was playing her cards close to her chest. Jayden let out a long-held sigh, and Hans was rubbing his jaw and thinking. They both looked at me. The confirmation of the existence of the "greys", the Vesna, had thrown me for a loop; yet I had recovered rapidly. As far as the rest of it was concerned, I wasn't fazed by any of it. I walk with God, and I don't fear death because I know of the eternal reward that awaits me. That doesn't mean I go looking for ways to claim it early. The risks I take are calculated. I looked at Jayden and Hans, smiled and sipped my coffee.

I cleared my throat while setting my cup down. I folded my hands in front of me and addressed the General, "Ma'am. You say that these Eridani don't want us on Mars. You say that I will probably be killed by them if I go." She nodded once to both statements. I leaned forward a bit and continued quietly, "… and still, you haven't told me *not* to go." Now it was her turn to smile, genuinely.

"General Rosewood, if all that you have said is accurate, and I have no reason or compunction to doubt you, then I have a few opinions on these matters. First off, this planet is ours. Earth is ours. It belongs to humans. If we want to stay on it or if we want to leave it, that's our business. You say these intergalactic bad boys are from a star system ten light years away. Epsilon Eridani is *their* star system. Sol and its planets, including Mars, is the *human* star system, *our* star system. If we want to go to the Moon or we want to go to Mars, then who the hell are they to tell us not to go?"

"They have very powerful weaponry, spaceships, and a highly motivated fighting force of drones", she replied. "Granted, they have been a bit preoccupied lately with a war on a different front, but when it comes to their threats, they can definitely walk the talk."

"So we humans are just supposed to roll over and give in to these bastards?" I was getting heated. "We're supposed to give up our rightful presence in the galaxy because they are trying to *scare* us? General, I can't believe for a second there is a single member of your armed forces who wants to run and hide from these jackals. I can fathom from what you've said that the only reason all y'all haven't forced this issue would be the lack of political will." She crossed her arms as I spoke, kept smiling and looked interested.

"Ma'am, if the politicos of this world are unwilling to step up and say *nuts* to these freak-a-zoids ..."

"Tantaloids," she corrected me.

"Fine, Tantaloids, then perhaps a non-political and non-nationalized organization is exactly what is needed." I looked at Jayden, he looked like he was going to barf. "I think that perhaps the absolute best thing we can do is throw down the glove and see where the chips fall. I personally am offended and incensed that no one has had the political will to do this before. Humans first, dammit! Humanity's expansion to the stars is not a matter of 'if', it's a matter of 'when'; and the "when" is *now*. We must not be scared away from humanity's destiny. I will not be scared from taking the next step in our progress. If they kill me, so be it. I walk with God and have a rich reward awaiting me in heaven. If they kill me, more will be sent. If they get killed, we need to send more. We need to show them that their time of dictating action and policy to Earth has come to an end. If they want a war, then give me something to sharpen my teeth with, and the ability to bite back. I don't like the idea of fighting. I don't like the idea of killing. That's not why I'm going to Mars. But I'm not going to cower in the corner and say, *'oh-pretty-please Mr. Grey, please sir, give me some more.'* My next two words were punctuated by my finger stabbing the table, "FRAK. THAT."

I looked around the table, and then looked back at the General. "I appreciate your efforts and taking the time to come here, but nothing has changed. Unless the United States Air Force or the United States Government plans to interfere with our launch plans, I'm going to Mars." I looked over at Hans and Jayden again, "I'm going to Mars, period."

I leaned forward towards the General and lowered my voice, "Give me something to fight them with, if they want to mix it up," I slowly finished with a creepy smile of my own, "Payback's a bitch."

I pushed my chair back from the table, and picked up my coffee cup. Quickly switching to a pleasant and disarming demeanour, I looked at the General and said, "More coffee, ma'am?" She smiled wide; it was a genuine, warm and laughing smile. She stood up, "Yes Mike, but allow me to get it this time." She took our two cups to the Keurig to make us coffee, leaving Jayden and Hans to get their own.

There was more I could have learned from her, but there was so much she had chosen not to share. I could have gone more fully prepared and with more support, but there were still some secrets that were too secret for her to let out of the bag at this point. It seemed to me at the time that she wanted me to go to Mars. I thought it was simply for the reasons I had stated. I didn't know that the U.S. Air Force had been on Mars since 1975. I didn't know about the Hybrid base, or the terms of the formal détente with the Eridani. I didn't know that she had spent three hours with Jayden and Hans outlining how the U.S. Air Force was going to get the Corporation's mission to Mars, and foot part of the bill. I didn't know about her terms and conditions for the assistance. The three of us certainly didn't know that Lt. Gen. Rosewood had a plan for dealing with the Eridani, and that this plan hinged on me going to Mars. It totally hinged on me going to Mars. She didn't care if I went or not, just that I played my role obediently, and without too much fuss. I was just a pawn in her game.

Chapter 22

The Drone

It had been some time since the little green Drone saw any movement outside the human's dwelling place. The Drone was concerned about failure of the Master's orders. Perhaps the human scum was outside, on the other side of the dwelling, and it was doing something important, and the Drone couldn't see it.

The Drone moved the vessel slowly back and forth across the ice field, trying to get a different angle of view. There were two spots on the opposite side of the human's dwelling that the Drone could not get a visual of. The Drone moved the vessel in a large circle around the human site. The Drone could not see the human anywhere outside. However, something had been done outside, because the metal pieces the human had taken off the dwelling had all been put back on. The scum must have done that during the night while the Drone's vessel was on auto-hover, and the Drone took the necessary rest period.

A bolt of hatred and a bolt of horror simultaneously spiked through the Drone at that thought. The Drone had missed recording this activity for the Master. *Failure!* The body wracking sob of rage and frustration at the thought of failure tore through the creature. It was so bad that very, very rare ink black tears came out of the Drone's eyes. The crushing terror of failing the Master was no longer just an abstract thought for the Drone. The Drone wanted to zoom in with the vessel, and annihilate the human for its impertinence, and for bringing the Drone knowledge of what failure felt like.

The Drone swung the vessel around over the plain between the ice wall and the dwellings. The ice wall's ragged structure would help with the camouflage system. The seething hatred in the Drone's mind was causing it to make a high keening sound, as the Drone fought desperately to not give in to the hatred and destroy the human. The Master had given observation orders, not kill orders. To go against the Master like that would be worse than simply being dissolved for the failure of missing the human's activities through the Drone's sleep cycle.

Hovering over the plains and glaring at the dwelling on the Drone's viewing screen, the human suddenly appeared in the window of the dwelling. At last, activity to record. The Drone started the recording equipment, and was able to focus again on the task at hand. The human was looking around, and looked like it was taking in sustenance. After a few minutes, the human disappeared, and then reappeared. It was holding something up to its face.

The Drone wondered what kind of tech the human was using to look out at the surface, and moved the vessel slightly closer. After a few moments, the Drone realized the human was looking directly at the Drone's vessel. The Drone had been discovered. With a cry of despair at yet *another failure*, the Drone rocketed the ship straight up in the air, not stopping until it was several kilometres above the Martian surface. DESPISE THE HUMAN; HATE THE HUMAN; KILL THE HUMAN; DESTROY THE HUMAN; ANNIHILATE THE HUMAN … The Drone was beside itself with fury and the wracking pains of failing the Master. The Drone hastily put the vessel into a low Mars orbit, as it tried to come up with a simple decision matrix that would reveal what steps to take next. The Drone's bitter hatred of the human was so unbridled and consuming, the Drone could barely breathe. The Drone continued to seethe with white-hot fury, as the Drone imagined what joy would be had; if only the Drone would have the opportunity to see the human's disgorged entrails, dripping from the walls of the human's dwelling place. The Lectra weren't the only ones with claws.

Chapter 23

No. 2 Hits The Fan

I was only unconscious for about three minutes. I moaned as I opened my eyes and stared at the white ceiling. My bedroom ceiling? No, it wasn't as high as my bedroom ceiling was. I wondered where I was.

Then I remembered; I remembered what I had seen. I sat up a little too fast and had to pause. My head was still spinning and I had to let the brief flare of nausea die down. It didn't feel like I hit anything on the way down, but I felt around my brain pan and kept checking my hand for any signs of blood. None was to be in evidence.

Well, so much for Mr. Unflappable. I didn't dwell on it too much. What I had seen had triggered an age old childhood terror reaction. Next time, I would be ready and wouldn't spaz out so bad.

I checked the COM system, and then realized that there hadn't even been enough time for that video feed of me shouting and fainting to get even part way to Earth. The audio-visual signal was direct feed. It wasn't a file that needed to spool up for burst transmission. If that had been the case, I might have been able to stop it but no, the signal was on its way. It would be another almost 40 minutes before I heard anything about it. I sent a quick text message to Hans to let him know I was okay. I took a big drink of water to get the cotton balls out of my mouth, and then plugged an Ethernet cable from my tablet into the COM controller. It would make things faster.

First, I pulled up the record of the Jalopy-Sat feed. I fast-forwarded from the start of the tracking over the ice field, across the plains, around the colony site; and then stopping on the plains between the site, and the ice fields. Then I played it in real-time, and watched the shimmer and the shadow until suddenly, the shimmer was replaced by a grey object that looked almost perfectly round, almost. It shot straight upward and quickly went off camera. There was a blur on the screen, as the targeting system caught up with the object, showing it achieving an orbital altitude, and then move off south and west from the Chasma Boreale area.

I sat back and thought for a few moments. I reviewed the topside panning camera from the W-Hab, and then the topside camera that was in motion detector mode. Neither camera feed revealed any more than I had seen with my eyes, it was basically the same thing but from slightly different angles. The panning cameras (#W1 and #L1) had both panned off object just before it took off, so only the motion tracker cameras (#W2 and #L2) caught its departure. It showed almost exactly what I had seen with my own eyes. I figured Mar-Sat would have similar, though differently angled feeds of this as well; but frankly, I had seen enough. There wasn't much else I could learn by watching those videos, at least not at this stage of the game.

I downloaded the video files, encrypted them with the secure video software, put them in the file servers outbox, and then executed the procedure to send the files to Mission Control. The topside cameras were on live feed as well, but at least I felt like I had done something. Carrie had once said something about copies of the local recordings containing much more detail than the live feed stream, so she would probably have asked for them eventually. Having done that, and it having taken almost a full hour to view, download, and prepare the videos; I saw that the messages were starting to pour in from Terra. A few were from Mission Control as the public message box was filling so fast it was almost a blur. There was not only a website dedicated to the mission, there was an email address the general public could write to me on Mars. I was obligated to spend at least an hour a day responding to these, but that obligation did not begin until the AtmoGen was fully hooked up, and the Stage 1 Wind Farm had been completed. Neither had been done yet.

The first Mission Control message was from Carrie, it was a video message. I opened it, decoded it, and then played it. Carrie's beautiful, concerned face under the ever-present Dutch Pancake braids filled the screen. Arno was hovering over her shoulder. He looked like he was going to burst with excitement. "Mike, we saw the whole thing. It's all recorded here. Arno and I are going to try and back track it. I hope you're okay and didn't hit your head too hard. You're in my thoughts and prayers Mike." There were tears forming in her eyes. She ended the recording with a weak, but brave smile, as Arno waved at me with wide eyes and a stupid grin on his face.

The next video was one of the Hab techs. He wanted to see if I had checked the Habitats' video feeds for any captures of the object. Well … duhhhh.

Next video was Hans. He too wanted to make sure I was okay, and offered his moral support. His face said more than his words. We both knew that things had changed radically in the last few minutes. He said Jayden was on his way down, and he would get back to me as soon as he had confirmation I was okay. He ended his message with a double entendre, "Remember Mike, you can always look up for help."

Next was an email from that mousey little ESA spook, Ernst. It said simply, "I stand ready to assist." A chill ran up and down my spine at the ominous words sitting so innocently on the monitor. I wasn't certain at this point, but I was forming the impression that people were over-reacting. I would need to think on it a bit but right now, I was still thinking about what Ernst's words meant.

I knew very clearly what he meant. The Jalopy-Sat's Support Module was so large, it had caused commentary by more than one person involved in the Space game. Our spin was that we were bringing along a significant amount of new technology to be tested and evaluated for future transit missions. In fact, the Support Module was so large on the Jalopy-Sat because as soon as the transit vehicle became Jalopy-Sat, it also became a weapons platform. I'm a pacifist by nature. I hated that a commercial enterprise for humankind's advancement became a player with weapons. That weapons platform was the price tag of the U.S. Air Force's help in getting the mission on its way. Conversely, it was also a bit comforting to know there are options when you are all alone, on an *alien planet*, one hundred million or more miles from home. I had, after all, asked Lieutenant General Rosewood to give me some teeth.

The Jalopy-Sat was armed with ten orbit-deliverable Thermobaric warheads (converted), and each had a 44 ton yield. These were an advanced design based on the Russian FOAB (Father of All Bombs). Thermobarics were used because they don't need high levels of oxygen as part of the explosion. Each of these was attached to a small bodied cruise missile modified for flight in Mar's atmo. They would be released from the Jalopy-Sat, and moved in an orbital position by OMP rockets (Orbital Manoeuvering Package). From there, the warheads delivery package could put it on the surface of Mars in about 40 seconds. That meant from the Jalopy-Sat to anywhere within a thousand kilometres of the colony, from button press to detonation was under three minutes. Delivery to the other side of the planet: nine minutes. Of course, there was no button to press. It would all be done by voice commands. There was even one, special, terminal voice command, just in case.

These Thermobaric weapons had the destructive power of a small nuclear weapon against anything on the surface, but they didn't have the consequence of radiation or radioactive fallout. They wouldn't do much to penetrate fortified structures though. That's why there was another five conventional cruise missiles with an OMP, like the Thermobarics had. The conventional cruise missiles would punch a hole, the Thermobarics would obliterate what was inside by releasing the fires of hell upclose and personal like.

This weapons platform idea and the weapons themselves had been arranged by the U.S. Air Force. They couldn't send it to Mars on its own; they needed to get it there under cover and without notice. That made our mission and the circumstances of our mission so fortuitous for them. They had their own reasons for getting that platform in place, and Lt. General Rosewood refused to comment on the why; just that it was the trade-off for helping us get on the way. I had my own suspicions: that she was hoping I would take on the

Eridani problem for them. That way the Eridani backlash would be directed at the colonists on Mars, and not on the U.S. Air Force or on Terra.

As if the Thermobarics were not enough, there were also two, ten *Mega*ton thermonuclear packages in the Support Module. They came with all required periphery and were added last minute. I imagined that Lt. General Gilda Rosewood had something to do with those as well, but Jayden would neither confirm nor deny my speculation. He just suggested that perhaps I should stop speculating, for my own health.

I wasn't happy about the nuclear packages in the weapons platform. Fat Man, dropped on Nagasaki had a 20 *kilo*ton yield. Little Boy, dropped on Hiroshima had a 16 *kilo*ton yield. These orbiting Hydrogen bombs were 600 times as powerful as the one dropped on Hiroshima. These multi-megaton thermonuclear bombs orbiting Mars meant a very impressive amount of destruction could be wrought with a few moments notice. It was definitely something to be upset about. For a few minutes, one day in transit, I fantasized about dropping them on the far side of Mars, just to be rid of them. However, the cultural fallout back on Earth from that would have been devastating. The irony that I was the one with the trigger hadn't escaped me.

The saving grace was, however, that when Jayden relented to the U.S. Air Force demands for assisting with the mission, he insisted that the actual "launch" signal for any of the weapons could only be sent from Mars' surface. They could monitor, track, assess and recommend as much as they wanted, however: no weapon would be released unless someone on Mars released it. They agreed to this, rather too quickly it seemed.

In my own view, we were going to Mars for colonization, expansion, and the furtherance of humankind's presence in the star system and inherently, in the galaxy. These were our first steps. I initially thought that bringing the weapons of war was distinctly against what we were trying to achieve. However, my feelings on the conventional weapons softened a little bit after considering the first briefing General Rosewood had given to me. Given the events at today's lunch time, I started to feel very appreciative of the conventional warheads being up there. I still wasn't happy about the thermonuclear packages, but so long as they stayed orbiting, they weren't falling.

On The Internet

The colony audio and video direct feeds were transmitted from the Hab's COM system to Mar-Sat. From Mar-Sat they were beamed towards Earth. In orbit around Earth was the satellite Relay-1 which was responsible for collecting the signals and beaming them down to the Corporation's antenna farm, just outside the complex where Mission Control was located. Once there, they went through a small bit of electronic delay (ten seconds), then were loaded onto a web server and streamed out to the internet. All the cameras at the Habitat, plus the Activity Suit cameras (when activated), had their own streams. Viewers could pick and choose which stream they wanted to play, and if their own bandwidth allowed it, they could play multiple streams, timestamp coordinated, side by side. They could also play back the archived clips as the stream itself auto-archived every one hundred and eighty seconds.

One of the ways the Corporation was paying for the whole colony operation was by collecting revenue from these viewers. It cost a certain amount of money each month for access to the Mars camera and audio feeds. You could also message the Mars colony with an email message system that only worked if you were logged into the site and therefore, a paying viewer. There were paying viewers from every nation on Earth, even Nauru.

When the small grey ship appeared and rocketed away into the sky, there had been a few thousand people viewing feeds and poking around the site. No one at Mission Control had thought to interrupt the feed until the delay time had passed. By then there was nothing to see, nothing to stop people from seeing, except in the archived clips. Now, so many years later, I can look back and say I'm glad that what was seen, was seen by everyone. Within a few days of this event, Jayden informed me that after some discussion, the live feed being broadcast would not be interrupted except in the most egregious of circumstances. That didn't mean, I later learned, that someone else might not interrupt it.

With the pause, rewind and playback features of the web site, those few seconds got played an unimaginable number of times. With word of mouth, within ten minutes of the word getting out, there were over thirty million people watching the vid feeds. The colocated servers eventually snapped under the strain, and the site went down for several hours. It came back up and was immediately deluged again. However, the propeller heads added so much scalable hardware that it was able to withstand the load.

Chapter 24

Getting On, With Getting On

I needed time to think, after my close encounter of the first kind. So much had happened in such a short time; and I still had so many things to do. I had only been on Mars one full day and a bit. I didn't need such a damnable distraction.

I finished responding to the messages I needed to, including one to my son, and one to Mary. I hit the Head, and then went to the lower level of the W-Hab. Entering the airlock, I unpacked my every-day Activity Suit and outer jumpsuit, inserted full air bottles in the harness, hooked up all the connections, and ran a full diagnostic. This all took only a half hour. I left my transit Activity Suit and outer jumpsuit hanging up in the corner, covering the secret weapons locker.

The Activity Suit had four main components to it. There was the mechanical suit itself that I wore over thermal underwear after taking off my indoor coveralls. This Activity Suit had been developed by MIT and was called "mechanical" because it used the mechanical strength of the fibres to hold my body intact in low vacuum. It could even function in the total vacuum of space if necessary. The suit had a hard seal with the helmet which was a bit bigger than you would expect because of the tech loaded into it. The gloves, boots, and helmet were all pressurized as the nature of those parts of the body would not be properly protected by the mechanical suit. The boots secured with pressure clasps, like ski boots. They were steel toed, and built to withstand anything, environmental or chemical.

There was a small life support system interface on the lower back of the Activity Suit. Over the Activity Suit I put on what was basically a one piece cover-all or jumpsuit. It was made of five layers of carbon nano-tube reinforced Kevlar. Even in low Martian gravity I could still feel the reassuring heft of the outer jumpsuit. The helmet and jumpsuit were jet black. Once suited, I slipped into the harness that held the two air bottles, emergency bottle, re-breather scrubber, suit heater, and systems regulators. Two small reinforced tubes from this system entered the outer cover-all through a small connection point in the right side of the suit, just above my hip, where it connected with the systems interface underneath the cover-all.

There was a COM unit that connected on four points on the air bottle harness, across my chest. It had the interface for the COM unit, an LED light pack, and at my insistence, a hardened, removable iPod that had been preloaded with my entire music collection. The outer-shell, the jumpsuit, I had been tempted to call the SOMP (suit of many pockets), because there were pockets all over it for everything. A set of emergency suit repair patches, signaling flares (although no one ever specified who I was going to signal with the flares, being that I was all alone on Mars), a signaling mirror, a hand sized emergency ratchet wrench, and a small suit repair toolkit were just a few of the many items. I had more than I would ever need.

After a low-g sprint up the staircase to pair the suit's COM unit with the W-Hab's COM system and to grab one item, I was back in the airlock and suited up in no time. With a bit more practice in the coming weeks, I would be able to be suited and sealed up, ready for outdoors, in under two minutes. The item I had grabbed upstairs was my K-Bar. I put it on the utility belt of the Activity Suit, around the right side and back by the air tanks. I had decided that I wanted it with me. Not that it would be any defence against guns, ray or otherwise; I just wanted it there to feel ... capable of defending myself I guess. I also grabbed one of the pulse-energy weapons from its hidden compartment, along with both spare charge clips and then slung the weapon over my shoulder. Taking the weapon wasn't a last-minute thought. I had been arguing the idea with myself in my head while I had been prepping the suit.

After shutting the airlock hatch behind me and descending the ladder with another Navy slide, I took a slow walk around both Habitats, to clear my head. I kept looking up at the sky. I kept looking over my shoulder. I had no idea where that thing had gone, but I refused to be controlled by the fear it generated. I had to set up the AtmoGen, and I needed to inspect the supply drops that were lined up just south of the Habitats. However, I looked over at the debris field from yesterday's Lander explosion and decided to start there. The debris field was an eyesore. Cleaning it up would be a statement to whatever had been watching me, and to those back on Terra. So this was how I spent the rest of my first full day on Mars: picking up garbage. The weapon kept falling off my shoulder, and although it was a nuisance, it was a comforting nuisance. I was glad to have it with me.

I looked around for Big Dawg, and then remembered where he was. I walked to the rear of the Habitats, near the solar collector connection point for the W-Hab. I had left him sitting there in hand signal mode, with no hand signals to follow. I gave the hand signal recognition command and then the hand signal sequence for "follow me". I headed back towards the debris field.

I used Big Dawg's cargo deck as a poor Martian's pickup truck. I used it to transport debris as I walked along. There were small posts around the cargo deck that could extend upward about 20 centimetres. These were for keeping larger objects from rolling off the flat surface, like pipes and poles. I extended these small posts, and lined the edges of the 100 by 130 centimetre cargo deck with larger pieces of metal ejecta. It wasn't a good ol' hillbilly pickup, but it was indeed a good ol' redneck mock-up for the job at hand. My redneck heritage finally became useful to me.

Most of the debris from inside the Lander, the lighter stuff that was blowing around, I walked around tossing it towards the center of the blast zone. You could get some good arc on thrown objects in low-g. A football game here would certainly be interesting; CFL of course. Bigger pieces went into the "pickup truck". The wind was at about 20 km/hr, and picked up to about 25 km/hr by the time I was done. I did have to worry about tossing larger pieces of the soft debris, and having them become sails in the wind. All of what I considered the "soft" debris was the fabric bag transport units, small boxes, and lockers, etc. I managed to cram into the mangled remains of the airlock, and the Lander's small toilet. I also got a fair amount of smaller pieces of metal in with them. These two pieces of the ship were still intact enough to act as garbage bins. The "hard" debris, the larger parts of the Lander itself, I dragged and carried back to the downwind side of the airlock wreckage. There wasn't actually anything left big enough that I couldn't move on my own, other than the Head and the Airlock. Downwind was south and west in this area, so despite my efforts, I would be looking at the debris for a long time as the Habitats were south and west of the about to be named, Cortés Crater. I'd also be picking up bits and pieces of memorabilia from yesterday's events for years to come. The tiny pieces were spread far and wide; and I was only one person. I was only really worried about the bigger stuff anyways.

During these efforts, I would stop every few minutes, scan the horizon, turn three hundred and sixty degrees scanning slowly. I saw nothing. Every once in a while I would lean back and look straight up into the sky, still nothing. Early in the local evening time, I got a priority message from Hans on the HUD interface. I decoded it and played it back in-suit, something very handy that I could do, now that I had a paired COM unit. Hans was reminding me that the PDV was due to arrive tonight, in about six hours. This had been on the work manifest for the day, but Hans rightly guessed I had forgotten all about it. I didn't actually have to "do" anything for the arrival of the PDV; but since they land so close to the Habitats, the protocol was that I had to be suited up during the final few minutes of the touchdown, just in case. This was the PDV my Lander had hitched a ride on top of while leaving Earth. If my Lander had been sabotaged, then perhaps the PDV had been sabotaged as well. Even though it had departed orbit slightly ahead of me, it was actually just a fraction slower. Due to its mass, it started braking before it was even in orbit. That was why it arrived after me, and not before me. As well, the PDV was using a direct atmospheric insertion approach. It would give a massive burn of its first of five RAD engines just as it reached Mars' atmosphere, hence the need for its slightly slower initial entry velocity. It would then drop right into the atmosphere to begin the atmospheric braking, before it had a chance to pick up speed, as it would in a typical orbital insertion.

Carrie checked in with a message about her video research a couple times, nothing significant found. I think she was just worried. I recorded an "in suit" video for her, full of smiles and a bit more good natured than I was feeling at the moment. I knew it would set her mind at ease. Jayden sent a message that expressed his concern and his happiness that I was okay, and hadn't injured myself when fainting. There was a touch of sarcasm in his voice, but I ignored it. Heavens only knew what he was dealing with right now. My son and some friends sent messages through the private channel they had access to. Every once in a while, I would take a wee rest break and troll some of the messages in the public channel. All mostly the same thing, how did I feel, was I scared, have I seen anything else, blah, blah, blah. Of course, there were a few requisite messages from the nut-bars and from some conspiracy theorists. I actually re-read the conspiracy theorists ones a couple times, and saved two of them for later perusal. The authors' names had become familiar to me over the last few months as they kept emailing me like we were old friends, even though I had not once responded to them. Perhaps tonight I might take the time to compose a short response or two. You never know when those guys were going to come up with a gem of truth.

After a full day of work, only going back inside to change air bottles once but not stopping for food, I had all of the soft debris I could find tidying up; and most of the hard debris gathered up as well. There were a few pieces still too heavy for me, even in low-g. I'd have to get Big Dawg to help me drag those, but not today. The Lander airlock and toilet, my makeshift garbage bins, were full. I bent, banged, and twisted metal over the openings to keep the contents inside, despite the building Martian wind. The wind always ramped up slightly in the evenings, just like on Terra, according to our historical readings sent daily by Big Dawg. The only difference was that after dusk they died down on Terra. Not so much on Mars, not at this latitude anyways.

I gave Big Dawg the recognition command, and then the "follow me" command. The recognition command was simply holding your fingers out straight, and holding your thumb at ninety degrees to your fingers, then chopping your thumb closed and open once. The recognition command indicated to Big Dawg that an actionable hand signal was going to be given. The recognition command was good for ninety seconds, any number of hand signals could be given before the next recognition command had to be given. The "follow me" hand signal was simply holding your hand out flat, palm down, then flip your palm upwards, and beckon with your fingers twice. Travel commands were good for five minutes. If no other hand signal was received within the five minutes, *and* the IFF of the issuer was not within 100 metres, then the rover would stop. This was a safety so that it wouldn't accidentally drive all the way around the planet … or off a cliff.

The only hand signal that did not need to be preceded by a recognition command was "stop". However, if there was no recognition command given with it, only the person who had issued the last hand signal could issue the "stop" command. More accurately, only the person with the same IFF signal could give the "stop" command without the recognition command.

I dragged my tired ass back to the airlock ladder, then stopped Big Dawg. I gave it the "release hand signal", the hand signal to put him back in normal operating mode. Big Dawg quickly turned away, and went about inspecting some items that had built up in its own work manifest. Since we were still in the land of the midnight sun and would be for another month or so, the rovers didn't need to go dormant at night. When winter hit, that would be another story. When we reached total darkness for the day, mid-winter, they would have entered hibernation mode had I not been there. However, one of the supply drops contained an upgrade that would allow both Big Dawg and Little Dawg to recharge themselves directly from the Power Aggregator on the Wind Farm Energy Distribution System (EDS for short), after I got it set up. This would allow them to be operable through all but the worst of the winter storms I would face in the months ahead.

Back in the airlock, brushed off, de-suited, suit and floor vacuumed, everything was finally plugged in and charging. I decided to take a moment and set up the air bottle system properly. Until now, there were only four bottles hooked up, and they had been hooked up since the whole contraption left Terra. I pulled the transport straps off the other twenty bottles. The bottle rack had three columns of eight bottles. It was on the left side of the suit racks, left of the secret compartment, and below the deep shelves for the helmets and gloves. These bottles were stored nozzle outwards in the angled racks. I took each bottle out of its rack, flipped it over, and slid it back in. When they made contact at the back of the rack, I pushed and turned to the right ninety degrees. This hooked them up to the W-Hab's atmo processing, and they would be automatically filled up. The bottles were full to begin with; this would just balance the pressure in them and top them up minutely. In future, all I would have to do with an empty bottle was return it to the rack and give it a twist, it would refill automagically.

Back upstairs, I had a protein shake and then checked the messages from Terra. Thankfully the ones from Mission Control didn't make too much more fuss about the grey ball thingy and got on with business. I complied with some system maintenance reading requests, installed some updated software in the COM unit itself, and did some climate readings for the peeps that cared about these things.

With some food and coffee in me, and a lot more work done than I expected, it was close to midnight local when I suited back up to head outside again. I didn't want to. I wanted to go down in the L-Hab, find my bed and just die for like twelve hours. However, it's not every day you get to see a space-ship landing on an alien planet. Even if it was just the PDV that was arriving, it was still a first for me and I was kind of excited. Just before exiting the Airlock, I thought about the energy weapon and decided that there had been enough of that for one day. I left the weapon and spare power cassettes hooked up to its charger in the secret compartment.

I grabbed the mini-cam I had the day before, and headed away from Cortés Crater and the Habitats. The battery had 82% charge and lots of space on the hard drive, so after hooking it to my utility belt, I just turned it on and left it on. I set the outward facing helmet camera to record mode as well. The supply drops had all landed south and west of the colony site; just shy of the Hyperboreae Undae sand dunes. Big Dawg had dragged the six supply drops from earlier this year into place, about 500 metres away. They were all nicely lined up on their self-leveling legs. The supply drop containers had the train wheels, like the Habitats, to assist with the re-positioning. They didn't have the walking legs like the Habitats. They just had thick support legs that would extend downward past the RAD nacelles to make the inside of the unit level, regardless of the pitch of the surface they were on. The landing legs would then act as stabilizers, keeping the cargo ships from falling over. This initial ground based re-positioning of the supply drops involved some careful plotting by Big Dawg's on board navigation system, to get them all in place. I have to admit, Big Dawg had done a pretty darn good job.

As I stood there admiring its work, Big Dawg pulled up beside me and just sat there. The whole idea of "dog" just struck me rather curious then. I think it was at this point I stopped referring to Big Dawg as "it" in my own mind, and started thinking of the large rover as "he". Just as fine an example of anthropomorphism as naming your car back on Terra.

So Big Dawg and I stood there, side by each, just looking around. I was swiveling my head inside my helmet, Big Dawg's camera head was panning back and forth. Touching the controller on my left forearm, I brought up a small COM window that displayed the automated signals from the PDV so I'd know when it was coming down. It was sequenced to land 200 metres further south and west to avoid the colony and avoid the existing supply drops.

Being a bit away from the Habitats, and looking at them from this perspective was powerful. The sun was low to the horizon and behind me, in the direction of the upcoming landing. I looked at the Habitats in that sweet light, and things really started to sink in. I had been so busy and so tired that while I had taken time to look around, I hadn't taken time to get philosophical. I took a sip of water from the sippy-hose in my helmet, and let my mind wander into the high-brow realm.

The ruminations started with the water I was sipping. The water I was sipping was still Terran water. It was Terran water that was nine months old and had travelled over a hundred million miles, yet it was here with me on the surface of this alien planet and ...

No, wait. It wasn't an alien planet. Not any more it wasn't. Mars was no longer an alien world to me. *Planeta Martes* was now home. It was my home. I had no way to return to Terra, and I would never go back to Terra again; for the rest of my life. I had made a very bold and permanent change of address: Mike Lane, PO Box #1, Mars.

From this point on, I was "from" Mars. If I stepped on a space ship right now, travelled across the galaxy, and landed on another world; when the inhabitants asked, "where are you from", I would have to say, "Mars". This was it. I had emigrated. There was no return to Earth for me. There was no return vessel, no return plan, no way back. Period. Ad infinitum.

I was okay with that. I had wanted this. I signed up for this. *I asked for it.* Granted, the original plan had some company coming with me; but hey, a few years alone could do the soul good. I hoped it would. I realized that I had been right about bringing the empty feeling, the long familiar heart ache, with me. Loreena would have hated it here; but she would have loved it for my sake. I remembered how freaked she'd been watching a movie about Mars and some ghosts, how she'd buried her Amazon body in my arms, and hid her face in my neck; her curly dark red hair tickling my nose. I smiled. There really was a ghost on Mars now.

I looked up at the paleness of the sky, it wasn't Terran sky, it was Martian sky and it was now *my* sky. I could see some of the stars in the low light of the Martian north polar midnight. I was close enough, in galactic proximity to Terra, for them to appear the same as on Terra. Still, there was something different about them, something ever-so-slightly different, that I couldn't put my finger on.

I looked down and kicked the regolith. Humphhh. Back on Terra I would have thought that I was kicking the earth. While technically, it could be considered "earth" that was beneath my feet, the word that my mind kept using was "soil" and "regolith". It's the small things I guess.

Tired from a very long day and still adjusting to gravity's effect on me, I hopped up on the cargo deck of Big Dawg, and then I just sat there swinging my legs like a child. I continued looking at the ground. There were no blades of grass. No tufts of green grass, or dead wheat coloured grass, sticking up anywhere. There were no leaves blowing around. All I could hear was the subtle hiss of my Activity Suit's air system, my own breathing, and the occasional low volume beep and twitter from the COM unit. The absence of

Terran normal sensory input and the future life ahead of me, imprisoned in a life of an isolated freedom, didn't bother me at all.

I think the events of the day showed what was going to be most challenging: keeping a rein in on childhood fears. Adult fears were no problem for me. I faced those head-on and squarely, confident that I walked with God on a daily basis. If I stood with Him, who could stand against me? I applied that to the childhood fears as well, but those fears still had some powerful psychological mojo that snuck up on me, and poked me in the ribs sometimes. When those fears hit, faith or not, it still takes a few minutes to corral those ponies and tame them down. I thought about that long ago night for a moment. That time when I was five years old and *they* came in the middle of the night. That was almost fifty years ago. I think the fact that General Rosewood had simply said, "We know", made it something even more terrifying for me. I only had partial memory of that night. As a child, it was scary; I remember most the helpless terror. As an adult, I can look back on those memories objectively, when I choose to look back on them. It's just that sometimes, those memories pop up and they surprise me at the oddest times. That's when the panic hits, the sense of being suffocated by the fear, the feeling of helplessness. So long as I could choose my own ground, my own time and place of facing these things, I knew that I could handle them calmly. I knew I could handle them without re-experiencing that middle-of-the-night-terror.

I sat there for another thirty minutes being all philosophical about my new life, and thankfully, other less weighty matters. I kept checking the PDV status, getting a little more impatient the closer it came to touchdown. It was ready to break atmo, and start descent.

That's when the PRIORITY indicator popped up on the HUD. It was a text message. I reached for the controller on my arm and opened the message in my HUD.

The message was from Ernst. It simply said, "Look behind you".

Chapter 25

Look Behind You

Ernst had not left Mission Control since the appearance of the grey ball almost twelve hours ago. He had been near the end of his shift when it appeared. After that, his replacement couldn't make him leave. So, the replacement just joined him. Two sets of eyes were, after all, better than one. Frankie was also an ESA spook, and shared duties with Ernst and one other person. Frankie had spent the early part of his life as a CIA analyst and then had moved on to private consulting for corporations with a global footprint. Finally, retiring at age forty-four, he had been picked up by the ESA to do things that simply interested him. Spooking on the Mars colony mission definitely interested him.

Ernst and Frankie were playing back Jalopy-Sat footage exclusively. Carrie had helped Ernst earlier or rather, Ernst request for help from Carrie had given her something new to pursue. It became a much more valuable lead after the grey ball shot away. She was now in her own office, also refusing to go home, conducting her own research. Arno was with her as well.

About an hour before the PDV was due to set down, Carrie and Arno were back in Mission Control. The big screen at the front showed Mike exiting the W-Hab. The night shift Mission Control Director, Karl, Hans' brother (no nepotism I assure you), announced that Mike was going outside to watch the PDV's descent. Many heads turned to just look at him a moment, causing a sheepish grin to creep across his face. *Master of stating the obvious,* was the immediate thought in his head, poking fun at himself.

Through Ernst's investigations, with Frankie's assistance, they, (Carrie and Arno) had determined that the "shimmer" effect had been present around the colony site from almost the same moment the Lander was touching down. It had even gotten very close, and then zoomed away just as the Lander exploded. Ernst was really tired by this time, and he didn't catch the significance of the twinkle of light that Carrie and Arno had questioned. It would eventually be Carrie that confirmed it was a pulse-energy weapon striking the Lander. In his defence, it looked like a glint of sunlight. That sounded like a perfectly reasonable explanation for the anomalous appearance of that tiny flash of light. Perfectly reasonable, that is, until Carrie and Arno had realized at the same moment, the twinkle was on the shaded side of the Lander.

Ernst and Frankie, however, had compiled the footage and tracker-cam telemetry that showed the exact position and route of the "shimmer" (or as

Ernst and Frankie now thought of it), the "cloaked ship". This data covered the Lander's arrival until the grey ball departed.

When the announcement was made that Mike was going outside to observe the PDV landing, Ernst and Frankie saved their research files, then switched to the current live-ish feed from Jalopy-Sat. I say live-ish because the feed was, technically, live. It was, *technically*, real-time as well, even though it was delayed a bit over eighteen minutes. It was live and real-time in the sense that as soon as it arrived from Relay-1, the feed was presented on their monitors. However, it was a live and real-time video feed of something that had happened eighteen minutes ago.

Viewing their live-ish feed, Ernst and Frankie watched Mike walk over towards the supply drop site. They saw the six existing drops lined up neatly, and saw Mike being approached by the big rover. They saw it stop beside him as Mike stood there looking around. They saw Mike hop up and sit on the cargo deck of the big rover. It was only a moment later when the image zoomed out on them. They hadn't touched anything, and were about to look at each other when the red capital letters displayed on the upper left corner of the screen:

ENGAGING HOSTILE REFERENCE

In unison, their eyes widened, and they both gasped quietly and leaned back. They both adjusted their glasses, and then both leaned in closer to the monitor, in perfect unison. They both pointed to the same point on the monitor at the same time, both nodding silently. Two peas in a pod, they both saw the "shimmer" was back, the cloaked alien ship.

The tracking system on Jalopy-Sat learned as it worked. Through the assistance of the techs on Terra (Ernst and his compatriots), objects on the surface that might move around were tagged and identified. If Mike's Activity Suit's IFF signal or the rovers moved outside the 500 metre exclusion zone, the tracker would identify them, and queue them to be followed if there was nothing more interesting to follow. The techs could also put the system in bypass mode to ignore all known and referenced objects. The alert for "engaging hostile reference" meant the tracking system had detected movement by something that was tagged as "hostile" in its database, or something that was not tagged in its database, could not be identified by its shape and size and was pursuing a direct course towards the colony site. The term "reference" meant someone sitting at the terminal. Ernst was sitting at *had* identified it as a potential hostile target in the database; something that might need to be destroyed. The "engaging" part meant that the tracker camera was following it, and ipso facto, so was the targeting system; and ipso facto again, so was a hellish death and destruction from orbit high above.

Whatever it was could have Thermobaric-Hell descend on it in under three minutes, if the man on Mars wanted it to be so.

In this case, the unknown reference was a slight surface shimmer, moving over the ice-field wall towards the plains and towards the colony. Earlier in the day, Ernst had tagged that shimmer as a hostile target, and the targeting system now recognized it optically. As they watched it, the shimmer moved over the ice-wall and across the plains, headed towards where Mike was sitting on the rover's cargo deck. Frankie stood up looking towards the Mission Director and inhaling sharply. Ernst quickly grabbed him and sat him roughly back down in his seat. He glared at him and held a finger up to his pursed lips. Truthfully, Ernst didn't really know why he made Frankie be quiet. In a few minutes someone else would notice the shimmer on the big monitor. As he thought about his motivation for silencing Frankie, Ernst realized it was just his own secretive nature. Given the parameters of his assignment on this project, maybe he would have to work on that. It would, however, would be something for later thought.

Focused on the monitor, the pair of spooks watched the shimmer stop moving. It was behind Mike's back and hovering over the plains. It was only about 100 metres away from Mike's position. Ernst drummed the desktop for a minute. They watched Mike just sitting on the cargo deck.

"We have to say something," Frankie said, strident and glaring right into Ernst's eyes, as Ernst turned to look at him.

"Yah, but not to them. Too much panic in here, and nothing vill be achieved. Ve don't know its intentions at zeh moment." Ernst turned back to the screen, his own words sounding hollow in his head. His fingers tapped the keyboard, and the priority COM window opened. It was a simple system that allowed one line of text to be sent to the Colony recipient, and it was transmitted ahead of whatever data may currently be spooled for transmission. Twitter for outer space, if you want. It could even be used terminal to terminal at Mission Control; but that would be frowned upon by most people as too secretive. This wasn't, unfortunately in Ernst and Frankie's minds, a black-op government operation. Openness and sharing were key words in the work environment here, and it was something they were both struggling to get used to.

Ernst paused for a moment and then typed his simple message: Look behind you.

Chapter 26

First Contact

If anyone else had sent that message, I wouldn't have had the body shivering chill hit my spine like an out of control locomotive. I jumped off the back of the rover and assumed a crouched position. As soon as my head popped up, over the edge of the rover deck, there was a brilliant flash of light coming from what I recognized as the "shimmer"; probably the one from earlier today. I ducked just in time. I swear I heard the crackling of electricity as the translucent energy ball passed over my head and exploded the ground only 10 metres from where I was crouched. I popped my head up quickly for a better look at the "shimmer", but it wasn't there.

"Frak me." It was a very poignant thought at this moment that whatever *this* situation was going to be, I had to handle it quickly. There was no backup, there was no aid, and there was no one to rescue me if I got injured. I turned my body and head slowly to look for the "shimmer". I thought about the energy weapons sitting in their secret compartment. They were certainly not going to do me any good in there.

I looked back at the W-Hab, but it was almost half a kilometre away. There was no way I could cover that open ground before the alien vessel could fire another round or four at me. I peered around the front end of Big Dawg; I was only a few metres from the first supply drop. I could make a dash for there, and maybe use that and the other drops as cover, but that was just going to wind up being a game of cat and mouse. I looked around the ground as I kept glancing upwards looking for the shimmer of the alien vessel. The only thing I had at my disposal was rocks, most of them a bit bigger than a hockey puck. I picked up one in each hand: they would have to do. I sighed, then muttered, "Just call me Grog, the Martian Caveman."

Chapter 27

Teviot Vallis

Located approximately 32 degrees south of the Martian equator and 83 degrees east of the Martian Prime Meridian, Hellas Planitia is easily visible from Terra with a telescope, even a cheap one. Unfortunately, it's just slightly out of range of the optics on Mar-Sat and Jalopy-Sat, due to its relative position to Chasma Boreale, and the steep curvature of Mars surface. Hellas Planitia is an impact crater that is 2,300 kilometres wide. Its depth is from 4 to 8 kilometres below the Martian datum (sea level). It is 9 kilometres deep if you count the rim of the crater. Yes, I said *kilometres*. To put this in more perspective, the area of the Hellas Planitia impact crater is approximately 4.15 million square kilometres. The area of the United Kingdom is only 243,000 square kilometres. You could fit the entire United Kingdom inside Hellas Planitia, seventeen times. That makes it big enough to hold almost one half of Canada's land mass, more than half of the United States of America.

On the eastern rim of Hellas Planitia, amongst the debris curtains, impact craters, and relatively smaller Planitias, Mons and plateaus, are three large valleys. These are regarded as the sources of the fluvial flow patterns and sedimentary deposits inside the Hellas' impact crater. They are Dao Vallis, Niger Vallis and Harmakhis Vallis. Hellas Planitia is actually deep enough to allow sufficient atmospheric pressure at its deepest levels, that if there were water at the bottom of the crater, it could exist without boiling off. At the top off the southernmost Harmakhis Vallis, ostensibly a large tributary to Harmakhis Vallis, is Reull Vallis. This flow channel stretches eastward almost 1,500 kilometres, and is 7 kilometres at its widest point. About halfway along Reull Vallis, east of the head of Harmakhis Vallis, is the much smaller Teviot Vallis. Teviot Vallis is only 140 Kilometres in length. It is barely noticeable compared to what is around it. Such inconspicuousness suited the Eridani just fine.

The Eridani settlement had existed in excavated subterranean tunnels and chambers on the western wall of Teviot Vallis for close to 700 years. Originally an outpost for secret propulsion experiments, it became an exo-biological research station that quickly rose to be the most prominent in this sector of the Eridani Dominion. Almost all of the Eridani warmongering came from their need to engage in biological research.

Critical to their needs, as it would be for anyone going to Mars, was water. Terran research missions and satellite measurements projected the terrain around this region is filled with water only a few hundred metres below the surface. The Eridani could confirm this, as they have an extensive drilled water system that supplied all their needs, it was the basis of the original propulsion research, and could supply a much larger footprint of consumers than it currently did. Without digressing too much further, I will say that in later years, their choice of location caused problems not only for themselves, but also for the colonist expansions. Thankfully that came later and not right now, as the region around Teviot Vallis, Euripus Mons specifically, was one that had been considered by the Corporation as a colony site!

While the Eridani had existed for only the last 1,500 Terran years, the genetic experiments and cloning process that originally created them hadn't been perfected at the time by the Eben scientists responsible for it. There were mistakes, and genetic drift; and it wasn't the type that brought about adaptations for the betterment of the new species. The original Eridani clones had a high incidence of Large Offspring Syndrome, and that condition persisted through the natural reproduction of the cast of Eridani Masters. It was also the chief cause of the statistically high maternal mortality rate during Eridani childbirth. Only three in twenty Eridani women survived childbirth, they had an 85% mortality rate. Needless to say, this was a very motivating factor in finding solutions, and in finding corrections. This investigation of biological and genetic solutions was, so far, the entire purpose of the Eridani society. Well, that and the headaches. Eridani males suffered what we call a migraine, almost constantly; from birth to death. Suicide was common amongst Eridani males, simply due to the lifetime of genetically inherited pain. They didn't care about conquest; the Eridani cared about survival as a species. Planetary and territorial conquest was just a welcome by-product of this pursuit.

Eridani males, while only about 165 cm tall, had enormous heads. It was like looking at a pumpkin head on an anorexic. Actually, that's quite an apt description of the Eridani males. They had no hair and very pale skin. In many places the skin was translucent enough to see the circulatory system at work under their skin. Their large and sunken eyes, along with their pointed and jutting jaws gave them a haunting, nightmarish look, which the few humans who had seen them never forgot. Even the humans who were memory wiped often retained nightmare images of the Eridani face, well after encountering them,.

The Eridani civilization, the Bsirutaeben (b-seer-ROO-tay-ben) in their own tongue (loosely, and politely translated as "Superior to Eben"), was initially created by Eben genetic experiments, hybridization experiments, and cloning processes about (as stated), 1,500 Terran years ago. Having a vastly superior jump start on species that simply evolved, the Eridani rapidly multiplied, and then took their independence from their Eben handlers, by deception. They then set out to grow and dominate the Orion Arm and the Sagittarius Arm of the Milky Way galaxy. Terra is located in the Orion arm, about two thirds of the way out from the galactic core. The Eben could have tried to stop them, but the fact that a cloned and hybridized life form had chosen to take their independence, was of more than a little scientific interest. The Eben put up a mild resistance to let the clones think they had actually outwitted their creators, and then the Eben spent the next thousand years watching the Eridani develop and grow as a society.

By the time the Eben began to wonder if they should do something terminal about the Bsirutaeben, they were too large in numbers for an easy campaign. Besides, the Eben had other newer pursuits to focus on. The ancient war that had almost wiped out the Eben was still a very present part of their cultural memory. While the Eben were considered by most races in the three galaxies to be amongst the most effective and fearsome warriors known, their numbers had reduced so much that they hadn't had the political will to launch an assault on the Bsirutaeben. The Eben also hadn't had the sociological will to pursue a war with the Bsirutaeben either. At the most recent count, there are over 50,000 Eridani Masters spread throughout the Milky Way galaxy. There are even more in neighbouring galaxies.

At this point in Eben history, the Bsirutaeben were a nuisance, not a threat. At least they weren't a threat to the Eben. Lately though, relatively speaking, there had been closer scrutiny of their actions and the direction their research was taking. The Bsirutaeben were indeed a problem for the humans, and the Eben liked the humans, even though they kept the humans at arm's length. While the Eben had stopped visiting Earth officially in the Terran year 1985, they still had assets on the ground, and they did have a significant presence at the Hybrid base on Mars. The Eben thought that humans had great potential. At a deep, sociological and philosophical level, the Eben found many similarities in the development of the humans to the ancient development of the Eben society over 10,000 years ago.

Eridani society has three casts, plus the drones. The upper cast is the Masters, the Voiya as they are called. They were the Eridani proper. They were the descendants of the original hybrids and clones. They were the shortest of the three casts, standing an average of only 165 cm tall. The Voiya were very sensitive about their height since they were almost as short as the average Eben male. In fact, the Eben were the only race known to be, on average, shorter than the Voiya. Within the other casts, the Trigla (pronounced TREE-la) averaged 40 cm taller than the Voiya. The Vesna (pronounced VESH-na) ran on average, about the same height as the Voiya, but without the Napoleonic complex. The drones, of course, were all much shorter than the Masters, but they were merely chattel, they were not real Bsirutaeben.

The Voiya always put themselves on elevated platforms, elevated walkways, or any position that would force others to look up to them, *literally*. Anything a Voiya could do to make itself appear taller than everyone around it, they considered it a good thing to do. At one point they tried mimicking the 70's fad of platform shoes, but they kept tripping and falling down in them, so they gave them up.

Only about fifteen percent of the adult Eridani were females. This was because of the unrealistically high maternal mortality rate I mentioned previously. About 40% of Voiya adolescents were females, but their high mortality rate burdened, burned and infuriated Eridani Society in general. The resulting glut of adult males created the sociological necessity for Voiya families to be polyandrous. One Eridani adult woman would bear the offspring of fifteen to thirty Eridani males, simply because there were not enough adult females to go around. A Voiya female would give birth to over one hundred offspring in her lifetime. There was only one female adult Eridani on Mars, plus about twenty adolescents, six of them female. They were all from the same household or "House". The current Eridani Mission on Mars simply wasn't of such a scale as to permit more than one House.

Each male in the household considered himself kingly … no … *godly* in his own right. This probably leads to some pretty interesting dinner parties, I'm sure. Unfortunately, the Voiya and Vesna have no concept of God, or deity, or *final cause* within their understanding. It simply didn't interest them to look at the origin of life and everything. They saw no gain or profit in such musings or theological considerations. Besides, the origin of life for the Voiya, based on appearances, was Eben scientists.

The next two casts were quite different from the Voiya. While the Voiya considered the Trigla and the Vesna to be equivalent, within those two casts the Vesna considered themselves to be superior to the Trigla. The Vesna knew they were superior to the Voiya as well, but they would never think that out loud. The Trigla, the servant cast, happened to agree with the Vesna on the point of their superior stature/nature, and were happy to agree. Any screw-ups were the fault of the Vesna, "hey, we were just doing what we were told". The Eben actually considered the Trigla to be very human like in temperament and societal constructs; though much more laid back and easy going individually, and as a society.

The Trigla are those in service to the care and well-being of the Eridani Masters and the Vesna. The Trigla are household servants, cooks, chauffeurs, tailors, shopkeepers, builders, skilled factory workers, and professional warriors. They are also one of the species that the Eben had used in the original hybridization experiments that had created the Eridani to begin with. When the Eridani made good their escape from the Eben, as soon as they had built up their numbers and acquired some space travel, they immediately captured and subjugated the Trigla out of spite. The Trigla have been a cast within the Eridani society ever since. Needless to say, there are a great many

150

hidden smiles and unshared mirthful thoughts amongst the Trigla when one of the Eridani Masters gets on about the superiority of their race, of their cast.

The Trigla look nothing like the Voiya. They average, as I said, about 40 cm taller than the Voiya, they have extremely long necks, and their heads aren't as disproportionately large. The Trigla are actually a sensitive and compassionate race, for the most part. Compassion doesn't dominate their thoughts, but they often feel bad about the things they are involved in; kidnapping other races and performing experiments on them, and so on and so forth. The Trigla have to keep these feelings hidden. There are stories of Trigla being thrown in acid vats along with drones, merely for showing compassion to one of the experimentation subjects.

The Vesna are a race with a single gender. There is no chromosomal difference in the Vesna, they are all female but have what humans would call male dominant traits. They have no outward sexual organs, and don't engage in any form of sexual activity. Reproduction is an endocrinal induced asexual process and can occur at any time, with no warning, after a Vesna reaches maturity. Occasionally, a Vesna adolescent will begin to show female dominant traits, as humans would define them. Vesna adolescents that develop this *disease*, as they see it, are immediately terminated. They don't have a problem with females in other races; they just see this trait as defective within the Vesna culture. The Vesna also have no skin pigmentation. Their epidermis is evenly gray-white throughout their entire race, though the skin of older Vesna tends to darken slightly. The tone of the skin is usually the easiest way to determine which of the Vesna in a pod of five (usually), is the Mahal, or the leader of the pod.

The Vesna are the intelligentsia of the three casts of Eridani society. The Vesna don't "hate" the way the Voiya and drones do. They don't suffer from compassion and caring the way the Trigla do. The Vesna are nature's perfect embodiment of indifference; they are nature's perfected example of sociopathic behaviour. Vesna have a well-defined concept of what is right and wrong, however, they simply don't care about right and wrong. The Vesna are the scientist, the doctors, the researchers, the inventors, the architects, the engineers, the designers, and the warriors' officers. The Vesna are responsible for all the mechanical, medical, and scientific advancements of the Eridani; including the genetic research that has been going on for more than a millennia. They are also responsible for the governmental and political machinations required by a large society. The Vesna come up with the ideas, the Voiya rubberstamp them, and the Trigla carry them out. It's a perfectly symbiotic relationship without competition for primacy. The Voiya, the Eridani Masters, well, they generally just strut around imperiously and yell a lot.

151

Earth culture through the 20th and 21st centuries would be familiar with the Vesna, by reputation if not appearance. Whenever there is a story of a UFO abduction and the abductees reported medical procedures by long-faced, white-skinned, indifferent aliens; it is the Vesna that are being described.

All Eridani Masters, the Voiya, are telepathic to a point. They have to be aware of an individual being to establish connection; but once that connection is established, they can often exert control over that being and retain the ability to reconnect with that being at any time. This is how humans are often able to be abducted. The often reported paralysis is simply caused by a Voiya, somewhere in proximity, exerting mental control over them. One of two exceptions to that rule is the Vesna. The Voiya can communicate with the Vesna but have, so far, been unable to control them like they do with humans. There is a trick to escaping that telepathic control over a being, however, it requires careful instruction and takes practice. Telepathy is how the Voiya Masters communicate with drones, exclusively. They only use their voices communicating with non-telepathic species, such as the Trigla, and that is only out of necessity. Usually they just thought-speak into the Trigla's mind to communicate. The Voiya exclusively communicate via telepathy with others in Eridani society, unless they are really, really, *really* pissed off. Then the social norms and niceties go out the window. The drones themselves are slightly telepathic. They can communicate simple thoughts and images amongst each other, but cannot force their thoughts on another, as the Voiya can. They cannot receive the thoughts of any other race except the Voiya and the Vesna. While the drones cannot project their thoughts to the Voiya, the Voiya and Vesna can easily read their thoughts.

Trigla are not the slightest bit telepathic, and don't want to be either.

The Vesna, are the most powerful of the telepaths in this horde. No Vesna has actually spoken out loud for several hundred years. They communicate and share complex ideas and concepts solely through telepathic contact. However, they have to be in very close proximity to do this. They have a maximum telepathic range of about 7 metres, much closer than the Voiya range of about 200 metres. However, the Vesna have an unlimited telepathic range when communicating with other Vesna. There is a whole section of Vesna in the Eridani Society whose sole job is to provide communication links with the many outposts and research stations in these two arms of the Milky Way galaxy. They communicate Vesna to Vesna, and then pass on the information to messengers that pass on the messages locally.

Lowest on the totem pole of Eridani society are the drones. In fact, the drones aren't actually considered part of Eridani society. To put quite a fine point on it, the Voiya do not consider the drones to be Eridani. They aren't even clones or clone descendants. The drones are genetically engineered life forms that started out as a form of semisentient plant, one that had a lot of genetic monkeying around (something the Vesna were very experienced with, though I wouldn't say all that good at). The drones are grown from vine pods in maturation tanks, reaching maturity of development and size in about four Terran months. They are then painfully severed from the vine stalks as they are brought to consciousness, and then taken to an education facility. Here they are taught how to understand the Masters, how to communicate when permitted, and how to perform the skills and functions required of them.

Many debates about the drones had taken place in Vesna circles over the centuries. The Vesna consider the drones to be sentient creatures, but barely so. There is no concept of supreme deity or of a Bsirutaeben soul in the Voiya mind. Therefore, there is not much more consideration given to the drones by the Eridani Masters; other than that a functioning drone is a useful tool. There is no such thing as medical treatment for a drone. There is no palliative care, no succour or nursing back to health of a damaged or injured drone. There is no burial for drones. Damaged drones and drones that fail to adequately carry out their Master's Order of Action are simply tossed in vats of acid, to be dissolved. Sentient or not, drones feel pain. The Voiya lack of consideration, therefore, is an even further incentive, beyond obedience and loyalty, to be successful. Destroying a damaged, useless, or disappointing drone is no hardship for the Masters. They are very easily replaced. Proper caloric intake and lighting are vital to the drones' overbearing survival; but they have no culture, other than the ever-present mindset of servitude. Many drones simply die from old age, when their circulatory systems simply wear out. At any given time, each of the Eridani Masters average a den of two hundred active drones with a daily revolving door of new drones arriving, while useless drones are being dissolved in the acid vats. Dissolving of these damaged drones, or drones that have failed their Master, occurs daily; even to this day.

The small size of the single Voiya household, or "House", meant that there were only about 2,000 of the drones on Mars. There are, however, over 30,000,000 active drones in the Eridani Dominion.

After four months in an education facility, a new drone is then handed over to the Drone Wrangler in the household of the Eridani Master that owns the drone. The genetic monkey-business of the drones' development has produced two significant traits that are common to all drones, without exception. The first trait is that all drones are blindly and unfalteringly loyal to their Master. A drone cannot conceive of violating their Master's Order of Action. In the rare instances where this has happened, no true blood Eridani would even consider admitting that it *had* happened, because the concept of an Eridani Masters' order not being followed to the letter is, well, inconceivable.

The second trait common to all drones is that they exist in a persistent state of hatred and rage of anything that is *not* of *their* Master. This trait is, coincidentally, also shared by all Voiya, adolescent or adult, both male and female. It is not uncommon for a group of drones to attack and kill another group of drones from a different household, for no other reason than they came into view. The Voiya are much better at showing restraint, though they have the same urges. For a period of time early on in the development of Eridani society, the Trigla and the Vesna were subject to these unprovoked killings by the drones. Since this definitely caused a problem, every Master issues the same first standing Order of Action to all new drones coming into their household which is, "No Vesna or Trigla may be killed for any reason, unless so ordered by Master". This is always disappointing to the drones, because the drones' highest form of pleasure and excitement is to kill something, kill it slowly, and then watch it die in agony. Consider cattle mutilations, as an example.

I think you can better understand now why the Drone that had an Order of Action to monitor the human, was so consumed with grief and rage at failing the Master. After an orbit and a half and not being able to come up with something positive to salvage the mission, the Drone returned to Teviot Vallis and reported what had happened. Telling a lie was not possible for a drone, given the telepathic connection a Master established to communicate with the drones. Upon arrival, this Drone was immediately taken to audience with Master Rillixiwen of Chernasai. The Master, already by its nature in a state of wrath, ordered the Drone be dissolved and a new Drone was assigned to monitor the human. The Order of Action clearly stated the human was to be studied and not interfered with, as this was the Master's pleasure.

While being led to the closest dissolving tank, the Drone did something unthinkable in drone hives or Eridani society. The Drone made a decision that went against the Master's Order of Action to be dissolved. The Drone broke away from the Drone Wrangler (the Wranglers are always from the Trigla cast), and ran for the hangar bay. The Drone Wrangler, stunned and confused, took a few seconds to process what was happening. By then the Drone was too far ahead of the Wrangler for the Wrangler to stop the Drone.

The Drone had considered how disappointed the Master was with the Drone, and so the Drone decided that if being dissolved was the future, the Drone was at least going to redeem the Master's view of the Drone before that happened. The Drone wanted the Master to truly know how much the Drone cherished the Master. The Drone was going to "do something" about the human, because the Drone did not believe the Master really wanted the human to be alive. The Drone considered that the Master was being manipulated by those other jealous Masters of the household. That was, obviously, the only explanation for the Master's order that the human not be killed.

The human the Drone had been assigned to observe wasn't like one of the abundant research subjects on the humans' homeworld. This human was an aberration, the human was a threat, and the human was something that needed to be destroyed so that the Master would not have to worry about the human. The Drone did not understand that the human presence on Mars was something the Eridani were concerned about because of the human expansion beyond Earth, after they had specifically warned the humans about such actions. Because of the long-reaching implications of the human presence, the Eridani Masters wanted the human and its technology studied as a threat assessment. It was vital to their position and posture in this region of the Orion Arm, that they know if this was a single incident or if these human creatures were beginning an expansion phase. If they were, that would have to be dealt with, somehow.

The Drone jumped into the vessel it had so recently vacated, passed through the hangar bays magnetic curtain, and swooped up from the valley floor. The Drone headed north and easttowards Chasma Boreale.

Chapter 28

Achael HofPin

Achael, Hlef, two of their pod brothers (one human dominant, one Eben dominant), two True-Blood Eben, a few of the human staff, and some of the hybrid residents were all sitting in the large conference room. They all wanted to watch the PDV landing on the big screen. They had gotten notice of it months before. While the Lander explosion had been shocking (and entertaining for some), the PDV landing was taking 5 to 1 odds for a successful landing, 3 to 1 odds for an environmentally induced or mechanical malfunction, and 2 to 1 odds on Eridani interference. This was, after all, the heaviest object that ever landed on Mars by the unsuspecting humans. Weighing in at close to 12 metric tonnes, the Payload Delivery Vehicle was setting a new benchmark, hence the interest at the hybrid base.

Achael had put down a hundred dollars on a successful landing. Her sister, Hlef, had put down a thousand dollars on Eridani interference. Oddly enough, they would both win and the bookmaker would give up bookmaking because of how much he lost to them and the others. The only people that lost on this event were the ones who bet on environmental or mechanical failure.

Achael sipped on the straw in her can of Grape Crush while reaching her hand into Hlef's bowl of buttered popcorn. Barry McMillan, a recently arrived forty-two year old human technician, was telling a joke about a minister, a priest, and a rabbi. Only the humans laughed. Eben culture has a very strong and devout faith in their Supreme Being. The Eben hybrids, as do the True-Blood Eben, consider this Being to be the same Supreme Being a lot of humans worship. Even the most liberal of Eben hybrids didn't muck about when it came to spirituality and religion. It just wasn't done. Barry knew that. Barry was a bit of an asshole.

They all turned their attention to the big screen as the image split into two views. One was from their own satellite in orbit, cloaked of course, that had a view of the Payload Delivery Vehicle. It was impressively large, and those in the room looked forward to seeing how advanced the human technology was in regards to the landing of the big container. The five massive staged RAD assemblies promised quite the fireworks show. While the Habitats that had landed had been a bit bigger in size, they only weighed in at seven metric tonnes each. Both Achael and Hlef had Masters Degrees from AFIT (Air Force Institute of Technology) in Aeronautic Engineering and Astronautic Engineering. That made this arrival of the PDV of special interest to both of them.

The humans on the Mars base were all single, with no families, parents or siblings. Human assignment on the base was until retirement, and those humans that did retire and return to Terra were given government housing for life, in a small, secure, and remote government community in Nevada. It was a nice community, nestled in the hills leading to Mt. Gant, above Walker Lake. A small number of the long serving humans simply opted to stay and live out their life on the Mars base. This was accommodated without much comment by those back on Terra. Having worked at the Hybrid base left a taint on a person for some small minded xenophobes in important positions.

The second view was a pickup (pirating if you will) of the Mar-Sat signal. Most of the hybrid base staff members were not aware of the Jalopy-Sat. Its own counterdetection status was in itself a testament to human technological advancement. The Mar-Sat feed showed the lone human colonist walking towards the previously landed cargo containers. Achael, Hlef, their human dominant brother Khlam, and Eben dominant brother Ahshuun, made small talk with a couple of the humans at the table. They watched the lone colonist standing there by his rover and then hopping up to sit on it.

That was when Helf leaned forward squinting at the screen. "Hey ...", she paused, brushing her curly brown hair out of her eyes, and then slowly pointed at the screen, "Do you see what I see?" The room went dead silent as everyone leaned a bit closer to look at the large half-picture.

Achael saw the "shimmer" of air immediately. It was like she had been slapped. She had watched the encounter earlier that day and it pissed her off, she was afraid for that lone human. She liked the human, liked what he was doing, and liked his chutzpah for coming to Mars alone. She didn't think he was an idiot like Hlef thought. Achael admired his bravery. She had thought for a long time that détente be-damned, the humans should tell the Eridani to kiss their ass and start going back to the Moon. She wanted the humans to become a spacefaring species. As many troubles as the humans had on their homeworld, they were basically good and compassionate people. They liked exploring, and they liked helping others. That desire to altruistically help others was a rarity in the three galaxies. Achael wished many of the other races would take a page from humanity's book. Achael set down her can of pop and leaned forward more in her seat.

"Bastards." Not one to use rough language, everyone looked at her then looked back at the screen. Achael rapidly drummed her fingers on the table as Hlef watched her.

"What are you thinking Sis?" was Hlef's question.

Achael looked at her, "We have to do something. We can't let it end this way."

"What do you mean", then added air quotes, "end this way?"

Looking at the shimmer on the screen and then turning her gaze towards Hlef, she said, "The only reason that Eridani *thing* is that close to the human is because it's going to do something, something bad. It's either going to kill him or destroy the ship that's landing."

Hlef simply replied, "Or both".

Hlef had been starting to worry about Achael the last couple of days, ever since that idiot arrived and survived the explosion of his space ship. Achael had been incessant in talking about what he was doing, his motivations, what it meant for humanity, how they would proceed after this, blah, blah, blah. Achael was a good and compassionate woman. She was intelligent, discerning in most things, and strong willed with a very strong emotional stability. However, she had a fault. Hlef knew from their thirty-nine years together that Achael would get something in her mind about someone, and then fail to see anything but that.

Hlef thought that Achael might be attracted to this human for some stupid reason, and it worried her. There had been that silly boy from town that had caught her fancy while attending AFIT. Their six years down-side, so many years ago, had been difficult enough without someone getting close enough to learn things he shouldn't. Then, having learned her lesson about townies, there had been the Captain at AFIT in their last year. Hlef had initially thought he was an okay guy, but then realized he was a playa and simply couldn't get Achael to see it. It took a massive heartbreak for Achael to wake up and since then, she had only allowed Hlef and their brothers Ahshuun, Khlam, and Pinpin (the other Eben dominant brother) to be close to her. Hlef thought Achael was headed for heartbreak again, and would do and say anything to stop it before it happened.

Hlefs reply "or both" had infuriated Achael. She was aware that she and Hlef did not see eye-to-eye on this human. In fact, most of the Eben hybrids thought the human was on a fool's errand. The humans on the base didn't say too much, but they were all secretly rooting for his success.

Achael's inner eyelid slammed shut. The hybrids inner eyelid turned their entire oversized eyeballs into orbs of black onyx. It made them look very Eben, and reminded many of the Eridani as well, specifically the Vesna, but no one dared say that to the hybrids. It would practically be a death sentence to insult them that way. Okay, maybe not a death sentence, but it would definitely be the precursor to an imminent ass-kicking.

The inner eyelid was an Eben trait. Eben had them to help protect their eyes from the bright sun on their homeworld. However, these inner and totally black eyelids also responded to anger and passion in the hybrids. Seeing a hybrid with the inner eyelid closed meant either they were in the thrall of passion, or someone was about to get hurt, and hurt bad.

Achael stood up rapidly, knocking her chair backwards, so did Hlef. Seeing Achael's rage also piqued Hlef's emotions and her inner eyelid slammed shut as well. Achael and Hlef loved each other; they were sisters after all. In Eben culture, being family was a bond with deepness and commitment that even the most committed of human families simply couldn't comprehend. It's known throughout this galaxy how strongly and deeply the Eben love their family members. It's also well known that no siblings can fight like Eben siblings. Especially two Eben female siblings. It should tell you something that the deadliest and most feared of military units in the Eben world was an all-female military special services unit. Entire armies had been known to surrender simply for the reason that this unit, called the PinShaah, showed up on the battlefield.

When the rest of the room saw their eyes go jet black, the room quickly emptied, leaving the two women alone. Everyone that had left the room hovered in the hallway while the on-duty security team was called. Even the True-Blood Eben on the base stayed out of the room. When the security team learned what the problem was, they went back to the armoury for larger weapons than just their sidearm. An Eben, especially an Eben hybrid, in a state of rage, could be very unpredictable. That unpredictability was something the Eben scientists had not been able to program out of them. It was the only thing that kept the hybridization program isolated to this one small outpost, instead of it taking place on a larger scale.

"I'm going to stop this" Achael said in a quiet voice, referring to the Eridani presence at the human colony site.

"No, you are not. You are going to sit down and stop being syrupy over this human *idiot*" was Hlef's equally quiet response.

After a momentary pause, Achael warned her, "Get out of my way, Hlef. This is my decision. I'm not letting that drone kill that man. I've had enough of this. They blow up his space ship, they terrorize him, and now that *thing* is going to do something worse. I'm going to stop it."

Hlef took half a step closer to her sister. They stared straight into each other's solid black eyes. "Wake-up sis. You've got a bug up your ass about this human and I don't know why. It's just another one of your pathetic 'save the animals' causes like you had in Uni. That idiot colonist is not one of us, he's not part of this base, and he's not part of this mission. You have no responsibility for him. He was warned."

"I. Don't. *Care*." Achael punctuated each word like it was its own sentence. Pausing to see if her sister would relent, she continued in a low voice, "Get out of my way Hlef; get out of my way now."

Ahshuun took this moment to gingerly walk back into the room. He held his long arms up with his palms facing forward. and a cheesy smile on his small mouth, "Girls, come on. Let's all be friends before ..."

Achael and Hlef turned to look at him at the same time. In unison, they said very quietly, "Get out." His eyes went wider and his face fell in sudden realization at what a silly thing he had just done. That was all he needed, he turned so fast he tottered, and then hightailed it out of the room, shaking his head at the others in the hallway. The crowd of people pulled back even further from the two doors to the room.

Hlef turned back to look at her sister, reached out and took hold of her shoulders, "Achael, I love you. You are my sister and I will die for you, but I am not going to let you attack that drone and destroy the détente we've had with the Eridani for the last thirty years. Let go of this puppy dog obsession and *grow up*."

In retrospect, that was what triggered Achael. That was exactly what did it. When Hlef told her sister to "grow up", that was the trigger. The events of the next few minutes would be talked about in hushed whispers for years. The security camera recordings were immediately downloaded and locked away; and to this day, have never been viewed by *anyone*. The level of destruction that occurred in the next few minutes was stupefying, especially when you considered it came from two average sized women; alien hybrid women.

Now some of you may be familiar with the term "catfight". To say this was merely a "catfight" would not be fair to either cats, nor to fighting in general. As I said before, no one can fight like siblings, especially Eben siblings. Compounding this was the fact that the two Eben siblings were women. It's well known on many worlds that one does not interfere with an Eben catfight; even the most hardy of warriors will turn on their heels and walk away from that thought. It *really is all that much worse* when the two Eben women are human-dominant hybrids. They have the Eben mentality, the Eben fierceness, the genetically inherited warrior reflexes, and they have human bulk and size.

There is the screaming, as well.

When Eben are in battle, specifically in close-up combat, the Eben Battle Scream instills such terror that enemies will flee or surrender just to make it stop. Likened to 1,000 finger nails on chalkboard by the few humans that have heard it, the sound could actually make the ears bleed in some races, including humans, if they were close enough. If it was closer than 2 metres, it could rupture human eardrums. For the Eben, it doesn't bother them; for the

Hybrids, only slightly so. Many warriors of old who went up against the Eben always wore some alien version of ear plugs and would flatly refuse to go into battle without the ear plugs. The Eben battle scream is just as effective over radios as it is in person.

With the screaming that started as the two women launched at each other, there also came the crashing and smashing of objects. Any object at hand can become a deadly weapon for an Eben. A few minutes into this flat out two-person brawl, one of the security members decided enough was enough. The women had had their fun and it was time to stop. The almost 2 metre tall, two-hundred and forty pound body building Special Forces Army Sergeant Tucker, handed his large weapon to his partner, stuck his fingers in his ears, and then walked up and stood at the door. He yelled in the room, "Ladies! Enough!" The only thing the people in the hallway saw was the blur of two fists connecting with him squarely in the middle of this face, and then the Special Forces Army Sergeant tipping over backwards like a felled tree. It would take two full days in the medical unit before he could return to duty, bruised and still sore.

Shortly after the unconscious Special Forces Sergeant had been dragged out of the danger zone, the battle erupted into the hallway. Every person there turned with a look of fear on their face and ran around the corner at the end of the corridor, empting the hallway outside the conference room. I think the fact that the Base Commander and his 2IC (second in command) were in the crowd that was running away in fear, was the real reason why the surveillance videos were locked away.

Achael had a thick wooden leg from the conference table in her hand. Hlef had a cinder-block in her hand. The two women had black ichor streaming from cuts on their foreheads, faces, and arms. Eben blood is black and sticky, much thicker than human blood. They both stood panting and staring at each other for a moment, then dropped what they were holding, and went fisticuffs.

It was a blur of swinging arms and legs. Had anyone stuck around long enough to watch it, they would have found it reminiscent of the old Saturday morning cartoons. The ones where the Roadrunner has his way with Wyle E. Coyote, after Wyle E. Coyote's latest Acme gadget fails to perform to spec. The Eben Battle Scream had, at this point, given away to simple screams of rage, laced with a few "you fraking bitch" thrown in as punctuation. Things seemed to be starting to slow down to those brave enough to peer around the corner from the end of the hall. Without any prelude or warning, the fight took another turn for the worse when Achael screamed at Hlef that she was a "drone fraker". That was definitely worse than telling them they looked like the Eridani. It was just so, so much worse.

In the end, the battle lasted twelve full minutes. It cost one conference table, two large screen monitors, six chairs, two book cases, a microwave oven, a refrigerator, three light fixtures, several gaping holes in the cinderblock walls, and the services of one Special Forces Army Sergeant (but just for a few days). The fight created two new doorways in the cinderblock walls of the conference room as well as destroying one solid wood door. That was all before they moved out into the hallway. It was after the smashing of two benches, a desk, and the catering office window in the hallway that the human dominant hybrid Base Commander finally had enough. He stepped around the corner, cleared his throat and at the top of his voice shouted, "ACHAEL! HLEF! STOP THIS! RIGHT NOW!"

Both women turned towards him and dropped to one knee on the floor with one hand resting on the floor, and one arm swept in the air behind their backs. The Base Commander turned ghost white, did an about face and sacrificing dignity for a much stronger survival instinct, he scurried around the corner as fast as he could without actually running.

The women had dropped into the Eben Death Stance. The Death Stance was an ancient battle tactic of the Eben. It made the opponent think the Eben warrior was tired and needed to rest, had given up, wanted to talk, or was confused and didn't know what to do. In fact, the Eben Death Stance usually indicated that something's life was about to end, quickly and violently. The Death Stance was designed to throw the opponent psychologically off balance, just a little. When an Eben went into the Death Stance, it lasted only a few seconds. They would then come out of it launching an all-out final physical assault, piercing the air with the Eben Battle Scream. This assault would be one-on-one, it would be in close quarters, and in almost every single case; it would be final for the opponent or the Eben. The Death Stance assault was always to the death.

The two women didn't do this though. They stayed in the Eben Death Stance for probably a full minute, panting, just staring at the floor in front of them. At the same time, they both realized how far they had gone, and both knew it had to stop. After some of the adrenalin slowed down, Achael looked sideways at Hlef and said, "I'm sorry Sis".

This surprised Hlef, she looked at her sister confused and then suddenly realized what had just happened. Achael had thrown Hlef psychologically off balance, followed immediately by her fist in the middle of Hlefs face. Hlef fell backwards, hit the wall and slid to the floor unconscious, as Achael stood up and ran full out for the hangar bay. The remnants of the security team looked at the Base Commander for direction as she ran towards them, turned the corner and headed away from them down the crossing corridor. The human dominant Base Commander threw his hands up in the air and shrugged his shoulders, saying wearily, "Let her go. Let her get it out of her system. She'll calm down before she gets there".

Chapter 29

Ernst & Frankie

18 Minutes, 2 Seconds Later

Frankie leaned over and whispered, "You didn't let me tell them ... WHY??"

Ernst closed his eyes, shook his head and ignored Frankie. The question was rhetorical anyways. They kept flicking their eyes back and forth between the Mar-Sat image on the big screen, and the Jalopy-Sat image on their own screens. Without announcement, Carrie was suddenly pulling up a chair behind them and between them. She leaned forward, her shoulders pressed against their shoulders and each hand resting lightly on their collar bones. With the intensity of her stare and pursed lips, she quietly dared them to say a single *verdammte* word.

When Mike had jumped off the cargo deck of Big Dawg and crouched down, most of those watching thought he had twisted his ankle. Then there was a bright streak and the ground exploded in front of him. It was about that moment when the room exploded with shouts and cries, and people trying to run around to do things but not knowing what to run around and do. Karl had to yell at them a few times to remind them that at this particular moment they were merely observers because the signal delay meant that whatever was going to happen, had already happened. He reminded them they were simply playing catch-up and even so, they had no real-time assistance to offer Mike. So sit down, shut-up and face your screens. Not exactly Management 101, but sometimes leadership through YELLING-REALLY-LOUDLY had its place. It was during Karl's rant that Carrie joined the two spooks.

Carrie saw Arno looking around for her and caught his eye. He had a quizzical look on his face, and gave her a 'wassup' head toss. She nodded her head back and to the left, beckoning him to come over. Ernst and Frankie started to protest to her quietly. She patted them both on the shoulder and with acerbic sweetness said, "Meine Herren, are we really going to do zis? Right now? In ze same room as everyone else?"

Ernst and Frankie both slumped their shoulders, and turned back to the screen. The secret squirrel stuff was now over. Jalopy-Sat would be common knowledge to the Mission Control staff. There was nothing they could do about that. Ernst sighed, reached over to his keyboard, tickled the keys a few times, and the Jalopy-Sat's main image caused the big screen at the front of the room to go into split screen mode. It was showing everyone a brand new angle that was clearer, crisper, and tighter than the other view. There was a murmur of questioning and heads turning this way and that. Everyone was familiar with what Mar-Sat could see, its angles, etc.; and there was a difference from that familiar image, to what the new image looked like. This was something new around Mars, and they had access to it. Ernst caught Karl looking his way and giving him the thumbs up. Neither Karl nor Hans had ever thought the stealth satellite would remain unknown for long.

In the few seconds all of this took place, everyone saw Mike crouching behind Big Dawg and peeking around the corners, looking for the shimmer they could all see plainly.

After Ernst had sent the first message, he had sat there for a few moments considering what options there were. Finally, he made his decision. He had sat straight up in his chair, typed a sequence of commands on his keyboard, and after confirming the commands were on their way to Mars, he sent Mike a second message, only two words long. Then, he was a spook after all, made sure his screen was clear of all references to Castle Cellar. That happened just moments before Carrie joined them.

Chapter 30

Dust Up

I couldn't see it. It had disappeared. I looked right, then looked left, then turned a full circle where I was standing and I didn't see ...

Ahhhh, there it was! I caught the shimmer between two of the dropped cargo containers. I stepped to the back of the rover, to put the rover between myself and the shimmer or more correctly, the cloaked alien space ship. I hefted the rocks in my hands, I felt stupid holding rocks while facing an alien space ship. Time to make a decision. If I stayed here, I had very little cover and was overly exposed. I really wished I'd brought the energy weapon at this point. I wouldn't make that mistake again. At least I hoped I would have the chance to not make that mistake again.

I decided to get out of the wide open, and into the narrow open. If I could get to the cargo drops I could gain some cover, what I was going to do after that was beyond me; but at this point, it was one step at a time. I jumped around the corner of the rover, and went into the hockey run to get to the cargo drops.

The Drone

Arriving over the ice field again, the Drone immediately moved the vessel far enough away that the Drone could barely see the human's place. The Drone sat there for several hours waiting and watching. The Drone noticed a shimmer in the air, and watched another cloaked scout vessel from the Eridani base fly around the human colony, and then start searching farther afield. That vessel was obviously looking for the Drone. Since the Drone's vessel was cloaked, motionless, and this far from the human site, it wouldn't be likely that the Drone's vessel would be located. The Drone had disconnected its transponder.

Eventually the Drone saw the human scum walking towards the row of human ships a little way away from the main living units, south of them, south towards Teviot Vallis, south towards the Eridani complex.

The burning anger and seething hatred was amplified by this. The Drone moved the vessel much closer to where the human was. The Drone wanted to know what the human was up to before the Drone ended the human's existence in the flash of a directed energy plasma explosion. There would be a great deal of gratification for the Drone, to see the human die. *PAIN, PAIN; IT WILL FEEL PAIN; IT WILL FEEL SUCH PAIN*, thought the Drone. That would wait though. The Drone would see what the human was doing so it could triumphantly return to the Master with news of the human's actions before it was obliterated (double entendre intended).

The secondary weapon on the Drone's vessel was one that used the mass and composition of the target to destroy the target. In its low setting, it would only affect biological material. At the low setting, hitting a human would cause indescribable agony, as the beam slowly excited the human's molecular structure to the point that molecular bonds started to fail. A long and agonizing death for the human, that would definitely please the Drone. However, the Drone went for the high setting. In the high setting, this weapon focused an intense beam of energy that caused the target's mass to instantly ionize, and since the ionizing matter, with instantly cascading molecular bond failure, was not contained in a magnetic field; all the objects potential energy instantly converted to release the inherent molecular energy as an electrical plasma ball. The plasma ball, still not contained and allowed to go as it would, would explode. The beauty of the design was that only a powerful energy source is needed for the emitter. The fuel, the explosive material, was the target itself.

The human was now sitting on the bigger of the two robots. The Drone hovered the vessel, watching the human for quite a while. The human scum was just sitting there. Was it aware of the Drone? Was it toying with the Drone? Was it setting a trap for the Drone? The Drone would never be accused of underestimating an enemy. The Drone took paranoia to a new height at the best of times; and this was not the best of times.

After spending too much time watching the human taunt the Drone with what had to be a rudimentary trap at best, the Drone started to slowly move the vessel closer to the human. The time had come for the human to die. As the Drone gleefully, with such focused intent, slowly approached the human from behind for the kill shot, the human suddenly jumped down off the robot, and hid from view.

A string of Eridani curse words screamed through the Drone's mind. *HUMAN THINK STUPID HUMAN TRAP SPRUNG?* The Drone stopped a short distance from the human, activated the directed energy weapon on its vessel, and then fired a burst of ionizing high-energy at the human. This weapon generated such an intensely powerful electric charge that when it left the emitter on the forward portion of the vessel, it delivered about three petawatts of energy on contact, at this range. Consider that a lightning bolt has about half a gigawatt of power, this energy beam was delivering roughly six thousand times more energy in a microburst passing only a few centimetres over the human's head.

The energy beam missed the human, but exploded the ground behind the human. Basic battle tactics flooded through the Drone's properly trained and conditioned mind. Fire, move, find cover, fire, and repeat.

Achael

Achael had run the whole way to the hangar bay where the six scout ships, four transports, two much bigger galactic transit vessels, and a myriad of research vessels were docked. The scout ships and transports were armed with defensive weapons. The galactic transit vessels were also armed, but much more heavily. It could also be called a heavy bomber. In fact, they were called "transit" vessels to keep those humans who might become "in the know", at ease. In reality, they were two old, but still very much serviceable, Eben Heavy Cruisers. However, they had never been used in this capacity in their two hundred years on Mars, and everyone on the base never wanted them to be used in that capacity. A method of deterrence was, however, at the end of the day, conducive to peacefulness.

As stated, the Eben are known as amongst the fiercest if not *the* fiercest warriors in the three galaxies, when their ire was raised. The galactic transports, in military configuration were a force to be reckoned with. So much so that even the Eridani feared the mere presence of them on the planet. It's probably what kept them in line and the détente in place.

Achael ran so softly and burst through the door so explosively that her Eben dominant brother Pinpin, the duty officer, came clear out of his chair with a yell of surprise while jettisoning a stack of papers in the air; leaving them to flutter down slowly in the low Martian gravity.

"Sis! What the hell??" he screamed through his office door at her while throwing his long spindly arms in the air.

Achael stopped right in front of his office door, not having even broken a sweat but breathing heavily with anger. "Ship. Now." Her eyes were still onyx black and her long-fingered hands were clenching and releasing at her side. In their years growing up together, Achael and Pinpin had been as close as she and Hlef were now. He had his noggin banged around enough times, in her surprise ambush games, to not miss the signs of the state she was in at this moment. Pinpin stopped picking up the papers, and looked even closer at her.

"Wow, you really are pissed. Was that you and Hlef I heard screaming?" he said as he looked towards the hallway doors, realizing now that Hlef had not followed Achael.

"Do you have a scout ready or not?"

Pinpin and Achael (as well as Hlef) held the rank of Major in the United States (Exo) Air Force. There was no ordering to be done in that respect. Pinpin just hated being bossed around by his sister, either of them. Pinpin looked at her for a moment, sizing things up. He straightened his dark blue jumpsuit, and stepped around the desk. Drawing himself up to his full 140 centimetre height, standing there in front of his 160 centimetre tall sister, he snapped his inner eyelids shut. They both stood there as two Eben; not two humans, not two hybrids. Putting on his most authoritative voice, he said in True-Blood Eben dialect, "Rahushi yi uhf spiksht?" (*What if I say no?*)

Achael took one step towards him.

Pinpin's inner eyelid opened immediately revealing what any 1950's teenage girl would have described as "dreamy blue eyes, just dreamy". That was a trait of all the hybrids, they all had dreamy blue eyes. He jumped backwards and started waving his hands in front of him, "KIDDING! JUST KIDDING!"

Achael took another step towards him, "Now is not the time Pinpin. Give me a scout ship NOW!!!!"

"Number two! Bay number two! It's preflighted and ready to go! Honest Achael, it's yours, go, take it!" Pinpin was not a stupid man. He had tested Achael looking for any sign of backing down. There was none. He knew from many, many past experiences he could not take her. Even the most advanced Eben battle tactics would not work on either Achael or Hlef with their relatively overpowering size. Achael and Hlef were both somewhat of a prodigy when it came to hand-to-hand combat. There was no hybrid or True-Blood Eben on the base that could take them in a fair fight. The humans were too smart to try. Well, the humans that had been there more than a few weeks. Every once in a while a new arrival would have a couple beers too many, and decide to show the "half-breeds" what was what. The sisters' three hybrid brothers almost always visited the recalcitrant fool in the infirmary the next day to give them the full rundown on Achael and Hlef. They felt it was their duty to keep the intergalactic feathers smoothed down when Helf and Achael ruffled them up.

Achael spun on her heels and parted with, "You're the brother that got the smarts in the family, you know that?" Achael loved Pinpin as much as she loved all her siblings. She so very much didn't want to hurt him, but she also would not have hesitated had he stood in her way as Hlef had. The image of Hlef hitting the floor unconscious flashed through her mind. She really hoped Hlef would be okay and not too pissed when she got back from dealing with this Eridani threat to the human. Of course, such fighting was second nature to them as children, as a form of play and energy release. It didn't carry the same connotations for inter-relationship solidity or have the cultural apprehension that such behaviour generated in humans. Eben children fought very, very rarely in a state of anger. In fact, they avoided fighting in anger because of their propensity to inflict great damage on one-another in such states. Still, that image of Hlef was on her mind. The image of Hlef's surprise, then the image of her hitting the wall hard and falling to the floor unconscious.

While that image ate at her a little bit, it didn't deter her. or stop her. If anything, it edged her on. To stop now would have made it worth nothing. She knew Hlef was right. She knew that she should mind her own damn business and stay out of this. The human did decide to come to Mars, notwithstanding what might happen here. She knew he had been warned. Achael and the others knew he had been given a very limited briefing by General Rosewood, overall Commandant of the Mars mission. She should stop, turn around, and let him sort it out himself.

She paused as she approached the dark grey triangular scout ship. It hovered on its antigravity supports while two umbilical lines kept the systems warmed up and ready. The scout ship in bay three was also in the same ready state. They could be in atmo in under twenty seconds from the sound of an alarm. The duty pilots were in the ready room twenty feet away, both of them, currently, human dominant hybrids. She stood there wondering if she shouldn't just forget it and turn around. The image of Hlef was really playing on her mind now.

Then she thought of the grey ball hovering around the human man out there. Before the fight had moved into the hallway, the one remaining working monitor had shown the flash of the Eridani energy weapon. It had shown the image of the human alone, crouched down behind his rover robot. That image came to the forefront of her mind. It had been so clear that she imagined she could see his face through the visor on this surface suit helmet. The thought of him facing this alone filled her chest with burning rage, at least it felt like rage. It definitely burned in her though. The anger returned in force. She thought of the drone in the little Eridani scout craft. It was always drones in those craft as the Trigla and the Vesna were too big, and the Voiya to self-important.

The anger and hatred towards the Eridani twisted and roiled inside her chest. She would have to be careful. She would have to be diplomatic. The hybrids and humans on the base had been in a state of mostly peaceful détente with the Eridani mission on Mars for thirty years. They allowed each other's presence on the planet without interference. Whatever she did, she would have to be very careful; and she could be very careful when she got there. She moved again, sprinting to the craft. She disconnected the two umbilical feeds, and then moved to the almost invisible and ever-so-slight recess near the nose of the craft. The two duty pilots stood in the ready room doorway watching her. Pinpin had already alerted them. She put three of her fingers in the recess, in a triangular pattern. If there was no pilot in the craft, this hand position caused the ships internal TransMat to move the one fingering the symbol inside.

The disorientation cleared in moments, and Achael stepped forward in the small, but not cramped, cabin. There was no real sense of transition when moved by the TransMat, first you were one place, and then a moment later you were simply someplace else. It caused a slight sense of disorientation for those experienced. The first time a True-Blood human used it; there were usually vomiting, vertigo, and stomach cramps that followed.

Achael sat in the pilot's seat of the craft, and then placed the palms of her hands on the touchpads of the controller units, on the arms of the chair. The advanced Eben control system then read a combination of her body's electrical system, her finger movements, and her brain waves to pair with her; much like a blue tooth device pairing. From that point on, until she exited the ship, it would respond to her thoughts and hand motions instantly; whether she was in the seat or not, with the lag time being measured in a very small number of microseconds.

Riding its antigravity field, the scout ship, the "Dart" as they called it, moved out into the central transit corridor, and rapidly accelerated towards the hangar bay doors. As she had started moving the ship, she had commanded the doors to open. Cutting it hair close by tilting her ship a few degrees sideways to reduce its profile width, she accelerated through the gravity curtain, barely missing the hard doors. She emerged into the deep floor of Shalbatana Vallis (7.33 degrees North, 317.91 degrees East), and then pulled up into a steep climb, going almost straight up before doing a turning overhead roll resulting in a vector almost due north. Since she needed to get there fast, but wasn't sure if the drone's scout ship was alone or not, she decided to come into the human colony site from about 100 kilometres out. She used the Folding Drive to move her almost instantly 5,000 kilometres north of her base, and then back at normal dimensional speed, she rapidly accelerated to just 1,200 kilometres per hour; almost one and a half times the speed of sound on Mars (879 km/h at the Martian datum). She wasn't wasting time.

Like Mike, Achael had also completely forgotten about the PDV arriving in a few more minutes.

Mike

As the alien ship moved overhead and into a new position, the Priority Message indicator came up in my HUD. *Damn it, what now?* I thought to myself. *The alien ship trying to kill me is the real priority here, but if this message is what I think it is, I really need to read it.* Then it dawned on me. Dammit, I forgot about the voice interface in the suit's COM system. Squatting by cargo drop #5, I looked down quickly to the controller attached to my left arm, and pressed the VOX button three times. I heard the soothing and calm, perhaps even a bit sexy, female voice in my helmet.

"VOX activated. Awaiting Command."

"Priority Message, Display" was my response as I lifted my head and scanned around for the alien ship. A bolt of energy passed between cargo drop #3 and #4, and I barely got my head out of the way. As the ground was exploding behind me, I was up once again and skittering around to the other side of the cargo container. The HUD displayed the message for me, "PLATFORM ACTIVATED"

"Oh Frak No!"

"Command not recognized. Please restate you command," her soothing voice said.

The alien ship wobbled a bit, and moved side-to-side. As it started to transit around the large cargo drops, I waited for it to hit a blind spot and then ran to the opposite corner of drop #4.

"Castle Cellar, Status," I said urgently. The message on my HUD was from Ernst. He had obviously activated the weapons platform so that a weapon could be fired. Castle Cellar was the term the VOX recognized for the weapons platform. I knew immediately there was no way I was going to bring a Thermobaric down on the area of the supply drops. Even though the Habitats were outside the 300 metre projected blast radius, I still wouldn't take that chance. It was still too close for my Earth-oriented mind. There was too much in the cargo drops that I needed to set up the colony properly, and to survive here.

The alien ship moved left and right, I guess it was trying to decide which side it wanted to kill me from. I kept jigging left and right in the opposite directions, while crouched behind the cargo drop. I was really thankful at that point I had an Activity Suit for the surface, and not a regular Space Suit. With all this running around and sliding on the regolith, the Kevlar outer jumpsuit had already paid for itself.

I still had the two large rocks in my hand, and decided it was time for Grog the caveman to rage against the machine. I stepped out from behind cargo drop #4, cocked my arm and threw the first rock at the shimmering alien vessel. It went so wild in the low-g that I won't even describe it. Suffice it to say, the next throw would have to be a lot different. It also, unfortunately, revealed my location. Another blast from the alien tore out a chunk of the nacelle skirting, and the side of the container of cargo drop #3 behind me. I turned and ran back around the ship, stopped and reversed my course. I had succeeded in fainting him out. I threw the second rock, it hit the shimmering spot of air. The sexy voice said "Platform Activated. Target Engaged. Bay number one is open. Thermobaric device number one is in prelaunch ready state. Your options are Hold, Safe and Release."

"SAFE! SAFE!" I screamed as I ducked back down, and ran behind cargo drop #4.

"Safe Command is recognized. You must authenticate."

"AUTHENTICATING, ALPHA KILO FIVE TWO SEVEN, AUTHENTICATE!" I said, running cross wise for drop #5.

"Command Authenticated. Thermobaric number one powering down. Launch bay closing," then after a brief pause, "Platform secure."

I watched the alien ship bob up and down a couple times, and do its own herky-jerky jig. Maybe the alien was just taunting me. As I ran back towards the cargo drop I had just been hiding behind, the ground exploded almost under my feet. I went flying forward and hit the ground hard. I didn't hit my head, thanks to the helmet, but the concussion of the impact still winded me. I shook my head and started to lift myself up. I froze, watching the green-and-white baseball cap, being drunkenly blown by the wind, flipping and flopping towards my helmet. I reached out and grabbed it, looking at it with disbelief. This was the baseball cap that Carrie's son, Hindrik, had given me on my last birthday before leaving Terra. I remembered the smile on his face. I had always grabbed his baseball cap from him whenever he was wearing it. For my birthday, he used his savings to buy me my own. I remembered the warmth of both of her boys hugging me, one at a time, wishing me *Alles Gute zum Geburtstag.* That baseball cap was one of the things I had brought with me. I had worn it at almost every day while in transit. I thought it had been lost forever in the explosion. I squeezed it, and looked at it. No burn marks, no soot, just a lot of red dust on it. The baseball cap had survived. I finally realized that after running from the pain for so long, I *wanted* to survive. I *wanted* to live. Enough maudlin distractions, time to put my head back in the game. I jumped to my feet, caught sight of the shimmer of air coming around to bear on me again, and then ran to the other side of the cargo drop I had been heading for.

I rolled up the baseball cap and stuffed it into a pocket on my jumpsuit leg. Crouching down, I took a moment to look around quickly. I figured if there was one, there might be two. Nothing else had fired at me; but then again, I didn't know alien battle tactics. If this had been Terra, the OpFor would have probably gone for some shock and awe. It struck me, that the fact I was only facing *one* of these alien bastards was ... disrespectful. *Hmpf. Frakers.*

"Command. Targeting system. Target designation."

Her silky smooth voice replied, "Target number thirty-eight engaged. Target lock confirmed." Thirty-eight? Oh yeah, it used a sequential target designation system.

"Command, use referential targeting designation."

"Command confirmed. Target number one engaged. Target lock confirmed." I had a bit of a chill for a moment. This appearance of the craft was number thirty-eight. The one earlier in the day would have been number thirty-seven. So what the hell were the other thirty-six ... and when were they? I'd only been here two days!

The alien ship wasn't a shimmer any more. I could see it plainly. It was round-ish, gray and about the size of a cargo van. There was a little nubbin thing sticking out of it like a small pitot tube. I rightly assumed that it was the business end of its weapon. The alien ship seemed to regain control. It buzzed forward over me, then suddenly lost altitude, bounced once hard on the ground, and then lifted back into the air. It swung around behind the line of supply drops, and I lost sight of it. It seemed to be moving a bit slower. I decided right then there would be no retreat. Hell, I just got here. There was no way I was leaving Mars, figuratively or literally. I thought that maybe this alien was sucking me into a trap; but maybe, just maybe, luck, providence, and certainly God were on my side.

I did the hockey-run towards cargo drop #6, the drop closest to the alien bastard. There are two kinds of run that work on Mars. We had worked these out in training, and I confirmed their effectiveness when I sprinted from the cover of Big Dawg. The hockey-run was something I came up with, being Canadian and all, eh? Because of the low-g it's easy to go ass over tea kettle if you try to run on Mars like you are on Terra. The hockey-run was simple. Lean forward until you were starting to fall forward, then turn your feet outwards so the inside edge of your boot was in contact with the regolith, and then skate-run like you were trying to get back over the blue line while your puck carrying teammate went for net. I certainly couldn't afford to be offside today. This precarious running position used forward momentum to keep you from falling. Without the high centre of gravity, you didn't have to worry as much about tripping or momentum imbalance as you would with a normal run. The hockey-run was much more exhausting than the gazelle-run; but it was much faster for short distances, and you were less likely to trip.

"Command, Target Count."

"There is currently one target. Target is engaged."

"Activate new target voice notification," I wanted to know if anything else came up to the site while my back was turned.

"Please state area of compromise."

"Area of compromise is 100 kilometres".

"New target voice notification engaged. Area of compromise is 100 kilometres. Known target has entered area of compromise. Designate target number two. Target number two is tracking."

"What??"

"Target number two is a known target. It is a scheduled supply mission that is in de-orbit deceleration. Second RAD is in burn."

Shit, I'd forgotten all about the PDV. I looked up at the flaming RAD engines coming down far up in the sky. As I looked at it, the RAD assembly cut out, jettisoned and another RAD assembly fired up. That would be the third of five. I looked at the round gray ship, almost in the right spot. I looked down, then started picking up rocks and throwing them. There was one possibility in my favour and suddenly I had to be a gambling man. *Tempus fugit* and I had to act fast. I guess this situation was of the same perilous outcome Pliny the Elder faced when he stated, while rescuing survivors of Pompeii, *fortes fortuna iuvat,* "fortune favours the brave". It was time to be brave, as well as bold. The stakes were my life; and I finally cared about seeing tomorrow.

The Drone

The human had no weapon with it. The human was throwing rocks. The Drone continued to burn with anger, and continued to seethe. *HUMAN WANT TO KILL DRONE; HUMAN TRY TO TRAP DRONE; STUPID TRAP; NO WEAPON; HUMAN MISTAKE; HUMAN MAKE MISTAKE; HUMAN DIE; HUMAN DIE NOW; SHOW HUMAN; SHOW HUMAN SUPERIOR RACE; SHOW HUMAN MASTER BETTER THAN HUMAN; SHOW MASTER DRONE LOYAL; SHOW MASTER DRONE LOOK AFTER MASTER; DRONE KILL HUMAN; KILL HUMAN.* The vessel lurched.

As the Drone fired its next shot at the human, the human managed to avoid being fried and vaporized yet again. The rage boiled over in the Drone, and the Drone started pin-wheeling long grey arms in a haze of frustration and anger with small, but solid fists pounding on instruments and control boxes. A drone would never normally react this way, but this particular Drone was already far off the scope of what was expected from drones. The Drone screamed and screamed with anger and frustration inside the helmet. Even though the Drone didn't have pain receptors in the pin-wheeling arms or hands, the Drone's hands and forearms started to feel numb from the repeated impacts. Finally the tirade stopped, and the Drone got a hold of raging emotions. The small vessel had been bobbing around as a result of the pounding on flight controls; but that was the least of the Drone's problems now.

Achael

Mars' surface raced underneath her unnoticed. Achael was forming attack plans in her head; attack plans for the Eridani ship, contingencies for other Eridani ships if that became necessary. Forming complex battle tactics on-the-fly came like breathing to the Eben. She was also running the political angels of what she was going to do, and what would lessen the impact on the detente.

The cabin filled with Hlef's voice from the Comm Unit, "Achael, stop."

Achael let out a sigh, she didn't realize she had been holding in. She was so very happy to hear Hlef's voice, to know she was okay, "Sis, I'm glad you're okay."

"Come back Turkey," said Helf, using her pet name for Achael. "The Base Commander is ordering you to return as well, if that matters."

"And who is going to look out for the human? He's out there alone, under fire, if he's not already dead."

There was a slight pause, "I feel ya Sis, but orders is orders, know what I'm ...", she had been cut off. Achael started in her seat, and looked at the Comm Unit.

"Ummm, Achael....."

Furrowing her eyebrows, Achael responded, "What is it Hlef?"

"I've just been informed that Mom says to leave you alone."

The Drone

The Drone looked at the ship's instrumentation as lights came on indicating problems from the careless fist pounding episode. All this did was piss off the Drone even further.

The Drone had moved the vessel around the line of ships sitting there, to find cover for the next attack. The Drone didn't need cover as the human had no weapons, but finding cover had been drilled into the Drone for years. The Drone heard a static sound, and then the camouflage indicator went out. The Drone hit the reset button several times, but the system would not reactivate. *HUMAN KNOWS; HUMAN KNOWS NO POINT; CAMOUFLAGE LET CAMERAS SEE, LET ALL HUMANS SEE; LET SEE SUPERIOR RACE KILLING HUMAN; HUMANS KNOW NOT TO COME TO PLANET;*

The Drone moved the vessel up and over top of the human to get a good look before taking up a new position. The human still only had rocks in its hands. Turning the ship so the emitter was facing the human, the Drone saw the human stand up. As more warnings started flashing the Drone depressed the button to send another stream of ionized energy towards the human. Something was wrong with the weapon's power. The charge fired at the human was only one one-hundredth of its normal power. The ground exploded behind the human, sending the human flying through the air. It didn't kill him, it just knocked him down. The Drone raged at the fire-control system.

Earth (18 minutes, 52 seconds later)

Nigara Kusiya, 72 years old, Niiyamahama, Japan - Nigara, long retired from the fishing industry, often snuck into the computer room of his not-too-small house, and went web surfing while his three adult sons ran the fishing boat. They would have been surprised to know he could even turn on the computer, let alone that he had a chat room nickname (Masaki23). Nigara had been following the Mars expedition with the avid interest of a ten year old. He had been watching the feed so he could see firsthand the landing of the next supply module. Now he sat there with his mouth agape, and his eyes as big as saucers (no pun intended). Just as the image dissolved to static he said out loud, "Rokkusu? Kare wa iwa o tsukatte iru?"

Anzhelika Rudnikova, 36 years old, Glazov, Udmurt Republic, Russia - The Journeyman Millwright with the Trans Siberian Railway had been home for about an hour. It wasn't too long after midnight. As a mother and wife she rarely had time to herself, especially since her husband Anton had been injured at work three years ago. He was underfoot even more than the twin girls. However, she loved him like life itself, so she stole those few moments alone for herself when he was asleep. Coming home after the swing shift was one of those times because everyone else was in bed, including her husband. Tonight she was enjoying some vodka and leftover dinner while watching the late news on Rossiya TV. The Molniya TV satellite service was still too expensive, so she usually had to weed through the rhetoric and nationalism in the Russian broadcasts to find out the truth. Tonight was different though. The producers at Rossiya TV were directly broadcasting the amazing events going on so far away on Marsovo. She sat there with her mouth agape, eyes as big as saucers (no pun intended), a shot glass of vodka perched unmoving just in front of her lips, and a piece of sausage dripping in the chubby fingers of her left hand. Just as the image dissolved to static she said out loud, "Skaly? On ispol'zuyet kamni?"

Bernadette Paquette, 22 years old, Bourges, France - Bernadette saw it was almost 23:00 hours as she ran up the front steps of her new apartment building. She had moved in two days before. She was still waiting for new furniture to be delivered. Until the new furniture arrived, she would be spending the night, again, on piled blankets on the floor. After work this evening, she had gone out for dinner with a new guy in her office. She quickly realized it was also the last dinner she would have with him. Still, he was a nice enough man and made pleasant conversation, so she stayed out a bit later than she normally would in that situation. Besides, all she had to go home to was her cat Mijou (a humorous contraction of Mon Bijou), her laptop, and a pile of blankets and pillows on the floor. When she did get in to the apartment, Mijou mewled and rubbed up against her incessantly; as he had been all day without fresh food, fresh cuddles, and fresh stroking of the fur. Bernadette took care of all those in reverse order, finally setting down a dish of freshly opened canned cat food. As Mijou purred and chewed noisily and sloppily on the food, the Rubenesque, dark red haired Bernadette (Adette to her friends) turned on her laptop, changed into a night gown, and lay down on the blankets. She looked at her email first, planning on binging a few episodes of her favourite show on the Canal+ streaming service afterwards. The last email arriving was from Claude, her brother, appearing at the top of her list. The email was only three minutes old and the subject line, all in caps, simply said, "REGARDE!!!!!" She opened the email and clicked on the link. It was a pirate site that was live feeding video transmissions from that silly, silly man on Mars. As the video loaded and she saw what he was doing, her mouth fell agape and her eyes were as big as saucers (no pun intended). Just as the image dissolved to static she said out loud, "Des cailloux? Il utilise des cailloux?"

Tommy Freemantle, 12 years old, Belchertown, Massachusetts, United States - Tommy was sitting at his computer watching events on Mars. His mouth was agape and his eyes as big as saucers (no pun intended). His friend, Carl, had called him two minutes ago and told him what was happening. Tommy was now raptly watching the action. Just as the image dissolved to static he said out loud, "Rocks? He's using rocks?"

The Drone

THIS HUMAN MOVED FAST. PERHAPS THIS HUMAN BETTER THAN MERE SCUM. PERHAPS THIS HUMAN WORTHY OPPONENT. The human stood up again and threw two more rocks. They were good-sized rocks, and the Drone heard the thump of them hitting the front of the ship. The Drone was not worried. The Drone's opinion was that the ship was far too advanced to worry about rocks. The Drone saw a bunch of indicators light up, and felt a tremble in the seat. *WHATEVER HUMAN DOING, ROCKS OR NOT, IS HAVING EFFECT.*

The Drone tried to get out of the way of the human, but the human kept tracking and throwing. The Drone didn't doubt the human would die, not yet anyways. In an even blinder rage, the Drone pointed the ship's weapon at the human, and pressed the firing button just as the human threw two more in its now almost constant stream of rocks.

Mike

One after another, pick up two rocks, throw two rocks. I was close enough and had thrown enough that they were all hitting the little ship, and hitting it near its little weapon nubbin; the little weapon nubbin with the big punch. One of the rocks, slightly bigger than a hockey puck, hit the nubbin dead on. Just as it did, there was a brief flash of light, then the area around the nubbin glowed briefly, then nothing. No energy ball.

"I hope that was the Hail Mary pass ..." I kept throwing more rocks.

The Drone

Instead of the longed for vaporization of the human, the weapon didn't fire. To add insult to insult, the full system control board lit up red. The ship bobbed and wobbled, and the Drone opened its helmet's faceplate and could smell something electrical burning. The Drone shut and secured the faceplate again. The futuristic radar went dark. The weapons system fire-control module shut down at the same time. This was a really odd situation for the Drone, because there wasn't that much that was traditionally electrical, not as humans think of electricity. The vessel used numerous localized power sources for each system specifically to avoid such cascading failures; but the localized power sources weren't joined together. The small vessel did not have a centralized power source. So why had two different systems shut down simultaneously?

The downside of multiple independent power sources to individual components is a lack of overall redundancy to any individual component. The Drone moved the ship over top of the human to try and get the advantage by firing from behind the human; but the ship momentarily lost all lift. It hit the ground and bounced back up as the lift engine re-engaged. That was the second time that had happened. The Drone needed a few moments to get the systems stabilized before pressing the attack. The Drone swung the vessel around behind the line of six ships on the ground to gain some cover.

Putting the vessel in hover mode, the Drone pulled out one of the guidance modules, found the leads from it, darkened by electrical energy overload, and began swapping out these leads with the few spares that were carried on board. The Drone couldn't afford to lose the propulsion engine on top of lift engine problems. Weapons were secondary at this point. The Drone was able to do all this without moving from the cockpit seat. Everything was within easy reach of the 130 centimetre tall creature.

More warning lights came on, and a klaxon sounded. The Drone looked at the external view monitor and could see the human crouched beside one of the ships on the ground. The Drone hurried to finish its work, and then dropped the guidance module back in place at the same moment the human stood up to throw more rocks.

The Drone tried to advance the ship, but it wouldn't go forward. The Drone tried backing up the ship and it moved back slowly. It would not go in any other direction. Backwards was fine, the now almost constant thumping of the rocks was distracting. Getting away from the human's annoying and distracting rocks would let the Drone focus on the repairs. The Drone reset the weapons fire-control system and tried firing the weapon again, but it still didn't fire. Another klaxon started bleating in the small space. The Drone started the small vessel moving backwards, away from the human, slowly.

The Drone pulled the same guidance module out again and realized one of the leads it changed was defective. The Drone pulled it off the module, and reached in the small supply box for another one. The Drone's hand came up empty. The Drone put the module in its lap, and pulled the supply box upclose and peered into it with one of its big eyes. Empty, completely empty. The Drone looked up at the monitor showing the human. The Drone suddenly felt the failure of the situation, and the failure of the day overtake it completely. Defeated by rocks? No! The Drone had underestimated the human.

The Drone had so utterly and completely failed; the Master it knew now, and all it could do was go back to the Eridani complex, in reverse, and jump in the acid vat in the hangar bay.

Watching the human on the small view screen, the Drone wondered, amidst that self-pitying inner monologue, why the human had stopped throwing rocks, turned around, and was running away from the Drone. Shouldn't the human, rocks or not, have pressed the attack?

Lt. Col. Gref KamPen

He had his hands full, yet again, thanks to Achael and Hlef. He had made a quick inspection of the physical damage to the base, and now he was walking out of the sick bay after checking on Sergeant Tucker. He turned left and headed to the Communications Room. They were good girls, really, but damn, they had to stop putting humans in the infirmary. He had tried the discipline route. It usually had an effect on Achael, but not on Hlef. Then Hlef would get Achael wound up, and pretty soon they would both be insufferable until he relented. Lieutenant Colonel Gref KamPen, United States (Exo) Air Force, had been accused of being a little easy on the hybrids more than once. Truth be told, he was. For all the obvious reasons. He hadn't chosen to come into life as a hybrid, neither had any of the others. However, they were what they were, and that was that. They had to stick together. In all the Verse there were only 216 Eben-Human hybrids in existence (twelve on Earth, seventeen on Sapro, and 187 on the base). There were four more gestating in growth tanks right now, but they hadn't been legally born yet; so he wasn't counting them.

Lt. Col. KamPen was appointed as Base Commander when he graduated from AFIT as a wide-eyed (literally) Captain, over thirty years ago. A few years later he was promoted to Major after successfully negotiating the terms of the détente, the accord, with the Eridani. Ten years ago he was bumped up to Lieutenant Colonel; and was now looking forward to getting his full Colonel bird next year ... if Achael and Hlef didn't totally frak things up for him. Gref KamPen (Gruffy to those close to him) had become a father figure to many of the younger hybrids, and he took great pleasure and pride in that. If he had been asked, point blank, where his loyalties were focused (career or hybrids): he would have had to admit he was more concerned about the pseudofamilial connection, than he was the uniform. Nonetheless, his career was important to him.

As Achael was approaching the new human colony site, the human dominant Lt. Col. KamPen (son of Kam) wandered into the Communications Room of the Mars base. He ordered the human corporation's Mar-Sat signal to be disrupted. The human tech on duty made the necessary calculations, pointed the pulse generator, and began assaulting the Mar-Sat with both radio and electro-magnetic waves that would disrupt all signals to and from the Mar-Sat, without damaging it. The video and telemetry signals back at the Corporation's headquarters, 18 minutes and 22 seconds later, dissolved into a solid mass of static.

The other satellite was a different story. That one was hardened against such interference by the same people who had built the interference generator. It required a different approach. Since Lt. Col. KamPen was the only one on the base that knew about that satellite, he would be the one that had to take care of it. He smiled a bit; the designers hadn't told the humans quite *everything* about that satellite. They had told them that the weapons could only be launched by a signal from Mars' surface, but they hadn't told them that the human wasn't the only one on Mars that could do it. There were a few other, shall we say, "quirks" that the human on Mars didn't know about as well. For now, the important one was that Lt. Col. KamPen had the same full access that Mission Control had, and he had that access without the communication signal lag time that the far, far away Mission Control had. Returning to his office, it took Lt. Col. KamPen ninety seconds to establish a connection and deactivate the data signals being transmitted to Earth from The Platform.

Lt. Col. KamPen sighed deeply. Now came the duty he was dreading. He had a good idea how it would go. He activated the ERB Communications unit and established a connection with the Wright-Patterson ERB Communications unit on Earth. He then placed a real-time, secure phone call to the 88th.

Mission Control

(18 minutes, 3 seconds later)

First the Mar-Sat display, and then three minutes later the new display were both lost and replaced by static. First there was dead silence. Ernst and Frankie fiddled uselessly with their controls. Then the room erupted.

Mission Control was once again, to put it nicely, going bugshit crazy. There was nothing Karl could say at this point, so he just sat there, waiting.

Mike

Crouching by the number five supply drop, I was wondering why the alien wasn't still shooting at me. I had expected to have to jump up and change position, but all it did was float slightly backwards.

Then sexy voice spoke up again, "New target detected in area of compromise. New target designated target number forty, referential target number three, is a classified reference. Tracking classified reference."

Classified what? Fraaaaakkkkkk!!! "Command, target number three, vector and speed."

"Target is moving north-north-east at one thousand, two hundred and 3 kilometres per hour."

Holy frak-a-doodle, that's less than five minutes away. At that speed it could be a spacecraft, an aircraft like an Earth jet, or it could be a warhead. *Fraking alien called for fraking backup. So why is it classified,* I asked myself.

Alright, never mind, prioritize. I can't do anything about whatever it was until it gets here. With spool up time and delivery time, a weapon from the platform wouldn't reach the object until it was here. Oh well, I had my faith in

God to look after me, and this was definitely turning into the valley of the shadow of death. Speaking of shadows ... I looked up and saw the fourth stage RAD engines jettison from the PDV. The PDV was almost directly over the gray space ship, and the gray space ship was still slowly backing up, exactly where I had hoped it would. The final stage, RAD unit #5, was about to light up.

"Ummm, shit."

Pliny-the-Elder-be-damned, I turned and ran away as fast as I could.

The Drone

The Drone was in the middle of bright red lights, there were two different, two-tone klaxons blaring, and a cabin filling with smoke. All of the rage and anger on the Drone's face had turned to despair. The Drone's hands were curled in a tight ball on its lap. The Drone screamed at the top of its lungs inside its helmet. Suddenly the ship screeched and slammed into the ground. The Drone saw the side of the ship buckle inwards, and then the Drone was spinning and bumping so hard it lost all sense of direction, and then all sense. For the first time ever, a Drone had been knocked unconscious.

Achael

Looking out the forward view screen Achael could now see the encounter site in the distance. She could see the habitats behind and to the left of the encounter site. She could also see the six supply drops, and the gray Eridani ship and ... and ... she shook her head and still couldn't believe her eyes.

She saw the cargo ship just as the final RAD engines fired for the landing. At the moment those engines fired, the Eridani vessel was right underneath it. The force of the roaring engines caused the Eridani vessel to move sideways - but before clearing the falling cargo container, the extending landing struts trapped it against one of the engine cowlings.

The PDV smashed the Eridani vessel into the ground. The number three engine cowling exploded in bits and pieces at the point of contact, and the two landing struts trapped the Eridani vessel, snapping back upwards with more bits of metal flying. She could see the Eridani ship cave in on one-quarter, before it plopped out from under the landing cargo ship, like an apple seed in a child's fingers.

As the Eridani ship rolled and bumped away on the ground, the now-landed cargo vessel's engines finally extinguished, it started tilting over to the side with the broken landing struts.

Mike

I stopped running when I heard the explosion, ducked and turned sideways. The supply drop was on the ground, there wasn't much flame, but there was a lot of smoke. I saw bits of metal, it looked like engine cowling, falling around me. I felt the impact of a few small pieces hitting me, but the carbon nano tube reinforced Kevlar fabric worked exactly like it was supposed to.

I saw the little grey ship, now deformed with a concave impact point, rolling and bumping away from the cargo drop, and rolling towards me. I stood up and was about run but I realized it was slowing down. It finally stopped about twenty feet from me, having rolled right by supply drop #6, without hitting it.

I looked over at the supply drop billowing smoke and saw it leaning over ... further ... further ... further ... and then it stopped. The spot it had landed on wasn't perfectly level, and the landing struts that appeared to still be functioning took its weight. It just sat there then, billowing smoke and listing about 35 degrees.

Then more movement caught my eye. I looked up and saw a triangular black piece of sky moving towards me. It was so black I couldn't make out any lines other than the outline; but it was getting closer, fast, and doing it silently. The closest cover I had, oddly, was the small gray damaged space ship that had so recently been trying to kill me. I ran over to it and crouched, although I knew at this point it was useless.

They had me.

This small spaceship was no real tactical cover. Heck, it might even explode any minute. Hell, whatever was in it might open a hatch and come out after me. This new ship was now almost overhead, and there was nothing I could do to hide from this one. I sighed. I took a deep breath and stood up. I stepped out from around the little gray space ship into the open.

The black triangular craft was now only about five feet off the ground. It hovered there for a few minutes doing nothing. I just stood there looking at it, glancing at the damaged craft on the ground every few moments, still half expecting some hellish creature to emerge from it.

When I looked back from one of these furtive glances I almost came out of my skin. There was an alien figure standing in front of me. It was wearing an environment suit and a helmet. The environment suit was a bit bulkier than mine, but not as bulky as a proper space suit. It was orange-red, the kind of orange-red that would blend in with the Mars surface. The environment suit and the helmet looked oddly human, like something NASA would have created. The helmet faceplate was opaque black. I couldn't see what was inside it. The one thing I did notice, as I took a single startled step backwards, was how long its arms and fingers were. Its hands hung at its knees, and its fingers were about half again as long as my own, even in the gloves of the environment suit.

This new alien stood there for a few moments, then turned toward the small gray ship and walked over to it. Not knowing what else to do I started following it but it stopped, whirled around and its left hand went to its hip. I saw then that there was a bulky piece of equipment that looked like a hand gun with a can welded around it. The alien didn't draw the weapon, but the implication was clear, follow any further and I'd find out for real what that weapon actually could do.

Achael

Seeing the dawning realization in his eyes, Achael took her hand off of the low atmo modified Desert Eagle, and started walking to the Eridani vessel again. Reaching the damaged section, glancing over her shoulder at the earthman, she then peered inside through the damaged and torn metal. She could just see inside the cockpit, and the control system lights let her see the little gray Drone.

She turned and faced the human again. She stared at him for a few moments, trying to understand the feeling in her stomach when she looked at him. Finally, she pointed at the ground in front of him then made a "stop" hand gesture. He must have understood because he nodded his head and crossed his arms. Through the faceplate of his surface suit she could see that his face was rugged, handsome, scared... and defiant. His fear would work in her favour, for now, defiant or not.

She walked around to the undamaged side of the Eridani vessel, found the over-ride panel, opened it and then triggered the hatch. All Eridani vessels had this identical access point, and everyone on the Mars Hybrid base knew how to access them, even though the Eridani didn't know they knew.

As the hatch swung up, she stepped back and looked around the craft to make sure the human was still where she left him. He was.

Achael then cautiously leaned inside the craft to look at the unmoving Drone. She didn't know if it was dead or if it was playing possum. She reached in with one hand and poked it once, then twice, then a third time; each time a bit rougher than the last.

At that point it started to move around slightly. It wasn't playing possum, it had really been unconscious. Unheard of. She had to move *fast* before it fully regained its senses.

Deftly, she flicked open the seat restraints, grabbed the Drone by the back of its own version of a space suit, and then quickly pulled it out of the craft. She bodyslammed it onto the ground, dropped to one knee on top of it, and reached behind her. She opened the pouch on her utility belt, and withdrew two plastic restraints.

When she had arrived, she had put her Dart in hover mode, and then she had to get into her surface suit quickly. Even though she was in a hurry, she had enough sense about her to make sure she fully kitted-up before activating the TransMat. It was quite by accident she wound up appearing right in front of the man from Earth.

With the Drone pinned to the ground, she pulled its suited arms behind its back and applied one of the restraints, then she half-turned and did the same thing around the Drone's knees. She'd apply more restraint once she got him in the ship. She picked up the now squirming and struggling Drone, and threw it over her shoulder. She turned and looked around the small Eridani vessel. The human still stood there, arms folded, and it looked like he was tapping his foot. She smiled at that.

She walked towards the Dart, reached up and activated the TransMat. Inside she set down the struggling Drone, opened a supply bay, and took out a roll of duct tape. She made sure the Drone wouldn't be able to struggle enough to get free.

Already knowing what had to be done, she TransMat outside again. She opened the service hatch under the craft, and took out a rescue toolkit. She then started pulling out a rescue cable. She pulled out enough to reach the Eridani craft, and walked towards it with the kit slung over her shoulder. The human was still standing where she had left him, arms still folded, foot still tapping. She stopped by the open hatch of the Eridani vessel. She looked inside for a connection point that would be solid enough to support the weight of the craft. She found a strut that looked strong enough and turned around for her toolkit.

The human was standing right behind her. She froze, just staring at him. After a few moments, the earthman bent down, picked up the toolkit and held it up to her.

Mike

187

I was tired of standing there just tapping my foot. I watched the bigger alien carry the squirming body of something small over to the triangular craft. She touched the craft and disappeared. I'm sure my surprisingly slack jaw slammed into the bottom of my helmet, but I was too shocked to really notice.

I didn't know what was going to happen next. Was the alien savouring the moment to kill me? Was the alien going to let me live? Was the alien a friendly, instead of a support operation for the downed craft? If it wasn't friendly, why had it restrained the smaller alien? If it was friendly, was there a bad-alien support operation on the way? Was I about to be in the middle of another fire fight? As these and other thoughts raced around my already overloaded brain, the alien was suddenly there again. I mean suddenly, as in one moment it wasn't; and then suddenly, it was. No flash of light, no materialization beam like on Star Trek, no sudden shimmer or distortion. One moment it wasn't there, and a single shake of a lamb's tail later - it was simply, there. The suddenness and visual disorientation actually made me feel nauseous.

The alien went under its ship, took a small box out of a hatch it opened, and then started pulling out a cable. It then took the small box (it looked like a really expensive toolkit for outer space) and the cable, and started walking back to the small crashed ship.

Ahhhhh ... retrieval. This alien was going to take the crashed ship away. I stood there while the alien walked around and out of view. I gave it a few moments, and then made up my mind. Kill me or not, I was done being the bitch of all these aliens. I walked around the small ship and saw the alien leaning inside of it. I walked up behind the alien and stood there. It stood up and turned around. I could see it give an involuntary jerk backwards, but at least it didn't draw that ugly weapon on its hip. I still couldn't see anything through the opaque visor so after a few beats I reached down, picked up the box that looked like a toolkit, and held it up for the alien. With the briefest pause, the alien opened the case in my hands, reached in and pulled out a 10 centimetre shackle and screw, along with a very human looking pair of pliers.

I watched the alien lean back in the craft, appearing to give me no further thought, and set to work. Standing on my tippy-toes to see over its shoulder, I could see the big alien wrapping the shackle around what appeared to be a support strut in an awkward location, and begin threading the shackle screw in place.

I was thinking fast and hard now. This alien hadn't killed me, even when I snuck up behind it. It was using equipment that would have been found in any hardware store on Earth. It had a surface suit on that looked like it came out of a NASA closet. Aside from the freakishly long arms and fingers, it appeared quite human; even though it was about a head shorter than I am. I knew that according to General Rosewood there were "friendlies" visiting our planet but this, this alien before me, well, seemed to confuse me in a way that "friendlies" wouldn't have. I was just starting to wonder what General Rosewood *hadn't* told me when the alien stood up, tossed the wrench in the toolkit and closed it up.

The alien bent down and picked up the cable. The cable had a snap hook on the end of it. The alien then reached in and attached the snap hook to the shackle that had just been installed. The alien in the red suit then stood and turned. It just stood there for a few seconds staring at me. With its helmets faceplate completely opaque, I imagined it staring into my eyes, if it had eyes. I refused to look away, to tremble, to even blink. Finally the alien took the toolkit out of my hands and without so much as a "by-your-leave" head nod; it turned and walked back towards the triangular Dart.

I started to back up slowly from the crashed ship. I could see, standing this close, the surface wasn't as smooth as it looked from any distance. There were faint seams of odd shapes. The surface actually looked like brushed metal rather than smoother metal. The cable tugged, and I looked up, the alien was making it taut and drawing the slack back into the bottom of the triangular craft. The alien walked back to the front of the craft, touched the nose of it, and then was (another shake of a lamb's tail later), simply no longer standing there. The nausea returned.

A moment later, the black triangular craft started to slowly lift up so I backed even further away. Moving right over top of the crashed ship, the triangular craft silently moved upwards, moving very slowly until the crashed ship had taken tension on the cable, and had lifted off the ground. I could hear some faint straining and groaning of metal, but it quickly quieted to nothing in the thin atmosphere. The two alien ships then moved slowly upwards in tandem, and then started moving away; moving a bit more south of the direction than second craft had arrived from.

I stood there and watched them until they were over the horizon. Once it was out of sight, I stood there some more. Once I was done standing there, I decided to stand there a bit longer and then a bit longer still. It seemed that the "take action" part of my brain had gone to sleep; perhaps it had gone for lunch. I fully expected to find a significant portion of my brain huddled in the corner, strumming a finger on its lips, and making senseless gibbering noises.

As if this wasn't enough on my plate, sexy voice spoke up again, "Unknown targets detected in area of compromise. Hostile targets designated target numbers forty-one, forty-two and forty-three, referential target numbers four, five and six. Tracking hostile targets."

I closed my eyes and took a deep breath then out a long sigh, "I don't fraking care".

189

"Command not recognized. Please restate command."

Sigh. Frak off.

"Command, cancel new target voice notification, and cancel referential targeting designations."

"Command accepted, cancelling new target voice notification. Maintaining 100 kilometre exclusion zone. Cancelling referential targeting designations. Resuming sequential target designations."

Sigh.

I decided to just stand there some more.

So I was just standing there for a while, not knowing what in the hell to do, and not having a clue what to make of everything that had just happened. From the time I got the heads-up message from Ernst, only twenty-five minutes had passed. The alien "rescue" ship had been on the ground for less than fifteen minutes. I decided that standing there was the right thing to do in these circumstances: so I just stood there some more, and then some more after that. At some point, I noticed that my HUD had not displayed any more priority message from Ernst or from anyone else for that matter.

Eventually, I looked around behind me and to the right, the Habitats were intact. I looked over the other shoulder at Big Dawg, it was sitting where I left it, but its camera mast was pointed right at me. I looked at the supply drops, the gaping wound in the nacelles, and lower side of cargo drop #3 (hydroponics equipment). I looked at the recently arrived cargo drop #7 (return pods, more on that later), and its scary and disappointing 35 degree list towards the other cargo drops.

I took a deep breath and let out a long sigh. I flapped my arms against my sides a couple times, turned to Big Dawg, gave him the hand recognition signal and then the "Follow Me" hand signal, and then walked back to the W-Hab.

Chapter 31

Achael

She flew low and slow, not able to use the folding drive with the damaged Eridani craft swinging freely below her at the end of the rescue cable. It took her almost five hours to get to Teviot Vallis and the Eridani base.

A few minutes after leaving the crash site, her proximity scans showed three Eridani vessels in formation behind her. She braced herself to cut the cable and engage in evasive manoeuvres, but they did not attack. Two stayed in formation, while one pressed close and did a circuit first above then under her ship. Obviously they saw the crashed craft, and that she had it in tow. That lead ship moved back into formation with its counterparts, and they flew with her the whole way to her destination.

Achael had been to the Eridani base many times. Once a Martian year, the Eridani and the Hybrid base exchanged two or three personnel for a few hours. Each was treated to some entertainment, a lavish dinner and a round table discussion of any issues that needed to be discussed. She hated those trips. The Vesna creeped her out, the Voiya were insufferable, and the place smelled like rotting sweat socks and dirty crotch. However Lt. Col. KamPen had been sending her more often. She suspected it was a form of punishment for all the fighting, but it was better than the brig. There was also the biweekly deliveries of biological material that she and Hlef seemed to get more than their fair share of.

The only positive thing to come out of all these visits was that she had made some friends amongst the Trigla. The Trigla weren't like the rest of the Eridani. Get them away from the Vesna and the Voiya; and they were friendly, solicitous, welcoming party animals. Many of them spoke small amounts of different Earth languages and were called upon by the Vesna, from time to time, to help interpret when circumstances didn't permit telepathy to work. Achael had learned some rudimentary Trigla and could get by in a pinch, but she wasn't fluent. Achael usually made her way from the state functions as soon as she could, and wandered down to the kitchens and maintenance areas where she would be greeted with hugs, backslapping, and the good food; not the pretentious crap they served upstairs. There was always music playing and the kitchen staff burst into unintelligible song and dancing as often as not. She had started bringing a case of human and Eben spices with her each year for the cooks, who were almost beside themselves with joy at such a bounteous, creative, and thoughtful gift.

This time, however, there would be no socializing, no gifts and no insufferable state dinner. She knew her arrival would not go over well, and there was a good chance they may just try to kill her on the spot. Key word being "try".

Lt. Col. Gref KamPen

He stood beside Pinpin HofPin in the Defense Office. They watched the Eben version of a radar.

"Damn it", the Base Commander said.

"I was afraid of this. There's only one place she can be going on that heading." mused Pinpin, while stroking his stubbly, but mostly Eben chin. The True-Blood Eben did not have facial hair, other than eyelashes. The Hybrid males tried growing facial hair, but usually wound up with patchy, odd coloured stubble only.

Lt. Col. KamPen scratched his head and looked at Pinpin, and then at Hlef and Ahshuun who had just entered.

"Straight to the Devil's doorstep no doubt," chimed in Ahshuun after seeing the track on the screen, "She must have a really big bug up her ass this time."

Pinpin looked at the Base Commander, "Boss, we have to do something. If she's alone and pisses them off, they won't hesitate to throw her in an acid vat."

The mood in the room changed at that moment. What everyone had been thinking was now being said, and now that it had been said, it demanded a response.

Lt. Col. KamPen held his head like he had a migraine. With squinted eyes he looked right at Hlef, "You girls are going to be the death of me, you know that, right?" Everyone smiled. He had just told them they were going to do something.

With a deep sigh, he put his hands on his hips, "You three meet me in the hangar bay. Get three Darts prepped," and they were gone so fast, he hardly saw them go.

He looked down at the techs working the defense consoles. "Big Martha", the True-Blood Eben tech turned her head slightly and looked at him from the corner of her eye. "What's the current status of those ground pounders?"

Big Martha responded in her swishy-slushy Eben dialect, "Thousis ab estend atta" (30 minute alert).

"How fast can you get one up, really?"

Big Martha (a nickname she'd had for forty years) paused a moment than said, "Thousis sri" (ten minutes).

"Do it. I may need some shock and awe," he spun on his heels, and headed for the hangar bay. He paused long enough at the Communications Office to order the tech to call the Ready-Team (10 Eben and 10 humans) to the hangar bay, with a full weapons kit for heavy combat. Shock and awe sometimes had to be upclose and personal.

The Battle Alarm started echoing in the halls when Big Martha activated the Heavy Cruiser alert. In addition to the ready team, many more pairs of feet, from all three races, started pounding towards the hangar bay.

Achael

She reduced speed a bit more as she started crossing Hesperia Planum, she didn't want the Eridani following her to think it was an attack run. With Hellas Planitia looming broadly in the distance and quickly filling her view screen, she searched for the telltale landmark of the kidney-shaped Teviot Vallis with its dog-leg entry. Rising another 700 metres in altitude, it only took a few minutes before she saw it in the distance. She changed direction to come in slow over Gunnison crater. She wanted to approach at an oblique angle with the entrance to the Eridani base on the west side of Teviot Vallis, just west of the dog-leg. She slowed and approached obliquely, so that the assholes following her wouldn't think she was on an attack approach.

Slowing to an almost stop, she crawled along the Vallis proper, while sending the challenge signal from her communications equipment. There was a lengthy delay. Long enough that she had to stop and hover in place with the damaged craft beneath swinging like a pendulum, ever-so-slightly. When the approach signal was received, she winched the small craft in close to the bottom of her Dart, and proceeded through the now visible entrance and through the magnetic curtain. The thick heavy doors had opened and recessed into the walls, she could see a large contingent of drones as well as a healthy ground crew of Trigla. She started running the mental exercises that would prevent the Vesna and most of the Voiya from reading her thoughts. This was something all the hybrids and humans on the Mars base learned very early on.

The ground crew halted her in mid-flight; while they ran underneath to have a look at the barely swaying damaged craft. Emerging from underneath, the one that had to be the Deck Chief guided her to a spot along one side of the landing bay, and indicated to her to set the craft there. She let out the winch slowly, and felt the change in buoyancy as the small craft rested on the deck. She waited a few minutes for the Trigla ground crew to disconnect the cable. It amazed her that Eben, Eridani, and human flight deck operations were almost identical, even though there had never been any purposeful collaboration.

The ground crew Chief gave her the all clear after only a minute. She winched in the cable, and followed another Trigla ground crew waving lighted sticks in the air. She was guided to the centre of the hangar bay where some drones and some Vesna had gathered. There was also a platoon-size force of Trigla soldiers present, all heavily armed. She smiled. There was an Eben hybrid arriving, they had to overcompensate. As her craft moved into the indicated position, she could see three Eridani scout ships alighting, and the pilots emerging on the far side of the cavernous hangar bay.

She settled the craft on its antigravity struts, and went to the back of the Dart's cabin. The Drone was still all trussed up in duct tape and its large eyes were staring at her while its mouth worked silently, gnashing its teeth and looking like it really thought it could bite her through its helmet. Thankfully, the helmet it was wearing meant she didn't have to listen to the damn thing. She still had her environment suit on, but not her own helmet. The Eridani base had Earth norm air pressure and breathable (though stinky) atmosphere. She took off her environment suit because she didn't want its restrictiveness if push came to shove; and when confronting the Eridani and their minions, push could quite quickly come to shove.

She picked up the trussed Drone, tossed it over her shoulder and then closing her eyes she thought-commanded the Dart, "Outside". Closing her eyes usually avoided the nauseating stomach lurch and slight disorientation of the TransMat, when her eyes were open.

The air around her was suddenly different. She opened her eyes and was standing on the Deck just forward of the nose of her Dart. She squinched her nose at the smell. The gathered drones were quickly moving to form a circle around Achael as the five Vesna approached her. She looked at the one in front and thought loudly, *MASTER, NOW*. Nothing happened right away so she knew the Vesna was trying to communicate with her. She refused to let her mental guards down though because, as previously stated, the Vesna just creeped the hell out of her. She refused to let them communicate with her directly. She adjusted the weight of the squirming drone slung over her shoulder. She thought again, louder if possible, *MASTER, NOW*.

Still, nothing appeared to be happening. One of the Trigla guards, the guard commander it looked like, stepped forward. She recognized him as someone she had sat at a table with during the last official visit she took part in. He smiled quickly, then went back to looking dour, "Vesna Mahal say down down quanni leave." His pidgin English wasn't half bad.

Having dealt with these assholes most of her life she looked right at the creepy Vesna Mahal (title, not a name) and said with her voice, "You bring the Duty Commander here right this minute. *You* bring him here. I'm not leaving until I speak with him." She reached out and poked her finger in his chest as she said this. This, of course, caused the circle of drones to rush in tight around her. One of them foolishly grabbed her arm. Unluckily for that particular drone, her lightning Eben reflexes let her withdraw her arm, and punch it in the head hard enough to kill it on the spot. It dropped lifeless and the other drones just stepped on top of it to get closer to her, but none of them touched her. She knew that could only be, because they were under direct orders not to. The dead one just got a little too excited. As far as she was concerned though, the only good drone was a dead drone. Push was indeed, coming to shove.

At this, the five Vesna turned as one, and walked away. She looked at the Trigla guard commander. He just gave her a wry grin and hunched his shoulders, "Wait now HipHip, Voiya come." (HipHip was what the Trigla called Achael, it meant 'gift bringer').

The little trussed up Drone on her shoulder was still wiggling. She could hear some faint sound coming through the helmet; it must have been in quite a state to be able to hear it. She hefted it up and flopped it not too gently onto her other shoulder. The drones circling her pressed closer to her momentarily, but then got hold of themselves and drew back. She had about 30 centimetres of space all around her, and they had to be twenty deep.

Sighing deeply, Achael did all that she could do at the moment, she waited. She amused herself by making sneering faces at the sea of drones, trying to see if she could provoke another one to go to it's death, quickly. These drones were well-trained though. They gibbered, snarled, and sneered right back at her, but none of them touched her. She really, really hated the drones.

Only three or four minutes had passed when a hatch opened at the side of the hangar bay. Two armed Trigla stepped through, then two Vesna, then the Eridani Master (one of the Voiya), then the rest of the original Vesna contingent, and four more armed Trigla. The last two also carried a lightweight, but ever-present platform between them.

The original Trigla guard commander watched their entrance, then turned back to Achael and said sotto voce with his deep voice, "Little big-big, korumph custy guards, fast move tut-tut." He had warned her that this was a low ranking Voiya, and that the guards with him would not be friendly to her: so don't make any sudden moves. She smiled. She could take half a dozen armed Trigla before they knew what happened. Still, she appreciated this one making the effort to warn her. It just strengthened her appreciation of the Trigla she had become friendly with.

Without even looking, a wedge of open space formed within the ring of drones. The ring itself pulled back a bit more, leaving Achael standing in a clear circle about five feet across. Clear that is, except for the body of the dead drone that had mistakenly touched her. She looked at the circle of drones and knew that they were the only thing she really had to worry about. A dozen or so of them would be no problem but there had to be at least two hundred of them around her. She wasn't entirely sure that she really could defeat that many of them on her own.

The two trailing Trigla guards scurried to the front of the pack and set down a wide three step platform, then retreated while bowing. The Voiya slowly climbed the three steps of the platform in front of her. He then stood there smugly, his head height above her eye line. He wasn't saying anything out loud, he was just staring imperiously down at her. She watched his forehead rise, his eyes widen, and nostrils flare. The Eridani Master was trying to communicate with her but she had her mental blocks up.

She said, "Speak to me, I won't hear your thoughts".

The Voiya recoiled like he had been slapped, the drones pressed closer again, and the Master's guard force unshouldered their weapons. Achael just smiled and waited.

"IMPERTINENT HYBRID!" he screeched in his whiskey and cigarette voice. All the Voiya on Mars spoke flawless English, it was just hideous to listen to. "KNEEL BEFORE YOUR MASTER!!!"

Achael laughed, "Like that's going to happen. We have business to talk about, Voiya, let's get on with it".

The Voiya fumed, she could see his fists clenched, he let out a yell of frustration and stomped around the small platform in a circle. He stopped, looked at the dead Drone on the hangar deck and screeched (they were always screeching), "WHY DID YOU KILL MY DRONE??"

"It touched me without permission."

The Voiya stared at her for a moment, and then screeched, ever the imperial host, "FOR THIS YOU HAVE MY PARDON." The Voiya looked at the lead Vesna, the lead Vesna made a hand motion. Four of the drones in the pack broke away, picked up the dead drone's body, and then carried it to a large metal tub in the far corner of the hangar deck, one of the acid vats used to rid themselves of dead or disobedient drones. Within a few minutes it would be nothing but liquefying grey goo.

Screeching at her again, "WHY ARE YOU HERE??"

Achael took the duct taped Drone off her shoulder and tossed it on the floor in front of her. "That thing attacked a human".

"HUMAN NOT WELCOME".

"That thing attacked a human on Mars, you do not attack humans on Mars."

"IT DID NOT ATTACK YOUR HUMANS. IT ATTACKED THE UNWELCOMED HUMAN. THE HUMAN GOVERNMENTS KNOW NOT TO SEND HUMANS TO MARS".

She took a step closer to the Voiya. As he raised its head imperiously, the Master's guard brought their weapons to bear on Achael. Achael put one foot on the squirming Drone on the floor and leaned forward with her arms crossed on her raised knee. "Who do I have the ... *honour* ... of addressing today?"

If possible, the Eridani Master drew himself even higher, with a face full of self-righteous, self-importance, and screamed, "MASTER BLITOWYN OF CHERNASAI"

"Master Blitowyn?" She smiled.

"YES."

"Of Chernasai?" She smiled broader. She could tell the smile was getting to him.

"YES!"

She chuckled, making the Eridani Master almost vibrate with rage, "Aren't you Master Rillixiwen's *little* brother?"

The drones pressed closer.

"I AM THE MASTER OF THIS BASE. I AM THE MASTER OF THIS PLANET."

Achael stood upright and did a bit of yelling herself, "You are the Duty Officer! You are not the one in charge! You're not the Master of anything except your own ass!" The Voiya screamed with rage and pointed at her. So far the encounter had been proceeding just about the way she had anticipated it would.

Before the Master could say anything, she went on, "However," she sighed. "I don't have all day to argue with a petty functionary," her inner eyelids slammed shut, "so let's just get this over with."

Seeing this, the Eridani Master's guards actually took a step back from her. The Voiya screamed with rage and reached forward for Achael out of instinct. She was too far from him for him to actually reach her. She held perfectly still and smiled. The army of drones pressed closer again, some of them standing unsteadily on the trussed up, one in front of her. The Voiya's guards held their new position and kept their weapons trained on her. Now that she was in battle mode, they actually looked a bit nervous. Out of the corner of her eye, she saw the original guard commander casting a very wary and experienced eye on the Master and the hybrid as the drama unfolded. The Guard Commander looked nervous. That suddenly made her a little less certain about her position. Something else was going on here, but she had no clue what it

197

was. She wondered why would Rillixiwen, the senior House brother, send his youngest sib to meet her?

As the Voiya got control of himself, the drones held their position. Two of them suddenly fell over from the movements of the squirming Drone bound and laying on the floor. The Voiya looked down at it, as did the Vesna. Again, without any words, four of the drones picked up the duct taped Drone and carried it over to the acid vat. Just before tossing it in, they removed the helmet and Achael could finally hear its screams of failure, angst, and rage. Thankfully she hadn't had to listen to that the whole way here. The screams were extinguished by a bubbling sound as the still bound Drone was tossed in the acid vat. She could just imagine its flesh and body dissolving into the grey goo, and actually felt kind of queasy about it. She didn't show that on her face. She remained impassive to the Voiya and the Vesna.

"Why did you attack the human?"

"YOU DON'T HAVE THE RIGHT TO QUESTION ME ON DEFENSIVE MATTERS!!"

"Defensive? Did you watch what took place? The human defended himself with rocks!"

"I DETERMINE WHAT IS DEFENSIVE AND WHAT NEEDS DEFENDING!!"

"You had to defend yourself from a lone human who fought with rocks?"

"YES!!"

"The great and mighty," she almost spat it out, "Bsirutaeben, so weak and scared they have to try to kill a man armed only with rocks?"

"YES!"

She said nothing. She just smiled.

"NO! NOT WEAK! NOT SCARED!" Master Blitowyn paused, "DEFENDING OUR BASE, DEFENDING OUR PLANET!"

She said very quietly, "Like I said, it's not your planet. You are guests here. We've been here far more than a human millennia. You have only been here seven hundred and three human years. My people laid claim to this place long before you arrived. Now you try to kill a human. Our humans are protected. You cannot kill humans."

"NOT YOUR HUMAN, YOU HYBRID. NOT PART OF YOUR BASE. IF THE HUMAN ISN'T PART OF YOUR BASE, THE HUMAN IS NOT PROTECTED", he paused, "IT WAS A DEFENSIVE MATTER, BY THE TERMS OF THE ACCORD WE HAVE THE RIGHT TO DEFEND OUR BASE".

Something about his tone, about how he had said that, gave her pause. Then she asked, "Who gave the kill order for this human?" She cocked her head to the side, and folded her arms.

There was a longer pause, then, "I DID. I GAVE THE KILL ORDER. I DEFENDED OUR BASE, AND I GAVE THE KILL ORDER. I WAS THE ONE!!"

She unfolded her arms and her inner eyelids opened. She stood there with her mouth open. "I can't believe it. You didn't give the kill order, did you?"

"I GAVE THE KILL ORDER. OF COURSE I GAVE THE KILL ORDER." He paused briefly then continued, "DRONE CANNOT KILL WITHOUT A KILL ORDER!! I GAVE THE KILL ORDER!!"

Achael looked over at the acid vat, and then looked back at the Voiya, "You didn't. You didn't give the kill order. The little fraker in the ship went rogue, didn't he? Didn't he?"

The Eridani Master just seethed and stared at her. It was much more acceptable to admit to giving an order that he never gave, rather than have it known that the Drone had indeed gone rogue, against its Master's actual orders. He looked at the Vesna, then looked back at her. The Vesna Mahal and the Master exchanged another glance and obviously, some unheard psychic chatter.

"WHAT YOU SAY IS NOT POSSIBLE!!"

"Yes, yes I believe it is. That little Drone went rogue, and now you have to cover it up. You don't have absolute control over your drones after all." She was enjoying pushing him around.

The thought that an Eridani Master did not have control over his drones was unthinkable. To actually say this out loud was an insult that went to the core of who they were (pretentious airheads with a Jovian sized ego). Questioning an Eridani Master's ability to control his drones was an incredible insult from an outsider. If true, it brought into question that particular Voiya's ability to rule and control effectively. It brought into question their right to have responsibility and power within the Eridani Dominion. It called into question the absolute right and power of all the Eridani Masters everywhere, because having lack of control over one drone meant they may not have absolute control over all drones, over all their Vesna, over all their Trigla. It called into question the nature of their very existence.

Having someone or something out in the Verse with the ability to correctly question this power was unconscionable. Having an outsider know for a fact that a drone had gone rogue could undermine and eventually destroy the whole Eridani sphere of influence ... or so this Master thought.

In reality, outsiders only submitted to the Eridani because of their large number of drones and the sociopathic viciousness of the Vesna. None of the power races believed the Eridani were as in charge and in control, as the Eridani thought that others thought they were. In fact, when the Drone went rogue, all the Voiya on the base went ballistic. The Drone's actual Master was Rillixiwen who along with several other Voiya Masters at the moment, lay dead in his chambers after a blood bath amongst the Voiya had ensued. Master Blitowyn was only one of three surviving Masters on their Martian base, and he was now in the hangar bay because he was low man on the remaining totem pole.

However, that's a subject for another day. For now, the Eridani had almost reached a very terminal decision for Achael. In interest of political détente, it was going to give her a chance to save herself.

A Vesna Mahal was sort of like a leader, but more like an elected group representative, but only with co-operative decision making ability. Nothing was ever simple with the Vesna. The Vesna Mahal looked at the Trigla guard commander. The guard commander stepped forward and said, "Vesna Mahal say no say what you say. Say that is bad bad. For you."

Achael was never one to respond well to passive-aggressive. She looked at the guard commander, looked at the Vesna Mahal, and then looked at the Eridani Master. Her inner eyelids slammed shut again, filling her face with two black orbs and then she burst out laughing. Probably not the best response given the situation. The Vesna Mahal jerked its head, the drones swarmed her and grabbed at her arms and legs. The Master's personal guards all pressed in with their weapons pointed at her head and chest. She ignored them and started killing the drones two at a time; no one there really cared about the drones. There would be lots more where these came from.

Achael was in a tough spot and she knew it. She could have taken the Trigla without the drones. She could have taken a lot of the drones on their own, but if (when?) the Master gave them a kill order, then she couldn't hope to take this many without some protective armour. Not wearing armour on this mission had been a mistake. She chalked it up to being blinded by rage and anger when she departed the hybrid base. As she struggled against the press of the drones she didn't let any of this show on her face. She couldn't lose face in front of a Voiya, in front of the Vesna.

The Voiya gave what could only be interpreted as a smile. He sneered and screeched, "I GAVE YOU A CHANCE HALF-BREED. YOU HAD A CHANCE TO RECANT." He folded his arms across his chest and continued screeching, "AND NOW YOU WILL DISCOVER WHAT ..."

As she shook off drones and killed one after another, the Master stopped mid rant and looked up. The Trigla guards looked up behind her, and the

Vesna contingent looked up behind her. Even though she was struggling with and killing drones, most of the drones were all looking behind her. She could see a look of surprise on all of their faces. She saw the Trigla ground crew running full tilt for the hatch at the back of the hangar bay. The Master stepped backwards and fell off the platform. His Trigla guards stood around him, and were now pointing their weapons behind Achael, not at her. The drones all went into a frenzy, looking behind her and looking towards their Master on the floor. They had stopped tugging and pulling at her, and she stopped killing them. Out of the corner of her eye she could see the Trigla guard commander with his hands in the air. Half his platoon also had their hands in the air, the other half had rushed around to surround the Master as he stood up and stepped back up on the platform. Even though answering the perceived call to duty, these inexperienced guards were looking mighty uncertain about having done so. The Master's personal guards had closed in tight around him. She could have turned around to see what they were all gawking at, but she didn't. She was in fighting mode and was keeping an eye on the Trigla with the weapons in front of her.

Then she heard it. The most welcome and wonderful sound she could have heard at that moment. Hlef's voice, "Well, aren't you the stupidest bitch in the Universe."

Mike

I had been having a very bad day. I stood in the airlock, outer hatch closed, inner hatch open, and my Activity Suit around my knees. I did some more of the just standing there, in despair. As I just stood there in despair, and noted an odd smell. I sniffed the air a couple times, lifted my arms and sniffed again. Yes, it was me. I realized that I hadn't had a wipe down since I left the Jalopy, and I hadn't had a shower in close to nine months. My mood brightened a bit. I had a shower here, just a few feet away.

With my mood brightened a bit, I stepped out of the Activity Suit, hung it up, swapped out the air bottles, put the helmet and gloves in the rack, lined the boots up against the wall, and then sighed heavily. I trudged up the stairs and over to the COM panel. I looked at the three blinking red lights that told me: a.) there was no communication with Mar-Sat; b.) there was no telemetry connection with Mar-Sat and; c.) that I was quite possibly totally screwed. I punched in the command to establish a signal with Jalopy-Sat and was presented with:

`ErrNo. 1 - Lost Signal Lock`

Sighing heavily again I turned around and trudged into the L-Hab. Just inside the entrance, on the upper level was the washroom. Toilet, sink and blessed Martian shower! With a brisker pace, I went down to my room, grabbed one of the two bath towels I now owned, and went back upstairs, peeling off my long johns and t-shirt as I did so. Hey, no signal meant no cameras. Buck naked wasn't going to be a problem. Of course, I forgot the Habitat cameras were recording to a local directory which would be spooled and transmitted when a signal with Mar-Sat was re-established.

I went into the bathroom and shut the door, out of habit I guess. I stood there for a tick, remembering the last time I shut a "bathroom" door. I turned around and then opened and closed the door twice, just to be sure.

I pulled the plastic wrap off the shower plumbing and primed the local pump. It took only a few seconds as the L-Hab had shipped with 100 litres of Earth water in its own buffer tank. As the two Habs were now connected, I had access to the main supply. At some point the air in the pipes would bleed out, but it would happen in its own time. It wasn't something I had to concern myself with. As the pump primed, I loaded the packed plastic dispensers of soap and shampoo. It would be decades before the hydroponics farms of Agri-Mars Corporation would let us grow the items we needed to manufacture our own soaps and shampoos; so for now, I would be totally reliant on Terra for these luxuries.

I activated the on-demand water heater, waited the requisite thirty seconds and then turned on the water flow. Nothing.

Frak. I didn't turn on the feeder valve. I opened the small access hatch and turned on the feeder valve, and the water started flowing. I stepped into the warm, low velocity water stream and let out a deep and relaxing sound of pleasure and comfort. I stood there for thirty seconds letting the water flow over me. I shut off the water at the showerhead, and then I soaped and lathered the body, soaped and lathered the hair. I turned the water flow back on, and rinsed all the soap off. As I ran my fingers through my hair, I decided it was time for a haircut.

With a final rinse and the water turned off, I looked at the readout panel as I was towelling off. I had used a whopping 11.3 litres of water. These combat showers were supposed to use only 8 litres with our advanced plumbing systems. Luckily, the recovery systems would make that 0.17 litres consumed, but still, more than anticipated. That thirty seconds of bliss I started the shower with was something I couldn't repeat ... often. I turned off the on-demand water heater as it was a huge drain on my batteries. I wouldn't have to worry about it once the wind farm was set up.

Towelled and dried, I dug out the shaving equipment and started scraping the hair from my face. A razor shave was a welcome luxury as the Jalopy only provided an electric space shaver hooked up to a small vacuum. It was better than nothing, but it was still annoying. As I stood there in the mirror, performing the manly ritual from out-of-time, I continued reflecting on the day's events. While I was still overjoyed to be on Mars and the adventure of it all still thrilled me, I was also getting tired of all this alien crap. There wasn't supposed to be anyone on Mars but me! Dammit ... I cut myself. I pulled out the styptic pencil and tooted it with some hot water remaining in the pipes, first blotting the cut with my towel, and then dabbing the styptic pencil on it to stop the small amount of blood flow. As I watched myself in the mirror performing this remedy, I remembered my father. He had taught me the manly art of shaving. He had given me my first styptic pencil way back when. The small plastic tube my current styptic pencil was in, was the same plastic tube he had presented me with forty years ago. I remembered my adolescent self, wearing with pride the little dabs of dried white powder, because it meant I had been shaving; shaving peach fuzz of course, but shaving nonetheless. It was a rite of passage. As I paused, hand in mid-air, looking in the mirror, I could see my Dad's face. I thought about what he would say about today's events, "Well son, you've got a job to do don't you? Do you want to sit down and wait for someone else to do it or do you want to be a man? If you got a job worth doin', it's worth doin' right; no matter how hard it is."

Teviot Vallis

"Hlef, not now," came Lt. Col. KamPen's quiet voice in the din of snarling drones.

Achael stood there staring at the Trigla as the drones suddenly peeled off her, and spread out forming a wide skirmish line, four deep, in front of their Master and his guards. The Trigla guards weapons stayed pointed behind her. She turned to look at her sister, then smiled and winked. Three of the Eben Darts were hovering inside the hangar bay. They had passed through the magnetic curtain unrestricted. The Eridani had never closed the outer doors when Achael arrived. Given the remoteness and lack of any indigenous life forms, the Eridani had never installed any point defense weapons at the entrance. Outside, through the magnetic curtain, she could see one of the Heavy Battle Cruisers, a ground pounder, coasting into position in front of the entrance. Its forward rail guns were now pointing directly down the middle of the hangar bay.

Spread out in a loose formation were ten human Special Forces, kitted up in armour for heavy surface combat, armed with low-atmo modified and highly favoured FN SCAR assault rifles. Perhaps even more daunting, ten armoured Eben warriors carrying Shil-7s. The impressive Shil-7 was an Eben weapon with heavy, high velocity 87-grain, exploding tip, discarding sabot rounds. It was less gun and more like a semiautomatic personal mini-missile launcher, but with magnitudes more destructive power than a shotgun could have. It looked very similar to the Austrian Steyr AUG, but the barrel was fatter and it had a 50 round canister clip instead of a banana clip.

She also saw, with great satisfaction, her three brothers in addition to her sister, all kitted up like the True-Blood Eben. Along with the Base Commander, they were the hybrid contingent. All of them had their inner eyelids shut, and looked all the more dangerous for it.

The human and hybrid warriors had .50 Cal modified Desert Eagles Magnums on their hips, just like Achael did, though she hadn't drawn hers yet. The Desert Eagle had too much kick back for the True-Blood Eben, but they were deadly enough in their own right, with the knives in scabbards on each hip, to care about not having a handgun.

Achael turned back to face the Eridani Master, "Shock & Awe" had arrived. Push had come to shove. The effect of the predominantly Eben arrival, on those in the hangar bay, was unmistakeable. Now free of the drones grasping hands, she stepped back a few feet and finally drew her sidearm. She stopped beside Hlef who had her own Shil-7 pointed right at the Eridani Master.

Now focused on the job at hand again, without looking at her, Achael said to Hlef, "Glad you made it. Things are just getting interesting."

"So we can see."

"Really, something's going on here. Something is wrong." She paused, "Did I tell you how glad I am you're here?"

Hlef rubbed her cheek with one hand, "Wasn't me Turkey. It was KamPen."

"Really? KamPen? I thought he'd let me rot after our little tussle in the conference room."

Hlef, smiled without taking her eyes off the enemy, "He talked to Earth and got his marching orders. Came out of his office full of piss and vinegar. This isn't the only place something odd is going on."

Achael reflected quietly on that for a moment. The USAF had been all about keeping the détente, not pissing off the Eridani, and maintaining the status quo. It would have been almost sacrosanct USAF policy to *not* come after a rogue operative, especially one that flew willfully into the middle of an enemy stronghold. Something had indeed changed.

"WAR!! THIS IS AN ACT OF WAR!! YOU ARE ILLEGALLY TRESPASSING ON OUR SOVEREIGN TERRITORY!!"

"This is not an act of war, Master Voiya", replied KamPen who was now standing directly in front of the Eridani Master, with only the skirmish line of drones separating them. Of course, his Shil-7 was also pointed right at the middle of the Voiya's head, "We are here solely to recover our operative who was on an unsanctioned mission. I'm also to offer my apologies to you for any inconvenience she may have caused."

Achael's skin around her onyx black eyes crinkled a little bit at that. She held her position though, she gave no further reaction to the fact that she suddenly felt like she was being spoken of as an addled little school girl sitting outside the principal's office.

"SHE INVADED SOVEREIGN TERRITORY!! SHE MUST BE PUNISHED!! WE DEMAND SHE BE KILLED FOR HER TRANSGRESSION!! WE DEMAND SHE GO IN THE ACID TANK SO WE CAN WITNESS THE PUNISHMENT!!"

"Not going to happen my friend," replied KamPen. His gun and body never wavered, "The terms of the accord clearly state that each of our bases will offer unfettered landing privilege to each other during time of crisis or emergency."

"NO CRISIS!! WE WERE DEFENDING OUR BASE!! HUMAN NOT PART OF YOUR BASE!! WE KILL, TO DEFEND OUR BASE!!"

"She had one of your damaged vessels attached to a rescue cable. She had one of your drones in her craft. She returned the Drone and the vessel to your compound. In our definition, that constitutes a rescue which by definition, would have been initiated by a crisis. Because the Drone could not survive for long in a damaged vessel, she was responding to an emergency situation. So, Master Voiya, since it was both a crisis *and* an emergency, you were doubly obligated to accept her request for admittance, *and* treat her with the respect and hospitality that the détente demands. The only one here that is out of line is the one that first pointed a weapon. Based on what I saw when we entered your hangar bay, you Eridani were the only ones pointing weapons *and* your drones were restraining our operative, also against the terms of the accord. The only one that deserves to be punished is the master of all this mayhem AND THAT, MASTER VOIYA, IS YOU!"

There was an uncomfortable pause. The arriving OpFor and the Master's personal Trigla guards held their opposing positions rock steady; the Voiya seethed; the Vesna huddled and gestured silently; the other Trigla guards all held their weapons slackly, and looked like they wanted to be anywhere else they could think of; the drones all chattered and gnashed their teeth making wild gestures of battle invitation with their arms, heads, and bodies.

"Whom do I have the pleasure of addressing today," KamPen finally said. The Eridani Master, the Voiya so full of himself, said nothing.

Finally Achael cleared her throat and said, "Master Blitowyn of Chernasai."

KamPen cocked his head to the side, and thought for a moment then looked up again at the Eridani Master, "Rillixiwen's little brother?"

The Voiya screamed with rage, his whole body vibrating with the emotion, his permanent headache had to be piquing. His personal guards didn't move, they weren't that stupid this close to a shooting match. The drones however all started to slowly advance on KamPen. Four True-Blood Eben along with the hybrids all stepped in closer and brought their weapons to bear on the Eridani Master, and the Vesna. One of the True-Blood Eben spoke up much louder than you would have expected, "Shri shesk shlom-pac!"

The Vesna Mahal looked at the True-Blood Eben and nodded. The drones stopped moving, obviously reacting to the Vesna's telepathic command. The drones moved back closer to the Master's podium.

Sighing with impatience, KamPen continued speaking to the Voiya in front of him on its raised platform, "Like I said, *fathead*, the only one in violation here is *you*. Shall we fulfill all the terms of the treaty and execute the one responsible for failing to fulfill the terms?"

At that, the Master's personal guards chose valour over reason, a truly stupid decision given the situation. They stepped forward and brought their rifles around to point at KamPen. It was less than half a second after this, that the six bodyguards dissolved, mostly, into sprays of fine mist as eight Shril-7's erupted all at once.

As the remaining goo slagged to the bottom of the hangar bay and pooled around the Master's platform, the Eridani Master looked like he was about to have a heart attack. The older guard commander, still standing there with his hands up, had his eyes and mouth clenched shut. His platoon members that had been standing behind the Master, were now all standing with their hands and arms straight up in the air, their weapons clattering to the ground in front of them.

"Nice," whispered Hlef.

No sooner had she said that, the large access door at the back of the Hangar bay opened. Armed Trigla, armed Vesna and a few hundred more drones started pouring into the open space that was suddenly growing smaller.

Mike Lane

I was showered, finally smelling clean, and my skin felt invigorated and tingly after months of no water to shower in. I had put on fresh long johns and t-shirt, and then I checked the COM panel one more time (still showing errors). I looked at the chronometer and couldn't believe it. It was only 21:50 hours local. I grabbed my tablet off the desk, and went back to the lower level of the L-Hab. In my room I mounted the tablet in its cradle near the head of my bunk, crawled into the sheets and was asleep in seconds.

Around 05:00 hours local the Com unit beeped, burbled, and buzzed a bit; and then clearly gave a chiming notification sound. I came clear of the pillow with wide eyes, looked at the COM panel and mumbled, "COMs are back. Awesome." I collapsed back onto my pillow, instantly asleep again.

Chapter 32

Mission Control

18 Minutes, 24 Seconds Ago

The telemetry techs at the front of the room all jumped up, raised their hands in the air, and yelled at the same time, turning in unison like a perfectly choreographed ballet, "Telemetry is up again!"

Numbers were pouring into all the idle consoles, and techs raced to get back to their stations. It had been hours since a signal had been received from Mars, and everyone had been milling around sipping coffee and impatiently whispering about what was really going on, on Mars. The large screen at the front of the room started scrolling biosciences and atmospheric numbers at the bottom edge. The static jumped on the left side of the screen (Mar-Sat), and with a few stills in between the bursts of static, finally resolved into a steady Hi-Def picture.

Many people gasped at the sight, Hans among them. Hans had promptly come in a few hours ago after being called in the middle of a sound sleep by his brother, Karl. Jayden, it seemed, never left the place. They stood with Karl at the back of the room, watching with everyone else. It was still Karl's shift.

The video feed showed the Habitat structures and the site of the supply drops. The gasp was the site of the most recently arrived supply drop. There were faint wisps of smoke coming from underneath it. It stood canted over to one side, obviously missing a nacelle. There were two broken landing struts hanging uselessly at odd angles. The aeronautical engineers in the room, on loan from the manufacturer, surmised that the undercarriage support legs, to be used after landing to support and level the supply shipment, had stopped the supply drop from tipping completely over. A later examination by Mike would reveal that the explosion of the engine nacelle had damaged the controller for the landing struts, and the two on that side had started extending on their own. Had they not, the one hundred million Euro cargo of sample return vehicles, the real money makers, would have been completely lost. For now though, it appeared they may be salvageable, but that wouldn't be confirmed until Mike could do a proper inspection.

"Carrie," Hans spoke loudly across the room, "Any sign of him?"

She and Arno were huddled over their screens, panning and zooming on the available feed. They both shook their heads and kept on with what they were doing. Karl was about to ask her a question when she turned around and said, "It looks like the COM unit is re-initializing, we should have internals in a few minutes."

One of the Habitat support techs turned in his chair with his arm in the air, "We're getting gas exchange telemetry from the L-Hab. He has to be inside."

Nodding at this piece of good news, Karl stepped away from his brother and Jayden, and slowly walked over to the other side of the room. He was staring at the floor as he walked, chewing on an unlit cigar, and rubbing his small pot belly under his cardigan. With a furrowed brow, and obvious mental machinations in overdrive behind his unfocused eyes, he stopped behind Ernst and Freddie. They both sat there, unable to do anything. They had no image and no telemetry.

Finally Karl looked up and saw Ernst, chair turned sideways, starring back at him through his black rim, 1950's style glasses. Karl spoke in French, as he knew none of the telemetry techs nearby spoke that language. "Étrange, non?"

Ernst nodded his head but never took his eyes off Karl, "Oui, c'est étrange." Ernst had already reached the conclusion that he suspected Karl was now reaching. He and Freddie had already had a whispered discussion on it.

"Il est étrange que votre vidéo n'a pas été rétabli."

"Oui."

"Le vidéo principal est de retour, mais pas le vôtre," then after a brief pause, "Pourquoi exactement?"

Ernst just stared at him. The Platform's video should indeed have returned when the Mar-Sat video returned. When the interference for the first one cleared up, the other one should have cleared up at the same time. That left only two possibilities. Either The Platform had been destroyed, or, Karl muttered, "Quelqu'un d'autre avait le contrôle du satellite."

There was someone else besides Ernst and Mike that had control of The Platform.

Freddie gravely looked over his shoulder at both of them, then turned back to watch the big screen, "Tu ma volé les mots de la bouche."

Karl nodded sagely, turned around and went back up the raised levels of floor in Mission Control, towards the back of the room. He quietly discussed his concerns with Hans and Jayden. Jayden looked pissed. Hans looked pissed. They looked at each other. They were all pissed.

"Phone her," said Hans. Jayden nodded, and headed to his office.

After closing the door he sat down at his desk and opened the top drawer, reached way in the back and pulled out a card taped to the back of the drawer. It contained a phone number for the one he had secretly started to refer to as the Puppet Master, because she had pulled so many strings in getting this mission on its way. He picked up the telephone handset from its cradle, and dialed the number. He waited for only one ring after the international connection was made.

"88th Air Support Wing, Commandant's office," came the friendly voice.

"Lef-tenant General Rosewood, please."

"I'm sorry, the General isn't here at the moment, may I take a message?"

Jayden suppressed a sigh of exasperation and gritted his teeth, "It's about Aquarius."

"Wait one."

There was a pause, then a beeping and gurgling sound. The same voice, a little less pleasant, came back on the line, "Is this line secure?"

"Ummm ..."

"The General will call you back. Stay by your phone," then the line went dead. Jayden stared at the receiver in surprise, and then slowly hung it up. He sat there tapping a pen on the desk and wondered how long it would take for her to call. He pondered forwarding his phone to Mission Control and heading back down there. After three minutes of waiting, his office door opened with no announcement.

Two men in black suits and black fedoras, perfectly trimmed crew cut hair, very square jaws, wearing Ray-Ban sunglasses walked into his office. They stopped in front of his desk. Wordlessly, one of them reached inside his suit jacket, pulled out a digitally encrypted satellite phone, and handed it to Jayden. They then stood there, hands folded in front of them, staring at him. The phone rang.

Jayden, usually nonplussed, almost dropped the damn thing. He swiveled up the antenna and pressed the talk button.

"What do you want?" came Lieutenant General Rosewood's voice, Gilda, Gabby to her friends.

"Have you been following events on Mars?"

"Of course we have."

"We have the Mar-Sat signal back but not," he paused, looking up at the two men, "the other one."

"I'm aware of that. Do you know why yet?"

"That's what I was calling to ask you."

Gilda sounded genuinely confused, "What do you mean?"

"Well, it's kind of odd we got one signal back, and not the other. When the interference on the first one cleared up, the second one should have cleared up as well. Those two signals are so far away that they are almost the same signal by the time they get back here."

"And why would I know why we aren't getting the second signal? If you are implying that we are blocking it; we aren't, we are relying on that signal as much as you are."

"Yes but if the ..."

"If the second signal hasn't returned it means that either the satellite has been destroyed, or someone turned off the signal. Someone at *that* end."

"Yes", Jayden said.

"Jayden," she sighed, "We want this mission to succeed as much as you do. We have invested billions in it, and we made a lot of political enemies getting your man off the ground and across the solar system. If we had been able to put someone there who could turn the signal off and on, why would we need your guy?" Jayden couldn't see her smiling at her own Oscar worthy performance.

"Okay, okay. I see your point. But it doesn't change the fact this is damn peculiar. Is there any way we can find out if the satellite has been destroyed?"

"*Humph*, I doubt it has. It's well defended."

They had never discussed that, "What do you mean, well defended?"

He could almost hear the contempt in her voice, "You didn't think we'd send it to orbit Mars, carrying what it carries, without defense did you?" Jayden felt kind of numb at those words. He started to get a queasy feeling in the pit of his stomach. He was getting the first inkling of the thought that he was more of a pawn, than puppet. There was a sound of an excited voice in the background as she muffled the phone. Then she said quickly, "The signal's back," and she hung up.

He looked at the phone and pressed the End button. He looked up and one of the two men in black suits and black fedoras, perfectly trimmed crew cut hair, very square jaws, wearing Ray-Ban sunglasses was already reaching across the desk. The silent man took the phone out of his hand, swivelled the antenna closed, and stuck it back in his suit jacket. Without a nod or a smile, they both pivoted on their heels and walked out of his office, leaving the door open behind them.

Jayden got up right behind them and walked to the door. He stepped into the hall and stopped in his tracks. They were gone. The hallway was thirty feet long and the exit was at the far end. His desk was only ten feet from the door. They couldn't have gotten to the far end so fast without him hearing them running. He swallowed nervously, and looked behind him in his office, then down the hallway again.

"What the hell have we gotten into," he muttered as he headed back to Mission Control.

Chapter 33

Teviot Vallis

When the Eridani reinforcements began pouring into the hangar bay, everyone on both sides held their position. The pilot in the lead Dart communicated with the Eben Battle Cruiser, and the behemoth edged frighteningly close to the entrance of the hangar bay, so close that two of its forward rail guns actually passed through the magnetic curtain. This had the desired effect of slowing down the rushing reinforcements, and convincing all present to keep their heads. If the Eben ground pounder opened up this close, nothing in the Eridani base would survive.

"It's time to leave," Lieutenant Colonel KamPen tossed over his shoulder. As his troops started to slowly TransMat back aboard the ships, he spoke to the Eridani Master again.

"As for today's events, Master Voiya, this matter is closed. The terms of the détente have been satisfied to my liking. As of this moment, that human is now under *my* protection. If you attack him, you attack us - and you will suffer swift consequences," he let that sink in. It hadn't actually been part of his orders to say that. He just threw it in to piss off the Eridani even more. It was counterproductive to the grand plan of his betters, but he didn't know about the grand plan, yet.

KamPen continued, "We'll leave you in peace and thank you for allowing our operative to wait here for us. If you choose to press this matter any further," KamPen smiled and looked over his shoulder at the now almost completely blocked entrance to the cave, "well, then we'll just have to begin some aggressive negotiations."

The Eridani Master was then looking at empty air where KamPen had been standing. The ground pounder started to withdraw from the entrance and the three Darts, turning in unison, accelerated out of the hangar bay between the nose of the battle cruiser and the rock wall of the entrance.

Master Blitowyn of Chernasai looked around him. He looked down at six pairs of bloody calves sticking out of combat boots and the gooey, bloody sludge around him and on him that had so few minutes ago been his loyal personal guard. He looked at the corpses of the drones, and he looked around at the hundreds of mostly armed reinforcements that had crowded into the hangar bay. He looked behind him and saw the other two surviving Voiya, the other two Eridani Masters pushing their way through the crowded space to emerge right by the steps of this platform. They looked as pissed as he was, but then again, the Voiya always looked pissed. This, for Blitowyn, was a special kind of pissed. This was beyond the garden variety pissed, and had moved into the realm of apoplectically pissed. That scurrilous half-breed had called him, "fathead". The hybrids were going to pay. Oh, they were going to pay deeply for that.

Chapter 34

Aboard the Eben Battle Cruiser "Shin Fa"

The TransMat materialized Lieutenant Colonel KamPen on the bridge, directly behind the ship's True-Blood Eben Commander, who also happened to be KamPen's uncle. The bridge was one of only three places on the Battle Cruiser with enough room for a hybrid, or a human to be TransMat aboard.

"Prill Foosh", he nodded. His Uncle Foosh, dressed in the traditional Eben black turtleneck and slacks, turned and acknowledged him.

"Looks like Master Eridani not a happy camper," said Foosh, using his well-practiced English, and one of the many loved idioms he studied carefully. He smiled.

"I don't think this is over, not by a long shot."

Commander Foosh ObooPen (Oboo was Kam and Foosh's father; Kam ObooPen was Lt. Col. KamPen's father) made a sound that was the Eben equivalent of "hmm". As the Battle Cruiser was now clearing the Vallis and arcing around to pass over Hellas Planitia, he turned to his nephew, "Wasn't that Rillixiwen's little shumshah?"

"Yes, it was," KamPen looked thoughtful.

He looked at his uncle, and his uncle, equally thoughtful nodded, "Yes, strange."

"Why was I dealing with someone so minor? I would have expected Tsweflon or Ufektin of even Rillixiwen himself. Why did they send someone so low down the totem pole?"

"Others busy maybe," his grammar wasn't as perfect as he thought it was.

"Perhaps, uncle, but they wouldn't have left Blitowyn in charge, he's too young, too new. He's only been here three years."

"Your think is correctly," Uncle Foosh paused and looked down at the deck, "something very strange is going on in Eridani base."

"Pol", yes, was KamPen's reply in Eben, "Pol rem" (for sure).

Uncle Foosh looked up at his nephew, looked him squarely in his now unguarded, dreamy blue eyes, "I think something odd is going on elsewhere as well."

KamPen met his uncle's gaze but didn't say anything. After staring at him a bit longer than was comfortable, Commander Foosh turned back to the bridge crew, "Achael is in my quarters."

217

Just like that, the uncle had dismissed the nephew.

KamPen turned around without saying anything else. He exited the bridge and ducked down to pass through the Eben sized corridor. Down one flight of stairs, whose walls seemed too close together, and then along that deck's back bending low ceiling corridor a few feet to the Commander's cabin. He didn't knock. He opened the hatch, ducked even lower, and stepped into the oddly spacious room. Achael stood up, but not all the way up. They stood there looking at each other's feet, shoulders hunched and heads bent forward, chins pressed into their necks, back of their heads grazing the low ceiling.

"Commander," she said in acknowledgement.

"Achael," he said, then added, "dumb ass".

Awkwardly, she managed to hunch her already hunched shoulders, flapped her arms against her side and tried to smile, "Everyone's a critic!"

KamPen tried really, really hard not to laugh, but it was pointless. He loved Achael in a fatherly way and could never stay mad at her. Besides, her actions had finally been sanctioned by the old woman, so technically, he didn't really have anything to be mad about. He wasn't, however, going to let that stop him from dressing her down.

"Can we please sit down?" she said.

He tried to nod, but only bumped his head on the ceiling. They both sat down. Notwithstanding the official sanction, he knew he couldn't let her actions this day go unaddressed. He proceeded to give her a military style dressing down that lasted ten full minutes. From the fight and the destruction of so much of that section of the base; putting the SF sergeant in the infirmary; her taking the Dart without clearance; interfering with the human colonist; risking exposure to the human's ... oh shit. He thumbed his communicator and ordered the base Communications officer to terminate the interference generator aimed at Mar-Sat. He then continued Achael's dressing down without missing a beat. She risked her own neck by towing that piece of junk a quarter of the way around the planet, arriving unannounced at the enemy base, and then stirring the pot up to the point they were ready to execute her.

By the time KamPen had finished, he could see that Achael was visibly upset. She was upset alright, she was upset she had to sit there and listen to this for so long. She had no regrets and no reservations about what she had done. She knew she had done the right thing, and the fact that she wasn't, at this moment, sitting in the Battle Cruisers brig confirmed that for her. She didn't say any of this to him. Even though she seemed to so frequently break his rules and disappoint him, she truly did respect and care for her Commander. She did try to please him in so many ways, and always defended him when the others questioned him behind his back. Right now she kept silent, looked at the floor for a moment, then looked up at him, "I'm not sorry for what I did, I *am* sorry that I disappointed you, and that I put you in the position that I did."

He sighed and shook his head.

"And thank you for coming to get me."

Fifteen minutes later the Battle Cruiser *Shin Fa* glided effortlessly through the magnetic curtain of the cavernous hangar bay in the hybrid base, a hanger bay five times larger than the Eridani's. The outer doors of the hangar bay slid almost silently shut after two of the Darts followed the ground pounder through the magnetic curtain. The third Dart, Khlam and a True-Blood Eben at the controls, maintained a Combat Air Patrol around their base just in case the Eridani showed some balls and were coming for vengeance. A chime sounded in the Commander's cabin and both Achael and KamPen stood up, hunched over. Then they were standing on the hangar deck, appearing right in front of Hlef and Ahshuun; who were having a heated argument, having materialized mid argue.

They both paused and looked at Achael and the Lieutenant Colonel. Hlef was too pissed with Ahshuun to do anything but glare. Seeing them materialize, heads bent and hunched over like they were talking to their feet, Ahshuun couldn't help but snort and guffaw loudly. The Commander straightened up, smacked him in the back of the head and muttered, "asshole" as he strode towards his office. He had to turn The Platform communications back on with Earth, pronto. No telling what those Eridani bastards might do.

Chapter 35
Mike Lane

Two hours after my tablet first buzzed, I slowly woke up with a stretch and a yawn. I had to pee. I was also hungry. As I tried to decide which was more pressing, I noticed the unacknowledged priority message indicator flashing on my tablet, which was resting in its bracket on the wall above my head.

I didn't even remember waking up two hours before. I never heard any of its subsequent buzzes or chirps. I plucked up the tablet, and carried it upstairs with me as I went towards the head. I sat there having a leisurely and looked at the priority messages. There were three of them. One from Karl, one from Jayden, and one from ... I'll be damned ... Lieutenant General Rosewood.

I read Karl's message first. They had gotten video and telemetry back about three hours ago. Internal habitat camera's came back online about twenty minutes after that. They couldn't locate me anywhere on camera, but they were getting telemetry indicating that CO2 was being processed. That told them that I was alive and breathing, well, something was alive and breathing; and they assumed it was me. It didn't tell them what condition I was in. Karl made the correct assumption I was in my quarters, and told me to let them know when I was awake.

I hit the reply button and typed one word, "Awake". Send.

Jayden's message said nothing about my condition, it simply asked if I had loaded and installed the secure video software yet. I replied for him to give me an hour, and it would be. Send.

With some mounting curiosity I opened the Lieutenant General's message. She was one person I never expected to hear from again. She simply asked if I was okay, told me to keep strong, and not give up and that "we" were pulling for me. The word "we" implied the United States Air Force Materials Command, 88th Air Support Wing, Wright-Patterson Air Force Base. I typed back to her, "Been better. Won't give up, and don't have any choice. Send a CIWS :-)". Brashly asking for a Close In Weapons System would probably make her smile. Send.

Finishing my business, I performed what was every man's ritual morning ablutions, and then went out to the kitchen area. I sat the tablet down, and made up a protein shake. I purposefully went and looked out the portal on the east side of the habitat, looking out over the sand dunes. Nothing out there. Good. Very good. Oh wait ... I watched a pair of dust devils spin by in the distance, one at a time, dissolving into nothingness. Those damn things were still a mystery to the climatologists.

I cleaned out my shake container, went to the W-Hab, and sat down at the workstation I had unpacked and already set up. I closed my eyes at that point and had a long talk with God about yesterday's events; what I was afraid of, what troubled me, and how I needed his strength and protection.

Now, in a better frame of mind, I booted up the workstation and launched the communications app (more than just email). First, I installed the software Jayden wanted online. Next, I went through the Mission Control emails, answering Karl, Hans, Carrie and Ernst. Then I answered a few of the techs emails, sending them local readings and observations. Surprisingly, everyone except Carrie and Hans had avoided the topic of the day before. Ernst just wanted to know if I had local connection with the Jalopy-Sat; and Karl told me to turn off the friggin' cameras if I was going to walk to the shower nude again. He said they were getting tired of seeing my junk. I have to admit, I blushed quite hotly at that one.

I checked my personal account next. I sent two less than quick emails to my son and to Mary. I shared some thoughts and fears with them, but reaffirmed my belief in the mission and my presence here. Mary had indicated she was ready to start a, "Return Mike" movement to force the U.S. Air Force to find a way to return me to Earth. I did have to pause a tick before responding that it wasn't necessary, and that I didn't want to return to Earth. I'd encountered these frakers twice and I was still alive. Granted, the second encounter was far worse than the first, but really, it simply *had* to be over for now, didn't it?

I moved on to the day's work manifest. I started taking care of mechanical checks and readings, and atmospheric observations to back up the telemetry, working my way slowly through the list that was much longer than the previous days.

I turned my attention to a pressing repair that one of the Mission Control Habitat techs had messaged me about. As I sat there going over schematics for the energy distribution system to find the L105-BR Auto Reset Circuit Breaker location, the workstation beeped beside me. I turned to look at it, and a small window was open that I had never seen or been briefed on. In the title bar it said MillChatSecure. In the window proper it showed:

```
User538: i see you still have your sense of
humour.
```

The cursor blinked slowly at me in the reply box. Chat software, on Mars. With that message it could only be Lieutenant General Rosewood. Was she nuts? Computer chat would be agonizing over this distance. I typed back to her and hit the send button, my message appeared on the screen:

```
MARCOL1: If I didn't laugh, I'd cry. No time to
cry in outer space. Send Cookies.
```

It would be close to an hour before I got a response back from her, if there was going to be any. I picked up the tech manual and headed downstairs to the small room with the power distribution equipment. Turning on both overhead LED lights, I moved very slowly to make sure I didn't inadvertently touch anything zappy. I was able to remove an access cover, swing out some circuit boards, root through some wires, and find the L105-BR Auto Reset Circuit Breaker. It had shown no connectivity in diagnostics. The techs needed a touchy-feely assessment before deciding what to do about it. I wiggled it a bit, and pressed inwards on it. With a silent snap that I felt in my fingertips rather than heard, it popped solidly into place. There was no indication that anything had changed, so I nestled the wires back in place, swung the circuit boards back into the box, and slowly reconnected the cover plate. I'd have to check the functionality back on the main system interface at the primary workstation. Doing a careful, procedurally driven safety check, I backed out of the small room, ticking off items in my head as I did so. Atmo, water, air and power were the big four of survival in this place. No mucking about carelessly with any of them. Procedures were life on Mars.

Exiting the electrical distribution room, I opened the other mechanical room to check water volume and available air supply. I ran some mechanical checks and took the time to properly inspect the CO_2 scrubbers. I then pulled some samples from the water and air tank to place in the diagnostic analyzer in the sick bay. I was supposed to do this once a week and hadn't yet done it since arriving.

Properly hooking up the AtmoGen was on this afternoons work manifest, and I had to put the intake system in a bypass standby mode. I disconnected the trickle feed from the main tanks and connected it to the empty reserve tanks. These, once filled, would be my emergency air supply. They depended on the trickle system staying operational. The Habitat then started running off of stored air in the main tanks. I reconfirmed the available air in the hi-pressure tanks. One person could last 72 hours on the stored air if there were no more than three airlock cycles in that time frame. I had just set an important clock ticking, and needed to get on with things. Backing out of this room and ticking off items in a different procedure in my head, I finished by making sure all the hatches were secure, and went back up to the main work space, stopping to boot up the sick bay analyzer, and drop in the samples.

As I sat at the workstation, I could see that Rosewood had responded to me.

`User538: good. im glad you are okay`

I checked the system utility monitor, keyed in the proper commands and was told that the L105-BR Auto Reset Circuit Breaker was in place, and had passed the integrity check. I replied to the tech-head email that had alerted me to the problem, and then went back to the MilChatSecure window.

I hesitated a moment, then decided to go ahead and ask:

MARCOL1: Do you think it will get worse?

In preparation for the AtmoGen connection, system charging and full activation this afternoon, I lifted the tablet to compare the atmospheric system readings between the tablet, where I had recorded them downstairs, and the desktop primary workstation. I no sooner started this when the workstation beeped. I glanced at the workstation with the MilChatSecure window open and saw:

User538: that depends

That depends on ... my head snapped up in shock. I stared at the wall for a few seconds as my mind tried to wrap itself around this. Then I looked down at the software window again. I really, really did see that there. It wasn't a hallucination. How the frak did she respond to me in seconds? That response should have taken almost thirty-seven minutes. What the hell was going on?

User538: surprise

MARCOL1: What the HELL is going on? Is this a programmed response or is this real-time?

User538: real-time

MARCOL1: HOW?

User538: need to know

MARCOL1: Can I communicate with Mission Control in real-time?

There was a pause.

User538: no

MARCOL1: Why not???

User538: because I said so

There was a pause at my end now.

MARCOL1: So it's like that is it?

User538: yes mike. yes it is. its like that

I was dumbfounded. I was flabbergasted. I was over 140 million kilometres from Earth. Telemetry and video between here and Mission Control was at about 18 minutes and 22 seconds each way, almost 37 minutes round trip. I could send a message, have lunch, inspect mechanics, do some clean up and then (only then), get a response to a very quick question with a very quick answer, from Mission Control.

Now, here I was, having a real-time chat with a woman who was also over 140 million kilometres away.

```
User538: ill be in touch.
```

The chat window remained open but grayed out in the text entry box. I couldn't type anything. Eventually I hit the "X" in the corner and the application disappeared. I searched around for an icon or link to launch it again, but couldn't find one.

I sat there feeling completely and utterly confused.

Chapter 36

Going Down-side

Achael had time to shower, change her clothes, and then she was standing in the Base Commander's office, again. Hlef was beside her, and they were waiting for Lieutenant Colonel KamPen to get off the phone. He was talking to Earth. He didn't look happy.

"I've been ordered to put you two on the supply transport, leaving in ten minutes. You are to report directly to the Lieutenant General at the 88th. I would not advise you be late."

"Why the two of us?" asked Hlef hotly.

"Because she wants the both of you," he replied just as hotly.

Achael grabbed her by the arm, "C'mon Hlef, we've no time for this, let's go."

Hlef pulled her arm out of her sister's grasp, "I didn't do this! I tried to stop her! I never wanted her to go frak around with the human! Why do I have to go to Earth, for frak sake?"

"GO!" he yelled at her, pointing at this office door with his long hybrid arm.

Hlef pursed her lips shut, looking at him with fire in her eyes, "Fine. I'll go." She spun on her heels, and led Achael out the door.

"Wear your dress blues too!" he yelled after them.

"FRAK OFF!" yelled Hlef from down the corridor. He smiled. Gilda didn't care what they wore. He knew it would just infuriate Hlef more, and she deserved it for getting prissy with him. Besides, Gilda had only asked for Achael. He kind of wished he could see the look on Hlef's face when she found out. He snickered to himself, "I'm a bad, bad man." He snickered some more.

For now, the two women were going to Terra. Peace would surely reign for several hours unless the Eridani attacked. At least he knew how to handle the Eridani effectively. He shut his office door with his extra-long hybrid arm, locked it, and then stretched out on the sofa for a nap. He so rarely got to nap. The True-Blood's never napped. They should try it.

As he settled on the sofa, Achael and Hlef practically ran outright to their shared quarters. When they arrived, Achael picked up the phone and dialed the hangar bay. Her brother wasn't on duty any more, she told his full-human relief to hold the supply shuttle as they had been ordered down-side most Riki-Tik.

They both flew out of their clothes and jumped quickly into their dress blues: nylons, skirt, button up blouse, neck tab, jacket, and hat. They both checked they had their sunglasses in their jacket pocket, and ran out of their quarters. They ran full tilt to the hangar bay, more to burn off Hlef's mounting anger and resentment than anything else. Of course, due to the hybrid's superior fighting physiology, they arrived without breathing hard, and not breaking a sweat.

The cargo shuttles looked like what you would expect a cargo shuttle to look like; if you were a spacefaring race that had exposure to, and experience with, cargo shuttles. This was one of the smaller shuttles. It was stubby, boxy, ugly, and uncomfortable. As it was Eben tech, the trade-off was that it was reliable, efficient, and had a top class NavCom for the top class folding engine; even more precise than the Dart's. It had to be able to fold them from extremely high orbit, precisely into an underground service bay at Wright-Patterson; without having them fold into a wall or worse, the bedrock surrounding it. It could even cross feed the NavCom figures to a Dart for the same precision folding. In fact, the only way a Dart could land at Wright-Patterson was if a cargo shuttle was in extremely high orbit to feed them the very, very precise coordinates.

The human co-pilot helped buckle them into their military seats then joined the True-Blood Eben pilot in the cockpit. They were in atmo in a few minutes. Five minutes later they were totally clear of the Martian atmosphere. As they were jumping a much greater distance than Achael had on the surface, the ship needed to be completely outside the atmosphere and magnetic field of the planet before activating the folding engine. They made the journey to Earth in about seven minutes. The cargo ship had a powerful folding engine, but it was small in comparison to the Battle Cruiser's folding engine. This meant they needed to make three folds to get there. The maximum distance a folding engine could move an object was exponentially proportional to the size of the folding engine core. In the case of this small size cargo vessel, the folding core was a 12 micron wide singularity encased in a self-powering magnetic bottle. The magnetic bottle was contained in several millions of layers of graphene. The Graphene container is insulated by methane gas, and it all sits nestled in a titanium-carbyne outer casing. To make the math simpler, a 10 micron wide singularity in the above described system could fold 0.83 AU, indefinitely. This small cargo ship's folding engine's entire assembly was about the size of a picnic cooler. The folding engine in the Battle Cruiser was the size of a Prius, the singularity being 32 microns in diameter.

Hlef gripped the seat and shut her eyes most of the way to Terra. She hated folding in the cargo ship. It made her queasy and bitchy. Well, bitchy-er. She had to keep letting go of the seat to scratch under her skirt and jacket. She despised the wool in her dress blues, they made her itch. She was now scratching herself like a flea infested pound puppy.

Achael just watched her sister as her mind wandered over everything that had happened in the last few hours. She had no idea why the Lieutenant General would be upset; she had gotten permission to proceed after all. She knew the Lieutenant General had briefed the human about the Eridani, and that the 88th had done a lot to get that mission and its human to Mars. She hoped that KamPen's boss wasn't going to dress her down the way KamPen had, at least not in front of Hlef.

Achael reflected on KamPen's dressing down less than an hour ago. It had only been about eight hours since they had been sitting in the conference room waiting to watch the human's supply mission land. She knew she had behaved very poorly. She and Hlef should never have gone into full battle mode on each other and destroyed so much property. Those follies of youth were supposed to be behind them. Taking the Dart without permission was also bad, but not nearly as bad as exposing herself to discovery; discovery by the human's site video equipment and satellite cameras. Luckily KamPen had shut down all transmission and data back to the human's base on Terra before she arrived. At least she wouldn't have to wear that millstone around her neck. However, she had still displayed flagrant disregard for protocol and procedure because of emotion and passion. "Ohhh, this isn't going to be fun," she muttered to herself. She didn't regret going to help the human but everything else about that decision started to weigh on her, heavily.

"Just wait till I'm done with you," her sister sneered, while squinting at her from beneath one slightly opened eyelid.

"You love me," said Achael.

"And your point is what?"

"If you stop being so fraking miserable for five minutes, I'll take you to the commissary at Wright-Patterson and buy you some chocolate pudding ... when she's done with us."

Hlef sat bolt upright with eyes wide open, "Chocolate pudding? For real?"

"Yes," said Achael, "for real."

Hlef had a very specific endocrine chemistry that was quite unique. Because of this oddity, it was discovered early in Hlef's life that cocoa acted on her system like 150 proof rum did on a teetotaler. Chocolate had an effect on all Eben and all the hybrids, but the most it would give them was a slight buzz and an upset stomach. With Hlef, it made her worse than a debutante hooted up on moonshine after a summer cotillion. The Eben mission had learned early on that this was one Terran delicacy that Hlef was never

229

supposed to have (no other civilization in the three galaxies had chocolate or cinnamon; they were both unique to Earth). It was also the one Earth delicacy she craved the most, like an alcoholic craving a '7 & 7'.

"Promise? You're not teasing me? That wouldn't be very nice of you," she sounded almost plaintively childlike.

"I'm not teasing you Hlef", smiled Achael, finally her sister was getting back to a more normal attitude, "I'll buy you two. We can also sneak some chocolate bars back with us, if we can."

Unfortunately for Hlef, the commissary had already been alerted by the shuttle's Eben pilot, through the ERB communications unit, that Hlef was on the way to the base. They kitchen staff had all run over to the desert cooler, and started to scarf back the remaining eight bowls of chocolate pudding that had been made that morning. Then they tackled the half of a chocolate cake that was sitting on the table. Their attitude was that it would be criminal to throw such delicious deserts in the garbage, so, chow down. They finished up by grabbing all the chocolate bars on display and putting them in the commissary storage closet, behind the bottles of bleach and Drano, to mask their smell. They finished operation 'Chocolate Gorge' just as the cargo ship folded into the service bay, located deep in the bedrock beneath Wright-Patterson AFB. The cafeteria on the lower decks never stocked anything chocolate, just in case.

After the cargo door opened, the ladies unbuckled themselves, stood up and straightened their uniforms. They exited the craft into a predominantly human world, but a closed world that was alien friendly, for the right aliens. Since the women were both half human and dominantly so, hardly anyone glanced at them.

They made their way along the corridors and up the lift to the real world. The elevator doors opened on the first sublevel of the 88th Wing's administrative building. Achael and Hlef put on their sunglasses, and without even thinking about it, they crossed their long arms over their chests, tucking their long-fingered hands, fists clenched, far under their elbows. Not everyone on this level was fully briefed, though they all had suspicions. Regardless, the human dominant hybrids took certain steps to prevent too many questions or ogling stares. The Eben dominant hybrids rarely ever came this far. The True Blood Eben never came this far. They did, however, have a small compound at the government community on Lake Walker, in the shadow of Mt. Grant, Nevada. It was a vacation spot for the Eben assigned to the Mars base. Highly protected and with Eben tech that made it invisible to long range cameras, like on satellites.

Achael stopped suddenly outside Lieutenant General Rosewood's suite of offices on Sublevel 1, Corridor 3, North Wing, Door #538. She put a hand on her stomach while biting her lip, turned to Hlef and quietly moaned, "Sis, I feel sick to my stomach."

Hlef, gave her a reassuring smile and rubbed her shoulder, "It's okay Turkey. You know she can only stay mad so long."

"Yes, but I did so many things wrong today, so many things."

"You better believe it. Made me proud of you."

"Proud of me?"

"Achael, I may ride you about that human and all your hair brained ideas, but really, you did what needed to be done, and what none of the rest of us were willing to do."

Achael was, for the first time, completely dumbfounded by her sister. Hlef had never given any indication that she had any understanding at all of what Achael was going through when it came to her compassion and passion.

"For real?"

Hlef smiled again, wrapped her long arms around Achael, and hugged her tightly, "You're my sister Achael. I love you without limits. One of the things I love about you is how responsible you are, and how incredibly gutsy. I may not always agree with you, but I always admire you." She kissed her on the cheek, then stepped back, and crossed her arms again.

"Come on," Hlef said, "let's go get our spanking. Remember, we have a date in the commissary!"

They stepped through the door to the offices, Hlef taking the lead. Major Billy Harper, the Lieutenant General's Adjutant, looked up from his desk in his office as the ladies entered the reception area. When they stopped to present themselves to the civilian receptionist (who's security clearance was higher than the President's), the tall, muscular, tanned, black-haired, black-skinned, former track and field star came out of his office.

"Welcome down-side ladies," he said with a smile. As they were all the same rank, the rules of formality were a bit relaxed.

"Billy," Hlef smiled, "Good to see you." She knew how nervous Achael was, so she wanted to run as much interference as she could until Achael went into the Dragon's den.

He nodded in acknowledgement, "The General's expecting you, Achael."

The two smiling women with dark wrap-around sunglasses just stood there, their arms crossed in front of them, smiling for a moment longer than comfortable. They looked at each other, and then looked back at Billy.

"Just Achael?" Hlef asked with a smile frozen on her lips.

231

"Yes, she was only expecting Achael. But I'm sure she is going to be absolutely thrilled to have you here for a visit Hah-Lef," he never could say her name right. "Would you care to wait in my office while Achael gets yelled at a lot?" he said with an apologetic and commiserating smile on his face. He'd been on the wrong end of Rosewood's ire more than once himself.

The girls smiles were frozen on their faces. Hlef looked down at the ground and chuckled a bit as she looked back up at Achael. She leaned a bit closer to her and in a very quiet voice she said through smiling lips and gritted teeth, "I'm going to fraking kill that son-of-a-bitch."

Rosewood's office door flew open at that moment and the compact, athletic old woman stood looming in the door frame. She wasn't smiling.

"You two, my office, NOW!"

Chapter 37

AtmoGen

I had a quick protein shake for lunch, still mulling over what the General's exchange really meant for the mission. Shaking it off and deciding to compartmentalize it, I'd worry about it when I didn't have other things more pressing to worry about. I got on with the work manifest. I was now at item number thirty-seven of forty-one items, "Atmospheric Generator Initialization and Full Umbilical Connection"

When the AtmoGen had first arrived and been towed into place by Big Dawg, it had a single unprotected hose connected to the W-Hab by Big Dawg and Little Dawg, working together. The AtmoGen had a small production/test system in place that provided a trickle supply of breathable air to the W-Hab for system testing and validation. This was the system that I had put on bypass this morning. This trickle supply would actually have met all the needs of a single person, but I needed to get the unit fully operational as part of my proof of concept mission. The trickle system would then become my backup system.

Once the AtmoGen was running at spec, I then had a lot of testing to do. Actually, the *computers* had a lot of testing to do, I just had to be there as the expensive on-call service tech. With my full surface Activity Suit and jumpsuit all donned and sealed, K-Bar on my hip, and Energy Weapon slung over my shoulder; I picked up the small toolkit and exited the airlock to the surface, closing the airlock door behind me. Navy slide down the ladder, one handed (still so very, very cool); and I was on my way.

I walked around the W-Hab to the backyard and headed towards the AtmoGen plant. It was about 100 metres away. The trickle feed hose was going to be replaced with an armoured hose, but that was the last step of the system conversion. I stopped every 10 metres or so, and did a scan of the sky as far as I could see. Nothing ominous, nothing shimmering. Reaching the AtmoGen, I dropped my toolkit and walked around it. The trickle system equipment port was open, as it should be, and a rectangular framed equipment carriage (the size of a bar fridge) was sticking out of it. This was the test system that extracted the O2 at the rate of about 400 ounces (just shy of two litres of O_2 and ten litres of nitrogen) per hour. The full system, once in full operation, would produce 12 litres of oxygen, and 53 litres of nitrogen per hour. In addition to this, separate equipment inside would also be separating carbon monoxide (CO) and oxygen (O_2) from the carbon dioxide (CO_2) at a slower rate; to be used as rocket fuels for the SRV's (Sample Return Vehicles).

As I walked around the structure of the space craft that was now going to be a processing station, I inspected the six ground anchors. After the craft had landed, Mission Control had sent the requisite commands that one at a time, installed the ground anchors. These were six tubes inside the craft that had openings through the floor/bottom of the craft/station. Small sealed explosive charges blew sharp pointed iron spikes (5 cm in diameter and 3 metres long) down into the regolith. Once in place, a secondary charge forced a firing pin down into the centre of the two part spikes which drove "teeth" out sideways into the regolith. These ground anchors were to keep the relatively light weight AtmoGen plant in place against high winds. In fact, only three of them were needed for the proper holding power, but it appeared that all six had functioned properly and were in place. That thing wasn't going anywhere any time soon, even in Martian hurricane force winds (90 to 100 km/hour).

Returning to the side of the AtmoGen facing the Habitats, I reached up above the nacelle skirting, and opened the human-sized access hatch, pulled out and installed a small ladder, and climbed inside. On this arriving space ship, the nacelle skirting was only about three feet high. The final RAD engines were much smaller than the others because, by comparison, this unit hardly weighed anything, regardless of how tall it was (9 metres high). This unit was not, and didn't need to be, pressurized, so I just left the hatch open. There was just enough room for me, inside the processing plant, to stand on a small square of decking, and reach everything I had to reach for normal start up and maintenance operations.

First I checked the battery levels. The solar collectors built into the top of the hull had been doing their job, and the batteries, in their solar powered heated compartment were completely topped up. The first thing I did was activate the electricity generating system. The AtmoGen required a lot more than the solar cells and batteries could provide. Flipping the correct switches and pressing the correct buttons caused four exterior panels to open up, high up on the top of the AtmoGen craft/station. The shape of the AtmoGen station provided a sharp curve at the top resulting in an almost flat "roof".

Next I extended the wind collectors. From each of the four openings, two poles extended straight up in the air with cylindrical objects at the end of them. They extended just enough to be clear of the top of the AtmoGen plant. Each cylindrical object was 25 cm in diameter and 80 cm long. They had composite discs and barrel ends, at each end. These composite discs were joined by 24 angled vanes that were just a bit over 5 cm wide. The extended poles holding the wind harvesters passed up through a hole in the middle of the flat discs and were capped with a larger nut at the top to keep the harvesters in place. The bottom disc of the harvesters had powerful magnets around the centre hole, which were matched by a ring of opposite polarity magnets on the armature itself. Inside the wind harvester vane assemblies,

234

there were a series of wires that would push against a series of spiky arms extending outwards from the centre line armature. When the wind harvester was turned, those wires pressed against the spiky arms, which caused the pole's core connecting rod to be turned. This turning connecting rod, protected below the wind harvester by an outer metal pipe shell, turned the 10 kW turbines inside the AtmoGen station. Due to the lack of resistance on the wind harvesters, thanks to the powerful magnets and free floating design, they had 58.5% efficiency, limited only by Betz law.

These were miniature versions of what I needed to set up in the coming days for the Wind Collector Farm and Energy Distribution System. Regardless of their smaller size, this station's high efficiency mini wind farm along, with some highly advanced and very efficient turbines, produced 40 kW of electricity per hour with a wind speed of only 15 km/hour. To put this in perspective, the eight 10 kW turbines produce approximately 900 kWh of electricity per day, or just over 325,000 kWh per year. That means this small AtmoGen facility would produce enough electricity for over 280 homes had it been on Terra. This was twice the energy that it actually needed for the atmosphere and RSV fuel extractions. The overage was planned as a backup for the Habitats in case something catastrophic happened to the yet-to-be-installed Wind Collector Farm. Redundancy in space.

Once the arms were up and spinning, the readings on the controller panel showed they were producing electricity at a wild rate. This would make things much easier. I flipped another switch, felt a soft *thunk* through the deck plate, and leaned outside to look. Ladder rungs had extended from the side of the station, right beside the access hatch. I unstrapped and removed the Boot Box from the small storage rack inside the AtmoGen station control area, attached it to a small tether on my utility belt, and climbed up the oversized rungs. I didn't need my toolkit as the Boot Box had everything I needed in it. I was happy with myself; I actually remembered this next part of my training very clearly.

Once on the top of the station, I reached in the Boot Box and pulled out a safety tether. I opened a small hatch near the centre of the roof. It had a hardpoint connection inside it. I connected the safety tether to a D-ring on my belt with an oversized carbineer clip, and attached the other to the hardpoint connection inside the small open hatch with another oversized carbineer clip.

Sand and wind is an ever-present commodity on Mars. A lot of design time and dollars have been spent accounting for this. The prevalence of the sand was one of the reasons our Colony was going to be relying so heavily on wind power, with solar power only as a backup. The NASA rover *Spirit* had been enjoying a mission far longer than planned, until it got stuck in the sand. Within a year, the build-up of sand on the solar panels caused its ultimate demise. Wind storms and dust devils had occasionally cleaned the panels for both *Spirit* and the sister rover *Opportunity;* but once Spirit was stationary, it wasn't enough. As the Colony's solar cells were all stationary, rather than making it a daily maintenance chore that would only get bigger and bigger as the colony grew; that would occupy larger and larger areas of real estate as the colony grew: the mission decided to go with Wind Collectors. Cleaning those existing Habitat solar collectors was what occupied almost all of Little Dawg's work time. Converting to wind energy would free up the little bugger for other important work.

The sand, however, could still be a problem. The openings at the top of the AtmoGen station would allow destructive amounts of sand to enter the inside of the otherwise protected area. That meant that I now had to manually close part of the openings and install Elastomer (rubber) boots around the remaining openings. The designs made this an easy task, and it only took me about ten minutes work at each of the four openings. Of course, after each one I had to stop for a minute and scan the skies around me, energy weapon still slung over my shoulder.

As I finished the last boot, I was about to unclip my safety line when I noticed some movement. Looking up quickly I saw it was a dust devil, headed right for me! The cyclonic wind pillar itself would extend high up into the atmosphere; but the destructive sand in this one was only about 800 metres high. As stated, it was headed straight for me. Pucker time.

I watched as it got closer and closer, whipping up sand in the regolith as it moved along, a fine mist of sand and small pebbles ejected from the sides, slowly falling back to the ground. It was probably moving at about a 50 km/hour ground speed. When it contacted the side of the AtmoGen station, the cyclone shape was warped by it a bit, and then continued right on over the AtmoGen station; and me along with it. I had to grab hold of the tether with one hand, and the hardpoint anchor with the other, and made myself as flat as I could.

The force of the cyclone tried to pull me free of the roof. I could hear the sand and pebbles rushing across my helmet. I could feel the wind tugging and pulling at me. After a few seconds, it was gone. I rolled over and looked behind me and watched it move off in a south east direction, totally missing the habitats, heading towards the sand dunes. Very cool! Mission Control would have caught the whole thing on video from the Habitat roof cameras. I wish I had turned on my helmet video camera for it, but I was more worried about pulling a Dorothy Gale.

The Boot Box, with its proprietary tools, however, wasn't as lucky. I looked over the side of the station and saw it lying on the ground, tools strewn in a line away from it. It was at that moment I said a silent thank you to the German engineer that had come up with the idea of the ground anchors. Since

I was still up on the roof and tethered, with the cyclone having gone right over the top of the station, I did a visual inspection of the wind collectors so recently elevated into place. They all functioned perfectly, and there wasn't a scratch of damage that I could detect with my eyes. The Elastomer boots had held perfectly in place as well.

Scanning the sky around me once again, energy weapon still slung over my shoulder, I unclipped my tether, and closed the wee hatch. I coiled up the safety line, hanging it from my utility belt. I climbed down the extruding ladder rungs, and stepped back inside the service hatch of the Atmogen station. Now that the power generators were online and functioning better than expected, it was time to get the critical part of the system up and running. This would take longer.

First I ran the unlock sequence, then ran the sequence of commands to open the two side doors that were three-quarters as tall as the station. One opened on each side. Each opening was 97 cm wide. As the doors opened, I went outside and did a visual inspection to ensure the built in operational hatch seals, the heavy Elastomer blades, extended properly. As these hatches would be closing onto pieces of metal, hoses, and power cords; the outer few centimetres of the door were actually hinged. When released, small armatures pushed them outwards and back against the hatch itself. There they were held in place by strong electro-magnets. The heavy Elastomer blades also hinged outwards from their interior transit position. Once extended, simple mechanical pressure held them in place when the hatches closed on the extended equipment.

Next I activated the extender motors, and had a flashback to the wing wells on the Jalopy. Two rectangular frames extended from each side, approximately 2.7 metres. Each of these equipment carriages held a collection of metallic fins, canisters, and armoured hoses. These were the actual workhorse parts of the AtmoGen plant. Due to their nature, they were made as tough as possible, but had some limitations. They were hardy enough to withstand the daily general blowing around of sand on the surface, and could even withstand moderate-sized dust devils such as I had just experienced. During a prolonged sand storm however, they would have to be retracted. Therefore, the extending and retraction of them was push button automated, so we didn't have to suit up and manually go outside to do it. Once they were fully extended, I ran the sequence to close the doors around them. I did a visual inspection outside and now with more room to move around inside, did a visual inspection there as well. The Elastomer blade's seams looked tight, as there was no light coming through them. Awesome, things were going like clockwork.

As this process needed to be automated and run from the habitats, it had to be tested from my tablet. I remembered that I had left my tablet back in the

W-Hab. I went back to get it, cycling in and then out of the airlock. I had now used up the three airlock cycle tolerance for the reserve air tanks in the habitat. This AtmoGen had better work properly or I was in the deep. As I walked back to the AtmoGen, my stomach suddenly sank and I froze in place. Out across the plain towards the ice wall I could see a shimmer in the air. I stood there feeling both helpless and enraged, not sure which one to go with. After maybe twenty seconds of this, the shimmer shot straight up in the air, becoming another gray orb, and disappeared from sight.

I stood there for a few minutes scanning the sky, energy rifle now at port arms. It didn't return, and I didn't see anything else to stress about, so, resigning myself to being the latest microbe in the Petri dish, I slung the weapon over my shoulder again, and went back to work.

I pulled a USB cable out of the small compartment on the back of the tablet carrying case and plugged it directly into the AtmoGen onboard controller. I launched the AtmoGen software, let it initialize, and then hit the "Storm Close" icon. I stuck my head out the hatch and looked from side-to-side to watch the hatch doors open, the equipment carriages retract, the Elastomer blades and the outer door rim rotate back into a closed state, then the doors finally closed, sealing and locking in place.

I climbed back down to do a quick visual inspection, then with the tablet still attached and sitting on the deck, I just reached in and hit the "Start Operations" icon. The process reversed and after a final interior and exterior visual inspection, I then pronounced the mechanical portion of the manifest item completed.

Next was the dicey part. I had very little to do with it, and yet my survival was highly dependent on it. In two years, I'd be better off. One of those future planned supply drops would include a hopper and feeder system/filtration system that would allow me to drop chunks of frozen water and frozen CO_2 into it. The hopper would crush, then feed these items into an as yet unopened port, and the equipment package coming with it would then process the ice just like it was processing the Martian atmosphere. The added benefit was that the solids processing system would also produce methane and hydrogen as well as oxygen, using the Sabatier process. The eventual production of methane and hydrogen would be used for a far more efficient lifting power of the SRVs; allowing them to return larger quantities. Right now, if they weren't damaged irreparably in yesterday's event, the carbon monoxide and oxygen lift for the SRVs would only put about 40 kg on its way to Terra. Using methane and hydrogen, with oxygen as the oxidizing agent, then they would be able to take about 150 kg.

Scrolling through all the readings from the AtmoGen control system on my tablet, then visually comparing them with what was on the screen inside the service area of the station, everything looked good. I activated the processing sequence. Panel lights started flashing and everything looked *A-OK*. I now had to kill an hour, while I waited to come back and check the progress. This first hour was as much system testing and validation as it was actual processing.

I pulled out the armoured umbilicals from their storage racks, just inside the service hatch, and started uncoiling them. I wouldn't attach them until all the system's checks had completed. There were two armoured umbilicals for gases, and one smaller armoured line for system's communication. I could Bluetooth with the AtmoGen plant, but the preferred connection was wired. After they were uncoiled, I took a stroll around the colony site, looking for anything that needed immediate attention with one eye, and watching the sky around me with the other. With half an hour left, I went back and sat on the deck inside the AtmoGen service hatch, legs dangling outside, and started going through email messages on my HUD. There wasn't anything from Mission Control that I could address right now, so I went on to the public email box. There were thousands. I looked at the latest ones, most had to do with yesterday's attack. I chose to ignore those, other than writing a quick reply to a few whose names I recognized, I'm fine and thank you for your concern. I typed these quick messages out on the controller unit on my suit arm. There were a few from schools and universities with real questions about the mission, and what I was doing. I answered three of those in more detail. I used the internal helmet camera to record video rather than type on the arm pad.

Realizing the systems had been running well over the required hour, I picked up the tablet (why hadn't I typed the messages on that? It would have been so much easier), and started running the evaluations and diagnostics on the AtmoGen controller, and the processed gases. Everything came up nominal, *A-OK*, or 100%; depending on what you were looking at. I was now producing oxygen and nitrogen to breathe, along with the carbon monoxide for the SRVs. I hopped down to the ground, and proceeded to connect the umbilicals. I realized both Big Dawg and Little Dawg had moved close to the AtmoGen station and were watching me. This gave me a momentary creepy feeling, but it passed when I realized from the angle of the cameras on the masts, Mission Control was just getting some upclose and uniquely angled video feeds.

Twenty minutes later, the two armoured hoses and armoured COM line were connected to the AtmoGen station, and the W-Hab. The service hatch was closed and secured; and I was feeling a lot better now that I knew I'd be breathing at the end of the week.

I walked over to the supply drop landing site and had a real close look at drop #7, yesterday's drop that almost ended in disaster. Getting down on my knees and peering under the canted craft, I could see what was keeping it upright. Two of the ground support/levelling legs had extended part way down. I couldn't tell if mechanical pressure or system commands were keeping them in place, but the controller junction unit looked like it had been blown to heck. As I was part way under the drop, seeing that, I backed up quickly, but carefully, to get out from underneath it. With that system controller blown, it would be mechanical pressure holding those support legs in place. The damn thing could still fall over at any time.

I turned on my helmet's exterior video camera, and gingerly made my away around the damaged side of the cargo ship so that Mission Control could get good visuals of what I was seeing. I stopped every few moments to point out something, my running monologue describing it in detail. After half an hour I stood up and headed back to the W-Hab, watching the sky as I went, energy weapon at port arms again.

I climbed into the airlock, got out of my suit and vacuumed it off, vacuuming up the floor as well. After returning the weapon to the hidden charging cradle, hanging my suit and exchanging the air bottles, I passed though the inner airlock door into the lower level. I went directly to the atmospheric system mechanical room and made the necessary connection changes. The day-to-day gas tanks for oxygen and nitrogen were now charging from the working AtmoGen plant. The AtmoGen really was a facilities plant now, and no longer a space craft. It was never going to go anywhere again.

I backed out of the equipment room carefully, procedure scrolling through my head, and went upstairs. It had been a good day so far, well, mostly good, aside from that one brief sighting. I decided to celebrate the successes of the day with a nice hot cup of the very precious coffee reserve.

Chapter 38

Achael, Hlef & Gilda

A Few Hours Ago

The girls walked into the office, neither hurrying nor hesitating. They stood at attention in front of Rosewood's desk. Lieutenant General Rosewood slammed the door shut, and stalked around behind the desk to face them. She stood there staring at them, fuming, finally leaning forward with her closed fists on the desk; and started the yelling.

"How many kinds of stupid are you??"

Hlef was impassive, Achael bit her lower lip.

"I have never seen anyone so blatantly and completely disregard procedure, protocol, and damn it, common sense!! How dare you go out to that site all by yourself Achael!? Anything could have happened to you, and then where would we have been?? Mike would have had no support, we'd have probably lost the Dart to the fraking Eridani, and we would have lost you!! What if that little peckerwood had others with it?? What if it had a cloaked strike force waiting for you?? What if they were baiting us Achael?? What if those bastards were trying to set a trap for you??"

Suddenly feeling the intensity of her shame at disappointing the Lieutenant General and the idiocy of her passion driven actions, Achael stopped biting her lip, and focused on not crying. Hlef looked impassive, Gilda got even hotter.

"You, young lady, are too damn valuable to us!! You are too damn valuable to me!! You are the shining example of joining Eben and Humans together!!"

Hlef glanced at the Lieutenant General with her big eyes, sunglasses in her jacket pocket. Gilda caught this and looked at her, "Yes Hlef, so are you ... and your brothers! And exactly why the hell didn't you stop her!! You're as much to blame for this as she is!!"

Hlef startled and snapped her head to look at the General, "Hey, I tried to ..."

"DO OR DO NOT, THERE IS NO TRY HLEF!!" Screamed Gilda, "Haven't you watched that fraking movie enough times?? You let her get the better of you, and because you were a lousy fighter when it mattered the most, Achael could have been killed, the Eridani could have killed Mike, and our entire operation could have been put in jeopardy!! You're as much to blame for this as Achael is!!"

Hlef wanted to respond, but instead she just looked straight forward again, lips pressed firmly shut. If Achael was in the thick of this, then she was too. Sistas' rules. No more trying to defend herself.

"Do you have nothing at all to say for yourself??" Yelled Gilda. Hlef just stood there, impassively, staring straight ahead.

Gilda threw her hands in the air at that point and roared, "ENOUGH!!"

Hlef looked straight forward again, stood a little straighter and could feel the first tingle of tears somewhere deep inside, though she didn't show it. She now knew in her heart she had also disappointed the General. Disappointing the General was, well, horrible. Thinking that maybe she had let her sister go into danger because of her inability to stop her, well, she hadn't thought of it exactly that way before, but now that a lantern had been hung on it, it started to eat at her.

Gilda paced back and forth behind her desk, a little bit calmer she continued, "KamPen got the Mar-Sat signal shut down before any images of our craft were sent to Earth, but I still have to deal with what's spooled on his local server." The girls didn't know about The Platform, "Mike survived the incident, and as fate would have it, he survived the incident without our help. He's a crafty bugger that one, he defeated the damn Drone with rocks!" she paused, "Ultimately, Achael, you were just the janitor that cleaned up the Eridani mess ... the Eridani ..." she drifted off into thought for a moment.

As she paused, mid-thought, Achael managed a brief glimpse at Hlef. She couldn't read what was on her face, but she knew that Hlef was upset now as well.

Gilda stopped and placed her hands on the back of her chair. She hung her head for a moment and shook it, looking up with a twinkle in her eye, "I can't believe you actually flew all the way to the Eridani base with that piece of tin shit hanging under your Dart. What the hell were you thinking woman?" Now with a much softer voice, "Did you encounter any problems on the way?"

"Ma'am, three of their scout vessels escorted me from just outside the colony site, all the way to their base."

"I see," she paused, "and the Drone? What did you do with his body?" Gilda already knew it hadn't been dead, she had already spoken to Gref.

"It wasn't dead ma'am, just knocked a bit doolally in the crash. I put it in the Dart, and took it to the Eridani Master."

"Really, it went willingly?" She didn't have quite all the details.

"No ma'am, I had to secure it in the Dart, it was extremely agitated."

"I'll bet it was," she thought for a moment, "what did you use to secure it with?" Those little frakers were famous for getting out of restraints and bindings.

"Duct tape, ma'am."

"Duct tape?"

"Ma'am."

The smile came first as she looked off to the side, then came the laughter. It didn't last long but it was genuine, "I really have to get your cabin video," she muttered to no one in particular.

The laughter had broken the mood; the Lieutenant General didn't seem as intense anymore. She walked slowly around the room and came to a stop behind them, "Girls ..."

Achael and Hlef looked at each other quickly, and then executed a military perfect about face.

Gilda smiled a bit, "Achael, Hlef, I'm so glad you two are okay. I'm so glad this didn't go the way it could have. I'm so very, very glad I sent the strike team after you Achael," she paused as her eyes started to get misty.

"Oh hells bells, enough of this formality crap," Gilda held out her arms, "come give your mother a hug."

The storm had passed.

Chapter 39

Teviot Vallis

Things had remained bad since the humans, Ebens, and hybrids had departed. Blitowyn of Chernasai had lost face in the way events unfolded in the hangar bay. He quickly regained face in his handling of the cleanup. He had immediately ordered the older Trigla Guard Commander and his entire platoon executed for their treasonous surrender in the face of a superior force. The recently arrived defense force opened fire on them immediately, lest they also be found treasonous. Blitowyn had mentally screamed very loudly about how the drones had failed to defend him, meaning they failed to defend his personal guards. He ordered forty of them dissolved. The fact that they had been ordered to be hands-off was irrelevant. In the drones' small minds, a Master was never wrong. The forty drones that he identified immediately ran to the acid tanks and threw themselves in one at a time, all fighting to get ahead of the others.

The Master was most displeased with the Vesna Mahal and his four cronies. To his credit, Blitowyn knew far better than to turn his ire on them for what had transpired in the hangar bay. The Vesna were far too vital to every single thing the Voiya wanted to achieve. Still, having a very good grasp of the politics, the Vesna Mahal prostrated himself before Blitowyn, while in front of the other two remaining Voiya Masters, offering his abject apology for the progress of events, offering his resignation and reassignment to a less purposeful position (the ultimate punishment of a Vesna). His four Vesna cronies, also being astute political players, prostrated themselves as well, and offered their resignations, and reassignments. Not a single one of them thought for even a moment this would be the case. They knew that by doing this, by aiding Blitowyn in regaining face, they would have more political power than before. The Vesna Mahal of this group was of the considered opinion that Rillixiwen's little brother was a serious player in the making and aligning himself closer and tighter now was going to pay off handsomely in the future. The payment would be, of course, the opportunities for more science and experimentation. Pure science, simply for the sake of science, was the first love of all Vesna. Everything else merely supported it.

After leaving the hangar bay, the trio of Voiya, and Eridani Masters each one of them, proceeded to the living quarters. Rillixiwen and the other seven Voiya's bodies, the Voiya who had killed each other in the aftermath of Rillixiwen ordering the Drone to harass the human, had all been removed. The three remaining Voiya had no idea what set off the blood bath, or what the problem was with Rillixiwen's orders. Since there were no recording devices

245

in the Voiya's private quarters, this would probably remain a mystery forever. Probably.

Trigla workers, supervised by Vesna, were in the process of removing the damaged furniture and repairing the walls. The largest contingent of Trigla staff were working at cleaning the copious amount of dark Voiya blood that soaked almost everything. It is very rare that the Voiya actually kill anyone themselves, but when they do, they do it in a grand way: always lots of blood and icky bits to clean up afterwards. This particular mess would take many days, and not a little reconstruction, to remove the last traces of it.

Arriving at the area of the underground base where their quarters were located, the three Voiya had immediately gone for massages and heated head wraps to help them deal with the stress of the day. Crequan, also of Chernasai, and Ochalz of Nejan were very, very distressed when they had heard about the massacre in the Voiya's quarters. Add to this the sudden arrival of armed human, Eben and hybrid soldiers invading their base, and a stand-off in the hangar bay; they were beside themselves. They had been in the Matron's presence at the time of the massacre, and did not know what was happening until one of the Vesna had come to call them away on an important affair of state. No one yet had the guts to inform the Matron of the massacre or the enemies' incursion, and none of the remaining three had yet volunteered to be the one to tell her. Since Blitowyn was last in line for everything at present, Crequan and Ochalz figured they would make him do it. They felt bad about that, him having to deal with the hangar bay, the cleanup, and now this as well. Okay, they really didn't feel bad, they couldn't care less actually. It simply gave them a reason to have the Trigla masseurs apply their craft longer than usual.

The three met privately so that Crequan and Ochalz could berate Blitowyn into the job of informing the Matron. Downing some of his favourite alcoholic nectar, without really tasting it, Blitowyn worked up the courage, and finally went to see her. The Matron was the female in charge of a certain house. As her name was Uudhoo, and she was the only matron on the base, that meant that everyone on the base belonged to the House of Uudhoo. The Voiya Masters, the Voiya children, the Vesna, the Trigla and the drones were all part of her house. Since females rarely survived childbirth, those that did were esteemed and revered as the leaders of the polyandrous families that formed around them. All of the children on the base had been born of her. The children were all fathered by the different Voiya, most of them dead now, except for Blitowyn; he had only been there three years, and had not yet had the pleasure. All of the children, reaching maturity, would either leave to join another house (the boys) or create their own house (the girls, if they survived their first childbirth). All of the male children would be known as "of

Uudhoo". All of the female children, that survived their first childbirth, would choose their own name for the new house that first birth established.

After Blitowyn had be gone only twenty minutes, a Vesna arrived, running into the room, to inform Crequan and Ochalz that Master Blitowyn of Chernasai had summoned them to the Matron's chambers. They looked at each other in disbelief, as only the Matron could summon a Master anywhere. The Vesna, seeing their confusion, conveyed that the breaking of the news had gone very poorly, and that Master Blitowyn required their assistance in comforting the Matron.

Well, Blitowyn or not, being summoned to the Matron's presence was something no Voiya would dare ignore. They all but ran to her door.

Upon entering the lavish and spacious sitting room, they found Blitowyn on his knees, and the larger Matron (females of the Voiya species were bigger than the males) collapsed in his arms. She was sobbing and screeching with a pain that a human would recognize as coming from deep loss. The Voiya males simply couldn't understand that concept, but they knew they had a duty, an obligation, to the Matron. Blitowyn looked up at them, his eyes wide, confused, and not knowing what to do. While the feelings of love, care, concern, and emotions in general were foreign to Voiya males, it was more than abundant within Voiya matrons. Something about surviving childbirth seemed to flip on a switch somewhere in their heads, or hearts.

Her half-opened eyes saw them entering, she turned her head to them and cried so hard she could barely breathe. She held out her arms to beckon them. They approached and without hesitation knelt beside her and Blitowyn. The four of them sat there for a long time. The three males had their arms wrapped around her, and tried thought-projecting words of comfort to her, perfunctory words they had all been taught by more senior Voiya males when joining the house. A Trigla attendant had a basin of water and was dabbing a damp cloth repeatedly around the Matron's head and neck, trying to cool her overheating skin and bring her some comfort. The Trigla attendant had no great love for the Voiya Matron, but she herself was a mother and wife. She recognized this could very easily have been her. The Trigla set aside her indifference for the present time, and responded with compassion; cooing the soft trilling sounds that soothed her own children when they were upset. The attendants' husband was a senior member of the guard force. Today he was in charge of the on-duty platoon in the hangar bay. She hadn't heard yet.

After watching this for some time and realizing that the Matron was not getting any better, one of the Vesna assigned to her detail thought-summoned the base medical team. Arriving promptly, the Vesna physician examined her quickly and efficiently. While the Vesna understood what love was, as an object of study, they had no experience with love towards another being.

247

Commitment they understood, sharing and obligation as well, but not love. Had they been able to understand it experientially, a few Vesna could have psychically flooded her with soothing emotions. Instead, the Vesna physician took a syringe and bottle from his portable med kit, charged the needle from the bottle, and injected it on the underside of the Matron's left wrist. She almost immediately fell into a deep slumber. Looking very relieved, the worried Voiya Masters inquired as to her prognosis, as such an intense display of emotion simply had to be caused by either a virus or a psychosis. The Vesna knew exactly what it was, though and even without experience of the condition itself, he knew that it would only be time that would heal her suffering. He tried to thought-project as much to the Voiya Masters, but they kept insisting if he was doing his job right, he would give her more injections or more pills. Finally the Vesna physician gave them yet another thought-projected lesson on emotions, their effect on the female Voiya body, how they were processed internally, and what it would take to heal her. He reviewed those things for a great length of time. One of the things the Vesna had long been studying in humans was their emotional responses.

The Voiya looked resigned, finally realizing that bluff and bluster would get them nowhere. They realized they truly were concerned for the Matron's well-being. Realizing they were going to have to make great efforts to aid her in that healing process, the three of them left the physician in charge of the Matron, and immediately went for another massage and heated head wrap.

To be fair to the poor devils, they each needed time to think and organize everything running around in their head. They also needed time to think about what would be their response to the day's events. They needed to have a firm grasp on their own thoughts before they could, as a group, work towards a consensus. Of course, when you have three aliens who border most of the time on bug-shit-crazy, the term consensus is probably going to be stretched a bit.

Chapter 40
Achael, Hlef & Gilda

After embracing each of the girls and kissing them on the cheek, Gilda had them sit down. It was only then that the girls realized there was a hot pot of tea on the small table by the leather sofa. There were only two cups on it, but Gilda opened a small cupboard and brought out a third. The tea service and the cups were not china, as you might expect. They were pottery. Gilda acquired them from a potter named Firça who was located in Avanos, Turkey. She flew there every few years for a big shopping spree. It was one of Gilda's weaknesses, but when you saw how colourful and ornately beautiful the items were, you completely understood. You could hardly move in her home kitchen for all the pottery she had collected. She had even taken Hlef to see Firça when she was a small child and still looked very human like. The teapot she had in her office was the one that Hlef had picked out during that trip.

Gilda asked after about her boys, the girls' brothers, then made small talk for a bit about their research projects in low atmo flight systems that didn't use alien tech. Finally she told the girls she had an important meeting to attend, but asked if they would stay down-side a while longer and have lunch with her, so she could meet them in the commissary in about ninety minutes. Hlef immediately spoke up for both of them indicating their pleasure to stay for lunch and meet their mother in the commissary when she was done with her meeting. She didn't fool Gilda for a second, but Gilda also knew that there was a protocol being followed when Hlef was on her way down-side. She had created the protocol.

She had to make a phone call so the girls showed themselves out of her office. Passing through the reception area, they told Billy they were staying for lunch. He excused himself for just a moment and asked them to wait. Major Billy Harper called the service bay and informed the Duty Officer that the cargo shuttle would not be leaving until after lunch, at the General's request. He also asked for the shuttle pilots to join him for lunch in the lower level cafeteria. They couldn't really risk having a True-Blood Eben come up to the commissary during the morning of a weekday. He secretly got a thrill out of sitting around and having lunch while making small talk with an alien. It made him feel special. Lots of things he did with the aliens made him feel special.

He went back out to the foyer, and informed the two of them that he had ordered the shuttle departure to be delayed until after lunch. They thanked him, and Achael shook his hand. When Hlef shook his hand, standing a bit closer than was comfortable, she felt his other hand on her hip, putting something in her jacket pocket. He just winked at her, and wished her a safe journey. As the two women walked through the hall towards the commissary, Hlef reached in her pocket and felt the unmistakable shape and wrapping of a chocolate bar, and smiled. It would be of course, a Mars bar. It wasn't the first time that Hlef and Billy had such an exchange on parting. She smiled at the other things they had occasionally done before parting.

Both Achael and Hlef felt a little bit better now that the drama was over. They were also glad to be having social time with their mother as well. They didn't get to see her as much as they used to, and given their upbringing, they both secretly craved her presence and attention just as much as they did from their father, Hof, whenever he visited from Sapro.

Achael said she wanted to stop in the Logistics Planning Office to see if there was any word or pictures from Tech Sgt. Moesby, who had recently given birth to her first child. Achael, Hlef and Sharon had been quite close a few years ago while working on the X-303 project. They had stayed in occasional touch and tried to do lunch once or twice a year. Achael even tried to get her to come to Mars for a weekend, but she flatly refused. "I'm an Earth girl," was all she would say. She didn't say that the thought of travelling by folding engine terrified her in ways she simply couldn't explain.

As it happened, Tech Sgt. Moesby, Sharon, was visiting the office with her newborn daughter, as new moms are want to do. Achael and Hlef walked in, Achael and Sharon both making sounds of welcome surprise. Hlef stuck with her, but she wasn't really a baby person. Too much poopy-poopy, and not enough party-party.

Sharon was holding her baby, wrapped tightly in a swaddling blanket, and Achael peered closely at her, making all the right sounds and facial expressions. Hlef marvelled at her sister as she watched on. Achael was one of the deadliest warriors in this galaxy; and she was going goo-goo and gaa-gaa, like she knew what she was saying.

"Oh, I have something for you Achael," Sharon said, surprised at herself for almost forgetting. "Here Hlef, hold Patty," and with that, she thrust the small bundle, sleeping again, smelling of baby powder, into Hlef's arm's. Achael winked at Hlef, and walked behind Sharon to her desk. Sharon had no qualms about this. Given the Eben predilection to family and children in particular, that little bundle resting in Hlef's arms was probably in the safest place it would ever be, for the rest of its life. Hlef looked at Achael and Sharon in surprise, looked down at the baby, then back up at them. She looked around the room, and several people, all with clearances that were beyond Ultra Top Secret, smiled at her. Seeing that little bundle of baby in those long gangly arms was indeed a little humorous.

Then it happened.

The bundle squirmed and made a *coo-oo* sound. Hlef looked down with her big dreamy blue eyes just as the baby opened her eyelids. The baby looked up at Hlef with her big (human-sized big) dreamy blue eyes. The fresh pink skin, the delicate amber coloured eyelashes, the brown hair, the warmth of the baby in the blanket, the smell of the fresh cleanliness of the baby, it all combined to have a profound effect.

Hlef made eye contact with the baby and couldn't look away. The baby looked up at the top of Hlef's head, and slowly wandered its gaze down to her chin. Then the baby focused again on Hlef's eyes. The baby smiled. With that one stroke of the brush of life, Hlef was changed forever.

Hlef looked up at Sharon, who was quietly talking to Achael, and then back down at the baby. Gunnery Sergeant Rina Michaels (U.S. Army, on special assignment) came up beside Hlef with a chair, "Would you like a seat Ha-Lay-eff?" her south Georgia twang made the mispronunciation sound almost like it wasn't one. Hlef smiled at her, and sat down slowly as Gunny held the chair for her.

She couldn't take her eyes from the child. The little bundle of potential was an actual person. It was a living human being, a seedling that was going to grow into someone big, strong, smart, and wonderful. Hlef thought about how Gilda reacted to them during the times both pleasant and rough; how Hlef wanted to please her, and to have her around whenever possible, sometimes wanted to be just like her. Those things would be felt by Sharon and little baby Patty as well. Only Sharon and little baby Patty would have that all the time, every day. This little one would grow up with one mother and one father, instead of being raised by a community, a very loving and doting community, but a community nonetheless. It suddenly hit Hlef what she had missed. What all her sibs had missed. Even the True-Blood Eben had families like this on base and back on Sapro, but not the hybrids. Not the ones of her generation anyway.

Damn, Hlef thought to herself, *I want one.*

The thought surprised her. Hlef was the carefree spirit, the party girl, the one voted most likely to never settle down. She had never had a steady boyfriend, and scoffed at the idea of marriage and commitment. She smiled at the irony of the wanting. It would never happen. So far, hybrids had not been able to breed with humans, or True-Bloods, or with other hybrids. They were effectively, for want of another term, sterile.

The baby yawned and blinked her eyes a couple times, she squirmed a bit in the blanket. She seemed to be trying to nestle closer to Hlef's not-too-small bosom. It took Hlef a moment to recall the tune and the words. She finally started gently rocking the baby from side-to-side, while sitting in the chair, softly singing:

Sleep, baby sleep,
The father guards the sheep,
Thine mother shakes the dreamland tree,
Down falls a gentle dream for thee,
Sleep, baby sleep,
Sleep, baby sleep.

Sleep, baby sleep,
Our cottage vale is deep,
The little lamb is on the green,
With snowy fleece, so soft and clean,
Sleep, baby sleep,
Sleep, baby sleep.

Hlef realized the room had gone dead silent. She looked up and everyone was staring at her. Sharon was smiling, Gunny Michaels had a tear rolling down her cheek, Achael's eyes and mouth were wide open. Glancing at her, Sharon reached over and pushed up on Achael's chin, who snapped her mouth shut.

The baby coo'd, gurgled, and (Hlef was sure) smiled at her again. Hlef smiled back down at the beautiful delicate bundle. Starting the gentle rocking motion again, she then lapsed into an Eben lullaby ballad she remembered, singing in a slow, lilting, alien accented voice:

Showa tao shumash, tre ota ola,
Kayam binta sa-kwo nah,
Labo koy ep-fran e amat tey ross,
Laba shpin shumash a-awa nah,
Koma hush e rel om tahsh,
Showa tao shumash, tre ota o--la.

As Hlef softly sang to the baby, Achael had tears forming in her own eyes at hearing the song. That song had often been chosen to sing her to sleep, so many nights, during her childhood visits to Sapro. Hof, their father, was the one that had first sung it to both of them. Achael quietly translated for the others in the room, while Hlef was singing.

Sunshine on baby, this brings life,
Kayam tree is just like night,
Mama holds your hand and loves you strong,
Daddy rocks the baby all through the night,
Safety sighs and dreams high sweet,
Sunshine on baby, this brings life.

The five women and two men in the room were all parents themselves. There wasn't a dry eye when Hlef had finished the lullaby ballad. They were the first humans to ever hear an Eben lullaby. The moments when an Eben child was being laid down to rest, the time for a lullaby song, was considered an intensely emotional and private time for bonding between Eben parent and child. It was closely guarded from the humans that occasionally visited Sapro. By the time Hlef had finished the song, the baby's eyes had closed, and she was fast asleep again. Hlef looked up, her own eyes moist, to see Achael standing over her, smiling.

"Sis, that was beautiful. I didn't think you would ever remember those."

Sharon was smiling and standing beside her. She held out her hands. Hlef stood and gently placed the small bundle in her arms. Sharon nudged her gently and said, "You've got the magic touch girlfriend. Maybe we need to find you a man?"

Hlef smiled, started to say something but stopped, did an about face; and walked hurriedly out of the room, arms tucked tightly under her elbows, and sunglasses back on her face.

Chapter 41

Teviot Vallis

Blitowyn, Crequan and Ochalz gathered in the privacy of Crequan's lavish quarters. He had banished his children to the common area, and after the Trigla servants laid out sumptuous plates of food and drink, ordered them out as well. About to sit down around the laden table, Crequan realized his Vesna assistant was hovering nearby.

Leave us.

The Vesna looked at him, *I must not Master Crequan, my Mahal has ordered me to stay with you.*

I don't care, leave us.

Arguing with a Master was unheard of, refusing to obey them was unthinkable. *With great and deepest respect Master, I ache to obey your command. With the recent turn of events, however, I must remain with you.* At that the Vesna turned over his hand to reveal a small weapon in its pasty white palm. *For your safety Master.*

Crequan paused and cast a dubious eye around his compatriots as they looked from the Vesna back to Crequan. They all stared at him expressionless. Crequan dismissed the Vesna from his thoughts.

As the senior member of the House, Crequan, began the meeting, *we have three items to deal with. The affront of the hybrids forcefully entering our base and the two human colony ships.*

There was no worry of being overheard by anyone outside the room. The Masters were communicating telepathically, and they were closely guarding their thought range. Of course, the Vesna attendant would be able to pick up most of it but as stated, the Vesna attendant had been dismissed from their minds, for now.

Is that not two matters Crequan?

No Ochalz, it is three. My advisors don't think the two human ships are working together. The second one has no support in place and there has been no outdoor activity around it. It is also of a significantly different design, I am told, from the other human ship.

It is under surveillance as well?

Yes Ochalz, Rillixiwen assigned a Drone when it landed. That Drone now reports to me.

That is outrageous! Blitowyn came out of his seat. *Rillixiwen was my brother! His possessions fall to me! That includes his drones!*

Sit down little 'Lixiwen, sneered Crequan, purposefully using the diminutive. *I am not possessing your precious inherited Drone. It has been ordered to transmit its recording to my advisors until a proper chain of command is established for it.*

I am its chain of command! My advisors I mean. They should be getting the data from the Drone, not you!

Does it really matter who gets the data at this point as long as we get it? asked Ochalz.

Everything matters Ochalz, responded Blitowyn with venom in his thoughts.

Attend me, Crequan looked at the Vesna.

Master?

Have the data from the Drone at the second site sent to little 'Lixiwen's advisors. Then turning to Blitowyn, *happy 'Lixiwen?*

Blitowyn came out of his chair and started to advance around the table towards Crequan with rage in his eyes and face. Raising both hands and pointing at Crequan he began, *Do not call me that you simpering ...*

As if by magic the Vesna was suddenly standing in front of Blitowyn. Blitowyn stopped short not to run into him and cut off what he was thinking at them.

Great and glorious Master, began the Vesna, *I am thrilled and delighted to see the degree and depth of your commitment to participation in these urgent discussions. Perhaps they would proceed more effectively, if I could humbly suggest, that you return to your seat?*

Blitowyn sputtered and looked up into the Vesna's eyes, he was so mad he used his outside voice, "YOU DARE TO ORDER ME VESNA?"

While smiling wasn't something that the Vesna did often, they were capable of it even with mouths as small as theirs. The Vesna smiled at Blitowyn as he raised his hand with the small weapon pointed in the middle of Blitowyn's stomach. He held out his other hand indicating Blitowyn's empty chair, *Master Blitowyn, I most humbly and regretfully must ask you to return to your seat. For your own safety.*

Blitowyn paused, staring at the Vesna and the weapon, Blitowyn's hands now curled into fists at his side, opening and closing rapidly. He spun on his heels, and as imperially as possible he settled once again in his chair.

Crequan was suppressing a snicker, Ochalz looked at the Vesna and felt very disturbed by what had just happened. He began the rudimentary steps of forming some of his own private plans.

Crequan continued, after they took a moment to have a few bites of food. He knew things would progress more productively if Blitowyn had a moment or two to calm down a little bit. He realized he had pushed him too far, and now with just the three of them, the odds of a power coup were all that much higher. With the current situation, having his leadership wrested away from him would not only be personally damaging, it would probably mean the end of the current Eridani mission on Mars. Not that it would be the end of the Eridani on Mars, just the end of their House.

I'm not that worried about the second ship for now, he continued as though he had never been interrupted, *it's the first one, the one setting up a base of operations out in the open. This concerns me, as it concerned many of our departed House-Brothers.*

It worries me as well, added Ochalz, *for years the human leaders have known that we will not tolerate their presence on this planet or on their planet's moon. This flagrant disregard for our warning and instructions must, MUST be replied to.*

Do we know what leader put them here?

Does it matter? responded Crequan to Blitowyn.

If we knew which leader it was, we could make our position clear by demonstrating our anger on his people. We could even have him taken and brought here to remind him of who is in charge of this system.

Blitowyn ... began Crequan.

What? You have a problem with demonstrating our strength and abilities to these infants?

You don't think things through Blitowyn! They demonstrated their own commitment and abilities at Dulce! Have you not heard the Vesna stories? Have you not read the historical accounts of our surviving Trigla warriors? Do you not think they have grown in power and ability of their own in the intervening years?

I am not afraid of the puny humans! They take almost a third of a Martian year to get here. We take ten minutes to get there! They can't match our accessibility!

All the more reason to be wary of how catastrophically they will respond. We are not without defense. but we are also not without our own weaknesses.

I am not afraid of the humans, chimed in Ochalz, *but Crequan is making a point. Do we want to risk the Eben Battle Cruisers? Do we want to risk* hundreds of nuclear warheads flying here from Earth? Only two or three would have to get through to destroy us. So far we have suffered a little affront from them directly. The loss of our House-Brothers was because of Rillixiwen's Drone failing to follow its Master's Order of Action, and the ensuing egoism of eight Masters all thinking they were the prime. As for the politics of confrontation, in addition to the logistical issues, we will lose the regular delivery of biological material. Do we want to go back to the wasted time and workload of night time snatches, stealthily taking test subjects and having to deal with their screaming and raging while our Vesna scientists try and perform the experiments we are here to achieve? We, you and I, have to put up with all of that because only we can erase their memories, and only we can apply the paralysis thoughts. The Vesna have still not been able to learn that skill regardless of years of trying. Crequan and I will have to go on all of those missions again! You've never even been on one! You have no idea how difficult it is!*

You are happy to work the samples they send us? You are happy to accept their meager offerings? You are happy to work with what they allow us to have, rather than select the stock that we desire? Are you their puppy? sneered Blitowyn to Ochalz.

Ochalz picked up an apple and threw it at Blitowyn, who dodged it expertly. Most of the food on the table was from Earth, it was just simpler than importing everything from Epsilon Eridani.

Blitowyn, adopting a tone of reason over bluster, continued, *House-Brothers, if we again establish the might and dominance that we once had, then we will have the samples and test subjects that we require and desire simply by commanding it to be so! If we show the humans we are still very much here, and still very capable of flowing wrath and destruction upon them, they will have no option but to bow before us and be contrite to our will! If we expose ourselves to their populace, their governments will be too busy and distracted to effectively mount a defense against us! If we strike first, fast, and hard against the half-breeds, we can take their base out of operation making them, essentially, insignificant. We all know the council has been displeased that our research is taking so long. We all know that the council is not happy with our détente and that we have not fully mastered the humans. How long will their patience remain with us? How long before they assign another House to this mission? What will become of our House, especially in as weakened a state as it is now, with this morning's deaths?*

Our house is not weak, challenged Crequan, *we still have our fighting and defense forces fully intact.*

Of course we do, pleaded Blitowyn, *but do you think the Council will see it that way, do you really believe Supreme Master Rheaum will see us still as strong without a full house of Voiya?*

Ochalz leaned forward, putting his elbows on the lower than normal table and sipped something cold from a large mug. He looked pensive as Crequan looked from Blitowyn to Ochalz. Ochalz raised his eyes and look at Crequan, *I'm afraid that our young House-Brother is also making some sense in this matter. I believe he is right about those in the council. Even our House-Brother Rillixiwen himself had to contend with questions and accusations from some on the grand council.*

Crequan sighed heavily and sat back in his chair as Blitowyn folded his arms in triumph. *I will deal with the human leader,* said Blitowyn.

No, you won't, said Ochalz.

You just said you agreed with me! That we could not appear weak!

Yes, House-Brother, that is mostly correct. However we must approach this smartly. We must play the long game here, and not accelerate our demise through the mistakes of haste.

Blitowyn started to sputter, but Crequan held up his hand, *continue Ochalz.*

Ochalz stood up and began to pace back and forth behind his chair. The Vesna attendant found things to straighten on that side of the table, and then stepped back against the wall, very close to Ochalz; and watched him closely without being overly obvious about it. The Vesna's Mahal and his work unit were in the corridor outside of Crequan's quarters. With them was a group of armed Trigla, just in case. Everything that was being said that the Vesna could pick up from the trio was relayed to his Mahal, and therefore the rest of his pod.

House-Brothers, began Ochalz, *notwithstanding our ability to neuter the half-breeds, I think that to attack the human leadership would be a provocation with responses we can't at present, properly identify. However, I believe there is a way that we can achieve part of our desires, and do it quite legally within the terms of our détente.*

This made both Blitowyn and Crequan curious. *How is that?* asked Crequan.

We must show the human leaders our power and commitment by destroying the human colony base they are setting up on our planet.

But they will consider that an act of aggression and respond to it as such. The half-breed commander of their base informed us this very day that the human was under their protection. We've agreed that right now, that may not be such a great way for things to proceed. Crequan had leaned back again, and folded his arms as he said this.

Yes, that is true. However, if we are merely defending ourselves, then by the terms of the détente, we are well within our rights to take the steps necessary to stop any attack or action against us. If the human attacks us, the half-breeds protection does not apply to our response.

Blitowyn sputtered a noise of disgust. *I told them we were defending ourselves when that half-breed brought back the scout ship.*

You were blustering Blitowyn, we all know that, sneered Crequan.

Of course I was dear House-Brother, Blitowyn of Chernasai sneered back at him, *we always bluster when we don't know what else to do. It's our way. Besides, have you not considered that the damaged ship is evidence of an attack on us? Evidence of an aggressive move by the human setting up his precious little base? Are we not within our rights to respond in kind right now?*

It wasn't attacked Blitowyn, and you know it, responded Ochalz. *That idiot Drone got in the way of the human's ship that was landing. All of our advisors have seen the telemetrics, and agree that's what happened. As well, Blitowyn, that Drone had gone off on its own. It had violated its Master's Order of Action, and it went to the human site and attacked the human. Anything that the human did or didn't do, from that point on, was in its own defense, according to the very terms of the détente we are going to use for our own purposes. According to the recordings of your encounter in the hangar bay, even the half-breed was able to figure it out; and she never believed you gave the kill order. A statement which, had she believed you, could have put us in violation of the détente. Idiot. We can also infer that they don't believe you gave a kill order, because the Eben ship of war did not turn this base to molten slag and us along with it.*

Blitowyn was ramping up to another tirade, Crequan could see it in his eyes. Crequan held up a hand towards Blitowyn and thought very calmly, *tell us House-Brother, how is it that we can use the terms of the détente to kill the human by defending ourselves?*

Easy, was Ochalz response with a plotting smile, *we scare him into attacking us directly.*

Chapter 42

Mike & Gilda

I was tired from the AtmoGen and the morning's business. I knocked off the last three items on the Manifest, and declared the work day done. Yeah, right.

I made up a chocolate and peanut butter dinner shake and sipped it slowly as I went through a few Mission Control emails, and then a few pages of public mailbox emails. I answered about 60 of them, including seven news agency emails about the night before. Those were easy; I just directed them to the Communications Office at The Corporation. Jayden had already instructed me to handle them that way. I was happy to, this time.

I sent a longer email to my son, and then decided it was time to relax. I had another combat shower, and then made a cup of Orange Pekoe tea from the supply of tea that was as precious as the supply of coffee. I tucked the K-Bar in my waistband, and then carried the steaming cup of tea and my tablet downstairs in the L-Hab to my quarters. I sat the tea on my fold-out nightstand, and sat down on my bunk. Using the tablet's carrying case strap, I hung it on the small clothes hook at the end of my bunk, uncoiled the charging cord to plug it in, and then opened the entertainment application. I had brought several Terabytes of TV shows, movies, and music with me. I decided to go for some total escapism, and queued up an old favourite, *Sense & Sensibility*. I leaned back on two of my pillows, grabbed a colourful afghan (which I had negotiated into my luggage), and pulled it up over my legs and stomach. I sipped a few times from my tea as I watched the unfolding story of the Dashwood ladies, formerly of Norland Park, seeking a permanent place to call home, and someone to pay for it. The irony was lost on me. My eyes grew heavy fairly quickly though, and within thirty minutes I had turned off the movie, turned out the light, and was sound asleep.

If I hadn't been sound asleep, I would probably have seen the alerts on the tablet screen that my system was being accessed remotely. In the stress, strain, and emotional aftermath of yesterday's attack, I had completely forgotten to check the local video feeds for footage of the craft that came to the rescue of the attacker. The recordings had sat there waiting to be reviewed and spooled up for delivery on the outgoing server. However, since I had forgotten about them, never viewed them, and no one had asked about them: they never made it to the outgoing server. Ten minutes later I was never going to view them, and would never send them to Terra.

The next morning, all evidence of the intrusion wiped from the computer systems records and screens, I obliviously went through the morning routine I was beginning to establish for myself. Hit the head, have breakfast (while reviewing the morning messages from Mission Control), review the day's work manifest, and then get on with it.

Number one on the list was an outside job. When I had inspected supply drop #7, the one looking like the Leaning Tower of Pisa; I had ignored supply drop #3, the one that had taken blaster damage from the alien ship. Hans wanted that to be a priority for this morning, so it was item number one on the manifest. They needed to know the extent of the damage, and if the exposed contents would survive the Martian winter. Supply drop #3 was hydroponics equipment; enough for me to set up a test system to see how well it would work prior to the main colony crew arriving. I wasn't due to set it up until the following Martian spring time.

I stood up and stretched, then rinsed out my mug. As I picked up my tablet and K-Bar and headed for the stairs, the desktop beeped. I looked over my shoulder and saw the MillChatSecure application open. I turned around, and with two steps was seated in the chair again.

```
User538: good morning mike, sleep well?

MARCOL1: I did, thank you. What time is it there?

User538: o'dark thirty
```

I chuckled.

```
MARCOL1: What do you want today?

User538: straight to the point. a man after my own
heart

MARCOL1: Stop flirting General.

User538: ha ha.

User538: there are some things you need to know

MARCOL1: You mean like aliens might be trying to
kill me? We covered that. Didn't help.

User538: you have ray guns asshole, why didnt you
have one with you?

MARCOL1: Touché
```

There was a pause in her response, and I started to wonder if I had gone too far with my glib comment.

```
User538: there is a lot that i didnt tell you.
there is a lot i wont tell you. there are things,
however, i need to tell you.
```

I thought about that a moment. The day was suddenly getting serious again. Why can't I just have an easy day here? Just once?

MARCOL1: Okay. Go ahead. I'm all ears as it were.

User538: this system wont let me use smiley faces dammit

Another pause.

User538: i cant tell you over this. it would take too long and some of it would be lost without the face to face component

I furrowed my brow at that one, she was coming here???

User538: NO Im not coming there if thats what you were wondering.

MARCOL1: You had me going for a moment. We have secure video software here, Jayden can give you an encoder.

User538: put it in a recording? AS IF.

MARCOL1: Okay General, you got me. Tell me how you are going to impart the secret information without using chat, without using video and without coming here yourself.

User538: i am sending my representatives.

MARCOL1: Sending them?

User538: yes. two of them

It was my turn to think before typing. Good heavens, was she going to send Men In Black? Finally I typed:

MARCOL1: It won't take them eight and a half months will it.

It was a statement. Not a question.

User538: no

MARCOL1: You're going to make me work for this aren't you?

User538: later today

I sat back and started to think about that, and then realized it was too much to think about. I'd think about it later. I had a more pressing concern to challenge her with.

MARCOL1: There seems to be an awful lot of people I don't know flying around here and trying to kill me and break all my stuff. How will I know this is your person and that they are not one of the ones trying to kill me.

User538: you will know

MARCOL1: HOW??

User538: I have to go now. you better go check that supply drop 3.

The chat window greyed out and I couldn't type anything else in it.

Frak.

I closed the application, then went down to the airlock and got suited up. Last piece being, of course, a fully charged energy weapon and two spare clips. I headed out to supply drop #3. Big Dawg followed me.

Chapter 43

Mother & Daughters

Hlef took quick steps towards the commissary, trying to make sense of the turmoil inside her. This was maddening. *I'm the party girl, not a mommy type*, she thought to herself. *I don't want to be tied down with just one guy and with a ... a ...* she stopped so suddenly Achael ran right into the back of her. Hlef caught herself but didn't even seem to notice.

The baby was all she could see, all she could smell. She could still feel it against her. It's breathing and it's coos were echoing faintly in her head. Her breasts were aching where it snuggled her. She stood there not even hearing her sister.

"Hlef ... Hlef ... HLEF..."

Finally she looked up at Achael's wide and concerned eyes. She didn't have her sunglasses on, her wide dreamy blue eyes were filled with questions, and the passion and all the feelings of love she had for her sister.

Hlef gave a weak smile and said, "It's okay sis, just going insane over here." Then she stepped off and continued walking down the hall. "Tra-lala la-la, Insanityville, party of one, here I come." She put on her sunglasses again, and so did Achael.

Moments later she turned through the double doors of the commissary, Achael right at her heels.

"C'mon crazy girl, let's get a table," Achael said with one hand on Hlef's shoulder, propelling her gently forward.

Habit was habit though. They were in the commissary, and a promise had been made concerning pudding of the chocolate persuasion. Hlef pulled out from under Hlef's hand and walked over to the dessert table. Then she just stood there, staring down at it. The table lay before her, devoid of chocolate pudding, devoid of chocolate anything. Well, not completely devoid. She saw a crumb that suspiciously looked like chocolate. She placed her finger on it, and put her finger to her lips. She didn't see Achael behind her giving a panicked looked to the commissary staff. They all stood at their stations, eyes wide in fear they had missed something; eyes even wider in fear that this time Hlef might actually hurt someone. Last time she had arrived to find no chocolate she had only broken dishes. It was always a possibility one of the hybrids might snap and break heads. They were aliens after all; well, mostly aliens. They all stood there holding their breath and watching Hlef.

Hlef just stood there. She was staring down at the table, finger still resting on her lip. They were waiting for the screaming and finger pointing but she just ... stood there. The few other diners sat there not knowing what the drama was, that was unfolding on either side of the serving line. They could tell something was up though. The air was filled with something that could be cut with a knife. They could see that the woman with the freakishly long arms and sunglasses looked upset.

Then it happened. Everyone heard it. The absolute last thing everyone in the room expected. Hlef let out a wracking sob of despair. She started crying, jet black tears started pouring down her cheeks, and she collapsed to her knees. Her body was wracked with soul-aching sobs of hopelessness, and she was hugging herself all the tighter.

Achael knelt down behind her, not knowing what was wrong and not caring. All she knew was that her sister was hurting, and hurting bad. It was all she needed to know for now. It wasn't the Eben way to try to take away pain, but rather to try to lighten the pain by sharing it. She wrapped her arms around Hlef, tears forming in her own eyes, and pulled Hlef back tight against her. She would sit there with Hlef as long as she was needed. Hours, even days. She sat there holding her, the side of her head pressed against Hlef's head, making comforting sounds. As she did so, she pulled down her sunglasses a bit and looked over them at the commissary Sergeant. The look communicated everything he needed to know.

The commissary Sergeant, Sergeant Danny Codrup, from Ohio, immediately cleared the few diners from the commissary. He then called for the facility security detail, the special one that dealt with alien issues. They arrived promptly, and he stationed them outside the commissary with instructions to admit no one, as there was an alien issue in the room. The Lieutenant in charge of the detail stuck his head in the room, saw the women in a tearful mess, and immediately shut the door again. No way in hell was he going to interfere with a couple of emotionally upset hybrids. He'd been foolish enough to do that once before, and had the scars as a reminder.

Once the room was secured from the hungry and uninformed, Sgt. Codrup looked over at his staff and with a few hand signals, had them clear out to wait in their staff lounge. He came over to the two of them and knelt beside Achael. He was late in his career, a career that had mostly been spent right here at Wright-Patterson. He had known Hlef and Achael since they were running around as adolescents.

"What can I do for you, sweetie?"

Hlef looked up at him through her sunglasses, and started crying harder.

"Okay," he smiled, "Some tea it is then. I'll be right back."

Achael let Hlef cry and snuffle her nose for a few minutes more. Then when she started the chuggy *hunh-hunh-hunh* of someone coming out of a crying fit, she lifted Hlef up, and guided her to a nearby seat.

Sgt. Codrup reappeared. He had a tray with a teapot and three teacups on it. There were three teacups because he'd made a quick phone call while he was preparing the tea. In addition to a box of Kleenex tucked under his arm, he also brought some of those little packs of moist towelettes. He included a fresh hand towel so that Hlef could clean the jet black tears off her cheeks and chin. Married and divorced twice, he was wise enough to know that he didn't need to say anything at this point. He just patted Achael on the shoulder, and then went back into the deep bowels of the kitchen area. He thought about going in the staff lounge with the others and locking the door, but valour trumped safety. He waited just out of sight, in case anything else was needed.

"Hlef?" Achael started.

Sniff, sniff, soupy snuffle, "Yes?"

"What happened? What's wrong?"

Hlef's face was already red, and got redder as she tried to hold back a fresh wave of tears. Achael just rubbed her back and slowly pulled her tortured sister sideways to rest her head on her shoulder. Hlef did just that, and the tears flowed again as she leaned submissively against Achael, "It was the baby," she finally managed to say. A chugging scream of loss and grief followed the words.

Achael's eyebrows furrowed. She took off her sunglasses, and tossed them on the table. She took Hlef's sunglasses off as well, seeing that Hlef's inner eyelids had slammed shut somewhere along the way, "The baby?"

Soupy-snuffle, head nod, take two Kleenex, dab at the tears, and then blowing of the nose. "Yes."

Achael was confused. She held her sister and would hold her for eternity if necessary; but she didn't understand what in hell the baby could have done to make Hlef cry like this, "What did the baby do?"

Soupy-snuffle, sniff, sniff, "Nothing." New crying jag launched fresh as Hlef reached up and was now clinging to her sister. Turning her face inwards to hide it from no one that was watching, she smeared black tears all over her sister's formerly fresh and clean Air Force blue dress blouse.

"IF YOU DON'T GET OUT OF MY FRAKING WAY NOW YOU'LL BE WALKING A FRAKING PERIMETER POST ON SHEMYA ISLAND BEFORE FRAKING DINNER TIME!! NOW FRAKING MOVE!!" and with that, the commissary doors blew open. Gilda walked in, scanned the room and walked with precision and intent over to the two girls. Momma Bear had just been roused, and she made the mental promise that only God would be able to help the hapless sonofabitch that made her daughter cry like this. She touched Achael on the shoulder as she walked behind them, and sat down on Hlef's other side.

Hlef's most recent crying jag increased in its intensity, she turned from Achael and latched on to Gilda, her tear and snot covered face buried in her mother's shoulder. Gilda gave Achael a very worried questioning look which Achael replied to with hunched shoulders and an "I don't have a fraking clue" expression on her face.

"There, there baby girl. What's all this about?" Gilda said as one arm held Hlef tight against her, and the other started raking her fingers through Hlef's long curly hair, the way she used to soothe her as a child.

"Oh ... Mom."

"Yes my darling, you tell Momma what's wrong."

"Mom ...", sniff, soupy-snuffle, soupy-snuffle, breathy *hunh-hunh-hunh*, sniff, sniff, "I want a baby and I know I'll never have one, and I can't stand the thought of being alone all my life, and I'm tired of not taking anything seriously, and I want someone to love me, just me, just for who I am, who I am on the inside and not because I'm some freak show they can show off and ... and who really ... who really ... who really sees me and really, really gets me, and who just wants to hold me, and protect me and share everything with me, and fight with me and love me and ... and ... and ..," sniff, sniff, blowing of the nose, sniff, "... and who wants to make a family with me," and cue the crying jag again. Tears, soupy-snuffles, deep sniffs, breathy *hunh-hunh-hunh's*, repeat as necessary, *ad infinitum*.

Both Achael and Gilda had wide eyes and slack jaws at that. Who was this woman, and what had she done with their daughter-slash-sister?

The crying slowly, ever so slowly, diminished. A significant portion of the Kleenex box wound up in snotty hand clenched balls on the table. At some point Sgt. Codrup came and cleared them off. As he started to do so, he first set a glass of water and a bottle of Advil on the table.

"Thank you Sergeant," said Gilda.

He just nodded his head and cleared away the refuse. He came back, his crisp kitchen whites still making him look like he was in a poor man's tuxedo. He poured three cups of well-steeped tea. Looking at how dark it was in the cup, he glanced at the Lieutenant General. She made the hand gesture to leave it, and he did. The next few minutes were spent coaxing Hlef back to a non-crying normal state, the job of all mothers in such situations. Human mothers that is. Eben mothers would have encouraged the crying to exercise the emotions that caused it, and most likely cried right along with her. Alas, such is the difference between the two races but a Mother's love, human or Eben, still knows no limitations. A trait shared by every race in the known galaxy, except for the Vesna and the Lectra.

Achael pulled a teacup closer and fixed it the way Hlef liked her tea. A dollop of milk, and three teaspoons of sugar. Achael preferred hers the same as her Mom did: cream, no sugar. Gilda would always add, "Because I'm sweet enough." Many of her associates and acquaintances, hearing this statement made with perfect seriousness, had wound up snorting hot tea out through their nose. Yes, Gilda was a bitch, but she was a funny bitch.

Neither Gilda or Achael had tried to get Hlef talking again, so far. They both knew that when she was upset, she needed processing time; and now that her emotional response had appeared to have peaked, they gave her some time to gather herself. Gilda tore open a towelette and started wiping the black stain of tears from Hlef's cheeks and chin. Achael, having already cleaned her own tears' black rivulets, assisted as she could. It took five packs to get it all, as there was a fair amount that had run down onto Hlef's neck, as well as across her cheeks. Both Achael and Hlef would be throwing their blouses in the garbage, they were beyond salvation. So was Gilda's, she would soon realize. Hlef, who sat there like a small child while her Mom cleaned her up, smiled at her with teary eyes when she was done, "I love you Mom," and then she hugged her, bordering on a new crying jag but holding it back through a few rounds of high-pitched keening. Getting control of herself, she then turned to look at Achael, "You too Turkey," more hugging.

"Now," began Gilda, "can you tell me what started all this?"

With a nod of her head, resting again on Gilda's shoulder, and some finger pulling on a piece of tattered Kleenex resting on her lap, Hlef started talking. She started talking about the baby and the effect it had on her. She told them about the baby looking at her; the smiling, the cooing, the snuggling, and the warmth of the little bundle. She told them how it flashed in her eyes what having a family of her own could be like; flashbacks to her childhood visits to Sapro. She talked about the family she had lived with there for two years, and then again when she returned as a teenager. She told them about the emptiness she suddenly felt inside, and how she was tired of trying to fill that void, she now realized, with diversion.

As she listened to this, Gilda was churning inside. She had expected something like this from Achael, not Hlef. Gilda understood very much what Hlef was going through. She was also smart enough to know that there was much more, much deeper, that she didn't and couldn't understand. The hybrids were far more Eben on the inside, in their psychological make-up, than they appeared to be on the outside. The urge to have a family, the urge to nest in an Eben, was stronger than the desire for self-preservation. Gilda herself had spent several years on Sapro, and knew through firsthand observation what the Eben familial bond was like. The only single Eben were children and elderly widows/widowers; and even they were very, very few. The Eben drive and instinct for family came earlier in the True-Blood adults; but again, in the True-Blood eyes, the forty-something hybrid girls were still only adolescents. Gilda knew now that one of them had the onset of the *fiat familias supremus* instinct kick in, the other sibs would be likely to start having it as well.

Many of the older hybrids had taken mates. Some of the hybrids had done so on the Mars base, while some had gone to Sapro. The dozen that were on Terra had all taken mates. Mates with very high security clearances of course. The one thing that haunted them all though was the lack of ability to procreate. None of the hybrids, man or woman, had been able to have children with other hybrids, humans or True-Blood Eben. There was a high incidence of adoption in these families, both on Terra and of orphaned children on Sapro. The hybrid-hybrid and hybrid-human couples on Mars had started taking guardianship of new hybrids being born. The last batch of hybrids, five years ago, had all gone to these families on the Mars base. The next batch would see younglings being placed with the two, recently formed, human-true-blood families as well.

Sgt. Codrup reappeared, some of his kitchen staff quietly back at their posts. He was accompanied by a timid looking Airman First Class. They had three trays with servings for each of the women. Meatloaf, mashed potatoes, julienned carrots, broiled asparagus and blueberry pie for dessert. He also had a small bowl of coleslaw he knew the General loved, but also knew the sisters hated. The last thing he sat down was a bottle of Frank's Red Hot sauce. The hybrids went nuts for it, and they put that s*** on everything.

"Thank you Danny," said Achael.

"Major," was his acknowledgement.

The women slowly enjoyed their lunch. Hlef realized that even though she was still sad, snuffling, and weepy; she was also starving. While at first glance the food may have seemed very pedestrian, it had been created by the commissary's Cordon Bleu trained Chef-Corporal. It looked like military food, but it tasted like a very satisfying afternoon on the Left Bank.

The conversation meandered away from Hlef's awakening and sauntered on to other topics. Eventually, Gilda brought the conversation around to something she had intended to discuss over lunch anyways. As the room was still secured by the security detail in the hallway, she could speak freely.

"Girls, I have a small job that I need you to do."

They kept eating their pie, but looked at her expectantly. Gilda wasn't exactly sure how this was going to go over, but it was something that needed to be done. It was an important step in a plan that had been a long time progressing, and was almost near its denouement.

"I need you to go see Mike."

They both paused, forks full of crust halfway to their mouths. It was Achael who spoke first, "You have *got* to be shitting me." The fork dropped to her plate, crust bouncing onto the table and into her lap.

Chapter 44

Teviot Vallis

Master Blitowyn of Chernasai looked up from his computer screen as the Mahal of his personal work pod of Vesna advisors walked unbidden into his chambers. It was a rare privilege, but one that had been won by the Vesna after demonstrating time and again that the Voiya needed to trust the Vesna's judgement in certain matters; including when to intrude on their alone time. Blitowyn was currently trying to figure out the complex inheritance rules of his elder brothers' offspring, versus the two brothers above Blitowyn. He needed to know how much of Rillixiwen's amassed wealth was going to be frittered away on the two boys and a girl, still in First Training, and on the two arrogant insufferable bastards he had to grow up with. He could have assigned the task to one of his team of Vesna advisors, but every once in a while the Voiya had to actually do something for themselves, just to prove how intelligent and capable they were. Of course, once the girl reached Third Training, he could always take her as a concubine, if she wanted him to, and then have access to her share of his brother's wealth since the females always got the larger part of the inheritance.

I have a report from the Drones on observation duty, Master.

Proceed.

The Drone that is standing observation duties on the single vessel that landed south of the main human colony site reports no activity since attaining station three days ago. The Drone confirms there has been no movement outside the Lander, there has been no egress or ingress to the Lander and no light is visible from within the Lander. There is a very slight radiation signature, but it is indicative of a power source, and not of the level we would typically consider to be a weapon - though that is not to say it isn't a weapon. Additionally, the electronic emission readings indicate that while there have been three very short and very high frequency burst transmissions, there is absolutely no other electronic emissions coming from the craft. In fact, between the Drone's observations and the lack of any activity, human or technological, we can't confirm that there are any life forms aboard the landing craft. It may be completely automated.

That's good then.

The Mahal hesitated, marvelling again at how stupid the Voiya were. It wondered how their race ever survived long enough to actually meet the Vesna, *No Master Blitowyn, that is not good.*

Blitowyn's brow furled, *Why not? If it doesn't have any humans on board, and it isn't doing anything, then it's inconsequential to us. Why are we wasting any more time on it?*

This particular Vesna had studied much of Earth history and was aware of the story of the trickery of Odysseus at Troy; a story that would be almost appropriate in this situation, but would be completely lost on the Voiya. Instead he used a story from the Voiya's own history that should be more illustrative for the dimwit in front of him.

Master Blitowyn ... distinguished One ... do you recall how the third Regent of Eridani Prime was removed from office?

Blitowyn thought for a moment, *yes, vaguely, someone brought him an obeisance on the first anniversary of his Regentship. A small box of something-or-other. Only it wasn't something-or-other, it was a bomb. As I recall, it eliminated the entire house, killing over 500 family, Vesna and Trigla.*

There was a pause between them. It went a little too long. Finally Blitowyn made the first move, leaning back and crossing his arms, *what does the third Regent of Eridani Prime have to do with this?*

The mental sigh was almost audible. Had the Vesna not already been aware of how thick his Master could be, he may not have been able to block the sigh of frustration from being transmitted. He may have potential, but right now the Master was being a dolt. The Mahal just smiled a little bit with its little mouth, *the landing craft is quite a bit bigger than that small box of Molyak Berries.*

It took a moment ... wait for it ... wait for it ... there. The lightbulb finally went on over Blitowyn's head, metaphorically speaking. He quickly sat forward, with an alarmed look on his face, slapping his hands loudly on the table.

You're telling me they landed a bomb? Why land a bomb there? Why not land it on the colony or land it here? What good would it do there? I thought you weren't sure it was a bomb?

The Mahal looked around him, took a chair and brought it close to the desk where Blitowyn was sitting, and now looking very anxious.

Master Voiya, I don't know if it's a bomb. It is only one of several possibilities we need to consider. It could be an unmanned research station, awaiting human arrival in the future as the colony site has done. It could be that the crew is hibernating or dormant. We know they use hibernating technology in their medical institutes, but we don't think it has been applied to their space programs. It could be a live and active crew in stealth mode using technology we are not aware of. Those sneaky Eben could have provided them

274

with something new. It could also simply be a supply ship awaiting future migration of the human colony. It could be a complete ruse to try and get us to act prematurely, thus breaking the détente, thus allowing the Eben to attack us. There are many possibilities rapacious One. We must not jump to conclusions, we must gather more intelligence, patiently.

I see, thought Blitowyn at him. With the painful expression of logic not coming easily the Voiya continued, *if there are no life forms around it, why don't we just claim it as junk, haul it into the base, and open it up?*

The Vesna Mahal put his elbows on the table in front of it, folded its hands, and rested its head against them. It was a very human like movement. He wished for a moment he had been born a Trigla, they didn't have to go through this type of thing. The Mahal looked up at Blitowyn and gave him one thought, *because it might contain Molyak Berries.*

It took another moment, and then the light went on again. *Oh, I see what your concern is.*

As I knew you would Master.

Let's just blow it up then and be done with it.

The Vesna Mahal worked at keeping a stunned expression off his face as he took another moment to process this latest bit of shocking lack of comprehension. Sometimes the sheer stupidity of these overly self-inflated narcissistic cretins just completely surpassed all understanding. The Mahal sat there motionless, staring at the Voiya long enough that it became uncomfortable again. Finally, with a deep breath, the Mahal explained

Master Voiya, if we blow it up and there are humans on board, the human governments will declare us in violation of the détente. If there are no humans on board, but it is a support post for the current human mission under way, then they may also see that as an attack on the present mission and also declare it a violation of the détente. If there are no humans on board and it's not part of the colony mission, they may well still see the destruction of their craft as an attack on humans in absentia and still claim it's a violation of the détente. We cannot bring it here, we cannot destroy it there; unless of course, you actually do desire to go to war with the Eben, the hybrids, and the humans.

Blitowyn stood up and paced back and forth a few times. The Vesna Mahal sat there and silently observed him, wondering if there was still a vacancy in the propulsion research facility at Proxima Beta Orionis.

Attend me.

The Mahal stood and began to pace back and forth behind the Master Voiya. He was being careful to stay out of the way of the Voiya's big feet in the heavy combat boots. They looked ridiculous, but they were the latest fashion amongst the Voiya males.

Mahal, I require you to maintain observation of this lone ship. Do so at a distance, and without interference. I want daily reports on the matter.

As you wish Master, the Vesna Mahal breathed a sigh of relief. Sometimes it was easier to just let them think they were being original. At least he was done with the stupidity.

The Master wasn't done though, he went on, *Mahal, was it not reported earlier that the design of this ship was of significant difference from the larger human colony ships?*

The Mahal paused a moment, a curious expression on his plain and pale face, *yes, Magnificent One, that was so reported.*

The Voiya Master paced a few more feet then turned to look at the Vesna with an expression of taxed and overworked mental processing on his face, *then perhaps we don't have to worry about the human colony after all. Perhaps the humans will take care of their own, as they so often do.*

The Mahal was thunderstruck. That thought had never occurred to him. It had not occurred to his work pod or any of the other Vesna pods in the loop of the reports. If this was indeed a rival Earth nation, perhaps they would indeed kill the human in the colony site for them. The Eridani would be rid of the interloper, and neither the human governments nor the Eben could claim a violation of the détente. Brilliance. And it was from the mouth of a mental babe. The fact that there would still be the interloper that had killed the other interloper had, for their immediate consideration, gone unrecognized by both of them.

The Eridani Master, Master Blitowyn of Chernasai, feeling quite superior for his lucky stroke of brilliance, walked to the sideboard and drew a large mug of the cold, golden, frothy, tongue tingling beverage they imported from Earth. He didn't understand why they called it *bear,* it had no correlation to that large and impressive predatory animal in their northern climates. Since the Mahal was here, might as well get on to the important business.

You have the humans' main colony site under observation still?

Yes Master, the still stunned and a bit more respectful Mahal responded.

We are going to proceed with the plan worked out with my house-brothers. We are going let the human provoke us to defense by attacking us.

Attack us with what Sire?

The Master Voiya just looked at the Mahal, and then continued, *do we still have only one Drone on picket?*

Three Drones, exalted One.

Make it five.

As you wish, Master.

Make sure the drones are properly briefed and that they clearly understand my Order of Action for this. I don't want any inconsistencies. He would never say "like the last one", because that would be admitting that a drone had failed to follow a Master's orders. That was something the Voiya, still, would never do.

Yes Sire. As you wish.

Repeat the Order of Action to me. I want to make sure you understand it as well.

That ended the Mahal's feeling of appreciation for Blitowyn's recent mental hurdle. The Vesna were usually unflappable about such things, but this Mahal had been dealing with this jackass so long he was more often finding it difficult to maintain his temper around him, promising future or not. Still though, he would have swallowed the acidic taste that would have been in his mouth if the Vesna actually had oral salivary glands, which they don't.

Master, your Order of Action has five parts to it Sire: one, that the drones observe and record all exterior activity at the human colony site; two, that they do this close to the colony site; three, that they do so without concern for being detected; four, that they harass and annoy the human when he is outside his habitat without taking any action that may be construed as an advance or an attack, and finally five, that they attempt to cause the human to fire a weapon at them, rather than merely throwing rocks, so that we can claim justifiable defense in obliterating the unwanted interloper.

Chapter 45

Supply Drop #3

I arrived at the damaged supply drop and spent a few minutes looking at the support struts holding up this Martian leaning tower of Pisa. It seemed to be holding its canted position, but I wasn't sure if that was by design or by prayer; perhaps a bit of both.

Walking back to supply drop #3, I could finally take a careful look at the chunk taken out of its north side. The missing piece was about three feet high, two feet deep, and covered an area about 20% of the circumference of the cargo ship. There was a bit of metal and ejecta on the ground, but most of it had been vapourized by the intensity of the alien weapon's blast. Supply drop #3 had hydroponics equipment, as well as an inflatable Kevlar Quonset hut to house the equipment. This was only a test system. It was supposed to supply me with fresh vegetables and greens; enough to survive on with a vegetarian diet. The future full colony version was going to connect to a utility access system so that we wouldn't have to suit up to get to it. For the purpose of my proof of concept mission however, I would have to suit up twice daily to go to the structure.

I had my exterior helmet camera in live feed mode. That meant the signal was going back to the W-Hab controller, and immediately sent on its way to Terra. I also had the hand camera recording the angles that the helmet camera couldn't. I did a close up inspection of the almost perfectly incised hole itself, to start with. I had expected jagged pieces of metal upon upclose inspection, but that wasn't the case. The entire outline of the hole looked like someone had melted it, and then smoothed it out. There were some spots on the edge of the hole that looked like the metal had turned to slag and dripped down to the exposed interior decking. With my gloved hand I pinched and pulled on this smoother, melted edge, and it broke away like brittle glass for about 8 centimetres from the edge. Then it toughened up again. I was able to do this same thing in several places around the recently added opening. Whatever that weapon was, it seemed to have altered the entire chemical, or possibly, the molecular make-up of the metal right around the perimeter of the hole. I shuddered at what it might have done to me. I looked over both shoulders at that point, having a wee case of the willies, but didn't see anything. I slipped the energy beam rifle from one shoulder to the other.

Peering inside, I couldn't see much either. This side of the cargo container had been where the inflatable Kevlar Quonset hut was packed. A great chunk of the material was missing. I could see several layers of the inflatable structure, so I knew right away that it was useless. It would have several great

279

gaping holes in it when unrolled. The Kevlar walls of the structure were 80 millimetres thick. On the inside of the structure were inflatable tubes to create a rigid frame. These inflatable tubes were 20 centimetres in diameter, with 10 millimetre thick walls of the same material, spaced every 60 centimetres. I could see some of those tubes had been damaged as well.

The process to install the Quonset hut would have been simple. Step one, clear the installation site area, 15 metres by 5 metres, of any rocks and debris larger than pebbles. Step two, unroll the Quonset hut structure, orienting the structure so that the rounded end faced the prevailing winds. We knew the prevailing winds at our colony site were North-North-East. Step three, with the help of Little Dawg and Big Dawg, install the ground pin system to secure the structure in place. These pins, plus the weight of the interior should (I stress "should") keep the structure from blowing away. The full system yet to be delivered would actually be installed partially below grade, to assist with its stability and wind resistance. The 80 millimetre carbon nanotube reinforced Kevlar shell with the inflatable structural support tubes, and the inherent flexibility of fabric would, I had been assured, withstand impacts up to 310 joules or newton-metres of energy. That would be approximately a one kilogram meteorite travelling at 90 km/hour. It would also withstand dust devils up to a certain, unspecified size. Step four, use the accompanying Mars Atmospheric Air Compression System (MAACS) to inflate the interior 20 centimetre wide inflatable support struts. Step five, install the graphene reinforced flooring panels. This included moving all of the necessary equipment into the Quonset hut. Step six, install and activate the airlock system. Step seven, hook up the atmospheric system. This procedure included steps to tie it into the AtmoGen, and then run the scrubbers to slowly replace the Mars atmosphere admitted during the installation. It would only take about three hours to remove the Martian atmosphere, and replace it with human breathable, and therefore plant breathable, Terran-similar air.

The system designers promised a three-day installation time frame. The mission planning team had changed that to a five-day installation time frame. Alas, it would be a zero-day installation time frame until they delivered a new inflatable structure. I was sure that this was already in the works, back home. The next launch window for supplies opened in sixteen months, lasting from July to September. They had more than enough time to get it ready. It just meant that I'd be eating protein bars, and drinking protein shakes a lot longer than anticipated.

I thought of Loreena. I thought of Carrie and her boys. I thought of the salvaged green-and-white baseball cap, now sitting on my bunk. I thought of the camping trip Hans and his family had invited me to tag along with. I thought about my son and his wife. I thought about Mary. I looked around at the nothingness. I looked back at the damaged cargo drop. This was my life now. I had chosen it. Those other things were memories. I'd just have to try and create some new ones here, by myself, until Colony 1 arrived in about six years' time. Neither Loreena, my Dad, or my Mom would have wanted me to dwell on the past when there was so much living left to do in front of me.

Holding the strap of the energy weapon slung over my shoulder, I turned around to scan the sky. I thought I saw a shimmer in the air, but it was almost in the exact same direction as the sun, West-South-West. It could have easily been the sun playing tricks on my eyes through the inevitable lens effect of my helmet's face plate. I moved around a bit, but couldn't make the same shimmer reappear, so I chalked it up to nerves. In fact, there was a cloaked Eridani scout vessel there, hovering about 600 metres away, and keeping itself in the line of sight against the sun. I didn't know that at the time though.

I walked around to the other side of the cargo ship #3 to the main cargo hatch. All of the supply drops were oriented so that the cargo hatch was facing south. I opened the small access panel, punched in the unlock code, and then turned the unlock handle. The door opened a few centimetres on its own. I grabbed the seam of the door, and pulled the right side hatch open first; using the cable attached to the inside to anchor the door open at a hardpoint connection that hadn't been vapourized. I opened the left hatch and secured it in a similar fashion.

I gave the hand signal sequence to Big Dawg and he came over dutifully, following my hand commands to stop right in front of the open hatch. I did a slow motion hop up onto Big Dawgs' cargo deck, feeling a bit like the Six Million Dollar man, and then stepped up onto the cargo deck of the cargo ship. Everything was packed tightly inside and secured against the horrendous mechanical forces of Terran launch and Mars descent. Nothing was out of place. The rolled up Mars Quonset hut was large enough that no light was apparent from the hole on the other side of the ship. There was no light visible around the remainder of the inflatable structure, packed tightly inside. Everything else looked secure and intact. The hydroponics equipment, exterior lighting packages, and the small lighting power generator all looked intact and ready to be used. I took a moment to record an in-helmet video for Mission Control, confirming the observations I had made on the inside of the cargo ship with what the camera was showing. I let them know that it looked like they would only need to replace the inflatable structure. Of course, waiting as long as I would have to, they would have to replace the seed stock as well. For now though, the remnants of the inflatable Quonset hut were packed tight enough against the opening on the far side that I felt the contents of the damaged cargo ship would survive the Martian winter.

With nothing else to do on my work manifest at the present moment, I thought about unpacking some of the lighting equipment. I could take out what was necessary to string up around the W-Hab and the L-Hab, and activate the lighting supply generator (wind powered with solar backup for battery charging). I could leave the rest of the lighting equipment in place until the other supply drops had been moved.

Supply drop #2 had a small, but powerful, electrically powered tractor inside it. It was for the water mining jobs primarily, but would also serve as an equipment mover. It was powerful enough to move the supply drops, fully loaded, with the assistance of the supply drop cargo ship under-carriage train wheels. It could move them without that assistance if they were empty. Supply drop number six also had a small flatbed trailer and a crane attachment, both designed to work with the small tractor.

I figured I should probably go off script and set to work unpacking the tractor, and then the crane and flatbed. They would be of more use to me at present than the lighting would. The lighting wouldn't really be in need for another six weeks or so. I would definitely need the tractor and crane attachment to salvage the last supply drop that arrived. I turned around and jumped down on Big Dawgs' cargo deck, then moved him out of the way. I unsnapped the securing line on first the left hatch, then the right hatch, and sealed up the doors on the cargo hatch. I turned around to head over to supply drop #2, and froze in my tracks. I was looking at four shimmering orbs hanging in the air between where I was standing, and the Habitats.

As I stared at them, a fifth one moved into place. That fifth one's movement unfroze me. I crouched down onto the ground, crouching behind Big Dawg. I pulled the energy weapon off my shoulder, pressed the VOX button three times on my forearm control unit, and brought the energy weapon up to my shoulder.

I didn't even wait for sexy voice to tell me she was awaiting my command. I simply began talking to her, "Castle Cellar, ready weapons platform, ready weapons one, two and three. Hold weapons one, two and three. Authenticate alpha kilo five, two, seven, authenticate. Activate referential targeting system, target unknown, hostile contacts one, three and five. Confirm."

Sexy voice now had her chance. After a few seconds pause, she responded. "Weapons ready. Weapons one, two, and three in a ready state; and at hold condition. Referential targeting system engaged. Thermobarics one, two, and three targeting unknown hostile references one, three and five. Confirmed."

I popped my head up with the weapon aimed, and saw the five shimmering spots of air in front of me. I pulled my head back down quickly, and waited for the ground to explode behind me but it didn't. I popped back up for another quick look, and the shimmering spots of air were still there. That was weird. There were five of them. They could have vapourized the entire cargo row, and me along with it. Why hadn't they?

I popped my head back up, and they were still there in place between me and the Habitats. I stood up quickly with my energy weapon shouldered. I stood there with the middle shimmering spot of air centred in the reticule of the targeting eye piece.

I stepped out from behind Big Dawg, and they didn't move. I kept the weapon trained on the centre small ship for no other reason than, the others would be equally far away from it.

Why weren't they firing at me? Why hadn't they destroyed me? Something was definitely odd here. I took a tentative step towards them. Nothing. I took two more steps. Nothing. I started walking slowly towards them and therefore, towards the W-Hab. Within a few steps they did start moving. The centre one was backing away from me slightly, with each step I took. The other four were slowly moving around me, encircling me. By the time I had moved 50 metres, I was in the centre of a Mexican firing squad. I stopped moving, and slowly turned a full circle; training my weapon on one after another, until the energy weapon was lined up on the first one again. Still nothing. They weren't killing me. They weren't doing anything except watching me.

"Castle Cellar, safe all weapons. Authenticate, alpha kilo five, two, seven, authenticate."

"Thermobaric one, two and three are powering down." After a pause, "All weapons are in a safe state. Bay number one is secured. Bay number two is secure. Platform is secure."

I lowered my energy weapon, holding it with both hands, but now pointing it at the ground. I turned a slow full circle again, watching the shimmering spots of air. Halfway through the turn, the shimmers were suddenly replaced by five solid-looking metal balls that looked exactly like the one from my last encounter, without the damage of course. They were no longer cloaked. They just hung there in the air, not even bobbing. That meant they were no longer concerned about stealth. This game they were playing had just changed, and I just wasn't sure what it meant.

I raised the weapon slightly to hold it at port-arms, and then started slowly walking, sauntering would be more precise, towards the W-Hab. As I slowly walked homeward, the five grey ships followed me in perfect step. They held their positions from each other and from me, keeping in step with me. This continued without change until the lead orb was about 20 metres from the W-Hab. It then moved its position to be directly above me. I stopped at that and looked up at it a few moments, having to lean back to do so. It didn't look any different from the bottom. No exhaust ports, no obvious propulsion system. The small round indentation with the nubbin of the weapon was visible, but that was all that was visible on the surface. I was too far away from them to see any of the faint seams or joints that could be seen when you were upclose to them.

I looked forward again, thought for a moment and then shrugged my shoulders to myself, "Whatever".

If they were going to kill me, they were going to kill me. *Yea though I walk through the valley of the shadow of death, I will fear no evil for Thou art with me.* I slung the energy weapon over my shoulder again, and finished my journey, walking at a normal pace, studiously ignoring the five alien vessels. I entered the W-Hab airlock without looking over my shoulder again. The small space pressurized, I took my surface suit off, and cleaned up the dust. I returned the energy weapon to its locker, and then headed upstairs. If they weren't going to fire at me, I wasn't going to fire at them. I had the sneaky feeling that they *wanted* me to fire at them. Knowing a little bit about what it's like to encounter bullies at school, in the workplace, and in private life; I was fairly confident I was now onto their game. I believed that they did want me to fire at them first, or to take some action that would appear to be attacking them. I was sure then, that had I indeed fired my puny energy weapon at them, the colony site would be a debris strewn series of blackened and smoky craters at this very moment.

I went to the control panel and activated the display of the exterior cameras. The grey orbs were no longer visible. I activated the Mar-Sat and Jalopy-Sat displays: nothing seen. I put the W-Hab COM panel on VOX.

"Castle Cellar, status."

"The Platform is in a safe state. Referential targets one through five are withdrawing from your location. There are no new targets."

"Vector and speed of targets one through five?"

"All targets are bearing 343 and moving at 3 kilometres per hour."

"Activate new target voice notification system."

"New target voice notification system is engaged. Please state the area of compromise."

Oh what the hell, "Five hundred kilometres."

"Area of compromise is 500 kilometres. New target detected, new target is an unknown hostile ref ..." there was a pause. I winced. That was totally not supposed to happen, but given how things had been going, I wasn't surprised. If Castle Cellar was failing, I was in more trouble than I realized. To my relief, sexy voice started again, "New target detected, new target is a classified reference, designate referential target number six."

A classified reference? Okay, not a dust devil then. What the hell is a classified reference?

"What is the classified reference?"

"Command not recognized. Please restate your command."

Oh for frak sake, this was getting silly.

"Castle Cellar, you identified the new target as a classified reference, provide the identification of target number six."

"You are not authorized for that information."

I was about to yell at the computer interface, when the panel suddenly displayed two red lights. Then the messages came up telling me that I had lost connectivity with both Mar-Sat and Jalopy-Sat.

"Umm, Castle Cellar? Status?" No response. Oh yes indeed, this was going to be another very long day.

Chapter 46

Pyongyang

Kang Hyo-Sang sat in disbelief. He couldn't believe his ears. He wasn't sure what was more incredible; what he was hearing, or the fact that he was hearing it. The Democratic People's Republic of Korea (North Korea) wasn't that big on openness and transparency. Mr. Choi had to be pulling his leg, "This has really happened?"

"Yes, it has," was the benevolent, smiling, simple response of Choi Je-Ha. "We have been working on this for many years under the auspices of the Great Leader, Kim Il-Sung. His plans have been carried forward most loyally by his son and grandson. You know, the West has accused us of making missile tests under the guise of satellite launches. They weren't always missile tests at all. Many of those launches were tests of interplanetary craft and their launching systems, one of the primary focuses of this project. I know for a fact that NASA has images of our test craft that landed on Mars ten years ago."

"I've never heard of this, why has it never been reported in their media?"

Mr. Choi smiled, "Do you think the Americans would publish pictures or reports of technology on Mars when they had no idea where it came from? We were very careful to make it as nondescript as possible; and to have no identifying features."

"Ten years ..." his mind did the simple calculation. "That was before the formation of the National Aeronautics Development Agency".

"Yes, its predecessor, the former Committee of Space Technology, was more than just a research institute. We did more than just build satellites."

"I'm confused. Ten years ago our country signed the Outer Space Treaty. You are telling me that since that time, our country has been working on more than just satellites? We have been working on manned Mars missions?"

Mr. Choi sighed benevolently and leaned forward to rest his arms on his desk. After pausing a moment, he sipped the last of the tea in his cup, and called the steward for a fresh pot. While waiting, he continued.

"Kang, there is much you do not know. In 2008 we landed our first robotic on Mars. This was many years after our robotics first landed on the Moon. On Mars, we landed our packages far away from the American, Soviet, and Chinese robots. They thought it was a satellite launch and paid not much attention to it when it disappeared and didn't fall back to Earth. It has been in operation ever since. After the new millennium, we had pursued a satellite program aggressively. We only have one satellite in orbit right now because of planned deception. The first three real satellite launches failed because we designed them to fail. We were making great strides in what we wanted to do, but we didn't want anyone to know that. The beauty of operating in our Republic is that we can be both open and secretive at the same time.

In 2013 we formed NADA to make the world think that we were scrapping old ways, and starting fresh, from the beginning; but we weren't. The hills between the launch assembly buildings at Sohae are riddled with underground research and manufacturing facilities. Our underground facilities have entrances at both Sohae launch sites. It was from that facility that we launched our missions to Mars last year, only a few hours, as it happened, after the Swedish colony company sent that Canadian."

"What about Tonghae?"

"We used Tonghae Launch Facility to misdirect the attention of the West."

Kang Hyo-sang was now getting excited, "You said 'Missions'. Plural?"

Choi Je-Ha smiled, "Yes, missions. Plural. We have landed two of our people on Mars, about 3000 kilometres south of the colony site being established by Sweden. We also landed two of our people on Deimos and two more on Phobos. This is in addition to the four people that recently arrived on Earth's moon."

"On Mars' moons? On our moon?" Kang practically came out of the chair. Eyes wide, mouth open, hands wanting to gesticulate, but having nothing certain to gesticulate to. His childlike enthusiasm and excitement was uncharacteristically evident. He sat down heavily, and snapped his mouth shut. Choi watched him carefully; he could see the young man's mind now working over several problems with the information given.

"They all arrived successfully?"

"Yes," Choi nodded.

"The men, they are all alive?"

"Men and women, yes, they are all alive."

"You sent women to space?"

"Each crew is one man and one woman. Each crew is married to their crewmate for the Mars missions. The mission on our own moon is all men."

Kang continued thinking things over. Finally he asked the two questions that were most obvious, the first was, "Why Mars?"

Choi smiled, easy answer, "Juche."

Kang nodded and continued to look thoughtful, then asked the second almost as obvious question, "Why Phobos and Deimos? Why on our moon?"

Choi got up and put his hands behind his back as he walked slowly over towards the windows in his office. He peered out from behind the heavy curtain; the curtain interwoven with electrically charged metallic threads, like the ones running through the walls. His office was, more or less, a Faraday cage. He looked down at the sonic device attached to the windows. It vibrated the glass at a subtle, but high frequency, which prevented laser intercept of their voices vibrating the glass. The room was swept twice a day for listening devices as well. Choi was confident no one was able to hear them.

"We landed on Phobos to provide overwatch. With its rapid orbital period, we are over our surface landing site three times a day. We also get to cover a significant portion of Mars visually and electronically without the higher cost and transparency of putting an actual satellite in orbit. We have placed our people on Deimos to provide a first response in case someone got the idea of sending reinforcements after we take over the colony site. They are armed heavily."

"Take over ... the colony site ... the Canadian?"

"Yes."

"And the astronauts, how long can they survive?"

"Each of the moon Landers carries basic food replacements and water with the same recycling systems used by the Mars colony missions. They can survive without resupply for four years. The surface crew on Mars can survive for six years." He turned to look at Kang with an intent expression, "Our people are dedicated."

"When will they come home?"

"Those on Mars most likely won't." Choi continued to face young Kang. "They went on a one-way mission. They volunteered for it. They know how it may end. Those on our own moon, well, their return is simple, and can occur at almost any moment's notice."

"May end?" Asked Kang a bit incredulously, "Wouldn't you say it was a certainty?"

"No, I don't believe it is. I believe there are options. These six on Mars and on Mars' moons are only the first stage. There are six more in transit to Mars as we speak, and there are more launches being prepared. We have a cadre of future heroes of the People's Republic in training right now, at secret locations." Choi paused, and then turned to face the young man about to be given a surprising opportunity, "I believe we have a good plan, and that it will succeed."

Kang adjusted himself in his seat as the steward came in with a pot of tea. The steward poured a fresh clean cup for each of the men, fixing the Managing Director's tea the way he liked it, a touch of milk, and three sugars. The old, leather-skinned and well-tanned steward took the few steps to Mr. Choi, and handed the teacup to him with practiced deference. The steward then withdrew from the office, bowing respectfully as he did. Kang could see the bulge of what could only be a handgun, under the back of his jacket, as the old man was bowing.

Choi sat down on the couch along the wall facing his desk. He watched Kang turn his chair around to him with a freshened teacup in his hand. His hand was slightly trembling. He lifted the cup and sipped the hot and sweet tea with focus.

"I have a question for you Kang Hyo-Sang."

Kang looked at the managing director of the National Aeronautics Development Agency. The old man continued to assess him carefully. The younger man, about to turn forty-eight years old, looked both excited and apprehensive. He set the teacup and saucer on the desk behind him, and gave Choi his full attention, sitting ramrod straight, with his palms flat on the top of his thighs.

Choi proceeded, "Do you want to be part of the most glorious and prestigious endeavour of the Democratic People's Republic of Korea? Do you want to be part of the most ambitious space gambit by any Earth power, acting solely on their own, that has ever taken place? Do you want to be a powerful part of a solar system that bows before the magnificence of Kim Jong-Un? Before you answer, I must warn you: if I proceed with what I am about to tell you, you become part of the inner circle. Once in, you may never leave this inner circle. Ever. If you try to leave this inner circle, well, serious consequences may befall you."

There was only one kind of serious consequence when it was referenced in that manner. Kang knew it was a serious consequence that ended with a deep hole, and a hollow-cavity lead bullet.

The septuagenarian Choi Je-Ha formalized the question, "Take a few moments to decide Kang Hyo-Sang, but I must have your answer before you leave this room. Do you want in or do you wish to return to your former life?"He stood and looked down at him, "There will be no repercussions and no punishments if you say no. There will also be no second chance to say yes."

Choi walked over to the small sideboard beside the office door. He set down his teacup and saucer, then stepped back, folding his hands behind his back. He looked up smiling and bright eyed at the portrait of Kim Jong-Un, the Dear Leader of the DPRK.

NADA Mission Control Room #3, Sublevel 6, NADA Headquarters, Pyongyang

The newly appointed Second Assistant Mission Manager, Project 57-3 (Deimos), held the door open for the Managing Director of the National Aeronautics Development Agency. As he stepped through the door, Kang's neck became a rapidly panning swivel for his head and his wide eyes. He was trying to take in everything at once, but there was just too much to take in.

The large room contained four distinct Mission profiles, each one wedge shaped and pointed to a not-too-small, raised round platform in the centre of the room. The wide ends of the Mission profiles were the four walls of the room. Kang could see telemetries and images that could only be coming from Earth's moon; and on the adjacent wall, telemetries and images that could only be coming from Mars' surface. The other two walls showed images and telemetries that had to be coming from Phobos and Deimos; the source being obvious by the sense of motion imparted by the camera's facing towards Mars. Phobos had a much more rapid transit profile than Deimos, due to its relatively shorter orbital period.

After leading him up the stairs of the raised platform, Choi Je-Ha took great pleasure, as well as his time, in explaining all that was displayed. He then explained the layout of the room, and gave a detailed overview of all the stations for each of the four missions. It was evident that the managing director took great pride in his own operational knowledge. He patiently answered all of Kang's questions. Two hours after arriving, Choi lead Kang down the steps from the raised platform and its workstations, to the side of the room specified for Project 57-3 (Deimos).

His new team was alertly on duty, and as they approached, the Mission Manager a few years Kang's junior turned to look at them. She stood and straightened her tunic, then stepped forward extending her hand to the Managing Director.

"Good afternoon Mr. Choi," she said in perfectly accented midwest American English. She smiled at his smile, and then bowed slightly.

Mr Choi very easily began speaking in English as well, with a perfect west coast American accent, "Allow me to introduce your new teammate, Second Assistant Mission Manager Kang Hyo-Sang." He turned slightly to Kang as the two new teammates shook hands, "This is my niece, Hahm Soo-Joon. She is the manager of Mission 57-3, and it is to her that you will report."

Also in flawless west coast English came his perfunctory but earnest response, "Ms. Hahm, I am honoured to be in your acquaintance, and look forward to working closely with you."

Looking over his shoulder and then back at the two of them, Choi Je-Ha said with gravitas, "They are about to make contact on our own Moon, I must excuse myself." He then turned away from them, and hurried around the raised platform to stand underneath it with the Mission Manager for Project 57-4 (Luna).

Kang watched him go with a confused expression. He asked Hahm, "Contact?"

The corner of her mouth started to curve up, "Wow. You really are new. Have you not yet been fully briefed?"

"No. When I accepted the offer, we immediately came down here. It wasn't part of his explanations after we arrived," he paused, "I guess I need to play a bit of catch-up."

She reached out and touched his arm as she looked over her shoulder at her own people, and then back at him. "Our mission is stable right now and we are performing routine diagnostics and observations. Let's go watch things unfolding closer to home, and I'll catch you up," she loved American idioms. She introduced Kang to the First Assistant Mission Manager, gave him a few instructions, and then led Kang around to the stairs. Smiling, she guided him up the steps again to the top of the raised platform.

As they topped the raised circle, they leaned against the railing over the control area for Project 57-4 (Luna), and she quietly began explaining, "Several years ago, we began sending robotics to the Moon; our moon. We landed three of those packages successfully. One of those packages went to the dark side of the moon. Almost immediately, we discovered that there was an infrastructure in place there."

"Infrastructure?" he looked at her.

"Yes. It wasn't human."

A sharp intake of breath indicated his surprise. Kang looked at her for a moment, and then looked up at the displays of the moon. The larger display showed an image that was just edging out around a ridge. A low structure along the face of a crater wall could be seen with dim lights in various places.

"Not human," he said very quietly.

"Shall I continue?"

"Please Ms. Hahm, forgive me, proceed."

She smiled as she straightened her shoulder length hair. She said, "We are going to be working very closely Sang. Please call me Joon."

He smiled and nodded. She continued, "Our robotic made discrete observations for quite some time. It observed their spaceships exiting and entering the base over a period of months. There was very rarely any surface activity, just arrivals and departures. One day a departing ship came directly towards the robotic, and the signal was then terminated. They destroyed it, we assume.

Two years later we landed another robotic, this one a bit bigger, and armed. That one was discovered much faster and was attacked. It was, however, able to defend itself twice."

"Only twice?"

"It only had two surface-to-air missiles. The extensive modifications for use in a vacuum meant we could only arm it with two. It had no defence on the third attack, other than its rugged good looks."

Kang smiled at her joke, "And now?"

She looked back at the screen and continued. "The third package that landed in the same area moved under a flag of peace. I mean that literally. A long arm popped up after landing, and it had a large white flag on it. It also contained both hard wired and portable communications equipment. Anyways, it approached the installation you are looking at now, and then just sat there. Apparently the flag of peace was understood. After several hours a few small figures in space suits," she shuddered, "horrid little creatures really, they came out and took the portable communications equipment inside. We then attempted to establish contact. We did have video both there and back, as well as audio. There were four distinctly different creatures that we saw. All were bi-pedal, but all quite different. They spoke at us, but their language was quite unintelligible. Well, to be accurate, only one of the creatures spoke at us. One of the other types of creatures spoke; but not to us. The other two types of creatures, while intently looking at us, said nothing. We assume they are telepathic, but I think we only assume that because the only other explanation is rudeness. The creatures that did speak to us, after much study by three specialists from the Pyongyang University of Foreign Studies, from the Ethnic Languages College, have asserted that the language seems to be quite similar to studied Proto-Slavic languages. They were only able to translate three words with some degree of certainty, 'Away', 'No', and 'Welcome'. We still have access to the video, I can show you later."

"Thank you, yes," he said quietly but enthusiastically.

As they watched the large monitor, first one, then two, then four pairs of legs moved around the camera, illuminated by lights from the terrain vehicle they must have been riding in. They were all obviously dressed in traditional Chinese style space suits. The figures came into view, moving very slowly. Kang and Hahm both watched in silence for several minutes.

Finally Kang spoke up, "So those are our people then?"

"Yes."

"The fourth mission is to the dark side of the moon?"

"Yes."

"Heroes," he almost whispered.

She gave a soft laugh, "If you say so."

He looked at her and smiled. At least she didn't have a stick up her ass, to coin an American phrase.

"The elite decided that it would be more beneficial if we could send our representatives there and attempt to establish first contact. They believe that by sending two astronauts, a party representative, and a linguist of Slavic languages, that they will be more likely to establish contact with them. More productive contact I mean."

"That would seem reasonable."

"The Commander of the landing team is my brother," she smiled. "He's scared shitless, but won't admit it to anyone."

Kang just looked at her and looked back at the screen.

"He's always lived at home. I can read him like a book. The last thing he wanted to do was go to the Moon on this mission to meet aliens."

Kang would have asked why he went, but already knew the answer. To refuse such a prestigious assignment would have meant the end of his career. He would have wound up a minor functionary in a remote government office if, and only if, he didn't wind up with a bullet in his head.

There were a few people stirring and talking excitedly down in the Project 57-4 "pit" as the four sections were called. Focussing on the screen, Kang and Hahm could see that the lighting had changed subtly, and the four suited Koreans were moving a bit, to allow a better view for the cameras. A door had opened in the structure on the crater wall, a small door, only about four feet wide. There stood a single figure in the doorway. It, too, wore a space suit but had a really, really large helmet. It was too far from the camera to make out any details. As if he had read their thoughts, the tech operating the camera slowly zoomed in on the creature. Unlike Sweden's feed from Mars, this truly was in real-time. What they finally could see was, to their perception, quite hideous.

Something dark moved across the camera, and then out of sight. As the camera started to release the zoom and show more of what it could see, dozens of smaller creatures in simple space suits came pouring through the doorway. They rushed past the side of the slightly taller figure, still standing by itself. The smaller creatures were all running towards the camera. As the camera zoom pulled fully backwards, the room was filled with gasps and then hushed silence. The four Koreans in their space suits were sprawled on the ground, as though they had just fallen asleep. The Medical techs confirmed they were still getting life signs' telemetry, so they knew the astronauts were not dead.

Kang glanced quickly sideways, and could see the concern for her brother was now evident on Hahm's face, even though she was trying hard to hide it.

The little creatures emerging through the doorway quickly approached the sprawled North Korean astronauts. The creatures surrounded each body, and then the bodies lifted up. It didn't look like the little things were actually touching the astronauts, but they were focused on them intently. The little creatures' faceplates were darkened so they couldn't really see what they looked like. The focus of intensity came from their posture, and the fact they were ignoring the camera and land transport it was mounted to. They started walking back towards the open doorway in the crater wall. The four North Korean astronauts seemed to be floating between them. The figure in the doorway stepped back, allowing each floating body and its retinue of creatures to enter the airlock, and then it turned out of sight. When the last one was through the door; the larger, hideous creature came back to stand in the opening. As he did so, nine of the little creatures re-emerged. This time they appeared to be holding some kind of weapon, though its abilities and ammunition could not be discerned. The nine creatures formed a line directly in front of, and across the field of view of the camera. They squatted down on their haunches, weapons held tightly in their hands, and there they stayed. In the background, the larger creature stepped backwards, and the airlock door closed.

Kang glanced sideways at Hahm. She had a hand over her mouth, and tears were rimming her eyes. All she said was the name of her brother, "Jin."

Chapter 47

Sapro

Oboo and Adla hurried up the path beside the infirmary. They were on the way to Kam's house to share the celebration dinner. It didn't take long to reach it. The singing had not started yet, so they rushed through the door without knocking. As they were old and dear friends of Kam and Falla, this was not considered overly rude, just slightly impolite.

Oboo joined Kam, Saklt and Piv in the dining/living area, while Adla joined Kam's wife Falla and the other two wives in the kitchen. Adla had been carrying an earthenware pot of wine braised vegetables. She loved the aroma of the sparing dash of the Terran spices from the closely hoarded supply in her kitchen. This one was called *sin-a-man*, she had been told. Her husband was an engineering mate on the off-cycle transport runs. He had made friends with the human kitchen staff on the Terrans' other planet, the red one, and they gave him samples from time to time. Oboo could have been a great trader, but he loved being in the Protective Service so much that Adla never made an issue of it. They lived comfortably, and to an Eben, that was all that was necessary.

The sound of laughing and teasing children drifted in through the open windows and doors on the warm semidusk of a Saproan winter's night. The candles around the dining area, and the increasingly laden table gave a warm glow that complemented the evening and the purpose of the celebration. The muted browns and dark orange-red colours of the smooth hand plastered walls of the adobe type structure (to use a Terran term) reflected the light softly, providing a very serene and inviting living space.

Little MuJu KamPen walked in with an armful of Alyak flowers, and placed them in the brightly painted pottery vase that his mother had set out for this. He placed the vase in the middle of the table with his little arms, straining under the weight of the pottery and water.

Kam hovered close by as he did this, trying not to embarrass his young son with overbearing behaviour, but also to not embarrass him by allowing him to drop or spill the vase in front of the others. MuJu was at that sensitive age where years of support were now being pushed back by the need for self-definition as part of the child's growth process.

All of the men watched out of the corner of their eyes. They all held their breath momentarily as the vase, heavy with flowers and water, tottered a tiny bit. They all exhaled together as MuJu braced his elbows on the table to steady the vase. Once in place, he turned and beamed up at his father. Kam wrapped him in his long arms, and praised him for a job well done; and for doing it so carefully. The other fathers all came over and touched MuJu on the head, in the Eben way of solicitous affection for children. They each complimented him on his selection of flowers and how beautiful they were. MuJu, delighted, ran outside to be with his sibs and the other children. The smiling men stood loosely together and blocked the kitchen occupants' view, as Kam pulled the poisonous Yinshi stalks out of the vase, surreptitiously discarding them before Falla noticed. The wives tended to be a little more firm and direct in such matters with the children.

The four families, all lifelong friends, were gathered to celebrate the birth of Piv and his wife Lata's third child. Three children were the limit on Sapro, and she would soon undergo the excision to prevent any more. This was a limitation that all Eben hated, but that they fully embraced and respected for its necessity. Many close galactic examples of top heavy societal collapses just reinforced the necessity of this concept. This limitation allowed their society to grow at a pace that could be supported.

For tonight though, minds were not on such things. Piv and Lata's family had just grown by one more child, and all thoughts were on the hopes and desires for the child's growth and his future role in society. More importantly, they were rejoicing at how the love in that family had just recently been given the opportunity to grow as well.

The women joined the men in the dining space, placing the last of the prepared dishes on the table - what we would call a Harvest table. Saklt and his wife Adla (she shared the same given name as Oboo's wife) called in all the children. The older ones sat at the table with the adults, while the younger ones (the ones younger than MuJu), all sat on a parent's lap. In the case of Saklt and his wife Adla, their third child sat on Falla's lap; as her children were all old enough for their own sitting place.

As the evening's host, Kam stood and the others, including the children, automatically stopped talking to listen to their host. Kam began by offering a prayer of thanks and gratitude to the Great Father. The Eben believed that wherever two or three were gathered, the Great Father was always present and therefore, always acknowledged His presence with humble and grateful hearts.

Kam then went on to speak about the blessing and responsibility of parenthood, including the special bond with the last child. The last child always got just a little bit more and stayed at home just a little bit longer. Both parents inevitably paid just that extra bit of attention, because they knew there would not be a fourth; although the Eben would gratefully and enthusiastically raise twenty or more if they could, as they had in the ancient times.

After his short speech, one that had been said in a similar manner millions of times for thousands of years across their society, Kam led his guests in the traditional song of family. It was a lilting and fun song that turned into a ballad, and then back into a light ditty. All of those present that knew the song, sang along. The children that didn't know it yet listened intently and repeated it as closely as possible.

The candlelight glinted off their solid black, large Eben eyes. For some, a slight sheen of perspiration on their bald heads allowed a bit more twinkle from the burning light. The men's black tunics were always countered by their wives' bright and deeply coloured ruffled blouses and ankle-length skirts. Modesty was not mandated by society, but only the adolescents would wear revealing clothing.

Gifting and presents were not the way of the Eben, instead it was personal interaction and involvement that was considered the truest gift of respect or affection. However, gifts were not unheard of, as was the case this evening. Saklt and Adla's eldest child, their daughter Keeva, was learning the skill of sewing. For this evening's celebration, Keeva had sewn two jumpers and a blanket for the recently born infant. After the gathered group had finished their song, Keeva (her name meant *breathe*, which was also the traditional Eben greeting) ran to the kitchen and retrieved these items from her mother's bag. As wrapping paper and such frippery were unheard of on Sapro, the gifts were wrapped the traditional way. They were tied up in big, green Kayam leaves. With great praise and much gratitude, Lata accepted the gifts on behalf of the infant. She invited young Keeva to come to their home the following day, after first sleep, to try them on the youngling.

In Eben society the eldest woman of the house is the master of the house, the owner of the house, and the one responsible for all the actions of those who live in the house. Kam's wife Falla was a model of Eben womanhood. She ran a tight ship, and everyone knew what was expected of them. She was also a giving, gracious, and loving hostess. As the hostess, Falla allowed Piv's wife Lata, the honour of serving the table. It was Lata's third child being celebrated tonight, so their culture would expect that she display her gratitude to the others for their sharing of love with her and her family. Being a good husband, Piv handed the child on his lap to the adolescent next to him, and immediately began assisting Lata in her service of their friends.

Eben meals are usually simple, quick, and perfunctory affairs; unless there is a celebration. Then they can last an exhaustingly long time, as many human visitors to the planet have found out. Eventually, the food was eaten, the small amount of Molyak wine had been consumed, and the tart and tangy citrus dessert had been portioned, shared and consumed.

The celebration caused the house to have a large complement of adolescents, eight in total. The eldest daughter of Kam and Falla, named Joose, was honoured with the charge of the kitchen and dining area for the remainder of the evening. Joose practically radiated with pride over the honour and responsibility handed to her so unexpectedly. She immediately lined up the five boys, and detailed exactly what they must do in clearing the table of dishes and serving pots. The actual washing up and drying of the cookery and table service was reserved for Joose and the two other adolescent girls, Keeva and Sela. The boys were just not quite reliable enough yet, at their tender ages, to be trusted not to break everything they tried to wash, dry, and place in the cupboards. Adolescent Eben males tended to be a bit, shall we say, clumsy.

Falla took the women out to the back terrace. She had secreted another small bottle of Molyak wine there. With surreptitious smiles, the woman with solid black eyes unabashedly held out their glasses. They all silently shared the sentiment that frankly, what the men folk didn't know wouldn't hurt them.

Kam, Oboo, Saklt and Piv took hot mugs of spiced tea and strolled down the lane in front of Kam's house. They soon wound up sitting on the bank of the creek that supplied their neighbourhoods fresh water needs. These four families all lived near each other. The four men, all military men, worked together at the Protective Services detachment in their province.

Kam had something he wanted to discuss with the men, and was trying to come up with a delicate way of broaching the topic. Oboo, however, wasn't nearly as politically astute as Kam. Having mulled over a similar thought, unbeknownst to the two of them, Oboo blurted it right out to start the conversation.

"Something is up with the humans. Does anyone think this is so?"

Startled, but pleased with the opening, Kam asked, "Why say you this young friend?"

"Well," he started, "Last cycle, when we were delivering the homeworld foods, the store rooms at the Mars base were not as roomy as they usually are. There was a lot of supplies from the human world there, but most of them were overbearing provisions, not much in the way of perishables. We also saw many boxes of what the humans call "Meals Ready to Eat", quite similar to our battle rations. We could see many of them."

"You are getting startled by the sudden appearance of food?" Piv rubbed his slightly paunch belly. Never one to say no to a second helping, he asked, "Are you getting skittish over preserves? I could most surely help with their overabundance problems!" The others chuckled, his gastronomic proclivities were well known.

"No friend, of course not. They did not appear all at once either. However, friend, I've been on this Mars run for almost forty cycles. It's only in the last five that I've noticed they are stocking up reserves. It's like they are expecting to go a long time without resupply. Even our own shipments have been increasing slightly for the last five cycles, more preserves and dried foods than perishables. Your own Adla provided dozens of pots of preserves in the last shipment."

The Eben liked fresh food. They would eat preserves and dried foods on campaign, on long interstellar or intergalactic voyages, and during droughts. When there was a source of fresh food, however, fresh food always won. With over seventy True-Blood Eben on the humans' second world, what Oboo had seen was odd and worth noting, though not overly worrying about on its own.

Saklt cleared his throat and spoke quietly, "My sister has reported to me that many of us, on their base, are growing more unhappy about the humans' shipments of live organic tissues to the 'dani base."

"Ahhhh," Piv threw his hands in the air and stood quickly, starting to pace. "They should obliterate that base of Tantaloids, and the one on the humans' moon as well."

Kam spoke up, "The humans don't have the power to take out the 'dani Piv, you know that."

Piv spun on his heels, the old argument coming back for another incarnation, "WE DO! It would take only one of the battle cruisers to eliminate the Eridani base on the humans' second planet. Then it could quickly make the jump to Earth and destroy the base on their moon! It would only take one battle cruiser and we have two stationed there! Why not just get rid of the bastards!"

"We all remember the stories of the Great War, that is why! Do we want to go to war with the Eridani? Do we know for sure the Lectra and the Ousoons will not join with them? The Trigla homeworld is bursting with too many idle hands!" Kam had made this argument more than once as well.

"The Trigla homeworld will never join in a war with the Voiya against us!" Piv was almost yelling.

"The Trigla are their slaves Piv!" jumped in Oboo, "They will do what they are told!"

"Ahhcchh, I disagree with you 'boo, the Trigla are slaves because it suits them to be so. It *suits them*. If the Voiya pushed them too far, the Trigla outnumber them ten thousand to one! The Voiya wouldn't stand a chance!"

Saklt quietly chimed in, sitting behind where Piv stood, "You keep forgetting the Vesna."

"Vesna, ahhcchhh! No better than the Voiya!" Piv spun around.

"You keep forgetting the drones too," added Saklt.

Piv didn't say anything but the frustration was evident on his brow. "Those drones are an abomination," he retorted sulkily.

"Yes they are," agreed Kam, "but at last estimate, there are almost 30,000,000 of those abominations in this galaxy alone."

This seemed to take the wind out of Piv's rant, as it usually did. He tossed his long arms in the air in surrender. Picking up his mug of spiced tea from the rock he had been sitting on, he drank deeply of it, "Forsake the one who created the drones" he muttered the time old curse. The others mumbled in agreement, and drank from their tall mugs of spiced tea as well.

"I agree with Oboo though," continued Kam, "there is something going on with the humans. I've noticed an increase in political communiqués with the central council and the industrial districts. The Protective Services division in the central city is also ... a bit different. Security seems tighter. Their training regimens of those at the academy are increasing in duration and intensity. Kala, my wife's brother's wife's sister told me that they have been conducting a lot of weightless combat training, and a lot of low atmosphere combat training."

The others looked at him, and murmured interrogatory sounds of concern.

"I've also heard," continued Kam, "that the *Shin Rol*, the *Shin Pey* and the *Shin Moff* have been ordered into the yards for refit," he paused, "all at the same time. They are sitting in the orbital docks right now."

This startled the others. He now had their full attention. The Eben, individually and as a race, are known as the fiercest and greatest warriors in the galaxy. While the Eben were victorious in the Great War, it almost eradicated their entire race; just as the Eben had entirely eradicated the Kuabatay during that war. Once a population of nine billion, there were now only about seven hundred thousand Eben on the homeworld, and another twenty thousand spread around the three galaxies. Some were on exploration missions, some were traders, and some were staffing remote outposts. Still, the Eben had never lost a skirmish or battle when forced into one, but they were also reluctant about going to war without far superior numbers on their side. Just because they were very good, didn't mean they didn't die.

The *Shin Rol*, *Shin Pey* and the *Shin Moff* were heavy battle cruisers. They were ancient, but fully functional and fully capable ships of war. In the last few centuries their business had been mostly commerce, and while heavily armed, they were old style arms and defenses. The newer and smaller battle cruisers like the *Lo Pal*, *Lo Long*, and *Lo Tow* were a bit more agile and packed as much punch with a lower overhead. Refitting the already

302

impressive *Shin* class of battle cruiser with the modern armaments and defensive technology would make them the most fearsome and deadly ships of war in the three (known) occupied galaxies. This new fact gave the Eben men pause, as they quietly calculated just one of the ships destructive capabilities. Though these men were peace-loving, as all Eben were, it gave them a shiver of both pride and fear.

Saklt spoke first, "If they are refitting the old *Shin* cruisers, then that can only be for the awe their presence would inspire amongst our enemies. Perhaps the council is merely making this a demonstration of resolve and intent, to discourage anyone who might get ideas about challenging us."

Piv spoke up, with a big smile on his face, "Were that true, friend, why would we be increasing our warriors training in low atmo combat?"

Another silence settled on the men. After a few moments Piv looked at Kam, holding his gaze for a moment, "Where is Hof?"

Kam, who had been staring at the babbling brook of water turned and faced Piv, "He should be arriving on the humans' second planet today."

Chapter 48

Hof

Achael was deep in conversation with Colonel Greff KamPen, sitting in his office. There was a sharp knock on the door and KamPen yelled out, "Enter!"

The door opened and Hlef leaned in, "May I join you?"

KamPen looked a bit taken aback, but nodded his head. Hlef would typically just barge in like she owned the place. She took a seat beside Achael. Looking at Hlef, Achael said, "I just told him what Mom wants us to do."

"I still can't believe she wants us to do this. It's ridiculous. Why should we make ourselves known to him? Why should we tell him about us? Why does she want to provoke the Eridani?

KamPen was fiddling with a pen, "The General has never steered us astray. She has always made decisions that, in the end, proved to be to our benefit and to the humans' benefit. While I'm not sure what her end game is," he had his own thoughts on that matter, "I'm sure that this is for a very good reason." He didn't know about any of the preparations on Sapro. He looked up and smiled, "And I can't think of two better people to do it."

The phone rang on his desk. He picked it up, listened then hung it up without saying anything. He stood up, "I have to go to the hangar bay, would you please come with me?" After the nasty surprise of sending Hlef to Earth unbidden, he now had a most pleasant surprise to make up for it.

They all stood and headed towards the door. Regardless of rank, Greff was a gentleman in both the human and the Eben way of thinking. He opened the door and held it for the ladies. As Hlef passed by him, she stopped and looked at him sweetly, reached out and touched her long fingers to his cheek. With a pert smile she said, "I haven't forgotten what you did," and then she slapped his face, playfully. He should have been incensed, but instead he just laughed; Greff had known there would be a reckoning for putting her on the shuttle to Earth, and if this was the piper's due, then he was getting off very lucky indeed.

As they walked towards the hangar bay, Achael recounted to him the meeting with Sharon Moesby and the new baby. Greff also knew Sharon from some work he had done down-side. Achael, of course, left out the part about Hlef's meltdown. She spent the rest of the walk to the hangar bay catching him up on some of the other gossip she had picked up from others she had spoken with. They reached the hangar bay doors, and Col. Greff KamPen pushed them open stepping through with the ladies behind him. He stopped suddenly, and they almost plowed into him. He said, "Keeva Hof!" and stepped aside.

Both girls screamed and ran forward at the same time, "DADDY!!"

Hof was standing with a small black duffel over his shoulder. He was talking to Pinpin, but turned quickly at the sound of his daughters' voices. They both practically plowed him over as they fell to one knee, grabbing him fiercely in their long arms, and hugging him so hard he could barely breathe. He wrapped his long Eben arms around both of them, and smiled despite himself; kissing them both on the forehead, and then touching them both on the head in a uniquely Eben way. He and his wife Pella had the permitted three children on Sapro, but he was also blessed with five more children here on the humans' second planet. It was something Pella held over his head when she was in one of her moods.

He could barely croak out in native Eben, "Nao ... keeva" (can't breathe).

Hlef and Achael both loosened their grip on him, but didn't let go. They started kissing his hairless head over and over again. It was an Eben familial expression of affection, but Hof always felt like he needed a shower afterwards. He had, after all, just gone through the same thing with Pinpin. The hybrids were almost as sloppy as the humans when it came to saliva and kisses. Finally the kissing stopped, the girls had thick black tears in their eyes at the joy of this surprise visit from their father. Their inner eyelids had slammed shut with the emotional surprise of seeing him and they, for the moment, looked very Eben kneeling next to him. Hof was very pleased as well, and had looked forward to seeing all of his hybrid children. The trip from Zeta Reticuli I Theta (simply known to the Eben and the humans as Sapro) had taken almost one hundred sleeps, about three months in human terms. Sapro was approximately forty light years from Earth, and even the heavy cruiser *Lo Pal* took time to fold that distance. The recently completed *Lo Pal* was a new generation battle cruiser, and was to remain on Mars while the *Shin Pu* returned to Sapro for refit. The *Shin Fa* would not go for refit until the *Shin Pu* returned.

Hof started to pick up his bag again, having dropped it when the girls tackled him. Hlef snatched it from his hand and threw it over her shoulder. The girls took a place on each side of him, each one holding one of his hands as they walked out of the hangar bay.

"Dinner together?" Hlef tossed over her shoulder to Pinpin. He gave her a thumbs up. This caused Achael to marvel again at the change in her sister. Hlef would never have thought of something so inclusive or family oriented like that before their trip to Earth, but now, it was like she was becoming, well, normal. Eben normal anyways.

As they walked down the corridor the girls had to let go of their father and jump out of the way quickly. Ahshuun and Khlam had come around a corner and repeated the screaming tackle so recently enacted by Achael and Hlef. When they heard that Hof had arrived, they had immediately headed towards the hangar bay to greet him as well. While Ahshuun, an Eben dominant hybrid, was the same height as Hof (about four feet tall), Khlam was a human dominant hybrid like the girls. He stood 161 centimetres, so he wound up hugging both father and brother, not even really being aware of it. Again, with the kissing of the head; Hof decided he definitely needed a shower after all this.

Hot showers were one of the perks of coming to the humans' second world. On Sapro, the houses only had small shallow baths, showers were seen as wasteful. The Battle Cruiser had showers, but they were low-pressure, lukewarm; and simply weren't of the same quality as those found in the human facilities. That was why Hof had one secretly built in his workshop behind his small house, although he rarely got to use it. Unbeknownst to him, Pella had discovered the shower and used it from time to time as well, more often than Hof. The luxury of it was mesmerizing to her.

The Eben father and four hybrid children walked towards the guest quarters. The air was resonant with native Eben dialect, as they all competed to tell him more than the other. Hof tried to get in words of encouragement, wonder, and how pleased he was. Hof wasn't a spring chicken any more, almost 320 Earth years in age, the wisdom of time finally told him to just let them ramble on and smile appreciatively while grunting in the appropriate places. Greff trailed along behind them, wondering if he would see Kam, his own sperm donor father, anytime in the near future.

Along the way, many people greeted Hof by word or gesture. He had been coming around the Mars base for about 150 years before the Hybrid program began. He was widely respected. He was both liked and loved by many.

Reaching his quarters, the children remained outside as Hof thanked them for their welcome, and promised that after freshening up, he would join them for dinner. He did have to meet with Col. KamPen first, he told them, but not until he had a shower and a change of clothes. His daughters told him they had a mission of their own to complete, so they planned on getting together in six hours.

They all left him to himself and headed towards the cafeteria. The Commander had offered the family his private dining room, and Hlef wanted to speak with the Chef about preparing some Eben dishes for their father. His created children knew that Hof had a fancy for carrots, something that had no corresponding vegetable on Sapro. They made sure that Chef prepared lots of them, oozing in butter and sesame seeds. Butter was something else unheard of on Sapro, and it was something that Hof indulged in when on the human worlds. Being strictly vegetarian, Hof's body usually had difficulty processing anything with lactose, but he tolerated it.

Twenty minutes later, Hof presented himself to the Commander, with the central council's compliments. Col. KamPen ushered Hof to the small conference table in the corner of his large office, and sat down across from him. As soon as they were seated, a human mess steward came in with a pot of hot spiced tea and a chinaware tea service. As this was being served, Hof presented Greff with a small bottle of Molyak wine, a gift sent from Pella, Hof's wife. Greff had spent some time on Sapro as a child, and for whatever strange reason, Pella had taken a shine to the young child Greff had been. Greff had been the first hybrid Pella had ever met, years before Hof's own hybrid children had been created.

Hof had brought several items of business to attend to regarding the operation of an interstellar outpost. It took about an hour to sort them out, including some personnel reassignments. Hof then went over some plans he had for the next generation of hybrids. The new advancements they wanted to incorporate would hopefully allow the next set of hybrids to be fertile, able to conceive and bare children. It was a major milestone they had been working towards for almost eighty human years. Greff, now 54 human years old, barely out of adolescence in Eben terms, had been in the third iteration of hybrids. Hof's children were in the fifth iteration of hybrids. The new batch about to mature would be the ninth iteration of hybrids. Hof's plans were for the upcoming tenth iteration, not yet started. The oldest hybrids were in their seventies, and showed no signs of slowing down. They didn't really have any clue yet what their life expectancy would be. Only five hybrids, from all the iterations, had died: three of them in accidents, and two of them in battle.

Finally, the formal business attended to, Hof stood and walked around the office in silence. His long arms tucked deep in his pants pockets; he was deep in thought as he slowly returned to the table and sat down. Greff had seen Hof like this before, and knew better than to interrupt his thoughtful cogitations.

As Hof sat down, Greff leaned forward and poured some more Saenggangcha spicy tea in his cup. Hof nodded in appreciation and slowly took a deep draught of the invigorating beverage. This particular blend was from South Korea and was imported quite frequently, via the 88th, by a few specialized merchants on Sapro.

Finally Hof looked at Greff and set down his cup. As always with Hof, they spoke in Eben, "I have been authorized by the central council and by the 88th to brief you on certain matters."

Greff wasn't totally surprised by this. Hof's visit had been a last-minute thing, and most of what had been discussed could have been done by communiqué rather than in person.

"We are finally going to rid Mars of the Eridani."

"Just Mars?" asked Greff.

Hof smiled.

Chapter 49

The Visit

Khlam did the quick prefight on the Dart as he waited for his sisters. After Achael and Hlef had given marching orders to the cafeteria staff, he had been surprised by them taking him aside. Now he was part of some cloak and dagger bullshit to the human colony site. Before he did the preflight, he had taken three minutes to access and disable the craft's transponder and IFF beacon. According to Achael, there could be no record of their visit to the human. The ship would still be visible because the Eben had never bothered with cloaking technology like the Eridani and the Ousoon had developed.

He wasn't aware of this, but Col. KamPen had once again interrupted the Mar-Sat feed and the Jalopy-Sat feeds. This was one alien encounter that could NOT be recorded. Greff KamPen knew that as soon as the visit was over, Lt. Gen. Rosewood would be scrubbing the spooled local files on the humans' servers.

Khlam only had to wait a few minutes when the women appeared. He waited impatiently while they suited up in environment suits, as he had done. He noticed Hlef putting an odd-sized plastic box in one of her environment suits' large pockets, but didn't question her on it. *Probably part of the whole cloak and dagger bullshit*, he thought.

Their brother Pinpin was the duty flight deck officer and he cleared them to leave. He knew they were going without transponder or IFF, but he didn't know where, though it wasn't hard to guess. Achael had given him the military code word that meant 'shut the frak up and don't ask silly questions'.

Khlam was a bit of a hot-dog when he was on the stick. He loved flying more than anything else. His ascent to a safe folding altitude involved several barrel rolls, one loop-de-loop, and Achael smacking him on the back of the head, yelling at him to stop fraking around.

She had told him she wanted the human to have some warning that they were arriving, so he folded 250 kilometres from the colony site. He then accelerated to a breakneck speed, cutting their travel time to about three minutes. As they moved in real space, the women put on their helmets and activated their suits' life support. By the time they were done, Khlam was bringing the ship to a stationary hover about 30 metres in front of the W-Hab.

He looked over his shoulder. This was easily done as his helmet was not on. Both of the women, with determined looks on their faces nodded at him. He activated the TransMat. The women were now standing on Mars' surface about 10 metres in front of the Dart. They had agreed that to TransMat inside the Habitat might be a bit much for the human. They needed to give him some breathing space to handle a couple aliens, expected or not, arriving at his Mars home. After the TransMat, Khlam's sisters immediately proceeded to the only visible Habitat airlock. He watched Achael climb up the ladder, swing the airlock armature, and then open the hatch. His sisters went inside, and the hatch shut behind them.

Khlam didn't like it. He didn't like it one bit. His instrumentation showed that there were five Eridani scout ships at about 100 km bearing 023, and were in a position to be observing what was happening. Now, his sisters had gone inside the habitat with the human. Humans could always be so unpredictable.

No, Khlam didn't like it one bit at all.

Mike

I stared at the error messages and wondered what the hell had happened. More precisely, I wondered what the hell was about to happen. The last time this occurred was when I had the second encounter with the little alien bastard out by the supply drops. This could not bode well.

Some movement caught my eye. I shifted my gaze slightly to the video monitors. Two figures were entering the airlock and then shutting the outer door.

Oh, uhmm ... frak.

I ran down the stairs and cautiously peered one eye through the portal of the inner airlock door. The two figures were standing there, blackened helmet faceplates revealing nothing. They were looking around. One of them stepped towards the corner where the weapons were hidden. I couldn't see that she was just examining the bottle recharging system. The green light came on the airlock control to confirm that the airlock internal pressure was balanced and human breathable.

They hadn't seen me in the portal yet. I closed my eyes, muttered a quick prayer, and then I swung the armature and pushed the airlock door inwards. Neither appeared startled, and both of them turned towards me. I stepped through the airlock door and reached around to the back of the Activity Suit I was still wearing. I grabbed the handle of the K-Bar, unsnapped the closure, and pulled it out in a forward grip. One more step and I was standing right in front of the closest alien, with the knife pointing right at its throat.

No sooner had I done this, I was looking down the barrel of the meanest, ugliest sidearm in the world. It looked like a Desert Eagle with a tin can welded around it. In fact, I would later learn, it was indeed a Desert Eagle with a pressure canister attachment that allowed it to be fired in low/no atmosphere. Regardless of knowing that, it still looked like a Desert Eagle, and that meant .50 cal; and that meant really, really big and messy hole. Not much of a combat weapon, but perfectly designed for upclose and personal.

I didn't flinch. I couldn't flinch. This wasn't a game of rocks n' lasers like before. This was, as stated, upclose and personal. This was for keeps. This wasn't the first time since the explosion that I was scared, and it probably wouldn't be the last. Scared or not, this was my home. I would give no quarter, show no hesitation, and show no fear.

Achael

The quick draw had been automatic. She had barely registered the weapon in his hand, and her sidearm was in her hand, cocked and pointed at him. Safety off. Eben reflexes.

She sighed heavily in her helmet. She had hoped it wouldn't go like this.

Hlef

Hlef had caught the movement of the human entering out of the corner of her eye. As she turned she could see the human with a big knife in his hand and her sister had already drawn her sidearm. As Hlef also had the Eben reflexes, her sidearm magically appeared in her right hand as well, but she didn't point it. This certainly had been a possibility, but she knew someone had to back down first. She knew that would *not* be her sister. Okay, it was up to her to handle this situation.

She holstered her sidearm and stepped to the side of Achael. She paused and looked at both of them. The human looked from sister to sister, but his knife hand never wavered. He looked scared, but he also looked determined. Now she understood the package in her pocket.

Hlef reached up very slowly and unlocked, disconnected and removed her helmet. She shook her wild tangle of long curly brown hair loose, then fixed the human with a pert, perhaps somewhat saucy, smile, and said, "Hello, sweetie."

Mike

She was the most beautiful woman I had ever seen. She looked like Loreena, but shorter. She also had freakishly big dreamy blue eyes, but they just made her even more gorgeous. I think I stopped breathing for a few heartbeats as I looked at her. After she said, "Hello, sweetie" she smiled and winked at me.

Still holding my knife on the other alien, and the other alien still holding their sidearm on me, I watched the vision of beauty who was obviously not human. Well, not entirely human. She slowly reached into a large pocket on the leg of her environment suit. She pulled out a plastic box, it looked like a Tupperware container. This breathtakingly beautiful alien woman pried the lid off, and held it out towards me. I smelled it before I saw it. I glanced down into the plastic box.

Homemade peanut butter cookies. My favourite.

Achael

She kept her gaze fixed on the human, but she knew that Hlef was stepping up to make the first contact. Achael did momentarily, unseen by the others, roll her eyes in her head when Hlef greeted him sexy-style. Her incredible peripheral vision allowed her to watch her sister open and present the cookies without taking her attention or focus off of Mike and the ridiculous knife.

As soon as the cookies were presented, the man first smiled, then chuckled. He dropped his arm holding the extended knife.

Mike

I slowly put the knife back in the scabbard and reached for the plastic box. I took out a cookie and slowly savoured its wonderful flavour. "Mmmmmm ..."

The beautiful alien nudged the other one who was still holding her space-gun on me.

"You will have to forgive my sister, she's a bit anal about having," she suppressed a smile, "a knife pointed at her."

The other alien re-holstered her weapon and started removing her helmet.

"Gilda sent you," I stated.

The other alien was pulling her helmet off as she spoke, "She said the cookies would be our calling card." The second most beautiful woman I had ever seen shook out her long silky black hair and looked at me, again, with the freakishly big dreamy blue eyes. What was it with their eyes?

"Don't you know you shouldn't take a knife to a gun fight?" she asked, smiling.

Two women, two very beautiful women, and they were sent by Gilda. They had to be safe. "Meh," I shrugged my shoulders, took another cookie and shoved the whole thing in my mouth. I offered the box to them, and the gorgeous one with the curly brown hair took one and slowly took a bite. The gorgeous one with the long silky and smooth black hair shook her head.

"Well," I said around the last bits of the cookie, "might as well come in. I'll put the coffee on." With that I spun around and headed towards the airlock, and up the stairs. The situation was what it was, no sense fretting. I heard them following me, and one of them said, "Tea, please". It was truly the most surreal moment I had ever experienced.

I set the container that still held nine cookies on the counter, and walked over to the supply cupboard. I had six mugs and had only unwrapped one of them from its transit packaging. I unwrapped two more, and set them on the counter. I emptied a stick of Starbucks coffee in one of the mugs. I dropped a Red Rose tea bag in the other mug, and one in my own mug. Filling them from the almost boiling hot water dispenser by the sink, I handed out the mugs and pointed them to the powder creamer. "Sweetener?" I hoped they would say no because at that moment I realized I didn't have any sweetener on Mars. The gorgeous one said, "Three please."

Frak, "Umm, ahh ..."

"Never mind," she smiled, "I imagine you haven't unpacked it yet."

With hot cups of coffee and tea we sat around the small work table I had previously unpacked. They had their helmets and gloves off. I could see they had really, really long fingers. They were still wearing their pressure suits though, so I wasn't sure if they maybe had an extra set of arms or boobs or something but hey, given the events of the last few days I didn't think there was anything that would surprise me.

"So," I began. "Gilda sent you to see me." The black-haired one nodded, she seemed to be the leader of the two.

"Mom sends her regards," she said, then sipped her coffee. I was suddenly very wrong about nothing else surprising me. She smiled at the look on my face.

"Mom?" I think I gulped.

"Yes, Mom."

"Ah-ha. So it's like that is it?"

The other one chimed in, "Yes, yes it is." They were most-def Gilda's daughters.

After a brief pause where I considered several things, I spoke again. "Okay, shall we start with introductions then?" The beautiful curly brown haired one slurped noisily on her hot tea.

The other one rolled her eyes, "I'm Ah-ooh-chhale and this is my sister Uh-oo-lef".

I smiled and tried pronouncing their names. She guided me through a couple attempts until I had them as right as a human set of vocal chords could get them.

"I guess you know I'm Mike Lane, Martian." I smiled.

The curly brown haired one laughed out loud, and the silky smooth brunette smiled. Maybe this wasn't going to be such a bad day after all. The brunette or, as I thought of her, the hot one's hot sister, got right down to business.

Achael

This guy actually seemed as nice in person as he did in the media and the monitoring they had done, she thought to herself. The dossier that Gilda had given them on this man summarised that he was disarmingly charming, thoughtful, and exceptionally intelligent; that he should not be discounted regardless of his circumstances; that he should be watched closely in any dealings with him. His responses could be interestingly unpredictable. Achael decided not to beat around the bush. She and Hlef did, after all, have a dinner date with their father and brothers.

"As you have noticed," she began, "we may a look a bit different." To his credit, Mike said and did nothing at that statement except sip his cup of tea. "We are Human-Eben hybrids. We are a product of inter-genome technology involving human ova and Eben spermatozoa.

Seventy-three Earth years ago, Eben scientists and human military personnel began experimentation with combining the two races. My sister, brothers and I are from the fifth generation of full-on trials that occurred forty years ago. The ninth generation is due for maturation in another couple of months.

The Eben themselves, we call them the True-Blood Eben, have been on Mars for over a thousand years. They used it extensively as a remote outpost for observation of humans on Earth. They made first contact by accident in the 1940's, which I know Mom told you about. After that, the True-Bloods attempted to form relationships with the Russians, the Chinese, and the French; but only the relationship with the Americans held up. While a formal presence on Earth was withdrawn in the 1960's due to the Earth alliances with the Eridani, the True-Bloods remained on Mars where the Eben-Human base had already been established. Currently there are about seventy True-Bloods, over two hundred Hybrids, and roughly one hundred and fifty humans assigned to the base."

Mike just nodded his head each time she made a particular point. He seemed nonplussed by anything she was saying. *Okay, a cool customer for sure then.*

The True-Bloods made contact at a time that coincided with the Bsirutaeben ramping up their own genetic experiments on humans. Theirs were not voluntary subjects where the Eben test partners all volunteered."

Mike furrowed his eyebrows, "The Seer-ROO-Tay-Ben?"

"Yes," she continued, "they are the Voiya and the Vesh-na and the Tree-la and their drones. I believe my Mother briefed you on them?" Mike changed his face to an expression of understanding and nodded his head.

"They are collectively referred to as the Bsirutaeben."

"Fraking Tantaloids," her sister chimed in sotto voce.

"Yes, technically the Voiya are physically Tantaloids. The Bsirutaeben had a relationship with the American government for a number of years. There were problems, it wasn't smooth. The relationship abruptly ended after a bloody massacre at an underground base in the New Mexico desert."

"At Dulce?" He asked.

She was surprised he knew this. The Dossier was right. She nodded and continued. "Thirty years ago we, the Hybrid base and the American government representing Earth, reached a détente with the Bsirutaeben after that incident. We signed a détente agreement. The highpoints of this agreement were that the Bsirutaeben would no longer involve themselves in human abductions or animal mutilations. Instead, every two Earth weeks we provide them with 20 kg of living organic material to experiment on."

Mike almost spit out the tea in his mouth, "YOU WHAT??" he almost came out of this chair. Both women were instantly on their feet. Hlef's right hand suddenly held her sidearm, and she didn't even spill a drop of the tea in her cup, which was still in her left hand. Achael, diplomatically, did not reach for her sidearm.

"Mike, we are against human testing without consent. We do not support it and would never engage in it. It's not the Eben way. The Bsirutaeben are provided with organic, biological material by the American government. I know only that it is sourced humanely, but not what those sources are. I can assure you that there are never any living creatures provided, human or otherwise. I know that because I am one of the couriers."

317

"Me too," chimed in Hlef, re-holstering her weapon and sitting down again, sipping at her tea.

Mike sat as well, but he looked pissed. All he said was, "Go on."

Achael sat down and continued, "There are some concerns at present that the Voiya are sourcing living subjects from other parts of the world. We can't prove it yet, but there are some indications of this." This was all a lie fed to them by Gilda, but Achael didn't know that. She continued, "As well, they are an ever-present threat here on Mars. We don't like them having their base here, we don't like them in this solar system, and we certainly don't like them interacting with those on Earth. There is always the risk one of your tribal governments will strike some kind of deal with them. Would you really want a new Cold War to start, with space aliens?" Her eyes crinkled with a brief smile.

Mike visibly shivered at that thought, "Certainly not. I had my own encounter with these bastards as a child."

Achael and Hlef nodded their heads, they had been made aware of this by Lt. Gen. Rosewood as well.

"So that's the Reader's Digest version of who and what we are. That brings us to the here and now," said Achael.

Hlef

As she sat there and watched him, she didn't have her usual train of thoughts about how cute someone was, about how frakable they were, or about how athletic they seemed. This guy was obviously older than you would expect, but he was ruggedly handsome, even if he was a bit dumpy. He wasn't very GQ, but he did have a boyish charm about him. She lingered over the thought that he looked very manly, very capable.

As she watched him, she had at first a fluttering, then a stirring in her chest. The surprising thoughts that came to her mind were: 'I could rely on this guy';'he would be a stand-up guy'; 'this guy can be trusted'; and 'This guy could be ...'

Khlam

Khlam was on guard but was bored. The sisters had been inside twenty minutes. The Eridani drones were still at the 100 km mark; and Khlam was trying to get a piece of duct tape off his fingers. Pull it off with one hand then shake, pull it off the first hand with the other hand, then shake. This went on for a couple minutes before the solution dawned on him. He stuck it to the corner of the console in front of him. Khlam was liked by everyone, but he was never considered the brightest of the sibs.

Khlam sighed deeply and drummed his long fingers on his knee. He also bored easily.

He heard the radio break squelch twice over the Bluetooth headset he had on. That was Hlef giving the "OK" signal. He wanted this to go quickly. He was hungry. Dad was in town. *Let's get this show on the road.*

Achael

She continued, "Mike, your mission was assisted for a very specific reason."

"Ahhh," he said. "Now we get to it."

She smiled. "We needed to get the weapons on board the Platform here without anyone knowing. There is too much oversight and prying eyes on everything that goes on in orbit around Earth." The platform and its weapons had been a surprise to Achael and Helf when Gilda told them. Being Eben and military, they liked it. Anything that would pound the Eridani was okay with them.

"That was rather obvious," he replied.

"Mom wants you to use the weapons to provoke the Eridani."

Mike

"WHAT?? SHE WANTS ME TO … WHAT??"

The gorgeous Ah-ooh-cchhale continued, "Mike, we need to rid this solar system of the Eridani. They are a threat to Earth and to humanity. They will aggressively stop any off world expansion so that you don't challenge their dominion in this arm of the galaxy."

This arm of the galaxy? They were worried that those freakish things were going to be worried about humans? Wow.

She continued, "Mike, we are in a precarious position with the Eridani, the Bsirutaeben. If we just go in and pound them to oblivion, something we can easily do, then we will risk the retaliation of the entire Eridani Dominion, as well as the Ousoon."

"The out who?" I was confused.

"The Ousoon are another race that are aligned with the Eridani. They are just as bad as the Eridani."

319

Too many names, "The Eridani, they are the Seer-ROO-Tay-Ben?"?"

"Yes."

"So you want rid of the Eridani, but you are afraid of the Ousoons?"

Hlef came out of her chair planting fists on the table, "We're afraid of NO ONE!"

"Yes, we are afraid of no one," Achael agreed. "However, we aren't in the mood for an all-out battle on multiple fronts at this point in time. If we go to war here, they may also attack our homeworld, and other outposts. While we can defeat them in the end, it will cost us heavily in lives and resources. We prefer not to go that route when there is another way."

I was even more confused than before they arrived. "So where does that bring me in?"

Achael and Hlef relaxed in their chairs and looked at each other. Achael turned towards me and continued, "As I said, Mom wants you to provoke them."

Hlef

She watched his face as Achael dropped that little bomb on him a second time. She felt something new, something she hadn't felt before. *This must be pity.* She had never felt pity before. She recognized the position this man was in. By the look on his face, this little bit of news had obviously affected him. A very strange feeling came over her with the new sense of pity.

She wanted to comfort him.

She had never wanted to comfort anyone except her sibs before. She realized she was changing and becoming someone new. That little meltdown on Earth had been the start. She finally understood *fiat familias supremus.*

Achael

She felt bad for him. She could see his face running through some complex thoughts, and she had a good idea what they were.

"If I provoke them, they will kill me. Do you not remember what happened last night?"

"There is some ... risk ..." Achael began.

"*Some* risk?" he snorted.

"We aren't going to hang you out to dry Mike. Mom wants us to work out a plan with you. We are going to support you and be there to defend you when

320

necessary. We have claimed you for protection, but luckily under the terms of the détente, it's a one-way relationship. What they do to you, they do to us; but what you do to them, you do on your own. It's complex, but the treaty was written by the Ousoons, who are to legalism, what oxygen is to life."

The human stared at her. Finally, he spoke, "So what is it you want me to do?"

Khlam

He knew better than to break radio silence, but he was getting more agitated. The Eridani scout ships had moved in closer, they were at 80 km range. He was about to raise the alarm, when they stopped moving and held position at that distance.

Khlam decided to move the Dart around to the north side of the human's growing complex of equipment, and pointed it right at them. He didn't do anything provocative, but he let them know they were being watched.

A few minutes later they withdrew to the 100 km mark. "Hmpph, that's strange" he said out loud. He keyed the transmit button on his COM unit. "Hey, Giggles," that was Hlef's nickname, "something's up with the drones. Shake a leg will ya?"

Hlef

She didn't react visibly to the radio message which only she and Achael could hear in their one-ear headsets. They did glance at each other, but left it at that. Hlef reached to the COM unit on her wrist, and broke squelch one time, the acknowledgement signal.

If the drones were acting up, they were acting up because of the hybrids' presence. The last thing they wanted from this visit was a shooting war, but a shooting war the drones would indeed get if they wanted one. Hlef stood up and walked to the North side portal, looking towards the distant ice field. She leaned close to the window and looked one way, then the other.

She heard Mike ask her, "Everything okay?"

"Nothing we can't handle, Sweetie."

Mike

Nice. I don't like being kept in the dark. I was about to go look out the window as well, but then realized these were the Pros from Dover. There was absolutely nothing I had to offer at the moment, so I just sat there.

The hot one's hot sister continued, "Mike, Mom needs you to provoke them into attacking your colony site. If you can do that, then they will have broken the terms of the détente. If that happens, then the Ousoons will not join in the retaliation, and there is a slight chance that the Eridani Dominion may not come to their aid."

"A very slight chance," confirmed the hot one with the curly brown hair.

"Use your handheld laser rifle to fire at them, which should get them to fire on you. Then rain hell down on them. We will plan this so that we are nearby. If we get the timing right, then we can come in and pick you up before they kill you."

"That's a mighty big '*IF*'" I said to her. I thought about it for a minute. The one called Achael kept silent while I went through it in my mind. Finally, I looked up at her and asked, "What if I refuse?"

The two women looked at each other. The sister came back and sat down at the table, and both of them looked very serious. Achael then put all the cards on the table, "If you refuse then your corporation will suddenly find it extremely difficult to get a paper clip off the ground, let alone any future missions to Mars."

The shoe dropped.

Khlam

A few minutes after returning to their original 100 km position, the Eridani scout ships, all piloted by the grotesque little drones, did something very unexpected. They all left.

Khlam stared at the monitor and ran a diagnostic to make sure there was nothing wrong with the equipment. They didn't cloak, they didn't suddenly disappear. They all rose up about 1,500 metres, and headed bearing 252 towards the Eridani base: all five of them.

This couldn't be good. But then again, this wasn't a known Eridani battle tactic either. They never let their drones retreat. They would destroy them in place along with the target rather than let them withdraw.

He keyed up the Hybrid base on the COM unit to confirm they were seeing what he was seeing. They confirmed it. Strange, very strange.

Khlam keyed the COM channel for his sisters, "Oy! Enough with the poodles already! Shit's happening out here."

Hlef

Both women looked startled at the same time. Hlef touched her forearm controller and said, as Mike looked quizzically at her, "'Sup Khlam?" She smiled and pulled back the hair over her right ear, revealing the Bluetooth headset.

"The drones just cleared out of Dodge."

Now it was time for the women to be surprised. They looked at each other, a bit confused, "Say again?" Achael said after keying her COM unit. Neither one of them had their COM units on VOX while they were having the meeting. This was so that the contents of the meeting would be private.

"They all just buggered off towards their home base. All five of them. They advanced to 80 km, then they withdrew, then they left. *Pfffttt*. Just like that."

"Ladies?" Mike said. Hlef looked at him and responded, "The five scout ships that were watching your base just left. No warning. They just left. That's strange."

"Very strange," added Achael.

"Ummm, perhaps this is the retreat before they start blowing the shit out of me? Us?" Mike looked worried.

"No." said Hlef. "No, the Eridani don't withdraw their drones just because they might get destroyed in an attack. That's unheard of in a thousand years of Eridani battle tactics. It has to be something else."

Achael

She was indeed confused by this turn of events. If anything, the drones should have pressed their advance, or at least had more drones join them. Having them withdraw actually made her breathe a bit easier for the human, but it was still damn odd. It might even be complicating the current situation, rather than simplifying it. She had to get a hold of the Lieutenant General.

She stood up and her sister joined her, "Mike, I think we need to get hold of Mom and talk to her about this. The drones leaving, I think that something is up, that we all may have missed. We need to talk about it, and get some direction."

"Sure, sure," Mike said, he sounded a bit prissy. "I'll just sit here and twiddle my fraking thumbs, shall I? All y'all bugger off for your secret meetings and decide my fate and fortune. That how we're going to play this?"

Achael got pissed at that herself. This human may be cute and admirable, but he just had no clue about interstellar politics or interplanetary war. She had a bit of an edge to her voice, surprising Hlef, as she responded, "Yes Mike. That's exactly what you are going to do. You are going to do nothing until we get hold of you again. Remember, we are on *your* side here, Mike."

Hlef forced herself to be calm and soothing, much to Achael's surprised irritation, "Yes Mike. We *are* on your side," Hlef smiled. "Don't doubt that for a moment. We knew your arrival would piss off the Eridani, but Mom has a plan to deal with them. Well, unless something has changed." She smiled again.

Achael watched her sister and wondered who the hell she was? That meltdown of hers certainly brought some changes with it. Her own temper flare-up towards the human had calmed down quickly, and she tried to be reassuring before departing.

"Mike, we'll be back as soon as we know something and bring you up to speed. We'll see what this change in tactics may mean, and let you know how you can handle it."

She glanced at Hlef and decided maybe a little fib would help settle him down. She stepped around the table and stood right in front of him. "Mike, you are a player now. You're at the table and part of this. We'll keep you in the loop and bring you in deeper after we get a handle on this," she smiled again.

She could tell Mike was holding his temper in. She didn't think he believed a word of the white lie.

Mike

I did a little mental deep breathing and held my temper. It wasn't this woman's fault. She was a pawn, like me. She had others to answer to. This was indeed going to be a very special report to Mission Control. The video of this meeting was going to rock a lot of worlds. I knew it wasn't transmitting, but the Hab system was still recording the internal cameras. Knowing I was playing with the big boys made me glad I had added a plugin to my laptop as I was having breakfast. The plugin would automatically back up the video files from the main Habitat server.

Not for one second did I believe her B.S. about me being a player. I was a pawn. Period.

She reached out and took my hand, her freakishly long fingers wrapping around my hand, a feeling I would soon become very accustomed too. She smiled and said, "We'll be in touch soon."

I forced a smile back at her and said, "You are welcome back any time."

She picked up her helmet and stepped back. The hot one walked over to me and smiled, giving me a wink, "We'll be back soon, Sweetie," she smiled again, "Very soon."

I couldn't help the genuine smile. Her hand was strong but soft, tough yet yielding. Her eyes, regardless of how big and odd they looked, were dreamy pools of invitation. "You are most definitely welcome back any time."

She couldn't have missed the slight emphasis on the "you" in that statement. By her slight blush and quick withdrawal of her hand, I could tell she picked it up. The one called Hlef, the hot one, my future wife, picked up her helmet and stepped back beside my future sister-in-law. As Achael reached for her COM unit on her wrist, Hlef said, "When we come back, is there anything you want, Sweetie?"

I chuckled, "Bring more cookies."

They suddenly weren't there anymore. I was all alone again.

I sighed heavily and made another cup of tea from my dwindling supply of tea bags. I sat at the table and slowly ate three more cookies with sips of tea while thinking about what had just transpired.

"Yep," I said to myself, "this is going to get a *lot* worse before it gets *any* better."

Join Mike, Achael, Hlef, Gilda, and the others in the sequel to Pathfinder...

On Mars:

Murder at Hellas Planitia

The Mike Lane Stories, Volume 2

Fall of 2015

Cultural References

This book is peppered with cultural references from some of my favourite books, TV shows, and movies. Here is a list of them from the book and the source they were taken from. These are all from people much bigger and better than I am. I did so, only to pay homage to those who have given me such joy over the years!

"*frak*" - As an author trying to appeal to wide range of ages, I have to be careful about too much cussin' and such. I used the word "frak" as an expletive. I first heard this word being used on Battlestar Gallactica (the original and the remake). It's been used in at least 17 other T.V. shows according to Wikipedia. Don't confuse it with "frackfrak" which has to do with oil drilling.

"*chew bubble gum and kick ass*" - My nod to a really great sci-fi B-movie starring the great Canadian wrestler, Rowdy Roddy Piper. The movie was called "They Live".

"*Spinning Wheels. Cue Blood, Sweat & Tears.*" - I'm referring to the song "Spinning Wheel" by the jazz-rock group Blood, Sweat and Tears. The opening lines of the song go like this: *What goes up must come down, spinning wheel got to go round, talking about your troubles it's a crying sin."*

"*I decided right then there would be no retreat. Hell, I just got here.*" – Battle for Los Angeles (movie). Aaron Eckhart's character in that movie was half the inspiration for the character of Mike Lane.

Feh-wu – A Mandarin phrase for "junk" from the greatest science fiction TV show ever, *Firefly*.

"*Miles to go before I sleep*" – From the Poem "Stopping by Woods on a Snowy Evening" by Robert Frost.

"*Ugly giant bags of mostly water*" – Alien lifeforms' description of humans, from an episode of ST:TNG (S1E18).

"*So much for the best laid plans of men, and mice.*" – Hitchhikers Guide To The Galaxy.

SOMP (suit of many pockets) - A nod to the Canadian adventure clothing company Tilley Endurables, in reference to their fisherman/photographer vest the VOMP (Vest Of Many Pockets). Read more at www.tilley.com.

"*most Riki-Tik*" – An occasional expression used by character Gen Thomas Ryan, played by Robert Patrick, in the TV show *The Unit*. The phrase is most likely derived from the Rudyard Kipling character Rikki-Tikki-Tavi in the Jungle Books, volume 2.

"*John Carter would have been proud*" – In *A Princess of Mars* (Edgar Rice Burroughs) we meet John Carter who impresses the Tharks with his ability to jump vast distances. A combination of low-g and his human strength.

"*Grog the Caveman*" - Was the hairy little quintessential caveman in the "B.C." comic strip by cartoonist Johnny Hart.

" *"I. Don't. CARE." Achael punctuated each word like it was its own sentence.*" - A nod to my hero, James Tiberius Kirk.

"*Rage Against The Machine*" - AKA RATM, they are a rap-metal band from Los Angeles, California, formed in the early 90s.

"*shake of a lamb's tail*" - Is a term used to denote the interval of sequential steps in a nuclear explosion. One shake of a lamb's tail is equivalent to 10 nanoseconds. I first encountered this term in popular fiction in the book, "Sum of All Fears" by Tom Clancy.

"*well, then we'll just have to begin some aggressive negotiations.*" - A nod to my much beloved Star Wars, mimicking something Anakin said in reference to his Jedi Master, Obi-Wan Kenobi.

"*I'm a bad, bad man.*" - One of my favourite lines of the character Malcom Reynolds, played by Nathan Fillion, in the greatest science fiction TV show ever, *Firefly*. Nathan Fillion's writer/crime solving character Richard Castle is the other half of the inspiration for Mike Lane.

"*I was more worried about pulling a Dorothy.*" - In the *Wizard of Oz*, the protagonist Dorothy was transported to the land of Oz by a tornado, a cyclone. My editor's name is also Dorathy (pronounced the same, just spelled with an 'a' instead of an 'o').

"*Pro's from Dover*" - a Nod to M*A*S*H, one of my fav TV shows growing up. The term comes from the 1968 book M*A*S*H by Richard Hooker.

"*Hello Sweetie*" - A demurely sexy line delivered by the character River Song, played by Alex Kingston, in the TV Show *Doctor Who*. Alex Kingston was who I loosely had in mind while crafting the character of Hlef. Closely associated, I was loosely thinking of Eve Myles, the black-haired lead character in the *Doctor Who* spinoff called *Torchwood,* as my character Achael.

"*Oy! Enough with the poodles already*" - From the Gilmore Girls, season 3. Great show!

"*Do or do not, there is no try*" - Do I really need to explain that one?

Check out the sites for the men who inspired me to actually start writing:

Rick Fearnley
www.lifeslessons.ca

Kenneth Lord
www.apoet.ca

Jim Melanson

Poet, programmer, procrastinator, sci-fi geek, coffee snob, actor, writer.

A devoted Christian, Jim is a quiet and thoughtful man who tends to think deeply, and act slowly. Much of this inner reflection and self-assessment shows up in his writing. "Capturing what truly motivates us," is how Jim describes his approach to both fiction and non-fiction. This author has a very direct, and sometimes *in-your-face,* way of writing. He tries to always use conversational language; and as one test reader of a work in progress put it, "made the complexities of space flight seem almost understandable."

Jim read his first novel by Laura Ingalls Wilder at the age of eight, and so this began his love affair with the written word. Jim's first foray into personal writing, as a child, was poetry. These and other poetic scribblings provided the content for his first book, *I Apologize for Nothing*, published in April, 2014.

Life, a child, a career with the Police Service, and a part-time business authoring software; all got in the way of pursuing his desire to write. In his 40's, Jim decided to turn his hand back to writing, mainly on topics surrounding self-development, spirituality, and Reiki. However, none of these really satisfied that craving for creativity. In 2013, Jim decided to pursue his creative yearnings, and he began writing for pleasure. Drawing on a solid work ethic from his experience authoring technical manuals and writing business proposals, Jim found writing for himself to be liberating and enjoyable. While working on his first fiction novel, he kept getting sidetracked by other ideas. He dusted off an old stage play he had written and published under the title, *Mama's Slippers*, with the hopes of attracting production interest. He currently continues work on both science fiction and Christian themed projects.

Originally hailing from the East Coast, Jim now lives just outside Cobourg, ON.